THE GENESIS PROTOCOL

THE GENESIS PROTOCOL

DAYTON WARD

A PHOBOS IMPACT BOOK
AN IMPRINT OF PHOBOS BOOKS
NEW YORK

PHOBOS
IMPACT

A Phobos Impact Book
Published by Phobos Books LLC
200 Park Avenue South
New York, NY 10003
www.phobosweb.com

Distributed in the United States by National Book Network, Lanham, Maryland.

Cover by Zuccadesign

Library of Congress Cataloging-in-Publication Data

Ward, Dayton.
 The genesis protocol / Dayton Ward.
  p. cm.
 ISBN 0-9770708-0-8 (pbk. : alk. paper)
 I. Title.
 PS3623.A7317G46 2006
 813'.6--dc22

2005030023

⊗™ The paper used in this publication meets the minimum requirements of American National Standard for Information Sciences—Permanence of Paper for Printed Library Materials, ANSI/NISO Z39.48-1992

" . . . before the trees of knowledge in their synthetic garden bear their strange fruit, the gardeners should heed the lessons of history."

—Oliver Morton
"Biology's New Forbidden Fruit"
The New York Times
February 11, 2005

THE GENESIS
PROTOCOL

IN THE BEGINNING . . .

PROLOGUE

Situated deep in the vast region of uninhabited terrain comprising much of the Hill Air Force Base, Project EDN was an expanse of lush vegetation measuring more than 225 square miles, though similarities to any natural jungle anywhere in the world began and ended with that description. Scientists—and, by extension, the United States government—had seen fit to "build" this wholly artificial environment, though they hadn't used wood and aluminum and plastic to do it. Instead, they had figured out a way to grow it, to bring it forth from out of the barren Utah desert.

It's still a jungle, Sean Godfried thought, and just as in any jungle it was hotter than hell here. For the fourth time in thirty minutes, he tried to wipe perspiration from his forehead, and for the fourth time his hand was stopped by the Plexiglas shield in front of his face.

You're gonna have to get used to that, you know.

The bright orange containment suit Godfried wore was cumbersome and tended to bind at the elbow and knee joints. His shoulders stung from where the straps on the combination respirator/environmental-control module he wore on his back were digging through the material of the garment and into his skin. As this was his first time venturing out into the jungle as part of a security detail, he knew he would need time to adapt to the discomfort, but for now the suit was a pain in the ass.

It was also the only thing keeping Godfried alive at the moment. All around him in this dark area of the jungle, he knew, the unearthly vegetation was emitting foul-smelling, highly lethal toxins. Contaminated water ran unimpeded through narrow rivers and streams into this region's various ponds and small lakes. Even the air was potentially hazardous, depending on such variables as wind speed and direction, temperature and humidity levels. There were areas in surrounding sectors that did not pose such hazards, but it was his misfortune that the purpose of his sojourn into the jungle had not taken him to one of those locations. Without the suit, Godfried knew that his life expectancy could be measured in hours, if not less.

"How's it coming, Al?" he asked, turning to his companion, Alicia Watts. The lamp molded into the top of his helmet bathed her in its powerful light, reflecting off the orange material of her own protective suit. She was crouching next to a large rectangular box that was as foreign to this environment as they were. Jutting out of the soil, the box itself was nothing more than a shell, intended to protect the delicate monitoring sensors it contained from the elements as well as the exploratory nibbling or pawing of curious animals. Its cover lay on the ground to one side, giving Watts access to its equipment.

"Almost done," Watts replied without looking up from her work, her voice sounding crisp in Godfried's earpiece as she spoke. "Just a couple of minor adjustments and we're out of here."

The interior of the equipment box was stuffed with a host of gauges, dials, and digital readouts that, as far as Godfried was able to understand, all worked in concert to report on various environmental conditions in this section of jungle. The ensemble also included a liquid crystal display monitor and computer keyboard which, like everything else inside the container, had been specifically engineered for use in harsh, outdoor environments. In particular, the keyboard featured oversized keys that allowed easier typing by users wearing bulky gloves like the ones protecting Godfried and Watts's hands.

The monitoring rig was one of dozens scattered throughout the region, all of which were connected via computer and communications link to observation and control centers situated both inside and outside the jungle's perimeter. Working in concert, the equipment provided constant environmental information to a team of scientists and engineers tasked with overseeing this, the most unusual ecosystem on the face of the planet.

In her left hand, Watts held a personal digital assistant, a larger and more ruggedly designed model than the types sold in electronics stores to civilians. It was connected by a length of fiber-optic cable to an interface port on the computer station, and its faceplate and keypad, like the keyboard's, allowed easy interaction for a user dressed in a containment suit. The light from the unit's backlit display shone up into Watts's face, giving her features an almost ghostly appearance as she studied the device and occasionally tapped instructions into the keyboard.

"Good," Godfried said. "I think something's wrong with my cooling unit." Checking the small gauge set into the wrist of his suit's right forearm, he shook his head. "I'm sweating my ass off in this thing. All I want right now is a cold beer and a shower."

"Is that an invitation?" Watts asked, turning to cast a wry grin over her shoulder at him. Though he was standing several yards away from her, Godfried could see the lines of sweat on the sides of her own face; they gave a glistening sheen to her ebony skin. Unlike many of the other science and engineer types working on the project, Watts lacked the desire to appear superior to anyone who might not have a doctorate. She had a wicked sense of humor, liked to flirt, and certainly looked a hell of a lot better in shorts and a tank top while working out on a StairMaster than most of her flabby counterparts.

Offering a smile of his own, he replied, "Absolutely." Even if it was nothing more than harmless flirting, it was still the best aspect of having to get up in the middle of the night and traipse through the jungle in order to repair the malfunctioning sensor unit. Both he and Watts had drawn the after-hours on-call duty this week, and with only one more day until turnover Godfried figured that if anything would go wrong, it would be the night before he transferred the on-call responsibility to one of his teammates.

Murphy's Law, and all that.

"Well, then, let's get this done and get out of here," Watts said as she returned to her work. In short order her hands were tapping the keyboard and moving back and forth between the different monitoring devices inside the equipment box.

Adjusting his grip on the strap of the tranquilizer rifle slung over his shoulder, Godfried redirected his attention to the outlandish jungle around him. Watts and most of the other science geeks had gotten used to their surroundings, but he had been on the job here only a few months. If anyone had thought to ask him, they would discover that he was still pretty damned amazed at the miracle of science and technology that had yielded a thriving jungle in, of all places, the middle of northwestern Utah.

"You'll get used to it, newbie," Watts said, and he heard her laughter in his earpiece.

Godfried hoped she was right. When he first signed on three months earlier, at the time not knowing how long the assignment would last, he figured it would be just like any other security detail overseeing a hard target, an installation, rather than simply providing protection for a person or group. He had participated in enough similar jobs around the world that he had the routine down pat. So long as he was properly paid, the arrangement suited him just fine, and his current benefactors were nothing if not generous with their checkbook, not only with him but with the entire cadre of professionals employed to maintain the project's security and privacy.

Upon his arrival in Utah, it had not taken Godfried long to learn why such measures were necessary, and why the project's overseers were willing to pay so handsomely to have those measures alleviated. They had briefed him, of course, but he had to admit he'd never understand it all. He had made the attempt, of course, had tried to take advantage of the briefings offered members of the project's scientific contingent, but even those shortened, dumbed-down sessions had at first proven too much to believe. It all sounded so much like something he might have read in a science fiction book as a kid. Genetic engineering? Cloning? Creating entirely new types of plant and animal life and putting them here, in a godforsaken place that was all but lethal to anyone who set foot inside? What the hell was that about?

Only when he was driven into the EDN region for the first time during his orientation briefing did he finally begin to comprehend the enormity of what the project had accomplished.

Driving through the area on that first day, staring wide-eyed at the world outside through the two-inch-thick glass windows of the sealed and pressurized bus, Godfried felt as though he were being guided through a set built in a movie studio. Some of it was familiar, though the green foliage was liberally mixed with colors from across the spectrum, and the leaves came in circles, squares, rectangles, and other shapes and sizes totally out of proportion with the leaves in the many jungles he had traveled. While some trees, the ones that struck him as being like oaks and pines if oaks and pines were covered in scales instead of bark, rose vertically out of the ground to tower above his head, others that he had no hope of identifying were bent and twisted, sometimes back on themselves. Equally bizarre underbrush ran rampant, climbing the trunks of the larger trees and creating impenetrable shrouds that choked smaller specimens—and the shrouds were humming, vibrating like the strings on a giant guitar being strummed by an invisible hand.

Everything about the region was unnatural, alien, as if he had somehow wandered off the planet Earth itself. And if two-thirds of it weren't poisonous to human life, Godfried thought, it might even be beautiful.

But it won't be poisonous forever, he reminded himself. *That's the whole point to this place, right?*

He heard the sound of metal scraping against metal behind him and turned to see Watts pulling the equipment box's protective cover back into place. "All finished," she said as she began putting away her tools and other gear. "I think I hear that beer and shower calling our names."

"Amen to that," he said, glancing at the clock built into the wrist-mounted keypad on his left sleeve. Just after 2:30. He didn't know about Watts, but there was no way he would get back to sleep by the time they returned to the observation station and got themselves and their equipment cleaned up.

Maybe she'll really be up for that beer, after all.

Picking up one of the toolboxes she had brought with her, Godfried helped Watts return her gear to their maintenance vehicle, parked on the narrow service road twenty yards away from the equipment cluster. It was essentially a large cargo van modified for all-terrain travel and, like everything else that ventured into the jungle here, was outfitted and hardened specifically for operation within the area's unique environment. Its passenger area was airtight and pressurized, providing an atmosphere free of the contaminants that permeated the jungle. Godfried for one was thankful for that, as it would finally allow him to get out of his now quite uncomfortable containment suit.

As they walked toward the road, Godfried's attention was caught by movement to his left. He tapped Watts on the shoulder. "Looks like we've got company," he said, the sight before him giving him yet one more reason to shake his head in astonishment at the wonders populating the EDN region.

As alien as the jungle they inhabited, the animal life thriving here also defied imagination. Though Godfried recognized some of the creatures as offshoots of more familiar species—monkeys, birds, snakes, and the like— so far as he was concerned the project's true accomplishments lay in what the scientists had seemingly conjured out of whole cloth. Such was the case with the pack of *malanters* that had emerged from the jungle and were now congregating on the narrow dirt road.

Godfried counted nearly two dozen of the large, lumbering creatures. When he had seen them for the first time he had likened the mals to buffalo, and had later learned that he wasn't far off in his comparison. According to the wildlife briefings he had received at the start of his employment, the animals contained genetic characteristics of buffalo and regular farm cows, just for starters. Capable of growing to weights in excess of fifteen hundred pounds and to heights of nearly seven feet tall at the shoulders, malanters possessed thick hides covered in long, thick hair that shone with the yellow of glow-in-the-dark paint under the dim moonlight, making them easier to see. Each of their four hooves could grow larger than twelve inches in diameter. Of course, bulk had its price; the massive muscles in their legs and flanks were incapable of moving the mals faster than a few miles per hour at their fastest sprint. They subsisted on the lush jungle vegetation, and had also proven to be all but completely docile, never once objecting to the approach of any human or other smaller animal.

Like most of the other species living in the EDN region, mals tended to stay within one certain area of the jungle. Godfried knew from his orientation that this was due in large part to a deliberate attribute built in at the genetic level, a measure designed to keep the wildlife population carefully restricted to designated zones. Animals were deposited into selected sectors, designed with genetic predispositions toward subsiding on specific plant life or other species as part of the larger research project that was the purpose for the EDN initiative in the first place.

But within their sectors, they liked to walk or just stand still wherever they damn well pleased.

"You've gotta be shitting me," Godfried said, making no effort to hide his exasperation as he studied the unmoving herd.

Laughing, Watts replied, "Just honk the horn a few times. They'll clear out."

"Like hell they will." He had read numerous reports, filed by maintenance and observation crews working inside the region, that mentioned the delays they had experienced while waiting for a herd of mals to make their way off one of the many service roads winding through the jungle. What the gentle creatures lacked in aggression they certainly compensated for with innate stubbornness. Normally he chuckled when hearing one of his fellow sentries bitching or complaining about having to wait, sometimes for an hour or more, before the gentle creatures decided it was time to be elsewhere.

Not this time, however.

Even from this distance, Godfried could hear the normal chorus of grunts and hums typically emitted by the mals as several of the animals helped themselves to patches of grass and weeds lining the service road.

"Start the truck," he called out over his shoulder as he started walking toward the herd. "I'll see if I can get them to move."

Watts chuckled again. "You'd have better luck just cutting another road through the jungle," she offered as she climbed into the van's driver's seat.

"Maybe so," Godfried replied, "but it beats just standing here waiting for my suit to drown me in my own sweat." As he expected, most of the mals seemed not to notice or care as he drew closer. A few looked up at his approach, but the others appeared content to continue their grazing.

Somehow, I don't think shooing them's gonna work. Nevertheless, he swallowed his pride and stepped forward, waving his arms in what he hoped wasn't a completely ludicrous attempt to get the animals' attention. "Hey! Yoo-hoo! Move it on out of here!"

To Godfried's shock, every mal stopped what it was doing, the herd acting as a single entity as the mals raised their heads to look around.

"Jesus, Sean," Watts said. "What the hell did you say to them?"

"Beats me," Godfried replied, watching as the mals stood motionless, though none of them seemed to be taking any interest in him. Several of them were sniffing the air, and after a few seconds he heard some of the animals uttering a new string of noises. This time there was a definite undercurrent of agitation. "Something's got them spooked."

Then all hell broke loose.

As if reacting to a signal that only they could hear, the mals began to scatter from the road, dozens of massive gray hulks moving as fast as their lumbering bodies allowed. Some took off on their own while others separated into smaller groups, but all of the beasts were scrambling into the jungle to the west of the road.

And some of them were heading directly toward him.

"Look out!"

Godfried felt Watts grab him by the arm the same instant her voice shouted in his earpiece, pulling him out of the path of three mals, which stampeded over the spot where he had been standing less than a second before. She pulled him after her as she ran for the side of the road, and he tripped as packed dirt fell away to grass. Godfried stumbled for several steps before his feet betrayed him and he crashed to the ground, landing hard on his side. Watts was able to maintain her balance, and she turned to come back to him.

"Are you all right?" she asked as she knelt beside him. Godfried rolled to a sitting position, wincing at the pain shooting through his hip from where he had landed on the stock of the tranquilizer gun.

Nodding even as he grimaced in discomfort, Godfried replied, "Yeah, I think so." Watts reached for his hand and he allowed her to help him to stand up, and he flinched at a fresh sting in his hip. Looking around, he saw the last of the mals disappearing into the jungle, their bulky forms quickly obscured by the thick underbrush.

"I've never seen them act like that before," Watts said from where she stood next to him. "Come to think of it, I've never seen any of the animals act like that."

"Listen," Godfried said, holding up a hand so that Watts would stop talking.

"What?" Watts asked a moment later, her voice suddenly subdued by what Godfried could swear was concern. No, not concern—out-and-out fear.

Moving to unsling the tranquilizer rifle, he replied, "I heard something." He checked the rifle to ensure that the dart was properly chambered and that the gun's safety switch was off, gripping the rifle tightly in his hands. Wasn't an M16, but it was better than nothing. Before coming to work on the EDN project, it had been almost second nature for Godfried to carry a sidearm, to say nothing of the larger weaponry that had been required for some assignments. His pistol was in the van, of course, but he couldn't use it while wearing the gloves that were part of his containment suit.

Standing still, Godfried allowed his eyes to move slowly from left to right, studying the trees looming in the darkness and concentrating more on what he saw in his peripheral vision than on what was directly in front him. He looked for unusual movement among the trees that might signal the approach of some other animal, but saw nothing.

Something's there. He could feel it, but what could it be? What other animals living in this part of the EDN region could frighten the mals? For that matter, what among the numerous species of animal life that inhabited any part of the project area could have that kind of effect? Nothing, so far as he knew.

The unmistakable sound of wood snapping came from some somewhere to his right and Godfried spun to look in that direction, tracking the barrel of the tranquilizer rifle wherever his eyes looked. He peered into the jungle, trying to separate trees and vegetation from shadows as well as whatever was most definitely moving among the foliage.

"Al," he whispered, "get in the truck." He started to step backward, each foot cautiously probing the ground behind him to ensure he didn't step on anything that might trip him. The hairs on the back of his neck were standing up, and a tingle was running down his spine. He was familiar with the sensation, one he had experienced on other occasions. The last time he had felt it was in the desert of Kuwait during Operation Desert Storm, mere seconds before two Iraqi soldiers appeared from behind a sand dune as they tried to ambush him and the soldier with whom he had been sharing a foxhole.

He sensed movement ahead of him and slightly to his left, just inside the tree line, and Godfried swung the rifle's barrel to sight in to see . . .

. . . something explode from the jungle.

"Holy shit . . ." he breathed, the words barely a whisper that died even as they left his mouth.

It was massive, and fast, and charging directly at him across thirty yards of open ground. He was only dimly aware of Watts screaming as the dark shape rushed forward, closing the distance between them with staggering speed.

Even as his mind screamed that the action was useless, he pulled the trigger on the rifle and saw the tranquilizer dart launch from the end of its barrel before the weapon was ripped from his grip. Something swiped at his head. The faceplate of his helmet tore away and he felt jungle heat on his exposed skin.

White-hot fire exploded in his vision as he was thrown backward off his feet, falling heavily to the ground. Something snapped as he landed flat on his back atop his suit's environmental-control pack. For an instant he thought that the fall might have broken the unit, but then he felt a tingling sensation enveloping his arms and legs.

He tried to roll onto his side but his body wouldn't obey him. Blood rushed in his ears, almost but not quite drowning out the sounds of Watts screaming again, but he couldn't even raise his head to see where she was before her shrieks abruptly stopped.

Then a massive weight crashed down on his chest, forcing the air from his lungs and stifling his own cry of pain. Something wet dripped onto his face, and the menacing snarl was the last thing he heard before he felt hot breath on his throat.

CHAPTER ONE

Gunnery Sergeant Donovan Hassler lay prone on the ground less then five meters from where the dense foliage opened up into an expansive clearing, using the trunk of a fallen oak to conceal his body and remaining absolutely still as the guard walked toward him.

Not that Hassler was worried. The darkness surrounding him was broken only by the feeble moonlight forcing its way through the irregular breaks in the clouds dominating the Colombian night sky. Precious little of the light penetrated the canopy of trees towering high above the jungle floor. He was all but invisible to the other man, his uniform along with the green and brown paint he wore on his face and hands to conceal his dark skin working to blend his body in with the vegetation surrounding him.

The same scene had played out at fairly regular intervals since Hassler and his team had moved into position just after 0100. Two sentries, the only signs of life outside the trio of small cabins inhabiting this small clearing, traced circular paths in opposite directions around the glade's perimeter. They walked their beats with their rifles slung, moving along the same path through the trodden grass and not really paying any attention to the surrounding jungle. It was obvious that the guards did not expect anything to happen out here, in the middle of the night, at the ass end of nowhere.

"These guys are boring the shit out of me," said a voice whispering in his earpiece, and Hassler recognized the New York inflection as belonging to Staff Sergeant David Maddox, the leader of Third Platoon's Team Two.

Hassler smiled at his friend's remark, knowing that it was just "Mad Dawg"'s way of passing the time. Meanwhile, the guard did exactly as expected, continuing to walk the same path he and other sentries had long ago pounded into the brush growing along the edges of the clearing.

Hidden by the jungle and the fallen tree and now safely out of the guard's field of vision, Hassler slowly rotated his wrist until he could see the luminescent hands on his field watch. According to it, the sentries had been on duty for almost two hours. They had been talkative and jovial earlier as they passed one another while making their rounds, stopping occasionally to smoke cigarettes and talk about what they might do for excitement the next time they ventured to the small town that was the closest thing to civilization in this part of the country. During one such conversation, which had taken place less then ten meters from where Hassler lay hidden, one of the guards had gone to great lengths to describe a waitress he had come to know at one of the local bars.

None of that was happening now, though. While the sentries still nodded and exchanged a few words in passing, it was obvious that both men wanted to be elsewhere. Boredom had definitely set in, and the early-morning guard duty was screwing with their circadian rhythms, their minds no doubt sending messages to their bodies demanding sleep.

Taking them out would be child's play.

Hassler felt another bead of perspiration running down the side of his face, unimpeded by the sweatband of his soft, wide-brimmed boonie hat. He made no move to wipe it away, of course, ignoring it as he had the others along with the humidity, the cramp in his thigh from lying still for so long, and everything else contributing to his discomfort. None of that mattered, not now.

So far, he was not thrilled with the way the situation was shaping up. The mission itself had been put together almost on the fly, with Hassler and the other members of his platoon carrying out the initial planning while in flight aboard a C-130 transport aircraft from their base at Camp Pendleton, the massive Marine Corps base located less than fifty miles north of San Diego. On alert for possible deployment anywhere in the world and with two of his platoons already engaged in assignments outside the United States, the commanding officer of the First Force Reconnaissance Company, Lieutenant Colonel Douglas Pantolini, had issued the orders to the unit's Third Platoon, of which Hassler was the senior enlisted member. They were airborne within one hour of the call, and it was only then that they had received their mission briefing.

While their units were equipped and trained for all manner of missions, from surveillance and scouting of terrain and enemy military installations and activity to limited raids in support of larger Marine Corps units, they could also carry captured enemy personnel and sensitive materials, as well as recover personnel or items of interest in danger from other parties. This last type of mission often took the form of a TRAP, or Tactical Recovery of Aircraft Personnel.

Less frequently, Force Recon units were assigned an IHR mission—In-Extremis Hostage Rescue—such as the assignment Third Platoon, First FRC, had drawn: the retrieval of two officers from the Drug Enforcement Agency assigned to one of several interdiction operations taking place in Colombia as part of the Unites States' protracted "war on drugs." The agents had been working a case that had taken them to Bogotá, the country's largest city and a hive of activity for the cartels, when they were abducted in broad daylight on a busy street while exiting their vehicle.

Given the target's location, the assignment would ordinarily have been given to a platoon from either the Second Force Recon Company based at Camp Lejeune, North Carolina or the Fourth from Mobile, Alabama. Otherwise, the mission might even have been given to a special operations group from one of the other service branches, such as a Navy SEAL team or a contingent from Delta Force. However, the current state of world affairs and the commitment of United States military resources to numerous trouble spots around the globe meant that Marine Force Recon platoons were getting a large number of assignments they might not normally receive as they and the rest of the services worked to cover the gaps in one another's operational tempo.

Working in the platoon's favor was Hassler's familiarity with the region, as he had been deployed here several times earlier in his career while assigned to Second Recon at Lejeune. He'd had no reason to return to the country in nearly a decade, and part of him was naturally disappointed that missions like these were still necessary. The war on drugs had outlasted even the most pessimistic estimates, with costs in lives and resources far outweighing any realized gains, at least so far as Hassler was concerned.

Not that anyone asked you, he reminded himself. Personally, he could not care less what some moron chose to drink, smoke, stick in their nose, or shoot into their arm, just so long as they inflicted no harm on anyone else while doing it. He considered the drug war to be a colossal waste of time, with one exception: stopping those who chose to sell the shit to kids. Disgust for that was enough to provide Hassler with all the justification he needed to carry out missions against anyone in the drug trade.

Well, that and when some of those same people took American hostages, of course.

"Heads up," said the hushed voice of Third Platoon's commander, Captain William Sorensen, in Hassler's earpiece. "Got a guy coming out of the south cabin."

Peering through the viewfinder of the thermal imaging scope affixed to the upper receiver of his M4A1 carbine assault rifle, Hassler could see the body heat of the man walking through the interior of the wooden structure, watching him as he stepped out of the building and began slowly to pace the cabin's low, dilapidated porch. Now that the man was illuminated by the dim light fixture hanging from the porch's ceiling, Hassler saw that he was dressed in khaki pants and a lightweight beige shirt. He was unarmed so far as Hassler could see, and he seemed to be doing nothing more than getting some air as he lit a cigarette.

"I don't recognize him," whispered another voice, one Hassler thought might belong to Staff Sergeant Brian Gerard, Team One's leader. "He wasn't in any of the pictures we got."

Though his own angle on the man was not a good one, Hassler was sure he had not seen him in the series of photographs the platoon had been shown during their briefing.

"Hired gun," Hassler decided, his own voice barely audible to his own ears, though he knew the sensitive mike at his throat would still pick up the reverberations of his vocal chords and transmit his words to the earpieces worn by his teammates. No doubt the man was a low-ranking member of the cartel, likely all but useless as an interrogation subject for anything save his immediate assignment.

Not that it mattered one way or another. Third Platoon's mission orders were simple: Retrieve the agents, eliminate all others, and leave behind no evidence that American troops had ever set foot in country. Everyone would know who was responsible, of course, but the directives were intended to prevent the capture of Marines, not to safeguard the lives of Colombian drug traffickers.

It had been a little dicey, parachuting into the jungle southeast of Bogotá in the predawn hours of the previous day. But all fourteen members of Third Platoon made it safely to the landing site only to have to hump nearly twenty kilometers over inhospitable terrain. They had battled oppressive heat and humidity and unrelenting attacks by jungle insects while remaining on constant alert for signs of human activity. Though the intelligence briefings given to the Marines indicated that the area was sparsely populated, experience had taught Hassler that such information usually lost its value within seconds of insertion into a hostile area.

Still, some information of worth had emerged. Witnesses in Bogotá, questioned by members of the local police force and other agents from the DEA, reported that agents Martin Elliot and Stanley Glover had been forced into the back of a dark blue Chevy Tahoe, which was last seen heading south out of the city. Working with that information, analysts at the Central Intelligence Agency in Langley, Virginia, scoured satellite photography of the region while people on the ground in Bogotá offered all manner of incentives to anyone with information on who might be responsible for abducting the DEA agents.

The reasons for the action had come soon afterward, when the Colombian National Police received a phone call demanding the release of Alejandro Ortiz, whom the CIA identified as the leader of one of the many upstart cartels feverishly working to insinuate themselves into the thriving cocaine trafficking network. Like many of the smaller, newer groups, Ortiz and his organization took advantage of everything the latest in cellular communications and computer technology had to offer—to say nothing of the vast gold mine of information- and intelligence-gathering capabilities the Internet could provide. He had taken bold risks where larger, older, and more traditional cartels had opted to play it safe, and in doing so had in only a few years' time garnered a respectable piece of the action. Scum-sucking bastard thought he had it all over the older cartels, with his high-tech toys, but Hassler knew better. Ortiz was a murderous prick, just like any other drug peddler.

American officials had celebrated when the drug lord was captured and extradited the previous year, but the party came to an abrupt and frustrating end as soon as they found out that the SOB had actually planned for the contingency of his capture. He had organized his group so well that his brother, Menno, was able to step in with little to no disruption in the cartel's operations.

This begged the question of why they might want Alejandro released, but brother Menno, according to the CIA at least, had not been forthcoming with that information. The only item of note in the message he had sent was that if his brother was not released from where he was currently incarcerated—at the federal prison in Leavenworth, Kansas—Menno would order the execution of Elliot and Glover. Taking a cue from various terror and other extremist groups operating in the Middle East, Ortiz's ultimatum had come with the promise to carry out the threat in a particularly grotesque manner, which would then be made available for viewing on videotape and via the Internet. No doubt thinking himself clever, dramatic, and in full control of the situation, he had even given the American government ninety-six hours to release his brother and have him on a flight bound for Colombia.

Gave us too much time. Hassler grinned at the thought. *They always find some way to screw up.*

Indeed, given the CIA's vast resources, it had taken less than a day to determine a list of possible locations where the agents might be held, based on profiles of the cartel's leadership and other major figures as compiled by the agency during the past six years. Many of the places the organization used to carry out its various operations—warehouses, safe houses, office buildings in Bogotá and elsewhere throughout the country, as well as facilities at airports and even ports long the coast in smaller cities like Guapi and Buenaventura—had long been under surveillance by American intelligence assets.

Analysts in Langley had suggested that Menno Ortiz would want them isolated and yet readily available in case he needed them for further bargaining, which narrowed the search field considerably when placed alongside witness accounts and satellite imagery that, while sporadic, had still captured the Tahoe more than once during its journey from Bogotá. Its journey had taken it in the general direction of Villavicencio before bringing it to what appeared in some satellite photos as nothing more than a pinprick of white in otherwise dark jungle, but with the magic of digital imaging had been enlarged and enhanced to reveal a small, unassuming glade populated with three small buildings.

The very clearing Hassler was watching now, a full thirty hours before the end of the time Menno Ortiz had granted for the release of his brother. Of course, key questions still remained unanswered: Had the hostages truly been brought here, or had the cartel been smarter than believed, transferring them to another location during a gap in satellite coverage? If they had been brought here, were they still here?

Keeping the man on the south building's porch in his peripheral vision, Hassler studied the clearing for perhaps the hundredth time since moving into his place of concealment. Along with the trio of single-story structures, two SUVs, one of which was a Tahoe, were parked underneath a shelter. The roof of the shelter was painted green and was covered in grass and other vegetation taken from the surrounding jungle. Hassler figured it was an attempt to camouflage the structure from aerial reconnaissance, and a pitiful one at that. He had expected better, given the information gathered about Ortiz and his cartel. Perhaps this safe area was one that had been arranged by brother Menno, whose own grasp of tactical thinking was not as developed or practiced as Alejandro's.

Hassler checked his watch again. 0328.

As if on cue, the voice of Captain Sorensen, sharp and taut, whispered in his ear. "Okay, boys. Almost showtime. Stand by." Normally, the captain was perfectly happy to joke around with the lively men of the Third Platoon, but he shifted to a no-nonsense demeanor once the time came to let bullets fly.

Upon arriving at the target area, Sorensen had dispersed the Marines equidistantly around the clearing's perimeter to reconnoiter it from every possible angle.

The plan was simple. Teams would take down one building each, sweeping and securing their interiors and eliminating anyone who was not Elliot or Glover. This was all in line with the training the platoon routinely received, but even close-quarters battle simulations with live ammunition could not compare to actual combat conditions, where the targets could shoot back.

On the porch of the south cabin, the man finished his cigarette, dropping the butt to the floorboards so he could grind it out under his foot before turning to go back inside the cabin. A shaft of light cut briefly across the ground in front of the structure as the man opened the door, disappearing again after a moment.

Hassler felt his finger tense on the trigger guard of his weapon. The barrel of the M4 rested across his left forearm, aimed generally in the direction of the clearing. A compact version of the M16A2 used by U.S. military forces since the mid-1980s, the rifle was lighter and featured a collapsible stock that made it perfect for the particular needs of a fast-moving special operations group. Evidently others agreed with him, because it had become Force Recon's preferred weapon for close-quarters battle situations, supplanting the still-reliable Heckler & Koch MP5. The weapon fired the same ammunition as the M16 and like that slightly larger rifle could be accessorized with a shortened version of the long-proven M203 grenade-launcher attachment.

Through the lens of the weapon's thermal sight, Hassler eyed the one guard who still patrolled the perimeter less than a hundred meters from his current position, presenting his right profile. At this range and equipped with the sound suppressor that he had fit to the end of the rifle's barrel, a single shot behind the sentry's right ear was all that Hassler would need. The man would drop to the ground without making a sound.

Sorry, pal, but you're about to have a very bad day.

"Ten seconds, shooters," Sorensen said, and Hassler kept his eyes on the guard as he counted down the remaining seconds.

When his count reached zero, a cloud of red mist exploded from the guard's head and he collapsed in a heap to the grass, dead before he had even started to fall. In the corner of his eye, Hassler saw the other sentry crumple in similar fashion even as he felt his own body springing into action.

"Team Two, on me," he hissed into his throat mike as he rose from his place of concealment and lunged forward. He crouched low as he emerged from the jungle and into the clearing, the butt of his M4 pressed into his right shoulder socket as he trained the weapon on the building in front of him. The stock of the rifle felt cool against his cheek as he sighted down the barrel, sweeping the weapon across the cabin's east wall in search of threats. There was no sign of anyone in either of the windows facing in his team's direction.

In his peripheral vision Hassler saw the silhouette of Team Two's assistant team leader, Sergeant Bobby Lipton, moving alongside him to his right. One of the best practitioners of small-unit tactics that Hassler had ever seen, Lipton was a master of ambush and counterambush techniques, and his accuracy with small-arms weaponry was unmatched by anyone else in the platoon. The sergeant was also coolheaded in even the most stressful of situations, rarely rushing into anything without first examining every factor. In Hassler's opinion, there was no better man to have guarding his flank.

The other members of the team, Maddox along with Corporals Kerry Stewart and Ronny Marks, were keeping pace to Hassler's left. Like him their weapons were trained on the cabin, ready to dispatch anyone or anything that might present a threat. He knew that at other points across the clearing, the rest of the Third Platoon was advancing in a like manner on their assigned targets.

Hassler slowed as he reached the cabin, coming to rest with his left shoulder against the wood slats that formed the wall. Still looking down his rifle barrel, he saw that he was three meters from the single door on this end of the building. Stewart took up station to the other side of the door as Maddox, Lipton, and Marks continued around to the front of the building, setting up their part of the two-pronged assault.

Reaching into the pocket on his left thigh, Hassler extracted a flash-bang grenade as Stewart produced a small packet of Semtex plastic explosive from a pouch on his assault vest. The corporal placed the putty-like compound on the door between the doorknob and the deadbolt lock positioned just above it. Next, he produced a length of primer cord from another pocket. One end of the cord was attached to a simple plunger detonator switch, and he inserted the other end into the wad of Semtex. He backed away from the door, keeping his right shoulder to the side of the cabin and uncoiling the cord until it extended to its full length of ten feet.

"Team One, in position," he heard Gerard say just as Stewart nodded to him.

"Team Two ready," Maddox reported.

Several seconds passed in silence before the leader of Team Three, Staff Sergeant Dillon Morrow, finally added, "Team Three, we're a go."

Muscles tensing in anticipation as his thumb moved the selector switch of his M4 from Auto to Semi, Hassler crouched down next to the cabin wall, lowering his head and covering it with his left arm.

"Go," Captain Sorensen said, three seconds later.

In his mind's eye, Hassler saw Stewart depress the plunger switch one heartbeat before the plastic explosive detonated. Even with his eyes closed he saw the flash as he felt the cabin rock from the force of the Semtex. Then instinct and training took over.

Stewart yanked the door open and Hassler tossed in the flash-bang he had readied, turning away and covering his eyes as the device detonated two seconds later. The resulting explosion was enough to rattle the fillings in Hassler's teeth. At the same instant, the night sky was obliterated for a moment as the flash-bang released its staggering light like a small sun going nova inside the building.

Sounds of pain and panic erupted from inside the cabin as Hassler rushed the door, sighting down the barrel of his rifle. Sweeping the weapon from side to side, he stepped to his right, keeping his back to the interior wall. He felt rather than saw Stewart enter the room and move to his left, mirroring Hassler's own actions.

Gunfire was already sounding from the building's front room, and Hassler recognized it as an M4 carried by one of the Marines. By then he had found his first target, one man holding a pistol and covering his eyes, still stunned by the flash-bang. In the near darkness of the room the man appeared to be a bright orange ghost through the filter of the M4's thermal sight. Hassler took him with two quick shots to the head. He saw another figure moving to his left, but it got no further before Stewart dispatched it, with similar ease.

It took only seconds to verify that the rest of the room was unoccupied before moving toward the hallway, and all the while Hassler's earpiece fed him the reports of other platoon members reporting their status as they proceeded through their objectives. Crouching low, Hassler maneuvered until he could look down the corridor and saw shadows flickering against the wall and heard footsteps echoing on the wooden floor.

Then a man appeared, carrying what the Marine recognized as an M16A2 rifle. The instant he saw Hassler his eyes went wide and he tried to bring the weapon up, but Hassler was faster. Two rounds exploded in the man's chest, dropping him in his tracks.

"Team Two, rear room secured," Hassler said as he stepped farther into the hallway. "Three down, moving forward."

"Two down in front room," Maddox replied. "Nothing in side room."

Five down in less than a minute. That should have been the end of it, according to their pre-mission briefing, but Hassler was hearing sounds from the room to his left. He swept the barrel of his M4 through the open doorway just as a bullet tore through the wall above his head.

Dropping to one knee, Hassler turned toward the sound of the weapons fire even as more bullets ripped into the wooden wall where he had been standing. One man, wielding what to Hassler's trained eye looked to be an MP5, was crouching behind a dilapidated desk. Thumbing the selector switch on his own rifle to Auto, Hassler held the trigger down and bullets tore through the desk, splintering wood and ripping into the man hiding behind it.

"Gunny," Maddox's voice sounded in his ear, "we've got them."

Lipton followed a moment later with "Rest of the building's secure."

Similar reports were coming in from the other teams, and Captain Sorensen was already issuing orders for the platoon to commence final sweep operations to ensure there were no stragglers hiding out anywhere as well as to search for anything that might be of intelligence value.

"Team leaders," Hassler said into his own mike, "deploy a defensive perimeter inside the tree line. I don't want anybody sneaking up on us while we wait for the helos." It was an unlikely scenario, but more than a few of Hassler's friends had been killed in the midst of unlikely scenarios. Now was not the time to start getting sloppy.

Moving toward the front of the cabin, Hassler finally allowed himself to relax a bit as he beheld the sight before him. Marks stood near the doorway of the building's only other room, keeping watch as Maddox and Lipton tended to a pair of bedraggled men, DEA agents Elliot and Glover, who sat tied to uncomfortable-looking wooden chairs. The Marines had already removed the gags placed over both men's mouths, and were now in the process of untying their hands and feet.

"Thank Christ," said Elliot, the younger of the two men. "Are we glad to see you guys."

"I'll bet," Hassler said, unable to suppress a smile at the man's unfettered relief. His attention instead was focusing on Glover, and the dark stain surrounding a tear in his left pants leg that had been tied back together with rope of some kind. "Are you okay?"

Glover nodded. "I tripped and fell when they were dragging us all over the place," he said. "Tore my leg on a nail." Sighing in relief, he added, "I'm pretty sure this was supposed to be the last stop, you know?"

Not knowing how well the agents had been informed about their situation by the people holding them captive, Hassler chose to sidestep the question. "Well, you can relax. We're calling for our ride right now."

"Works for me," Glover replied, his voice determined. "I'm more than ready to get the hell out of here."

In his earpiece, Hassler heard Sorensen reporting that the helos were inbound and would be here within the hour. The only thing left to do here was wait for their extraction.

To Hassler, that only left one question.

Wonder what the next mission will be?

CHAPTER TWO

Reginald Christopher was not in the habit of waiting, for anyone or for anything.

After nearly thirty years spent in professional politics, his demand for punctuality was far too ingrained to be changed. Though he had been in office as a United States senator for less than a month, he was already garnering a reputation as a stickler for promptness in the halls of the Capitol. His subordinates actually admired this in Christopher, especially as he held himself to even higher standards of conduct than he expected from those who worked for him.

He had long ago earned a similar reputation in the offices of the Utah state senate. He strictly adhered to schedules and disdained those who could not find the discipline to do likewise. He started meetings on time, remained on schedule with regard to agendas, and ended such gatherings with equal precision. More than once he had barred fellow members of the state congress from participating in meetings to which they had arrived late, in order to respect the schedules of those who had seen fit to show up on time.

Simply put, whenever someone kept him waiting, it pissed him off.

"Where the hell is Bates?" he asked without turning away from the large picture window dominating the foyer of the building identified to him by his driver simply as "the main building." Glancing at his Rolex, Christopher noted that it was 7:42, more than ten minutes after the time Bates had scheduled for their early-morning meeting.

At the far end of the lobby was a desk, behind which sat a guard dressed in a black battle-dress uniform, its only accoutrement an identification badge over the left breast pocket with the man's photograph and name printed on it. Christopher had noted the Beretta 9-millimeter pistol in a holster on the man's right hip, as well as the pair of M16A2 service rifles in a locked weapons cage mounted on the wall behind him.

"The professor's running a bit late this morning, Senator," the man offered. "He's involved with a critical experiment that's taking longer than expected. Can I get you anything while you wait, sir?"

Christopher shook his head. "No, thank you." While it grated on his nerves to be kept waiting, perhaps Bates deserved a modicum of leniency on this occasion, the senator decided. If what he had seen of this installation was any indication, the professor was indeed one very busy man.

The rest of the room in which he stood was unremarkable, its floor covered in alternating black and white tiles of a type that Christopher had seen in government buildings across the country. The walls were painted a generic off-white color, and a row of chairs lined the wall behind him, all of which looked to have come from the same warehouse as the guard's desk.

Not that he cared about the building's interior furnishings. It was what lay outside that captured his attention. Beyond the window, Christopher could see the edge of the plateau on which the building sat, overlooking what should have been a vast, uninterrupted vista of desert wasteland. Three miles away, according to his driver at any rate, was what the senator could only describe as an oasis: 225 square miles of teeming jungle.

"Amazing, isn't it?"

Christopher was startled by the new voice from behind him. It was old and raspy, much, the senator suspected, like its owner. Turning from the window, he saw the man he recognized from photographs he had seen during his initial briefing on this project.

Sixty-three years old according to his personnel file, the man was rail-thin, though his Caucasian skin was tanned almost to a deep brown as a consequence of his years spent living in the Utah desert. Balding, he wore what remained of his hair trimmed closely around the sides and back of his head, leaving the top of his skull smooth. A pair of wire-rimmed bifocals sat perched on the edge of his nose. His hands were stuffed into the pockets of his rumpled white lab coat, the breast pocket of which was stuffed with three pens, a notepad, and the mouthpiece of what Christopher recognized as a smoking pipe.

"Senator," the man said, pulling his right hand from his coat pocket and extending it to Christopher, "Professor Geoffrey Bates, administrator of this facility. It's a pleasure to finally meet you." The two men shook hands, and Christopher noted that the man's smile appeared to be genuine.

Returning the smile, Christopher actually felt himself relaxing in the face of Bates's undeniably warm personality. "The pleasure's mine, Professor. I have to admit I'm still a bit in the dark about this place." His friend and colleague, Senator Jonathan Dillard, had given him only the most cursory of briefings on this facility, referring to it simply as the "EDN project" and insisting that he had to travel here to receive the full briefing from Bates himself. The senior senator from Utah had warned him to keep an open mind, and to be ready for, as he put it, "some remarkable shit."

"Don't you worry, Senator," Bates said, assuming an almost paternal demeanor. "Jonathan is on his way to join us, but we've plenty of time to get acquainted before he arrives and he insisted we not wait for him." As he began to lead Christopher toward the door at the far end of the lobby, the one behind the guard at the desk, the professor offered, "Elizabeth has told me so many wonderful things about you."

That was just one more minor shock that Christopher had experienced since the strange meeting he had taken with Dillard the previous day. As part of the vague briefing he had given, during which he had managed to offer not a single shred of information about the facility's purpose, his friend had also revealed that Christopher's own daughter was playing a role on the project. "I knew that Elizabeth was working for the government these past few years, but most of her work is classified. I thought she was at a science lab over at Hill," he said, referring to Hill Air Force Base near Ogden, Utah, eighty miles away on the far side of the Great Salt Lake and almost due east from where he currently stood.

After receiving her doctorate in molecular biology from the Massachusetts Institute of Technology and after a brief tenure in one of that prestigious institution's renowned laboratories, Elizabeth Christopher had, for reasons she had yet seen fit to reveal, been attracted to some hush-hush government research. It was unnerving—hell, downright frustrating sometimes.

"You know your kids are gonna grow up and start edging you out of their day-to-day lives," Christopher said, "but this top-secret stuff can be hard to deal with." It was as though the longer he knew his daughter, the less he knew about her.

"An unfortunate aspect of the security surrounding our work here, Senator," Bates replied. "Now that you've been granted the so-called need to know, we'll be sure to spare no details. In fact, Elizabeth herself wanted to give you the tour." He waved to the window, indicating the jungle region that lay in the distance. "But she's been involved in some work out at one of our observation outposts. She sends her love, though, and promises she'll be back in time for you to take her to dinner."

Chuckling at that, Christopher replied, "Some things never change." His daughter had always been the type to let her work consume her attention to the exclusion of all else, a trait that, he honestly admitted, she had acquired from him as well as from her mother. Of course, sometimes she took the work ethic too far, just like her parents. If she ever settled down, the senator hoped she'd spend more time with her family than he'd spent with his. "In the meantime, what can you tell me about what we've got here?" he asked, returning his focus to the job at hand.

Nodding in the direction of the window once more, Bates replied, "You'll find we've been busy these past years. The jungle you see out there receives much of its water from a subterranean irrigation system that channels and desalinates water from the lake, allowing Mother Nature to bring forth life to this once barren wasteland."

Christopher's eyebrow rose at the odd choice of words. Did the professor consider himself a romantic, or was he simply suffering the effects of too many years spent inside a laboratory, shut away from the real world?

As if reading the senator's mind, Bates said, "Worry not, Senator. As Jonathan no doubt warned you, it is very likely that this is the most normal aspect of the facility that you'll encounter during your visit." Smiling again, he added, "As it happens, we've been giving Mother Nature a bit of help."

The conference room was like everything else Senator Christopher had seen of the building. It was furnished modestly, and its most striking feature was the large oval-shaped table occupying its center. Polished oak, the table was empty except for a single laptop computer situated near its far end, along with various fingerprints, smudges, dried moisture rings, and other assorted blemishes. A faint odor of cigarette smoke and old coffee lingered in the air, testifying to the uncounted hours of honest work that had taken place here.

Christopher could appreciate that. It told him that the people assigned to this project were focused on results rather than on their image. So far as government-funded endeavors were concerned, he was pleased by the refreshing change of pace.

"Please, Senator, have a seat," Bates said, gesturing to the chair at the head of the table. Like its eleven companions, the chair was standard-issue, black vinyl over a metal frame, its back stenciled with a national stock number and a description rendered in typically redundant government parlance: CHAIR, CONF, BLACK.

As he took his seat, Christopher noted that a three-lens projector hung from the ceiling, aimed at a large white dry-erase board mounted on the room's front wall. There were no windows, and while various pictures and generic artwork adorned the remaining walls, the only decoration of note was a monstrous full-color map of the immense Hill Air Force Base hanging to Christopher's left.

Bates said, "Now that we're officially behind closed doors, so to speak, we can talk freely." He smiled as he stepped around the table to the laptop, tapping a few keys on the computer as he withdrew a remote control from his pocket. In response to his actions, the lights in the room slowly began to dim and the projector activated, casting an image onto the white board. Christopher recognized the photograph as an enlarged version of the Hill Range and the western shore of the Great Salt Lake.

"In 1962," Bates continued, "this site was selected as one of several areas across the United States to be used as a toxic-waste depository. It's far away from any real population centers, so it seemed as good a place as could be found to dispose of various noxious substances that are the inconvenient and unwanted by-products of modern civilization."

It was an unfortunate truth, Christopher knew, but a disheartening one nonetheless. Such sites, those both known to the public and several others which like this one were closely guarded secrets, were scattered around the country, to say nothing of similar sites maintained by the world's other industrialized nations. Regulating the disposal and containment of toxic waste was no easy task, though the United States had a better track record than most. Still, the senator knew that when it came to how too many people treated their planet and its natural resources, the distinction was small, with the U.S. acting the part of the rapist with the nicest assortment of prophylactics.

That will change, if I have anything to say about it.

"As an offshoot of the disposal program," Bates continued, "government scientists also enacted a plan to monitor the prolonged exposure of various toxins on different environments." He tapped the remote, and the picture on the whiteboard changed to what Christopher recognized as rows of giant greenhouses.

"The facility pictured here was originally constructed in 1974 and designed to simulate dozens of regions from around the world. The ecosystems were re-created as close to the original as possible, including plant and animal life indigenous to a variety of locations from around the world. For years, the protracted effects of these substances on the different environments were monitored, begetting all manner of subsequent experiments as more knowledge was accumulated."

"You mean you deliberately exposed plants and animals to toxic pollution?" Christopher asked, making no effort to hide his revulsion at the idea.

Bates nodded. "I admit it doesn't sound pleasant. In fact, it was undeniably cruel. Trust me, though, when I say that it ultimately served a most noble purpose. As the experiments proceeded, theories began to emerge about how contaminated soil, vegetation, and animal life might be treated or even freed of the debilitating effects of different toxins. Soon, we started considering the notion of genetically engineering new breeds of plant and animal life designed specifically to thrive in these tainted environments."

"Why on earth would you want to do that?" Christopher asked, his expression now a combination of equal parts confusion and disgust.

An almost paternal smile appeared on the professor's face. "Think of the possibilities, Senator. There are animals that rid us of pests like insects, rodents, and other undesirable creatures. The vegetation around us removes carbon dioxide from the air we breathe and returns oxygen to the atmosphere. But, what if we had species of plant and animal life that were specifically engineered to break down those toxins and impurities caused by industrialization? In time, such plant and animal life could conceivably reclaim regions that have been ravaged by the effects of pollution."

Frowning, Christopher leaned forward in his chair until his arms rested atop the conference table's well-worn surface. "Is that what you've got out there? You've grown a jungle and fed toxic waste to whatever the hell you've got wandering around out there? They eat the plants or bushes or grass, and then what? Shit out new pollution-free fertilizer? Are you kidding me?" What the hell had Dillard gotten him into?

Annoyance clouded Bates's features for the first time. "This is not some pork-barrel government grant program, Senator. I should think that Jonathan would have made that clear before sending you to me. The scientists assigned to this installation, as well as our secondary support facility at Nellis Air Force Base in Nevada, are leaders in their respective fields, and they've invested a significant portion of their lives and careers to bettering the world in spite of the best efforts of those who seek to pillage it for their own interests."

Uh-oh, Christopher mused. *Looks like I hit a sore spot.*

"We employ the latest in scientific, medical, and technological advances here," Bates continued, tapping the table for emphasis. "Let's take DNA mapping, for example. You'll be interested to know that the human genome was charted right here, in this building, seven years before it was made public knowledge that such a venture was even under way." Placing his hands in the pockets of his lab coat, the professor began to pace a circuit around the room. "Perhaps that makes you think about cloning.

Well, we're way ahead of you in that area, too, Senator. Once we developed the blueprint, re-creating the simplest microorganisms was child's play."

Bates turned away from the whiteboard and locked eyes with Christopher, his voice taking on a hard edge. "Given all of that, and everything that you do not yet know about the work taking place here, I would appreciate it if you refrained from dismissing me and my people like so many government-supported crackpots who waste taxpayer money studying the effects of soft-drink mixtures on rodents."

"I apologize for my outburst, Professor," Christopher said, attempting to mollify the other man. "But you have to admit that, on the surface, what you're describing sounds pretty outlandish."

In other words, what have you been smoking, and who's your dealer?

The smile returned to Bates's face, though it lacked much of the energy it had previously possessed. "By the end of the day, all of your questions and concerns will be addressed to your satisfaction." He nodded and chuckled to himself, as if acknowledging a joke only he had heard. "I realize that the notion of creating all of this simply as a tool for protecting the environment might seem like so much 'pie-in-the-sky' wishful thinking. Believe me, you're not the first to express skepticism." He released another small laugh, only this time Christopher noted a distinct lack of humor in the professor's demeanor.

"There are also other applications for which this technology might be employed, Senator," Bates continued. "For example, when the armies of the world wage war on each other, they tend not to concern themselves with the havoc they wreak on the environment around them. Everything from the pollution cast off by vehicles to nuclear waste from the reactors powering aircraft carriers and submarines to the very real dangers brought on by nuclear, biological, and chemical warfare."

Stepping around the table, the professor gestured to Christopher with outstretched hands. "We both know that the military has spent decades devising methods for its soldiers to survive in such environments, particularly in recent years as we continue to face a very real threat of attacks by enemies using such dreadful weapons. Now, consider the possibilities of a species of animal life that not only could survive in the inhospitable conditions that would be generated in the aftermath of an attack by a weapon of mass destruction, but which also could thrive in that environment."

Realization was beginning to dawn on Christopher. "You mean . . . ?"

Bates nodded as if anticipating the senator's next words. "That's right, Senator. Our goals here are quite multifaceted. Some, naturally, are driven by the desire to heal the wounds humanity has inflicted on this planet. Others have more martial applications." He paused as he said that, his expression melting into a frown before he added, "For better or worse, that is."

Despite his initial reservations, Christopher found himself being drawn in by the professor's presentation as well as the obvious enthusiasm he held for his work. Leaning forward until his elbows rested atop the well-worn conference table, he asked, "How have you managed all of this?"

Bates pressed a button on the remote he still held in his hand, and the projector responded by displaying a photographic montage of various animals. Mice, rabbits, snakes, birds, a tiger, a chimpanzee, even a fish that Christopher recognized as a large-mouthed bass.

"After we mastered the craft of re-creating single-celled organisms," the professor continued, "we spent several years advancing upward through different orders of plant and animal life as we perfected the process. Cloning was just the first step, Senator. Then came our efforts to understand the potential of resequencing DNA in order to produce hybrid species. It was not until we graduated to creating life-forms designed specifically for our rather unique environment that we began to see the realization of the vision we had when this project began."

"Genetic engineering?" Christopher asked. He had read about this subject, if only sporadically, over the years. The idea of artificially manipulating DNA by taking genes from one organism and combining them with genes from another had long been fodder for scientists looking to "improve the world" or, more precisely, "improve man." Everything from creating animals with near-human levels of intelligence to developing an improved breed of human had been bandied about for decades. The concept of the "supersoldier" was one from which Christopher himself had derived much amusement, as the notion usually took the form of escapist entertainment in books or movies.

Jon, what the hell have you been hiding out here? The senator also had to wonder what could have compelled his daughter to involve herself with something that—to him, at least—was little more than an outrageous fantasy.

Shaking his head, Bates waved his hand as if dismissing the notion. "Genetic engineering is at best a haphazard concept, Senator. Simply depositing fragments of one DNA strain into another is not the way. Our genes are not isolated components that can just be shuffled and rearranged as we see fit. They are constantly evolving in response to their interaction with one another, the organism as a whole as well as the environment it inhabits."

It was obvious to Christopher that the professor was in his element now. There was no mistaking the passion in his voice or the way he waved his hands about while speaking, all of it signifying the sheer, unqualified trust he placed in whatever the hell it was he and his comrades were doing here.

"With that in mind," Bates continued, "simply rearranging the DNA of a bird or snake so that it can better live in an environment we choose for it is impractical. It is far better to create an entirely new animal, from whole cloth if you will." Pausing in his dissertation, Bates returned his hands to his coat pockets, offering another wistful smile.

"For this project to succeed, we've taken what Mother Nature provided and developed our own schema, which over time has acquired the admittedly arrogant designation of the Genesis Protocol."

CHAPTER THREE

Still sweating from her workout, Dr. Elizabeth Christopher entered the small locker room and sighed in relief as cool air played across her exposed skin. A glance to the clock on the far wall told her that it was just past eight in the morning, and she tried not to dwell on the notion that this would probably be as good as she would feel for the remainder of the day.

She received no comfort from the image of the mountain of paperwork that surely had accumulated in her office back at Central Operations during her three-week absence. With that in mind, Elizabeth was sorely tempted to spend an extra day out here, tucked away within the tiny observation outpost deep inside the EDN region, her and the rest of her team almost safe from Professor Bates and his notorious long reach. After all, fieldwork beat administration or labwork every time.

He'd still find you.

Such was her lot in life as a senior member of the EDN project, Elizabeth knew. Previous experience had taught her that simply participating in a government-sponsored undertaking all but guaranteed a certain level of bureaucracy and paperwork, itself far beyond even the absurdity she had observed during her brief sojourn to the private sector. The irony of her more recent assignments was that the higher the security classification surrounding a particular task, the more paperwork it seemed to generate, and the more red tape Elizabeth Christopher was forced to endure.

At least today there's something to look forward to.

Elizabeth had been surprised to get her father's message notifying her that he had been cleared for a tour of the EDN facilities. It was a welcome break from the routine here, one to which she had been looking forward for the past three days. If her father was being briefed about the project, then chances were good that he would soon play a part in its oversight. This would have the added benefit of allowing her to see him more often than had been possible in recent years, a change she welcomed.

More shocking even than that was his having called himself, rather than delegating the task to one of his assistants. He had always been a busy man, sometimes too busy to make time for family. She understood her father's work ethic, having acquired it herself, and also knew it was one of several things that had eventually driven him and her mother apart.

As for Elizabeth herself, her own work had always conspired with her father's political career to keep her from seeing him on anything resembling a regular schedule. Once or twice, the gaps between visits had been more than a year. After her mother's death the previous summer, her father had been making efforts to spend more time with each of his three children despite a manic campaign schedule. Elizabeth had appreciated the effort and done her part to reciprocate.

Today was one of those precious few occasions, and she had no intention of squandering it.

Stripping off her socks, shorts, and sports bra, she stepped into one of three shower vestibules, each composed of translucent Plexiglas that helped to assuage the feeling that one was stepping into a closet or coffin. The shower's series of eight water jets activated automatically as the door was closed, the warmth of the water combining with a gentle massaging action that immediately soothed the kinks out of her stressed muscles.

She enjoyed the water spray for another minute or so before getting on with the actual business of washing, doing so for a few minutes before she heard the sounds of someone stepping into the stall next to her and noted a shadowy figure through the hazy film of the Plexiglas. Even though their outline was indistinct and distorted, Elizabeth was fairly certain of the person's identity.

"Didn't I flip over the Ladies Only sign before I came in here?" she asked, nearly shouting to be heard over the streaming water.

"I'm sorry, miss," a male voice responded. "Are you decent?"

Elizabeth smiled, having correctly deduced her neighbor to be her colleague and friend Dr. Paul Sanchez. She had seen him running his normal circuit around the outer corridor of Observation Station Four's subterranean compound. Every day without fail, the man ran thirty laps around the building, equaling just over three miles of distance. She had tried to run with him on a few occasion but had found the exercise of running in a big circle mind-numbingly boring. It was a testament to Sanchez's self-discipline that he was able to do it day after day, whereas she instead preferred the collection of free weights, treadmill, and stair-step machine stuffed into the storage room that had been converted into Ob-Stat Four's makeshift gym.

"You just behave yourself over there," she offered in mock warning. "Otherwise, I'll have security throw you out."

Sanchez laughed. "And here I was hoping you'd wash my back."

Constructed nearly a decade before the first woman signed onto the EDN project, the outpost offered little in the way of true privacy to those who worked here. The bathroom facilities were small and functional, and though the entire structure and interior of the outpost had been renovated and modernized over the years, the all but subterranean building simply offered no further room for separate facilities based on gender. Therefore, while team members still made efforts to respect one another's privacy as much as possible, most, including Elizabeth and Paul Sanchez, had long ago abandoned any notions of shyness.

"Hey, how are the fish biting this morning?" Sanchez asked a moment later.

Her mind quickly refocusing on the work she had performed the previous evening, Elizabeth replied, "Everything is within norms. The greps are really taking to the crude we dumped in Beta Pond. They're going after it like frat boys to cheap beer."

She had spent the majority of the past five days observing and cataloguing information about the region's newest inhabitants. Named *greplers* after Wyatt Grepler, the scientist who had proposed their creation, the fish were one of the first ideas pursued once the true potential of the EDN project was realized: a species engineered for the express purpose of breaking down crude-petroleum spills in waterways.

Once perfected for real-world use, the greps would live and breed in oceans, lakes, and rivers while consuming the impurities introduced by petroleum and other pollutants, breaking it down over time and removing harmful elements from the water.

It was a concept that had evolved over several years, with earlier generations of the greps used in discreet tests performed at different locations around the country, including the Philadelphia Naval Shipyard and even the area around the sunken wreck of the U.S.S. *Arizona*, from which oil had been seeping since its tragic loss during the attack on Pearl Harbor. The range of tests had spanned nearly a decade, and everything learned during those earlier experiments, good and bad, had been incorporated into this latest generation of greps.

Elizabeth had overseen the program for almost three years, since Dr. Grepler's passing after a long bout with prostate cancer. It was but a single aspect of the overall EDN initiative, though one she knew would attract a lot of attention from environmental-protection groups and oil companies around the world once the project was revealed to the public.

God help me when that day comes.

She reached for the door, the water shutting off as she stepped from the vestibule. Goose bumps rose on her still-wet skin in response to the cool air, and she quickly wrapped herself in a towel before crossing the changing room to her locker. She had just begun to dress when she heard a door open behind her.

"Hello?" a tentative voice called out. It belonged to Rory Maguire, one of two security agents assigned to the observation station's field team.

Knowing that Maguire would not enter the locker room so long as any women were inside, Elizabeth smiled as she stepped into a pair of khaki pants, both amused and charmed by the man's mix of propriety and embarrassment. "It's me, Rory," she said. "Paul's in the shower. What's up?"

Keeping the door closed save for a narrow gap through which he could speak, Maguire replied, "Have you heard from Dr. Watts or Sean this morning?"

"Not yet," Elizabeth said as she ran her towel through her damp blond hair. That done, she donned a blue sweatshirt emblazoned with an MIT logo before reaching for her running shoes. "It's okay to come in now, Rory."

She nearly laughed at the man's hesitation when Maguire poked his head through the doorway, as if to verify her claim. "You know that Dr. Watts had the late watch last night," he said. "According to the trouble log, she took Sean and they went out last night around 0130 to fix a sensor that was out of alignment at Remote Pod Six. They never came back."

Running a comb through her shoulder-length hair, Elizabeth frowned. "Are you sure?" No sooner did she speak the words then she waved a hand as if to erase them. "Sorry, of course you are. The repair job must have taken longer than she expected."

"I thought about that," Maguire offered, "but Dr. Griffin told me that the sensor listed as malfunctioning is now working just fine. According to him, it's been transmitting data for almost five hours now."

Behind her, Elizabeth heard Sanchez enter the changing area. "Five hours?" he asked as he stepped toward his locker, a beige terry-cloth towel wrapped around his waist and rivulets of water still dripping from his black and gray hair. "Pod Six is three miles away. They could have walked there and back by now."

"I know," Maguire said. "Their truck's GPS locator shows that it's still parked on the road near the pod, but when I tried to call them on the radio, I got nothing." Shaking his head, he added, "I don't like it."

Elizabeth felt a knot of worry forming in her gut. Though the project did not operate within strict military protocols or even the parameters of overbearing corporate policy, there were still rules followed by all personnel. One decree was that anyone venturing into the EDN region was to maintain regular communication with their given base of operations.

Both Watts and Godfried in particular were unswerving in their compliance with that rule, and would certainly have called back to the outpost if they had encountered difficulty, either with the sensor pod or their truck. So far as Elizabeth was concerned, that they had failed to do so on this occasion was cause for concern, not irritation.

A crackle of static spit out of the intercom speaker mounted to the wall near the door, followed by the distressed voice of Dr. Joshua Griffin, the fourth member of the science team stationed at the outpost during the current three-week rotation.

"Liz? You need to get up here right now."

There was no mistaking the distress in Griffin's voice, which itself was unusual. Normally unflappable and reserved almost to the point that Elizabeth had been tempted on occasion to check his pulse to ensure he was actually alive, she had never heard him so much as raise his voice during the two years she had known him. Given the current situation with Watts and Godfried, hearing Griffin's anxiety now put her immediately on edge.

Crossing the room to the intercom, Elizabeth pushed the Talk button with her thumb. "What's the matter, Josh?"

There was a moment's hesitation before Griffin replied, "It's . . . uh . . . I think you should just come up here, please."

The camera shack, as it was called by various project members, shared one key characteristic with most of Ob-Stat Four's other interior areas in that it was small, cramped, and stuffed to the ceiling tiles with too much equipment. The air-conditioning fought a never-ending battle against the heat vented from the collection of computers, printers, and television monitors, and the bodies of the three or four people who might be working in the room at any one time.

Elizabeth felt the warmth inside the shack even as she and Maguire jogged through the door, quickly locating Joshua Griffin seated at his usual place at a desk in the far corner. He looked like a typical fiftyish ex-hippie, with receding gray hair gathered in a ponytail that fell between his shoulder blades and a gut that lapped over his belt, straining the threadbare material of his faded black Grateful Dead concert T-shirt. A laptop computer sat atop a chaotic pile of papers, notebooks, and other assorted office detritus littering Griffin's desk, but Elizabeth saw that he was ignoring all of that and everything else in the room as he sat slumped in his chair. Instead, he was directing an almost vacant stare at the array of display monitors dominating the shack's forward wall.

"Josh?" she prompted as she walked up to Griffin. He did not react until she placed a hand on his shoulder, and then only directed the empty stare up at her. Elizabeth felt her blood grow cold as she beheld the anguish and fear in her friend's eyes. "Jesus, Josh. What's wrong?"

It took an additional moment before Griffin replied, clearing his throat and removing his glasses to wipe his eyes before saying, "When Rory came to me this morning asking about Alicia and Sean, we tried calling them on the radio. That didn't work, but the truck's locator was still active, so I thought maybe their radio just might be broken or something."

Reaching for the wireless mouse situated to the right of his laptop computer, he continued, "There aren't any cameras in that area, so I tried to remote-activate the truck's dashboard camera. The signal was full of static, but I kept playing with the settings and I was finally able to tune in a picture. It's grainy, but it's . . . it's enough."

Not saying anything more, Griffin navigated his mouse pointer across the laptop's display monitor and selected an icon marked VIDEO FEED ENABLE. In response to his commands, the bottom-rightmost monitor on the far wall, one of eight atop shelves bolted into the concrete, flickered to life. The only thing visible was a multicolored blur, obscured by a dull gray mist.

"What is that?" Elizabeth said at first, unable to discern what it was she was seeing on the screen.

"The truck's windshield," Griffin replied as he moved the mouse again, and this time the dashboard camera's lens pulled back until Elizabeth realized that the gray film that seemed to cover the windshield was in fact the windshield itself. The safety glass had been struck by something large and heavy near the passenger side of the vehicle, with a web of cracks spiraling out from the point of impact. Dark splotches speckled the glass, and Elizabeth felt a shiver grip her body as she realized what the stains were.

Blood.

"Holy shit," she heard Paul Sanchez say from behind her as he entered the shack. "Did they hit something?"

Griffin shook his head. "I don't think so." He moved the mouse again and the truck camera responded by rotating to the right, panning across the interior of the truck until it was aimed through the passenger-side window.

Outside the vehicle, Elizabeth could see the muddy browns and muted greens of the ankle-deep swaygrass bordering the service road, spanning several dozen meters before being met by the tree line of the dense, deadly vegetation dominating this sector of the EDN region. She noted that the swaygrass was missing in many places and clumped together in others, as if it had had to move quickly to avoid being trampled by a herd of large animals and had not yet wandered back into its regular evenly spaced position.

Even more disturbing to Elizabeth were the remains of an equipment kit, along with its tools and some components she could not recognize, lying scattered across the ground, twisted and broken as though the box had been ransacked and ripped to pieces.

Then the camera panned until it focused on a pair of crumpled shapes lying in the grass, perhaps fifteen meters from the truck.

"Oh God."

The words were a tortured whisper just audible to her own ears as she saw the shreds of orange material, what could only be the tattered ruins of a containment suit, barely covering the prone form of its wearer. Elizabeth felt bile rising in her throat as she beheld the site of one decapitated body. What remained of it was covered in blood, almost impossible to identify even as human save for the right arm, the only extremity which had not been severed from the torso.

The second corpse was in far worse condition.

To her right, Griffin turned away from the screen, one hand moving to cover his mouth, and Elizabeth could hear him drawing several deep, rapid breaths in an effort to keep his own onrushing nausea at bay. Turning to her left, she locked eyes with Sanchez, whose ashen expression was certainly a match for her own. Even Maguire, who she was sure had seen far worse during his tenure in the army's Special Forces, appeared disturbed by the grotesque scene. Thank God he still had the presence of mind to reach for a phone and call it in. They were too late to help Watts and Godfried, but if there were other teams out there . . . Elizabeth shivered.

"Looks like they were mauled," the security specialist said after he hung up.

"Yeah, but by what?" Sanchez replied.

Orienting herself so that the televisions were behind her, Elizabeth took her own set of calming breaths, thankful that she had been able to keep from vomiting all over the shack in response to the horrific images on the screen. "Josh, turn that off, would you?" To Maguire, she said, "He's right, Rory. Every animal in the region is genetically coded to stay within restricted areas."

"The most dangerous thing near Pod Six was a bunch of mals," Paul said.

Individual species had been designed to subsist on a limited variety of plant or other animal life, and the project's genetic engineers had also encoded allergies into their DNA. Predisposed dislikes of other vegetation or animals or even the chemical balance of various bodies of water scattered throughout the EDN region had been ingrained in the animals' genetic makeup. They worked in concert with the layout of the region itself, which had been designed to offer natural barriers to keep the animals in their specified zones without the need for fences or other obstacles.

In theory, anyway.

"What about a security breach?" Maguire suggested, but almost as quickly shook his head. "No, of course not. If anyone or anything could even get inside the perimeter, chances are they'd be dead inside of an hour."

Elizabeth nodded in agreement. The EDN region was, by its very nature, protected from unwanted trespassers. It was true that a handful of sectors had been created throughout the artificially engineered jungle so that humans could work outside—at least so long as they had been properly inoculated upon joining the project, of course. The area immediately surrounding ObStat Four fell into that category, but a significant portion of the region was, by design, an extreme biohazard. Anyone luckless enough to venture into its environs without the proper protection would be signing their own death warrants.

"Why aren't they responding?" Griffin said, his voice still trembling. "You'd think they'd at least have sent out some sort of rescue vehicle by now—"

He stopped talking when he saw the others staring at him. Elizabeth felt a pang of embarrassment for him. No one needed to say it out loud. It was too late for a rescue. With a little luck, though, perhaps it wasn't too late to warn anyone else out there.

As if in response to her thought, an alarm blared, echoing in the shack's confined space and nearly causing Elizabeth to jump out of her skin. A warning light mounted over the row of television monitors flared bright crimson, flashing in rhythm with the klaxon.

"Perimeter warning," Maguire shouted above the siren as he moved to another desk, atop which sat a pair of larger flat-screen computer monitors and their accompanying keyboards. Tapping keys, he said, "Something's approaching without authorization."

"Put it up front," Elizabeth said. In response to her request, Maguire entered new commands to his computer and one of the middle monitors on the upper row of display screens shifted to a view of the grounds above the buried observation station. Using his mouse, the security agent pivoted the camera providing the feed, first to the left and then back to the right, searching for whatever had tripped the alarm.

A dark figure ran past, moving much too fast for the camera to keep up.

"What the hell was that?" Sanchez shouted, before cursing again and, much to Elizabeth's relief, stabbing a control on his computer that silenced the racket caused by the alarm.

Shaking his head, Maguire replied, "Damned if I know." He rotated the camera again, this time completing a 360-degree circuit of the compound, showing nothing but vegetation along with two exhaust vents and the array of antennae that were the only aboveground signs of ObStat Four's existence within the camera's range.

Then she saw the shadowy figure again, running near the tree line at the edges of the clearing, followed closely by another one. "There!" she said, pointing at the screen before the sprinting shapes outran the camera's view once again.

They were visible only for an instant, but Elizabeth was sure that, whatever they were, they had been running upright, not on all fours like a mal. There were no simian-based animals in this or any of the surrounding sectors, and even if there were, what she had seen had not looked like an ape.

Another alarm sounded, this one not nearly as loud or obnoxious as the previous alert, but Maguire turned to investigate it with the same fervor. "One of the exhaust vents is offline," he reported. "Hang on."

Reaching for his computer mouse, he panned the camera around again. This time, the video feed showed that the rotating hood on the closer of the two exhaust vents had been ripped away and was now lying in a crumpled heap on the ground next to the vent opening itself.

"Look!" Maguire shouted, and Elizabeth saw a dark, fleeting shape moving away from the port and heading toward the other vent. It lashed out at the other vent as it ran, smashing its cover with a single blow and causing the unit to halt its spinning just as another warning alert sounded in the shack.

"Jesus, did you see that?" Sanchez cried out. Even though the camera offered no audio feed, Elizabeth imagined she could hear the groan of protesting metal as it ground to a halt under the force of the blow.

Then something stepped in front of the camera, and the video feed went dead.

"Damn it," Maguire said, reaching for the mouse. "Let me pull up another angle."

"Forget it," Elizabeth said, trying to ignore the pounding of her heart as it apparently tried to force its way from her chest. "Make sure all the outer doors are secure."

"They can't get in here," Griffin countered, though she heard the concern in his voice. "I mean, can they?"

Maguire shook his head. "Beats the hell out of me, but I'm not taking any chances. All outer doors are secure, along with inner doors." Tapping keys on his computer once more, he added, "I'm securing all sections adjacent to the exits, too." As he worked, a new alarm sounded from his desk, and the security agent grimaced. "Another vent is out."

"Shut the others off," Elizabeth said suddenly, moving to stand next to Maguire. "And kill all power to anything that's exposed on the surface."

"What are you thinking, Liz?" Sanchez asked.

Shrugging, she replied, "Maybe they're attracted to rhythmic noises, or the hum produced by a power supply. Something about the equipment out there is pissing them off."

"Oh dear sweet Jesus," Griffin said from behind her, the panic evident in his voice. "Elizabeth, look."

She turned to where the other scientist was pointing and saw that Griffin had brought up the image of another camera, this one aimed in such a manner that it displayed one of the station's entrances. The image was clear, showing stairs descending from ground level between a pair of concrete walls until they met a heavy metal door, in front of which stood . . . something.

"Look at this," Griffin called out as he moved his computer mouse. "That's the south door," he said as he moved the camera, the external unit responding by turning to get a better angle on the doorway. Its image raced out of focus in reaction to the hurried movements before the picture abruptly exploded into static.

"What the hell is that thing?" Sanchez asked rhetorically.

Then a thump, dull and distant, echoed in the hallway outside the shack.

"No way," Sanchez said, his eyes wide with disbelief and growing fear.

"This is nuts," Maguire said as he rose from his desk, and Elizabeth watched as the man ran out of the shack and toward the room across the hallway. She figured she knew what he was after, and her suspicions were confirmed a few seconds later when he returned, this time carrying a pistol belt and an M16 rifle in one hand and a flak vest in the other.

"You think they can get in here?" she asked.

Donning the flak vest and zipping it closed, Maguire next reached for one of the vest's pockets and extracted a magazine of ammunition. "You saw what one of them did to that vent cover. If they decide to really start wailing on that door, there's no way it'll hold for very long."

Elizabeth fought to keep her voice calm. "Call for help. Have Rolero come and get us."

Maguire reached for the M16. "It'll take time for her to get here." Inserting the magazine into the weapon, he slapped its bottom to seat it and loaded the first round into the rifle's chamber. "Until then, we're on our own."

The man's statement was punctuated by the echo of more pounding in the passageway, only this time the sounds were louder and more insistent.

CHAPTER FOUR

"The Genesis Protocol."

Senator Christopher repeated the words. They sounded significant, revolutionary, and pretentious all at the same time.

The fundamentalists are gonna have a stroke when they hear about this.

Of course, given what Professor Bates had told him over the past several minutes, the moniker was an appropriate one. Using science, humans had dared to attempt what many believed was the purview of something far more powerful than themselves.

"You're creating entire species of animal and plant life," Christopher said. "They're products of your imagination, existing because you see fit to construct them to your specifications. You've been playing God, Professor, something I would think that a great many people would find disturbing."

If what Bates was describing truly was possible, then it would unleash philosophical and ethical discussions of a nature so profound that similar debates surrounding cloning, stem-cell research, genetically engineered foods, and even artificially grown organs and tissue would pale in comparison.

Assuming it ever became public knowledge, of course.

Nodding, Bates reached for a glass of water near his left hand, taking a drink before replying. "Our allusions don't stop there, I'm afraid." Tapping a key on the remote once more, he switched the projector to an aerial view of what Christopher now realized was the jungle expanse three miles from their present location.

"The greenhouses that harbored our experimental habitats outgrew their usefulness years ago," the professor continued. "As we perfected the Protocol, it soon became apparent that we had to craft an entirely new ecosystem to house the life we had brought into our world. The culmination of that work is what you see here, and what we refer to as the Environmental Development Nucleus, or EDN."

"E-D-N," Christopher repeated, shaking his head again. "Eden. Of course."

As if embarrassed by that, Bates replied, "Given the Genesis Protocol itself, it seemed appropriate, though I myself prefer to call it 'New Eden,' not that it really matters." He pointed to the picture on the wall. "This region is a living, breathing laboratory, replete with all manner of artificially engineered plant and animal life developed right here on this site. Senator Christopher, what you see here—and what you will see for yourself in due course—is the culmination of nearly forty years of work. In time, it could very well change the face of our world as we know it, for the benefit of everyone and for all time."

The professor tapped the remote again, and this time the still photographs were placed by video. Each time Bates pressed a control, the image shifted to display a different location in the EDN region. What struck Christopher first was that, although he recognized the general outlines of what he supposed was trees and other foliage, their shapes and colors were unlike anything he had ever seen.

Then the video feed shifted once more and Christopher forgot about the bushes.

"What the hell are those?" He rose from his chair, transfixed by the images on the screen that depicted a grouping of what at first looked to be monkeys cavorting among the high branches of several trees, jumping from limb to limb with practiced ease. Their orange-red fur gave them the appearance of baboons or orangutans, but the senator saw almost immediately that the resemblance ended there.

"We call them *dilmores*," Bates explained after a moment. "We've established a tradition of naming the different species after the scientist responsible for creating them." Pausing the video, the professor pointed to the hands of one of the animals. "As you can see, they do possess many simian characteristics, though note here the opposable thumbs." Smiling again, he added, "This particular breed has shown remarkable intelligence, greater than even the most gifted nonhuman."

"Just so long as they don't start riding around on horses and burying the Statue of Liberty," Christopher retorted.

Bates resumed the alternating series of video feeds, and with every new image the senator found himself increasingly drawn to what he was seeing. Different species of animal life, each one more bizarre than the last and all of them engineered artificially on this site. The very idea was staggering.

"All of this," he said, "just to populate polluted areas in an effort to reclaim them?"

Shrugging, the professor replied, "That was the original goal, yes. The idea was to introduce such animals into regions determined to be poisonous to indigenous life. For example, specially designed fish could be brought to oceans, lakes, and rivers polluted by oil spills, refinery waste, and so on. Living and feeding in these compromised environments, they would, over time, break the contaminants down into inert compounds."

"How have you paid for this?" Christopher asked. "I'm certain there are a great number of people who wouldn't like taxpayer money going to something like this."

Bates looked at his feet for a moment, then met the senator's eyes. "New Eden is funded mostly by the development and patenting of different technologies, many of which have found legitimate uses far beyond the project's classified environs." Shaking his head, he added, "It may interest or even amuse you to know that my people have toiled for years in anonymity, watching as those small snippets of their work which are revealed to the public have been used in all sorts of ventures that have brought great wealth and recognition to others."

Christopher nodded in understanding. Though he imagined that at least a significant number of the EDN participants were content in the knowledge that they were working toward a higher purpose, there had to be those who resented seeing their efforts being exploited by some of the individuals and corporations responsible for the very pollution and environmental damage the project was intended to heal.

Irony. What a bitch.

"Obviously," he said, "you must have some plan for deploying these . . . creations of yours to different parts of the world. How long before you'd be ready for something like that?"

"The project has enjoyed rapid progress and success in recent years," Bates replied. As he spoke, he reached into one of his lab coat's pockets and extracted a small medication vial. "Our latest variations of plant and animal life have shown a measurable effect on the toxic substances permeating the EDN region. We believe that tangible results can be achieved within two decades of introduction, with permanent arrest and even reversal of environmental damage possible within a century." Retrieving two bright blue pills from the vial, the professor popped them into his mouth before taking a drink from his water glass.

Christopher shook his head in unqualified wonder. The possibilities were endless. Both he and Senator Dillard had always lobbied for environmental causes. This would be like manna from heaven to his supporters. Sure as hell wouldn't hurt his chances in the next election.

Getting ahead of yourself, aren't you?

An outdoors enthusiast since childhood, Christopher had always portrayed himself as a pro-environment politician while maintaining a respectable distance from the more extreme activist segments. There were practical considerations for which to account in a modern civilization, he knew, but that did not mean that companies and individuals could not be held accountable for actions that harmed the environment for personal or corporate profit. He had long campaigned on such issues, promising his constituents that the country's natural beauty, particularly that of his home state, would be safeguarded.

Something like the EDN project, harbored right here in his back pocket, would be nothing less than a guaranteed ticket straight to top of the political ladder.

Assuming he had the upper hand, of course.

"Already figuring out how this will work for you, Reg?"

The voice jolted Christopher from his reverie and he looked to the front of the room to see Jonathan Dillard— friend and longtime U.S. senator from the state of Utah— standing in the doorway and smiling with all the practiced warmth and charm one would expect from a man in his position.

"So," Dillard said, "is Geoffrey here taking good care of you?"

Christopher nodded. "Of course." Indicating the projection screen, he allowed his eyes to widen and a note of wonder into his voice. "Jon, this is incredible. How long have you known about it?"

"Eleven years," Dillard replied, turning too see the artificially engineered dilmore on the screen. "You haven't seen anything yet."

"Who else knows about this?"

Shrugging, Dillard replied, "A few senators, but the list is very short for the time being, at least. There's a hearing scheduled for next month in Washington where we plan to announce the existence of the project and discuss in detail its accomplishments as well as our future intentions." Christopher noted the fleeting glance his friend shared with Bates as he said that last part, and could not help the feeling that there was more to what was being said here than met the eye.

Of course there is, he reminded himself. *We're just getting started, after all.*

"I'm surprised you've been able to carry on your work here all these years without encountering at least a few headaches," he said. "Given the economic and budget woes of the past few years, particularly with the last administration, I'd have thought a project like this would have bitten the dust long ago."

Dillard offered a knowing, almost weary smile. "Well, as I'm sure you'd guess, the project has had to make a few concessions in order to be seen as useful by some of the more conventional folks in Washington." He indicated Bates with an outstretched hand. "Geoffrey will be attending the hearings and answering what will undoubtedly be a very long list of questions, including ones just like those you've posed, Reg."

Stepping closer to the two politicians, Bates said, "That's why you're here, Senator. As you are probably already thinking, there's so much potential on so many levels. Those who properly position themselves before the project is revealed to the public stand to gain the most. Jonathan knows this, of course, just as he believes that you are the person who can best put a face to what is sure to be the prime political topic for many years to come." The man's expression faltered a bit before he added, "He's even become quite . . . excited . . . about it in recent months, possibly due to your election to the senate and the potential you bring to the party."

Christopher chuckled at that, noticing the hesitation in the professor's voice as he had spoken. Though Jonathan Dillard had never himself aspired to the presidency, the two men had discussed the younger senator's possibilities of ascending to that position on more than one occasion.

Twenty years to introduce lasting environmental change for the better? If Bates was right, it was a bold idea that could inspire people across the country in a way not seen since the days of World War II or the race for the moon, and this time it would be for a far more moral objective: curing their own ailing world.

And leading them toward that objective? Reginald Christopher, president of the United States, the man who would save the planet.

Has a nice ring to it.

There would be obstacles to overcome, of course. Given the nature of the EDN project and what it involved, battling misperceptions would be critical.

"Naturally we know this isn't going to be an easy sell," Dillard said. "After all, there are those who'll believe this is science run amok. Some will understand the larger picture, but there will be those who'll fight it at every turn, be it on religious or ethical-treatment grounds. That's where you and I have our work cut out for us, Reg."

Bates sighed at that, and to Christopher it sounded as though the professor had endured this and numerous other arguments against what he and his people were doing here. "The promise of what New Eden can offer the world is well worth any resistance we're sure to encounter," he said.

"What about the more predatory species in the region?" Christopher asked. "I'd think people will worry about some of them finding their way into a populated area, perhaps contaminating or killing innocent people. This isn't like an alligator crawling out of a river in Florida into some old lady's garden."

Christopher noted how Bates paused in response before replying, his eyes narrowing as if trying to gauge how much information he should offer.

"We have anticipated that very thing, actually," the professor finally replied. "In addition to the region's isolated location, we've taken certain precautions with the breeding of our animals. They're designed to live exclusively within the EDN habitat. Indeed, the area is the perfect environment for them, their ability to traverse the outside world being the equivalent of a fish attempting to walk from one pond to another."

The hint of uncertainty in the professor's voice was subtle, but Christopher picked up on it nonetheless. What was Bates not telling them?

"But if this project is to be implemented on a global scale," Christopher said, "then what about once those areas are reclaimed? Won't animals engineered to live within a contaminated jungle just die off once they've . . . cleaned it?"

Bated nodded. "Some will, of course, while others adapt to the environment as it is altered. It is a price, to be sure, but the benefits to the entire world would seem worth the cost."

"To you, maybe," Christopher countered, shaking his head. "PETA's going to go apeshit when they hear about it, though."

"Which will only matter if we're trying to get campaign donations out of them," Dillard countered. "Don't worry, Reg. Once people see the larger picture, caterwauling from PETA or whomever will just fade into background noise."

"There will of course be plenty of time to address all of those issues," Bates offered, his tone once again paternal. "First things first, however." He indicated the door leading from the conference room. "Senator Christopher, Jonathan here was quite explicit in his instructions that you be spared no details. If you'll follow me, I'll guide you through the rest of the facility, though I'll leave the tour of New Eden itself to your daughter."

Any response Christopher might have given was forgotten as the calm atmosphere of the room was shattered by the shriek of a siren. The sound was brief, but it was enough to startle the senator and make him look around the room, searching for whatever might have caused the alarm.

"Professor Bates," a voice called out over an intercom speaker at the far end of the room, "please report to Central Operations. Professor Bates to CentOps, please."

"That doesn't sound good," Dillard said.

To Christopher's surprise, Bates actually seemed to ponder that statement for an odd moment before responding.

"No," he said quietly. "No, it does not."

CHAPTER FIVE

Whereas the other areas of the complex Christopher had seen were functional but sparse, Central Operations was a different story.

It took his eyes a moment to adjust to the subdued lighting, and at first appearance the room resembled a smaller version of the NASA mission control room in Houston. Thirty workstations, each richly appointed with its own multi-line phone as well as state-of-the-art flat-screen computer monitor along with accompanying ergonomic keyboard, mouse, and chair complete with lumbar support.

The workstations were situated on tiered rows of ten apiece and arranged in a wedge formation facing a large flat-screen monitor that the senator saw was actually composed of twelve smaller screens, each fifty inches across and all networked so that they could display individual images or operate in concert to produce a single larger picture. Through a smoked-glass wall to his left, Christopher saw rows of network servers and other assorted computer hardware.

Christopher expected to see a beehive of activity as he and Dillard followed Bates into the room. Instead, he was struck by an eerie silence. The tension in the air was palpable, and he quickly counted fourteen people working at various stations, each with their own version of apprehension clouding their expression. Only one of the people did not turn at the professor's approach, a young African woman wearing a set of headphones with her right hand pressed to her ear, her concern evident by her deep frown and furrowed eyebrows

Something bad was happening. Right now.

"What's going on?" Bates asked.

In response to the question, one of the other technicians rose from his chair and stepped toward the professor. Like most of the others in the room, he was dressed in casual clothing—khaki pants and a dark long-sleeved shirt with three buttons near the neck, typical attire for someone accustomed to spending their days in a cubicle or in a computer lab. His hair was blond and noticeably thinning despite his best efforts to conceal that fact with artful brushing and use of gel. His eyes were blue, bloodshot, and underscored with dark circles, which at eight in the morning was itself disturbing.

"We just got a call from ObStat Four," replied the man, who Christopher now saw wore an EDN badge displaying his picture and identifying him as Clifford Meyer. "They say they've been attacked."

"Attacked?" Christopher repeated. "By whom?"

"Not who. What," Meyer replied as he directed the trio to follow him back to his desk on the room's uppermost tier of workstations. Settling into his seat, the man began dragging his computer mouse across the rubberized pad to the right of his keyboard. "Dr. Christopher said they only got a glimpse or two of something, but they're definitely animals."

That got the senator's attention. "Christopher?" he said, anxiety momentarily heightening the pitch of his voice. "Elizabeth Christopher?"

Meyer looked up from his desk, first to Christopher and then to Bates. "Yeah, that's right. She's the leader of the field study team assigned to the station. They're supposed to rotate out later today."

"Is she all right?" Christopher asked, ignoring Dillard's hand on his right arm. "Is she hurt?"

"She's fine," Meyer replied, and the senator detected the younger man's nervousness. "She's on the phone now, telling us what's happening out there." Reaching for his phone, the man tapped one button corresponding to a green light illuminated on its control panel, and Christopher heard the tense voice of his oldest daughter.

" . . . destroyed three exhaust vents and two cameras. At least one tried to get inside the station but the outer door held. We think they're gone now, but there's no way we're going outside to get to the garage, so we could use some help getting out of here."

Despite the strain behind her words, Christopher sighed in relief as he listened to Elizabeth, doing her best to maintain her bearing as she relayed her team's current situation.

As Meyer turned in his chair, his expression was pale and dismal. "Professor, Dr. Christopher thinks that whatever attacked the station may also have killed Dr. Watts and Sean Godfried."

"What?" Dillard said, shock lacing the word. "What are you talking about?"

Rattled somewhat by the senator's outburst, Meyer nevertheless maintained his composure as he brought the others up to speed. "Dr. Christopher says that a camera feed from the truck they drove out to the site shows . . . " He faltered on the words, swallowing and wiping his mouth before completing the sentence. "The camera showed what looks like a body."

"It's all right, Clifford," Bates said, placing a gentle hand on the other man's shoulder. "Is everyone else on the team safe?"

Meyer nodded. "Yes. Dr. Christopher says they've sealed up the entire complex and are moving to a secure area away from any external doors." Pausing to swallow again, he added, "Apparently, Mr. Maguire is concerned that the . . . whatever they are . . . might break through a door and get inside."

His patience wearing thin, Christopher stepped forward until he stood next to Bates. "Just what the hell do you have running around out there?" As soon as he asked the question, he waved it away. "Never mind. Enough of this horseshit." He pointed to Meyer. "I want to talk to my daughter, now."

He felt Dillard's hand on his arm again. "Take it easy, Reg. Everything will be fine."

Ignoring his friend, Christopher maintained eye contact with Meyer. "I'm waiting, son," he said, biting down on each syllable.

Bates nodded to the younger man and Meyer tapped two keys on his phone. "You're on speaker, sir."

"Elizabeth?" Christopher called, his voice shaking as he called his daughter's name. "Can you hear me?"

"Dad?" Elizabeth replied. "Is that you?"

"Yes, sweetheart. It's me." Christopher made no attempt to suppress his sigh of relief at hearing her voice. "Are you all right?"

"We're fine, Dad. I think we'll be okay so long as we stay inside and wait for the security team to arrive." He heard the uneasy confidence in her own voice, which sounded so much like her late mother's. Elizabeth had always been strong and independent, more than capable of taking care of herself. Even when she was a little bit of a thing, she had never been prone to the usual childhood fears. Hearing even a hint of fear in her voice now made his own blood run cold.

He scowled at Bates, who by way of reply looked to the other side of the room. Christopher turned to see a lithe, athletic-looking Latino woman walking toward them. "Ms. Rolero," Bates prompted. "What is your status?"

She had an air of confidence, accentuated by her black battle-dress uniform. Her hair was also black, cut short on the sides in a womanly style with her ears and the back of her neck visible. A Glock semiautomatic pistol was tucked into a shoulder holster beneath her left arm, the only obvious weapon on her person.

"Alpha Team has just taken off. ETA twelve minutes." Turning to Christopher, the woman held out her hand. "Senator Christopher? Shannon Rolero, head of EDN Security."

Christopher took the proffered hand and shook it, not completely surprised by the power radiating through the woman's grip. There was real strength there, enough to show respect without overdoing it, but he held no doubts that she was holding back for his benefit.

She can probably kick the ass of everyone in this room without breaking a sweat.

"Reginald Christopher," he offered in greeting. "I can't thank you enough for taking care of my daughter."

Nodding respectfully, Rolero replied, "Just doing our job, Senator. She and the others will be just fine."

"Don't worry, Reg," Dillard said from behind him. "Liz and the others are in good hands. Shannon here is one of the very best there is at her chosen profession, with a track record as long as your arm." Christopher heard the attempt at calming in his friend's words, but he still picked up on the edge of nervousness in Dillard's voice as the other man looked to Rolero and asked, "Isn't that right, Ms. Rolero?"

He knows something.

Pulling Dillard aside so that he was out of earshot of Bates and Rolero, Christopher locked eyes with his friend.

"There's something else, Jon, something you're not telling me. What is it?"

Dillard did not flinch as he replied, "Reg, please, try to get a hold of yourself. Liz will be fine, okay? Trust me."

His gut telling him he was right about this, Christopher pressed, "You haven't answered my question, Jon."

This time there was a reaction. To Dillard's credit, it was one he almost succeeded in hiding, but Christopher saw the doubt flicker across the other man's eyes, if only for an instant before the elder senator reasserted control over his composure.

"I'm honestly not sure what to tell you right now, Reg. Even if I did, this isn't the place or the time. Let Rolero do her job and get Liz out of there, and then we'll get to the bottom of this. You have my word."

Christopher reined in his anger and nodded curtly. "Fine, Jon. We'll do it your way, for now."

Turning his back on Dillard, Christopher moved back to the row of workstations where Rolero and Bates were continuing to oversee the operation. Rolero had donned a cordless headset, and Christopher could see that she was dividing her attention between the conversation in her ear and the forward wall screen, one portion of which was no displaying what looked to be an aerial view of jungle terrain.

"Team Alpha en route," Rolero replied, her tone reserved and businesslike now. "ETA nine mintues." She pointed to the wall monitor. "The feed is from a camera mounted on the front of the transport vehicle. Each team member has a small camera mounted to their headgear, and we'll patch in those feeds once they're on the ground. You'll be able to see the whole extraction, Senator."

Christopher nodded, pleased with the report and the woman's demeanor. "Do Liz and the others know what to do?"

"Their instructions are to sit tight and wait for my people to come and get them." A frown abruptly crossed her features, and her right hand reached for her headset. "What just happened?"

"They stopped transmitting," Meyer said, his fingers all but a blur as he typed at his computer keyboard. "We're not getting anything from them."

"From whom?" Christopher asked, his gut tightening in trepidation once more. "What's going on now?"

Not looking up from his computer, Meyer replied, "We lost comm with the station, and I'm showing alerts from the power transfer block in Sector Thirty-one. Main power's off at their location."

"What's the cause?" Bates asked, his tone still amazingly calm and composed.

Meyer shook his head. "I'm not sure yet, but indications are the master circuit box is offline."

"Power surge?" the professor prompted.

"Not showing anything like that. Whatever it was, it happened at the station itself. Other lines from the transfer block are reading normal, and I'm not picking up any other problems anywhere in that sector."

Unable to stand still, Christopher had taken to pacing the narrow aisle behind the row of workstations and the operations room's rear wall. "So what the hell happened?"

No sooner had Elizabeth begun to relax, comforted at last by the reassuring sound of her father's voice, than she was thrust once more into a pit of anxiety.

Still gripping the now dead phone receiver in her right hand and with her eyes trying to adjust to the abrupt loss of lights inside the barracks recreation room, she instinctively reached for something to hold on to as emergency illumination kicked in. A pair of halogen bulbs above the door helped chase the majority of shadows away, but much of the room still lay shrouded in darkness.

Elizabeth could already hear the sounds of the backup diesel generator kicking over at the far end of the corridor, echoing in the near silence of the currently powerless facility. The generator, triggered automatically by a switch that closed the instant main power failed, was designed to support the station's essential systems. It would tend to environmental control and keep juice running to the outpost's multitude of computer and other monitoring equipment, though the lighting would stay low to save power.

"Did you hear it?" Griffin asked from where he stood near the door leading into the corridor. "It sounded like the main box blew."

"Guess that means our luck is holding," Sanchez said, the weak attempt at humor falling flat as he crossed the room to a gunmetal gray cabinet in the corner of the room. Opening the cabinet's double doors, he extracted three flashlights and carried them back to the pool table in the center of the room that had become the repository for the haphazard collection of supplies the group had gathered on their way here from the observation shack.

Elizabeth remained silent, but in her mind a notion had been playing over and over from the moment she had found her way to a chair in the near darkness following the power failure. Could the creatures glimpsed on the camera feed have destroyed the power junction? How and why would that have even been possible?

"Still think the exterior equipment was riling them?" Maguire asked from where he sat in one of the rec room's overstuffed chairs.

She had offered that off-the-cuff theory without really pausing to consider if the idea had any weight to it, but this latest development was something that could not be ignored. The circuit boxes would almost certainly have been emitting a similar, albeit more powerful, type of rhythmic and artificial sounds. Perhaps the equipment on the surface attracted or even somehow aggravated the things.

Pulling that right out of your ass, aren't you, Liz?

"It's as good an idea as anything else we've got," she offered. She knew that there was precedent in nature to support her line of thinking. Still, the simple fact was that none of the animals created for the project acted in the manner Elizabeth and the others had witnessed earlier. Likewise, none of the species had been engineered with the kind of strength or ferocity demonstrated by the creatures that had attacked the station.

Or Alicia. Or Sean.

"Well," Sanchez said, "the big question for me right now is where the hell those things came from. Even if they had found a way to get inside the perimeter, there's no way they could have survived the jungle."

Turning from the doorway, Griffin shot the other man an exasperated look. "Come on, Paul, they didn't come from outside, and you know it."

"That's bullshit," Sanchez snapped. "We never created anything like that, and even if we did, why the fuck would we let it run around loose out here?" Cocking his head in Elizabeth's direction, he added, "Besides, if that was the case, Liz would know about it. Right, Liz?"

Even as she nodded in reply, Elizabeth felt doubt clouding her thoughts. As a senior project leader and department head, she was aware of everything pertaining to the Genesis Protocol, the EDN region, or anything either initiative had spawned throughout their lifetimes. She had participated in or provided input to nearly every effort undertaken in the last five years. There was nothing pertaining to the project stored anywhere—in any computer file, laboratory, or jungle zone—of which she was not aware.

Supposedly.

"All I know," she said a moment later, "is that somebody's got one hell of a lot of explaining to do when we get back." Pausing a moment, she felt a sudden chill on her skin as she considered their current situation. "Assuming we can get out of here anytime soon, of course."

"Don't worry," Maguire replied. "Alpha Team will get us out of here in fifteen minutes, tops. All we have to do is wait for them to come and get us."

As relayed to them by Shannon Rolero, the plan was simple. Their instructions were to remain in the barracks area of the complex until help arrived. The rescue team would enter the subterranean station and sweep the building, making their way to the science team's location and escorting them back to the surface into the waiting transport for the ride back to Central Operations.

It sounded almost too easy, but after the morning's events, Elizabeth was in the mood for easy right about now.

"Listen," Griffin said, holding his hand up in a gesture for everyone to remain quiet. "Does anyone else hear that?"

Elizabeth heard it, too. A faint, dull, mechanical sound just barely audible through the complex's reinforced concrete walls.

"Truck," she said, feeling the beginnings of a tired smile teasing the corners of her mouth.

Grinning himself, Maguire nodded in satisfaction. "Oh yeah. Cavalry's here."

Elizabeth allowed a small wave of relief to wash over her. There was no mistaking the telltale drone of an EDN all-terrain vehicle's heavy-duty engine, closer now. In just a few minutes, they would be able to leave the now very unnerving environs of the observation station and return to the project's main complex.

Still, her mood remained sober. While their surroundings would by comparison be much more comfortable, she knew that she might well be walking into something even more dangerous. Her worry—that someone assigned to the project might be deliberately conducting experiments that had heretofore been kept from her and other members of the team—was growing with each passing moment. That such work might have been in any way responsible for the deaths of Alicia Watts and Sean Godfried only added to her agitation.

I want answers, damn it.

"What's that sound?"

The question jolted Elizabeth from her reverie, and she looked up to see Griffin, still standing near the door, looking upward as if he might be able to peer through the concrete and earth that lay between him and the surface and ascertain the source of whatever he had just heard.

"I only hear the truck," she said at first, her next words cut off as she picked up a string of faint, indistinct popping sounds. They were followed almost immediately by another series of similar noises, and yet again by another.

"That's gunfire," Sanchez said, moving closer to the door. "I'm sure of it."

Saying nothing, Maguire instead stepped to the center of the room and retrieved his M16 from where he had placed it atop the pool table. Elizabeth watched as he checked to ensure a round was chambered in the weapon, and she felt a twinge in her gut as the security agent locked eyes with her.

"They wouldn't be shooting unless there was something they thought they needed to shoot at."

Shit.

It was all she had time to think before Maguire was out of the room and running down the corridor toward the heavy fire door, beyond which lay a stairwell providing access to the surface. With main power offline, the elevators would be out of commission, leaving the stairs as the only option for moving between floors.

Elizabeth and the others were ten paces behind Maguire as he put his shoulder to the door, slamming the handle bar with the palm of his left hand to open it. He was through in an instant and already halfway up the stairs beyond by the time they entered the stairway.

"Rory, wait!" she shouted, but Maguire ignored her, climbing the stairs two and three at a time like a man possessed. Reaching the landing for the first level, he yanked on the fire door and barreled into the hallway, his footfalls echoing back into the stairwell as he sprinted down the corridor.

Despite that, to say nothing of the racket she and the others made as they clamored up the stairs, Elizabeth could still hear the distinctive report of weapons fire. Now, however, they were accompanied by a new sound.

Screams.

CHAPTER SIX

"Wes! On your nine!"

Hearing the shouted warning over the noise of the all-terrain transport truck's still-rattling engine, Wesley Lucas swung the barrel of his M16 rifle to his left in search of a target. He was in time to see a dark, indistinct figure darting into the tree line and heading toward the landing dock that served as a loading point for transport and patrol boats used to traverse the toxic man-made river winding through the EDN region. The thing, whatever the hell it was, moved with incredible speed and was gone before he was able to get a bead on it.

Weapons fire chased after it from behind him, three quick volleys of three-round bursts. Lucas did not have to look to know that the shots had come from Jeri Boam, his partner and the one who had yelled out the alert to him. Arguably the best shot on the team, she had wasted no time firing after the . . . whatever it was. If anyone could hit the damned thing on the run, it was her. A high-pitched shriek made him figure she'd tagged it until he traced it to the trunk of a scaly tree that one of her rounds had penetrated.

"Shit!" she snapped, loud enough for him to hear over the screaming tree. "I had the bastard clean!"

His eyes scanning the perimeter of the clearing that also served as the roof for the buried observation station, Lucas saw nothing. Whatever it was, it was gone now, concealed by the unearthly multicolored foliage.

"What the hell was that?" he called out. The thing had a tail, of that he was sure, but beyond that he had not been able to discern any real details. It had run almost upright, propelled by two large legs, unlike any of the larger, potentially dangerous animals with which he and the rest of the project's security force had been trained to handle. Was this something new?

Nice of them to tell us, Lucas mused bitterly. *Fucking science geeks.*

"No clue," Boam said as she jogged ahead of him on their way across the open ground and away from the transport vehicle. Four more members of Lucas's eight-person team, three men and one other woman, fanned out to either side of him as he ran toward the nearest recessed doorway leading down into the observation station. The remaining two men were taking up station outside the truck, providing cover for the rest of the team, with the truck's driver remaining inside the vehicle, keeping the engine running and ready to get the hell out of here the second the team and their charges were aboard.

Humidity hung in the air like a thick blanket, and Lucas also noted the cloying scents of copper, sulfur, car exhaust, and other unidentifiably noxious odors coming from the chemicals intentionally added to the artificially engineered environment around him. He ignored all of that, just as he ignored the first hints of perspiration he could already feel under his arms. Despite the warm temperature, he kept the sleeves of his black battle-dress uniform rolled down and buttoned at the cuffs, as was normal during field operations. The black Nomex gloves he wore would prevent sweaty hands from slipping on his weapon, but they did nothing to alleviate the slow buildup of his own insulated body heat. He ignored that, too. Lucas could handle the discomfort for the short time it would take to complete his mission.

The rescue operation had been put into motion almost totally on the fly, with Rolero scrambling Alpha Team just as Lucas and his people were returning to the complex following their morning run. They had scarcely finished gearing up for the op before they were aboard one of the two oversized and field-rated transport vehicles—essentially, armored buses with all-wheel drive and steering—assigned to the project's security force, with Rolero providing their briefing via radio while the team was on the move toward the observation station.

Something had attacked ObStat Four. Not some*one*. Some*thing*.

That was enough to worry the shit out of Lucas, and he considered himself the kind of man who did not scare easily. He had learned to handle and channel fear the hard way, first as a misguided teen running around the streets of Atlanta with the Brownside Locos—a life from which he had been saved after his older brother jerked a knot of reality into his ass—followed by eight years in the army, two spent in the Persian Gulf during Operation Iraqi Freedom. Hell, he had even found time for college during his service career. All of that, in Lucas's opinion, should have provided sufficient opportunity for a man to figure out how to grow a set of balls.

So why am I so jumpy now?

The answer, he knew, was that he should not have been. Whatever was running around out here, they were still animals, right? Pitting dumbass animals against automatic weapons should be a no-brainer.

But according to Rolero, at least, this did not appear to be true.

To her credit, she disapproved of sending her people into the EDN region to fetch Dr. Christopher and the rest of the field surveillance team. She had been light on the details, offering only that the animals that killed Watts and Godfried were big, fast, and dangerous.

As for the current situation, all Lucas knew was that four people, including Rory Maguire, were sitting inside the observation station waiting for someone to get them out. Whatever had attacked the station, it was strong enough to disable power to the whole complex.

This is one awesome critter. Probably chewed right through the power cable like it was a licorice whip.

Lucas had been with the EDN project long enough to have seen some supremely weird shit. The jungle was like something Tolkien and Heinlein might have created together—provided everyone involved had been taking hits off the same bong.

None of that bothered him, but then again, none of that seemed to be stacking up against what Rolero had described.

Enough of that shit, Lucas chastised himself. *Keep your mind on your job.*

He moved to stand at the top of the stairs leading down three meters to where the station's main entrance had been set into a concrete frame embedded in the soil. With Boam backing him up, Lucas would enter the complex while the other four members of Alpha Team provided security. According to everything the team had been told by Rolero, Dr. Christopher and her group were safe inside the station with instructions to wait for an escort. Lucas liked the plan's simplicity and that it offered few, if any, potential problems.

Get in, get out, get gone.

"I've got movement!"

The alert was from Ray Collins; Lucas heard the man's distinctive nasal twang in his earpiece. Collins was one of the men left behind to provide rear security for the team, and Lucas turned toward the transport to see him pointing toward the tree line to the left of the truck, an area of the jungle blocked by the vehicle itself. Standing a few feet away, his partner, Dwayne Marshall, was raising his M16 and aiming it at something Lucas could not see. Rifle fire echoed across the clearing as Marshall fired into the jungle.

"Incoming!"

The call came from his left, where Alan Virdon and Peter Burke had been advancing on Lucas's right flank as the team approached the complex entrance. It was immediately followed by the sound of weapons fire as both men opened up. Lucas caught sight of something big, dark, and fast dashing through the foliage. Virdon and Burke tracked after it with their rifles, loosing three-round bursts that all seemed to be a heartbeat behind the . . .

"Look out!"

Boam's shouted warning was enough to alert him to pending danger, but it was instinct that made Lucas duck and roll to his right in the instant before a shadow fell across the ground where he had been standing.

Lucas felt swaygrass moving nimbly away from body as he continued the roll and scrambled back to his feet, the stock of his M16 already in his shoulder and the muzzle tracking upward in search of a target. There was only time to register a massive shape moving directly toward him before his finger pulled the trigger.

Reginald Christopher stood transfixed at the butchery displayed before him on the monitor at the front of the room. He could not move, could scarcely breathe as gunfire along with screams of pain and terror echoed through Central Operations. Transmitted with startling clarity from a suite of cameras mounted around the outside of the armored transport vehicle as well as the truck's interior, the images spared no detail as Rolero's security people came under attack.

One monitor was a blur of color as it caught something moving with blinding speed, ignoring the bullets fired at it and barely breaking stride as it cut down the man shooting at it. Blood and tissue splattered everywhere as the animal's arm swept across and through the man's torso, dropping him in two parts to the soft earth as the thing changed direction. The action was immediately met with a chorus of stunned gasps and screams from various people in the room, and Christopher heard at least one person retching nearby. His stomach heaved as the pungent odor of vomit reached his nostrils.

"Jesus fucking Christ," the man sitting next to Meyer said, the words a choked rattle.

On the screen, the creature's movements carried it off camera, but it was picked up just as quickly on another monitor receiving imagery from a different angle as the thing attacked a second man. His arms were still trying to bring his own weapon to bear even as his head was separated from his body.

"Dear god," Christopher heard Jonathan Dillard say, and turned to see his friend covering his mouth with one hand, his eyes closing tightly as if that might keep at bay the appalling images they were witnessing.

Moving like a crazed person between various workstations, Rolero was attempting to maintain some semblance of control over the rapidly deteriorating situation. "Lucas, what's your status? Report!"

The only responses to her anxious queries were distraught shouts and more weapons fire. Christopher could make out several clipped, disjointed conversations overlapping one another, cries of warning interspersed with screams of horror and agony. Some of it was interrupted by sounds the senator identified as animalistic snarls and howls, and all of it was joined in chorus by the sounds of rifles discharging in a chaotic frenzy.

"Rolero, get them out of there!" Professor Bates yelled over the din.

She ignored him, her attention instead focused on the display monitors and the jumble of comm traffic spilling over the CentOps intercom system as well as her headset. Turning back to the screens, Christopher's eyes locked on one monitor showing a view of the transport vehicle's cab.

The picture was dark and muddied, but it was enough to show the last moments of the driver's life as something grabbed him by his head and yanked him completely out of his seat. Behind him, another member of the security team was scrambling to bring his weapon around as a dark shape leapt into the cramped space. The picture shook as a brief melee ensued, with something jostling the camera and distorting the image it transmitted. What it did not fail to relay were the men's futile shrieks for help followed by the sickening sounds of flesh and bone being torn apart.

Then something struck the camera itself. Its lens struggled to bring the picture back into focus, and Christopher realized that what he was seeing was blood spattered across the interior of the cockpit, coating everything including the camera.

"Oh dear God," he blurted as the dark figure thrashed around the inside the compartment. Sparks exploded from various consoles as the creature's legs, arms, and tail smashed anything they assaulted.

The next instant, every image on the monitor wall dissolved into static.

"Power failure," Meyer reported, his voice barely a whisper and choked with anguish. "I'm not getting anything from any onboard system."

"What the hell are you doing?" Bates shouted, his voice laced with horror and fury. "Rolero!"

"Shut up!" Rolero snapped, not turning away from her work. The tension in her voice broke through a confident and composed demeanor upon which Christopher suspected she was long accustomed to relying. It was obvious to him that she was livid at herself at sending her people into a situation for which they had been unprepared. They were now paying the price for that lapse, and Christopher could see that it was already having an effect on the woman, as she channeled angst into anger.

"Lucas, can you hear me?" she called into her headset. "Answer me, damn it!"

"He's gone!" someone else answered, a woman, and there was no mistaking the terror in her voice. More weapons fire erupted from the intercom speakers and Christopher heard a male voice, this one more distant, shouting something he could not discern. Had the man's microphone stopped functioning? His voice was lost amid the reports of at least two rifles as well as the woman's own frantic, labored breathing.

"Jeri, is that you?" Rolero called out. "What's happening? We're blind here!"

Instead of a reply, Christopher only heard another volley of gunfire, followed by the woman cursing at something before the channel went dead.

Elizabeth scrambled up the concrete steps to where Rory Maguire had taken up position at the stairway's parapet, her ears ringing as the sharp bursts of his M16 echoed in the narrow space. Above and around her, she heard the sounds of other weapons fire and the screams of the rescue team as they tried to fend off the attacks of the . . .

. . . *the things*.

Crawling until she lay beside Maguire, she looked in the direction he was aiming his rifle and saw several of the creatures moving in and around the transport vehicle. Two of the animals appeared to be feasting on the remains of a couple of fallen men, with another thrashing about the interior of the truck's front compartment.

"Jesus," she heard Paul Sanchez say from behind her. "Look at them!"

Elizabeth felt her jaw go slack as she got her first good look at the creatures. She estimated them to range from seven to eight feet in height, with massive legs that were surprisingly agile, like those of wolves or large predatory cats. Instead of fur, the animals had what she at first took to be a thick skin, leathery like elephant or rhinoceros skin. Looking closer, she realized that the creatures' hides were covered with rows of ridges and ripples that must have offered a great deal of protection against harsh environments. They looked kind of like alligators, or even armadillos.

Huge, fast, violent god-damned armadillos, you mean.

"Alan!" Maguire suddenly shouted. "Look out!"

Elizabeth saw another of the creatures sprinting into the clearing, coming from the direction of the river and the landing dock. It covered the open ground at a phenomenal rate before pouncing on one of the security people, who never saw the thing coming. A single savage blow with one paw and its long claws was enough to cut the man down, but the creature swung again and again. The man's blood sprayed in all directions and clothing shredded as the animal continued its attack in a mindless frenzy. Its arms—that's how Elizabeth thought of them, anyway—and its long and angular face, its mouth lined with rows of sharp teeth, were covered in the blood of the luckless soul who had been unable to escape its assault.

"Oh Christ," Josh Griffin said from where he crouched next to Sanchez, and Elizabeth reached out to place a reassuring hand on her friend's shoulder as he turned away from the grisly scene and put his head down. His breaths were deep and rapid, and she worried that he might throw up.

"Damn it," Maguire hissed as he brought his rifle up again. He never got there, though, before weapons fire erupted from someplace else. Elizabeth watched as bullets tore into the creature's thick skin. It flinched in reaction to the shots, howling in pain as it scampered backward, but that was the limit of its response.

Turning toward the source of the rounds, Elizabeth saw a woman, dressed in black fatigues and brandishing an M16 like Maguire's. Instead of trying to run or seek cover, she was standing her ground and aiming her rifle at the hulking creature.

"Jeri!" Maguire called out, trying to sight in on the animal as it lunged toward the woman, rapidly closing ground on her. She fired two more three-round bursts and Elizabeth could see blood spurting as the bullets ripped into the animal. It even stumbled for a few steps before continuing forward, almost seeming to accelerate as it charged the woman. She continued to shoot at it, and

Maguire was firing after it as well. Elizabeth was forced to cover her ears in response to his rifle's echoing report, but he could not seem to hit the sprinting creature.

Then the woman's weapon was empty.

Elizabeth saw the look of panic on her face as she dropped the M16 from her shoulder, one hand triggering the rifle's magazine release as the other reached for a replacement. She never had a chance, as an instant later the creature was on top of her.

"No!" Maguire cried as the thing decapitated the woman with a single strike. Her body remained standing for an additional few seconds, not even beginning its fall to the ground before the creature had shifted direction. Elizabeth's heart leaped into her throat as she realized the thing was charging directly at them. Though she could see that it was bleeding from the numerous wounds the woman's rifle had inflicted upon it, the creature did not appear to be otherwise affected.

And it was not alone.

Moving in concert, as if reacting to some sort of signal, the two creatures that had been feeding on the fallen members of the rescue team seemed to turn their attention on the one of their number heading toward the stairs before giving chase. Elizabeth saw two more emerge from the transport vehicle, with a third still inside the cab and kicking and punching its way through the front windshield before jumping to the ground.

"Back inside!" Maguire snapped, and she felt his hand on her shoulder. "Now!"

She pushed herself to her feet as Maguire rose from his position, bringing his M16 to his shoulder and aiming at the onrushing creature. It was close enough now for her to make out the rippling patterns in its dark green hide, which had an oily sheen that reflected the late morning sunlight.

"Move!" Maguire yelled as he opened fire, and Elizabeth flinched as the report from the three-round bursts echoing once more in the narrow stairwell. She scurried after down after Sanchez and Griffin, taking the stairs three at a time and nearly losing her balance before Sanchez reached out to steady her.

The heavy metal door was open and Griffin had already made his way inside. Sanchez was right behind him, but Elizabeth stopped in the doorway. Looking back, she saw Maguire firing one last time before turning and making his own descent. The security agent was reloading on the run, fumbling a fresh magazine from a pouch on his belt, when a shadow fell across the stairway.

"Behind you!" Elizabeth yelled as she reached for the door handle, preparing to yank it shut the instant Maguire was inside.

Then the thing was there.

Maguire was less than three feet from the door as the first creature leapt over the parapet, dropping down into the stairwell and landing on top of the man. He twisted around, both the M16 and the new magazine dropping from his hands as brought his arms up in an attempt to defend himself.

"Close the door!" he shouted as the thing reached for him. Elizabeth screamed in shock as the creature gripped Maguire by the neck and swung him across the narrow stairway, slamming the man headfirst into the concrete wall. Blood sprayed through the air, some of it smacking Elizabeth across the face as she screamed again.

"Come on!" she heard Griffin yell as she felt hands on her from behind, pulling her back into the complex. Pushing past her, Sanchez reached for the door and wrenched it toward him, but not before Elizabeth caught sight of Maguire being thrown about the stairway again.

Arms and legs flailed in all directions as the creature slung the man's body around relentlessly in the narrow space, and she was certain she heard bone snapping again before Sanchez finally succeeded in closing the heavy door.

She could only stand there, trembling in panic as Sanchez and Griffin worked together to secure the door's locks, and listening to the sounds of carnage and death drifting to her. The thing was continuing to pummel whatever remained of Maguire against the walls of the stairwell. She heard several shrieks, one after another, some of them overlapping each other. The other creatures had arrived at the stairs and were joining in the harsh chorus. To Elizabeth, the eerie vocalizations almost sounded like euphoric cries of victory.

Relishing their kill?

The odd, errant thought was forced away by a massive impact slamming into the door, the sound echoing in the corridor and making her jump backward.

"Get back," Sanchez warned, pushing Elizabeth and Griffin farther into the corridor as the door shuddered again, followed almost immediately by a second and third strike. This time she could see the door reverberate under the force of the blows, and she wondered if the creature was strong enough to break through the reinforced steel hatch.

It was only after they returned to the supposed safety of the barracks recreation room, with Sanchez securing the fire doors behind them as the trio descended back to the second level, that Elizabeth finally allowed herself to collapse. Dropping into a recliner, she hugged her knees close to her chest, her body racked with sobs as she finally succumbed to the strain of the past hours. She made no effort to wipe away the tears that stung her eyes and ran freely down her cheeks.

Sagging against the pool table, and rubbing his face with one hand, Griffin looked ashen, also visibly shaken by what he had seen.

"Somebody made them," Griffin said, some small amount of emotion returning to his voice. "Otherwise, they'd have been dead long before they could have gotten this far into the jungle. Somebody made them, and for all we know, they're making more." Pushing off from the pool table, he began to pace the room. Elizabeth noted that while he had regained a bit of his composure, his hands were still visibly shaking.

"I mean, Jesus," Griffin said a moment later. "Did you see the way they acted? It's like they were on safari, and the rescue team was the game. Those guys never had a chance." Pausing in his pacing, he looked down at the floor, shaking his head as he let a heavy sigh escape his lips. "Poor Rory," he said, before looking at Elizabeth with a new gleam of anger in his eye. "Why the hell would anyone make something that could do that?"

The images of Maguire's last moments flashed in Elizabeth's mind, bringing forth more tears and even a wave of nausea. While there was no denying the lethal efficiency with which the things had dispatched the rescue team, had the creatures actually savored the bloodshed? Even if their behavior could be explained, it was the question of their very existence that still demanded answers, but from whom?

A single response screamed in Elizabeth's mind.
You know who.

CHAPTER SEVEN

Standing alone in his office, which featured a large window overlooking the main floor of the operations center, Geoffrey Bates watched as his people attempted to carry on with their work. He could see that they were having little success focusing on their assigned duties, and that there was no denying the air of despair enveloping CentOps.

He felt a strong hand grip his shoulder an instant before he was whirled around and spun nearly off his feet. The hand darted to his chest and stopped his motion by grabbing a handful of his lab coat, and Bates found himself staring into the menacing eyes of Shannon Rolero.

Had he been so lost in thought that he missed her entering his office? It was more likely that the woman's formidable talent for stealth had served her yet again. She could well have killed him without his ever having heard her approach.

"What the fuck just happened out there?" Her tone told Bates that she suspected him of possessing more knowledge of the situation than he had previously conveyed. Likewise, he knew that his own troubled expression would be more than enough to convince her that she was right. He felt the hand gripping his coat clench tighter, and Bates could not help but wince as his own skin was pinched between Rolero's fingers. "You know what those things are, don't you?" she asked, her eyes boring into him.

Finally, Bates yielded, nodding slowly. "Yes, I know what they are."

Leaning closer, Rolero's voice dropped almost to a growl. "Tell me."

She released her grip on him, pushing him back a step the process. Without thinking, Bates felt his hands move to smooth the wrinkles in his coat before returning to his pockets. Looking up, he saw Jonathan Dillard and Reginald Christopher stepping into the office, Dillard with more than a bit of dread while Christopher looked on with an expression of confusion mixed with fury.

"What's she saying, Bates?" Christopher asked. "You've known about those things all along?"

"Reg," Dillard began, "this is obviously a very complicated situation—"

Christopher turned on his friend. "No, Jon. It's very simple. There's a pack of savage, bizarre animals out there killing people, and they've got my daughter in their sights. This guy knew what they were from the start." He jerked his thumb to the left, indicating Bates. "And I'll bet my state's budget that you did too."

Christopher slammed the door of the office, muting the buzz of activity in CentOps and returning Bates and his office to their cocoon of near silence.

"Ms. Rolero," Christopher said, making an obvious effort to keep his emotions under control, "what can you tell me about Elizabeth and the others?"

Rolero reached out and placed a hand on the senator's shoulder. "They know the procedures for power outages and other problems, sir. They have portable comm gear, so we should be back in touch with them in no time. They'll be fine so long as they stay inside the complex, and we'll figure out how to get them out of there, I promise you that."

"Shannon is nothing if not as good as her word, Senator," Bates said. There was very little Rolero could not do once she put her mind to it, he knew. Her former career as a field operative for the Central Intelligence Agency and brief stint as a freelance mercenary bore ample testimony to her abilities, which was one of the reasons he had taken Jonathan Dillard's recommendation to hire her as the director of security for the EDN project in the first place.

He motioned the others toward the small circular conference table at the rear of the room. Taking one of the chairs for himself, Bates removed his glasses and rubbed the bridge of his nose. He had a migraine coming on. If only that were his biggest problem.

"You must understand that as with any other natural environment, there is a constant state of evolution in progress inside the EDN region. Of course, this ongoing development occurs at an accelerated rate and within specified parameters thanks to our involvement, but it is evolution just the same."

He leaned forward in his chair, resting his arms atop the scuffed surface of the cheap table. "Several of the species currently inhabiting New Eden have done so for decades, in some cases spawning their own offspring to complement the more advanced specimens we continue to introduce to the environment. All of this is done with the knowledge that there will, on occasion, be unexpected and unintended occurrences."

"'Unintended occurrences'?" Christopher exclaimed, his eyes wide as he leveled an accusatory finger at Bates. "Is that what you call that massacre back there? What the hell is wrong with you, you bloodless sack of shit!"

Bates held up his hands again. He knew that no matter what he said right now, Christopher's primary concern was the safety of his daughter. His emotional reaction to what he had so far learned was understandable, of course, but Bates feared that it would blind the senator to the larger picture EDN represented. With that in mind, he looked to Dillard for support.

The elder senator nodded impatiently. "Get on with it, Geoffrey. Tell him."

Bates regarded his friend for a moment. Had he detected a hint of distance in the man's voice? Was Dillard already looking for a way to separate himself in some manner from the project?

You son of a bitch.

Forcing his attention back to Christopher, Bates said, "Once we developed the Genesis Protocol to the point that we could use it to engineer plant and animal life to our precise specifications as part of the EDN project, other uses for this knowledge immediately began to present themselves. Several of our scientists were enamored with the idea of creating new life-forms for all manner of reasons. New breeds of predators that could be used to control the populations of nuisance species, things of that nature."

Indicating the main floor of CentOps with a nod of his head, he added, "The animals we saw on the video appear to be what we call *harbingers*. They are by far the most aggressive predators we've ever introduced to the habitat, combining characteristics from many of the world's fiercest known species."

Bates paused, knowing how this next part would likely be received. "It was our intention to have a series of specimens that could be introduced into an environment once the task of reclaiming it from contaminants was complete. Their purpose would be to eliminate other artificially created animal life without the need to subject humans to the dangers of trying to collect and dispose of animals that are, in effect, walking biohazards."

It was a not a total lie, of course, as that had been the initiative's original intention. Only after the results of experiments conducted on the first generation of the animals were studied had the true potential for the new species become clear. With that in mind, Bates sensed Dillard eyeing him, no doubt worried that more information than the senator might consider appropriate would be shared here and now.

Relax, Jonathan. I'm not a complete fool.

"So the idea is to send these harbingers out to do what, exactly?" Rolero asked. "Kill the other things you've created?"

Bates replied, "That is essentially correct. Bear in mind that, just like every other animal in the region, these first generations of harbingers were designed to thrive within a specific zone and feed upon those species of animal life that provide them with needed nutrients. This same principle would be applied with regard to the environments where they were to be used, but we've noted over the past few years that the specimens have been showing remarkable adaptive capabilities. We think they may have discovered food sources outside their home zone that fulfill their particular nutritional requirements."

"In other words, they evolved, so now human kibble is on the menu." Christopher sat down on a hard chair and put his face in his hands. When he lifted his head again, he looked more sad than angry. "And the way they tore into those armed guards, was that behavior bred into them, too?"

"Of course not," Bates snapped, his own patience finally beginning to falter under the strain of the past hours. Was it his imagination, or had the temperature in the office actually risen during the past few minutes? "Though it's obvious from their actions that at least some of them have formed a pack of sorts," he continued, "not unlike tigers or wolves. They were designed to assert their dominance over any region into which they were introduced, so in effect they're simply following their instincts." Lowering his gaze until he was staring at the table, he rubbed his face with one hand. "But we didn't anticipate this level of ferocity."

"Still, you let me send my people in there," Rolero said, each word delivered in a measured cadence. "If I'd known what they'd be facing, I might've been able to do something to protect them."

Bates wiped his brow. "Believe me when I tell you, Shannon, that no one foresaw the harbingers escaping from their containment area. I . . ."

He let the sentence drift away, shaking his head in futility. It was an oversight, yes, and people had died as a result of it. There was nothing else to say. "I'm sorry."

Raising a hand, Dillard said, "I understand your frustration, Ms. Rolero, and I share your sadness over the loss of your people, but in Geoffrey's defense, this aspect of the project *is* highly classified, with only the strictest need-to-know clearances having access."

Rolero turned in her seat. "You knew about it, too, Senator, which puts you on my shit list right below the professor. I'm holding you responsible for what happened to my team right along with him."

His voice hardening, Dillard straightened in his seat. "I'd take care with my tone if I were you. I'm not accustomed to being addressed in that manner. Trust me when I tell you that one phone call from me will end your participation in this project, to say nothing of its effect on the rest of your career."

"Trust me when I tell you that you won't live long enough to reach a phone," Rolero replied, her own demeanor unchanged from the moment she had sat down at the table. "I suggest you reevaluate any threats you toss in my direction." She leaned closer, almost to the point where Bates thought she might lunge across the table and attack Dillard.

"Maybe you think I'm an idiot," she continued, "but I've been around long enough to know that Washington would never spend the kind of money that was needed to get this place up and running if there wasn't something in it for certain people. You might also be hoping I didn't know or that I've forgotten the fact that you're on the Armed Services Committee. Put those pieces on the table, seeing all the possibilities this place—and those things—have to offer starts to get very easy."

"Enough," Bates said, surprised at the force of his own voice when he delivered the command. "We have greater concerns here, people." Accusations, even accusations that contained a grain of truth, wouldn't help them extract themselves from their current predicament.

"Yes, we do," Christopher said. Tapping his finger on the table for emphasis, he added, "I want to know how you propose to get my kid out of there."

His statement went unheeded for several seconds, and Bates watched as Dillard and Rolero continued to stare one another down. Then a knock on the door startled everyone at the table, and the door opened to admit

Clifford Meyer. He was slightly out of breath, as if he had sprinted up the two flights of stairs separating Bates's office from the CentOps main floor.

"Sorry for the interruption, Professor," he said, pointing to the phone on Bates's desk. "All of your calls were being forwarded to voicemail. Dr. Christopher just called in from ObStat Four. They're using a portable radio unit, and I've patched the connection into our intercom system." He waved one hand in the direction of the desk again.

Senator Christopher was the first to react, bolting from his seat and rushing to the younger man. "Elizabeth? Is she all right?"

"Yes, sir," Meyer replied, "but there was another casualty." Looking to Rolero, his expression turned grim. "I'm sorry, Shannon. It was Rory Maguire."

Rolero's only reaction was to close her eyes and shake her head, and Bates thought better of trying to offer any words of consolation just then. Instead, he rose from his own chair and crossed the office to his desk. "Thank you, Clifford." Moving behind his desk, he shifted aside several haphazard piles of papers and file folders until he had excavated his telephone, and pressed the unit's intercom button. "Elizabeth? This is Professor Bates."

"It's good to hear your voice again, Geoffrey," Elizabeth Christopher replied, and Bates heard the anxiety in her tone. "I don't mind telling you that we're scared shitless down here right now. You want to tell us just what the hell is going on?"

As Elizabeth updated them, Rolero rose from her seat. "You should be fine for now, Liz," she said. "We're sending another rescue team after you, but it might be a little longer this time. Just sit tight. We're coming."

Bates regarded Rolero with skepticism. "What exactly are you planning?"

"Go in armed to the teeth," she replied. "I call in some friends of mine who can bring more firepower than I've got here, and we go in balls to the wall. We can lay waste to the entire area surrounding the compound before setting foot in there. Once that's done, if we plan it right, we're in and out in three minutes."

"Now, hold on, Shannon," Bates said. "I understand you're angry at what's happened, but let's not forget the amount of time, money, and technology that's been invested in this project. I can't allow wanton destruction within the region, even for a cause as noble as getting Dr. Christopher and her team out of harm's way. There has to be a more reasonable alternative to what you're suggesting."

"Geoffrey," Elizabeth said over the intercom. "We can clean up the mess later. Now your one and only priority is to make sure we all get out of here safe."

Predictably, her father nodded with great vigor.

Bates clenched his fists, his jaw, and anything else that would prevent him from dignifying her comment with a response. Why did these people keep casting aspersions on his humanity simply because he was the only one who could take a long view of the situation? Elizabeth's attitude was particularly disappointing. She of all people should understand that the interests of science took precedence over all else.

"I don't think anyone here would argue that point, Dr. Christopher," Dillard said, casting an unnecessarily nasty warning glance at Bates. "But I am concerned about bringing outsiders into the compound. The security issues would be a nightmare."

Turning to face the senator, Rolero said, "With all due respect, Senator, I'm not some rookie at this sort of thing." Her voice still held an edge from her earlier face-off with the politician. "I can call in reliable people who'll keep their mouths shut." Shrugging, she added, "Of course, they're strictly work-for-hire, but they'll take a pay cut for me."

"And with all due respect to your abilities, Ms. Rolero," Dillard responded, "I'm not about to entrust the security of this project to a band of mercenaries recommended to me by an ex-agent of the CIA."

"Then what the hell do you suggest, Jonathan?" Christopher asked. "While the two of you are standing here bickering, my daughter and her friends are stuck inside a hole in the ground. I don't give a damn what you have to do to get them out of there. Just do it."

Dillard held up his hand. "Calm down, Reg," he said. "We'll take care of it." Looking to Bates, he added, "I've got more than a few favors banked here and there. I can have a special operations team here by morning. They can go in and get your people."

"What?" Rolero exclaimed. "The last thing we need in here is a bunch of grunts."

"They'd certainly be more qualified for a hostile engagement than your security forces," Dillard replied. "Besides, we can keep SpecOps units on a shorter leash than any pay-to-play types you call in. Security concerns can be minimized."

Bates shook his head. "Unacceptable. A conventional military unit won't be as concerned about preserving the environment." Bates didn't believe crude stereotypes of military personnel as mindless thugs who killed anything in their path. Nevertheless, regardless of their level of training these people would simply not be prepared for the unique situations they would encounter inside New Eden.

"It's the option with the greatest chance of success," Dillard said a moment later. "I don't think we can risk the safety of Elizabeth and the others with anything less."

Bates knew the senator was playing the angles. Dillard had allowed the lure of the EDN project's as yet un-tapped political power to all but consume him, and he would not do anything to jeopardize all that he had so carefully planned to this point. He might well be worried about Christopher's daughter, but only to the extent that rescuing her avoided any kind of embarrassing incident with the potential to damage the political power New Eden offered.

You poor, deluded soul, Bates silently offered his friend.

Leaning closer to the phone, he said, "Elizabeth, are you still there?"

"God damn it, Geoffrey," she snapped. "Are you com-ing to get us or not?"

"Don't worry, honey," Christopher offered. "Ms. Rolero is preparing another team to go in and bring you out. Just stay put for now, okay?" His own voice seemed buoyed by the idea that a full-scale rescue operation was being readied.

Stepping forward, Rolero said, "Liz, this will take some time to put together, so you should take steps just in case you're there for a while. Shut off anything that's not absolutely essential, to conserve your generator fuel. Otherwise, just sit tight. We'll be there as fast as we can."

"Okay, Shannon," Elizabeth replied. "Thanks."

Rolero turned her attention to Dillard. "Let's get one thing straight, Senator. I'm taking my own team in. We're the ones with the knowledge of the area. I don't give a shit who else you bring in, but they're my backup, and they'll answer to me. Understand?"

"Absolutely," the senator replied. "I have no intention of usurping your authority here. In fact, I expect that you'll do everything necessary to protect not only the safety of Dr. Christopher and her team, but also the se-curity of the entire project."

Rolero shook her head. "I love politicians. Never use two words when twenty will do. I know my job here, Senator. Also, just so you know, you and I aren't done yet. If I find out you're still keeping things from me, you'd better hope one of those things breaks out and finds you before I do."

CHAPTER EIGHT

No sooner had Dillard closed his cellular phone than Christopher regarded him with no small amount of suspicion.

"Not that I don't appreciate it, Jonathan, but how in the hell can you just retask a Special Ops unit? The military doesn't send their people anywhere on a whim when someone calls."

An understatement for sure.

Currently facing a high operational tempo, conventional U.S. military forces and special warfare units were in especially high demand. They were sent anywhere and everywhere, gathering intelligence on the military activities of evolving enemies such as China and North Korea, hunting down and quelling terrorist cells in the Middle East or Asia, or recovering hostages taken by extremist groups in all parts of the world. These and other unconventional and low-intensity engagements that seemed to characterize twenty-first-century warfare were the prime assignments given to such elite units, making them perhaps the most valuable weapons in the United States military arsenal.

Christopher, therefore, found it unlikely that warriors of such caliber would be dispatched to rescue his daughter from a herd of testy genetically engineered zoo animals.

Moving to the black vinyl chair situated behind a cheap wooden desk—the sole furnishings of the small office that Dillard had commandeered to provide him and Christopher with a little privacy—the other senator replied, "Ted's on the Armed Services Committee, and he owes me a few favors. He'll know who to call to get a special forces unit sent here, and keep it quiet." Dillard offered a knowing smile. "Keep in mind, Reg, that there are a few people on the Hill who know all about this project. They've got a lot riding on its success, more so even than me. They'll know what to do in order to keep this quiet, and who to call to make it happen."

"Oh, yes," Christopher said as he began to pace the width of the small office, "more secrets. Just what we need."

Dillard sighed. Maybe it was from fatigue, but Christopher suspected there was an air of annoyance in his friend's sharp exhalation. "Damn it, Reg, I'm worried about Elizabeth, too, but you have to understand that there's a larger picture to be concerned about here. There's too much at stake here to simply throw away. Not now, not when we're so close to success."

Turning to face Dillard, Christopher leveled a withering stare at the other man. "I'm no fool, Jonathan, but we're talking about my daughter. Do you actually expect me to stand here while someone else attempts to prioritize Elizabeth's safety with anything else? Could you do that if it was one of your kids out there?"

To his credit, Dillard did not offer any attempt at a placating answer. "I honestly don't know. I'd like to think I could be as resolute as you are." He allowed his gaze to drop to the desk before him. "I guess that's just another in a long list of good reasons why Joanne and I never had any children."

For a fleeting moment, Christopher's irritation began to subside. He watched as Dillard wiped his hand across the desk's unpolished surface, lost in thought as though he were reflecting on choices not made, roads not taken.

The anger returned when Dillard opened his mouth again.

"But while I may not understand how you're feeling," he said, "you have to make an effort to look around here, to see what New Eden has to offer. We're talking about global changes, Reg, for the betterment of everyone living on this planet. Entire industries will be created, practically overnight. The scale of this will be unlike anything seen in history, and we'll be right there at the forefront of it all."

Bored with his pacing, Christopher dropped himself into the office's only other chair. "Positive impacts? What about those things running around out there killing people? What positive impact are they supposed to have?"

And then he saw it.

Perhaps it was the way Dillard tried too hard, if only for an instant, to appear duly concerned about the situation Elizabeth and the others faced. It might have been the manner in which the older man shifted in his seat and cleared his throat, which at first seemed at first to have sprung from genuine discomfort, though his agitation appeared to have been induced by something else entirely.

Guilt?

"There's even more to those things than Bates told us," Christopher said, his voice barely a whisper. "Isn't there?"

Dillard said nothing at first. Then, after several seconds had passed and perhaps after realizing that his silence was itself a confirmation of Christopher's suspicions, he nodded slowly. "Yes."

Feeling his ire rising again, Christopher rose from his chair, placing his hands flat on the desk and leaning down until he was at eye level with Dillard. "What are they?"

"I can't tell you," Dillard replied, already working to reestablish control over his composure. "At least, not now."

"Why not?" Christopher pressed.

Slamming his open hand down on the desk hard enough to make the inexpensive wood shake in response, Dillard barked, "Because it's classified, damn it!" Rising from his seat, he glared at Christopher, "Don't you get that?" He waved his arms, indicating everything that surrounded them. "This entire place is a secret for a fucking reason, Reginald. Everything you've heard today is true, and it was developed for the very reasons that Bates laid out, but of course there's more to it."

"There's always more to it," Christopher repeated, contempt lacing every word.

Dillard shook his head in disgust. "Don't be so damned naive," he said. "Of course there's always more. Do you really believe that we'd sanction the development of this place if there weren't other applications for its technology? Take a look around, Reg. The world is a shitty place, and we're the ones who have to carry the shovels. Every technological advancement for the past fifty years has been rooted in how it can help us fight our enemies. You know that."

"Oh, here we go," Christopher said. "'Can't help it, Reg, it's the price we pay for protecting the world'? Don't you give me that horseshit, Jonathan! We've gotta stop trying to rationalize every decision we make by wrapping ourselves in the cloak of the world's savior."

Granted, there were occasions where such a mindset was justified. Events in recent years—war, global terrorism, despotism, and genocide, to name just a few—had certainly given Christopher cause to reflect on his own feelings about such matters. Despite the challenges facing the United States and, yes, the world, he still believed that such a philosophy was not the all-encompassing validation that some people in positions of power desired.

Oftentimes, it was just plain bullshit.

"Like it or not," Dillard said, "and whether we're right or wrong, it's a reality we deal with every day." Stepping back, he wiped his face. He drew a deep breath, as if to calm himself, before saying, "We're losing sight of things here, Reg. Let's get Elizabeth out of there safely. All of this'll still be here when that's done."

"A lot of people died today because of the secrets being kept around here," Christopher said, ignoring his friend's attempt to pacify him. "You can bet your ass I'm going to make sure their lives weren't wasted."

Dillard held up his hand. "Of course, all in due time. Right now, though many aspects of the project remain classified, even to the majority of people assigned to this facility. The best thing you can do for Elizabeth right now is not to disrupt that and let these people continue to do their jobs. In other words, we have to do our part to maintain the status quo." He fixed Christopher with a steely look. "Do you understand?"

There was no mistaking the hard tone in Dillard's voice, as close to menace as he had ever used in their uncounted private conversations together. Christopher had heard it directed at others enough times in the past to know that Dillard was not to be trifled with when it was employed in that manner. Careers had ended with pronouncements made in that tenor.

Sensing that there was nothing more to be gained here, Christopher drew himself up to his full height. "Fine," he said. "We'll play it your way, for the time being, anyway. Now, if you'll excuse me, I'm going to go talk to my daughter."

He turned away from Dillard and moved toward the door, but as his hand rested on the handle, he looked back over his shoulder and locked eyes with the other senator. "But if anything happens to Elizabeth, you and I are just getting started here. Do *you* understand?"

Perhaps Dillard realized he had crossed a line drawn between them, as Christopher watched his features soften in reaction to the terse words. Nodding, he stepped from behind the desk and reached out to place a hand on his shoulder.

"I'm sorry, Reg," he said, his voice subdued now. "That wasn't fair." He sighed again. "Look, I can only imagine what you're feeling right now, and I hope you know I'm praying this all works out."

Christopher felt a wave of fatigue descend over him, trying to discern if the words were heartfelt or a calculated attempt to mollify him. If it was the former, then he could appreciate his friend's candor.

His gut told him it was the latter.

Elizabeth Christopher switched off the portable radio, her father's words of encouragement still echoing in her ears as they had countless times during her life. In that gentle manner which had so characterized his demeanor throughout her childhood, he reassured her that she and

Paul and Josh would be fine, and out of there by this time tomorrow.

"One more night," Joshua Griffin said as Elizabeth laid the radio's microphone atop the unit. He leaned forward in his chair, rubbing his hands through his thinning hair and exhaling audibly. "God, would you believe I never thought about how much this place is like a prison before today?" He looked around the room, and Elizabeth followed his gaze, taking in the dull gray walls, the bunk-style beds and other drab furniture. The lack of windows only added to the claustrophobic atmosphere.

Jesus, prison would be a step up, wouldn't it?

"We can handle it until tomorrow," she offered as she rose from her chair, wondering if the doubt in her voice was as obvious to Griffin as it was to her.

That uncertainty had been laced with panic in the moments after Sanchez pulled the outer door closed, sealing them back inside the observation station. The creatures—harbingers, as Professor Bates had called them—continued to throw themselves against the door's heavy steel exterior for several minutes afterward. After the assaults ended the trio of scientists had listened for any signs that the things might still be nearby but heard nothing. Where had they gone?

Since then, Elizabeth's imagination had tortured her with visions of the harbingers returning their attention to the luckless security agents, who had been wholly unprepared to deal with the animals' ferocity. The thoughts came whenever she tried to rest, giving her all the incentive she needed to find any kind of activity with which to occupy her time until Shannon Rolero or whoever mounted their next rescue attempt.

"All I know is that somebody better have some goddamned answers when we get out of here," Griffin said, sounding very much like someone whose confidence had been betrayed. "I can't believe those things have been running around out here all this time with nobody knowing about them."

As angry as she was over what had happened, her anger took a backseat when compared with the human losses that had resulted. "I hope they do something for Rory," she said after a moment. "He saved our lives."

Rory Maguire had acted without hesitation, holding off the creatures long enough for her and the others to retreat back inside the complex. Did he know he was doomed even as he stood his ground? Had he remained in place for too long, or just long enough to give to his friends the precious seconds needed to reach safety?

"Not just Rory, but everyone out there today," Griffin replied. "And what about Alicia and Sean?" He closed his eyes, holding them tightly shut for several seconds, and Elizabeth saw his lips moving silently before saying aloud, "Jesus, I can't believe I didn't remember them before now."

Elizabeth felt a momentary burst of rage, directed at herself, for she too had nearly forgotten that Alicia Watts and Sean Godfried had also died. With fresh resentment to fuel her, she added their names to the unofficial mental tally of those whose horrific death demanded explanation.

"That's okay," she offered. "We won't forget about them, not again, and neither will anyone else."

Shaking his head, Griffin grunted in frustration. "All those people, just dead. What the hell was Bates thinking? Why create those things at all? I don't buy that horseshit about needing some kind of special animals for cleaning up the other ones." Holding up his hand, he added, "I mean, okay, that might be one reason for them, but come on. Do those things strike you as some kind of fucking amped-up sheepdog?"

The answer was simple, of course. Arguably the most advanced scientific endeavor of the last century, the EDN project's success to this point was as much a result of the continued generous funding provided by the United States government as it was a result of the combined talents of the scientists, engineers, and other support personnel who had contributed to the venture's ongoing efforts. The promise of having the answers to most if not all of the planet's environmental woes in one's hip pocket was a seductive siren's call to those politicians privy to the project's details.

Further, Elizabeth knew that the generosity visited upon the project by those holding federal purse strings had to have come with its own price. Representatives of the government had always taken a marked interest in the development of New Eden and the Genesis Protocol. It was easy to see that those in power would not settle for the revolutionary potential the project offered, at least not in and of itself. For those people, such ideas and technology would have to possess several applications—not all of them peaceful—in order to be perceived as worth the effort to develop them in the first place. Elizabeth could only guess as to what those other uses might be, but based on what she had witnessed of the harbingers' formidable abilities, several scenarios were playing out in her mind, none of which she found appealing.

"Don't worry," Elizabeth said as she rose from the desk where the radio had been set up, stepping past Griffin on her way toward the barracks room's small kitchen area but pausing long enough to give her friend a reassuring pat on the shoulder. "We'll get to the bottom of all of it when we get back." She did not care whether it was Bates who provided the answers, just as long as somebody gave up the truth about exactly what was going on here.

Griffin frowned in response to the bold statement. "What, you think the suits writing the checks are gonna tell us anything?" He waved the suggestion away. "You can bet those fascist pricks are already washing their hands of anything even remotely embarrassing."

Elizabeth was too tired to argue, even if she had been so inclined. Josh was right. Washington would turn its back on the project. If word were ever to get out about the gruesome death and dismemberment of project participants at the hands of artificially created predators, it would almost certainly dampen the chances that the controversial EDN project would ever gain public support.

The very notion that humans could harness nature after forsaking it for so long while in pursuit of their own selfish needs—and to do so by manipulating and twisting it into forms and substances once again suited to their own agenda—would fuel raging ideological and philosophical debates for months, if not years. The cries of protest from religious factions all over the world would be loud and vehement, deploring people like Geoffrey Bates and even herself for their attempts to emulate God. Everything that had transpired here over the past decades—all of which had been driven by the simple yet noble goal of making the world a better place—would be lost in a sea of intellectual, emotional, and spiritual chaos.

Yeah, she decided, Bates *will probably be shit out of luck when Uncle Sam decides to cut his losses. So will you.*

"I'm hungry," she said as she moved toward the small yet functional kitchenette occupying one corner of the room. "You want anything?"

"Lobster tails and a cold beer would be great," Griffin replied, offering a humorless chuckle and shifting around in his chair in an attempt to get comfortable.

Elizabeth smiled weakly.

Stepping to the kitchenette, she sighed as she took stock of its meager contents, which consisted of a small refrigerator and an L-shaped counter containing overhead cupboards, a no-frills microwave oven, and a pair of sinks. A small hotplate sat on one corner of the counter, along with a toaster and coffeemaker. The appointments were not luxurious by any means, in contrast to the station's main kitchen and dining room, which featured a complete set of appliances as well as full pantry and deep-freeze storage. Located down the corridor from the sleeping area, that portion of the complex had been powered down, with the exception of the refrigeration and freezer units, as part of the trio's power conservation efforts.

Too bad, she mused as she opened one cabinet door in search of something interesting to eat. *Those lobster tails of Josh's sound pretty good right about now.* The standard military-issue field rations she and the others had been subsisting on for the past day—MREs, or Meals Ready to Eat, as they were called—had already lost their allure. Elizabeth found it hard to believe that the men and women who served in uniform, if constantly subjected to the substandard contents of the ration packs while deployed to various hostile regions around the world, did not revolt against their superiors at least long enough to find a McDonald's.

She had retrieved one of the prepackaged meals from the cupboard, its dull brown vacuum-sealed pouch already working to diminish her appetite, when she heard the sound of running footfalls out in the corridor and getting louder with each step. Turning to the door, Elizabeth was in time to see Paul Sanchez, visibly out of breath and brandishing one of the security detail's remaining M16 rifles. He also carried a pair of belts slung over his left shoulder. One held a pair of pouches that

Elizabeth recognized as the type used to carry extra magazines for the M16, while the other held a holstered pistol. The look of fear on Sanchez's face was unmistakable.

"They're inside."

Lurching up from his chair, Griffin was aghast. "What? How?"

Stark, cold fear gripped Elizabeth's spine, still-fresh images of the harbingers and the horror they had wrought flashing yet again in her vision. What carnage would they be able to unleash within the confined spaces of the underground complex? "Where are they?" she asked.

"I heard them up on one," Sanchez replied. "They must've busted through the outer door, or maybe they found another way in."

The color had all but drained from Griffin's face. "Can they get down here?"

Shaking his head, Sanchez replied, "I don't know. The door leading to the stairs on this level is secure, and I closed the two fire doors between here and there. I think they're gone now, but that doesn't mean they won't be back." He shrugged. "I guess it comes down to how determined they are."

Elizabeth regarded the radio sitting silent on the desk in the barracks room and briefly considered using it to call for help before just as quickly discarding the idea. How long would it take for Shannon Rolero to mobilize another team and send it out here? What would the team find when they arrived? What if the things had managed to force their way down to this level before then?

If they could get down here, they'd have done it by now. Right?

Maybe. Then again, maybe not.

Forcing the disruptive thoughts away, Elizabeth looked to Sanchez and noted that he did not look at all comfortable carrying the M16. He must have seen the concern evident in her eyes, as he glanced down at the weapon and grimaced.

"I should have let Rory teach me how to use this damned thing when I had the chance," he said, his voice low. "I'll probably end up shooting myself."

Griffin replied, "Don't look at me. I'd probably shoot you, too." He offered a dry chuckle, as if knowing that his attempt at gallows humor would fall flat.

A few of the security agents assigned to New Eden had offered weapons training to any of the project's interested civilian personnel, but Sanchez was one of the many who had chosen to decline the invitation. Elizabeth had taken Maguire up on the offer once, during a lull in the science team's work the previous year. She did not consider herself proficient in the rifle's use by any means, but she figured she could remember enough of the basics to avoid killing herself or the others.

Holding her hand out, she whispered, "Give it to me." The expression of gratitude on Sanchez's face was unmistakable as he handed over the M16. Memories of the few times she had fired a similar rifle under Maguire's discerning supervision came forth as she gripped the weapon in her hands.

The recollections were accompanied by images of Maguire himself. Though Elizabeth had never told him, his disarming smile, and charming shyness, had helped her through the boring extended stays at the remote observation outpost. She had even considered asking him out, but the right opportunity never seemed to present itself. Besides, she had always figured there would be time to get past her own hectic schedule and Maguire's timidity.

So much for someday.

Pushing away the bitter, useless thought, Elizabeth recalled what Maguire had taught her about the M16, checking to ensure that the rifle's safety was on and that its magazine was properly seated. Satisfied, she nodded to Sanchez.

"Now what?" Griffin asked.

Shrugging as he dropped into a chair, Sanchez exhaled audibly as he replied, "What else? We wait."

"Pretty much it, I guess," Elizabeth added, attempting to muster some shred of confidence. Shannon Rolero and her father had told them that help was on the way, but until then, their only course of action was to hold fast and await rescue.

Her ears already straining to hear any sign of unwelcome company, Elizabeth tried to relax, and take heart in the knowledge that they would be gone from this place tomorrow.

One more night, she reminded herself.

It was not a very reassuring thought.

CHAPTER NINE

As he followed Captain William Sorensen through the door leading to the conference room, Gunnery Sergeant Donovan Hassler felt his jaw go slack as he got his first look at who was waiting for them.

Near the far end of the room's oval-shaped conference table sat four people. The man at the head of the table was older than his companions, balding and with a pair of bifocals perched on his nose. He wore casual clothes beneath a rumpled lab coat, the pocket of which held an assortment of pens.

To the man's right sat two Caucasian men, each at least sixty years of age, their expensive-looking suits and well-coiffed hair telling Hassler that they were either bigwig businessmen or government officials. Given the security measures he had encountered since the team's arrival and the fact that their plane had landed at an Air Force base in Utah, he was betting on the latter.

But it was the room's fourth occupant who caught Hassler by surprise.

"Are you kidding me?" he asked no one in particular as he stepped into the austere room and made eye contact with Shannon Rolero. Unlike her companions, she was dressed in the same sort of black battle-dress fatigues Hassler had seen worn by most of the security staff he and his team had encountered since their arrival. Rolero's old-style black leather combat boots were polished to a high gloss, and the creases in her trousers and shirt looked sharp enough to draw blood. Her hair was cut shorter than when he had last seen her, and there appeared to be a few new lines in her face, but Rolero otherwise looked almost the same as she had the last time their paths had crossed.

She looked tired, but she still offered a small smile to him. It wasn't the same confident expression he remembered as her trademark.

That can't be good.

"Captain Sorensen," the older man said he and the others rose from their seats and he made his way around the table, "I'm Professor Geoffrey Bates, administrator of this facility." As he drew closer he extended his hand in greeting.

"Bill Sorensen," the captain replied as he shook the proffered hand before introducing Hassler and Staff Sergeant David Maddox, who had accompanied them from the lounge that was serving as the Marines' staging area. "But, you already seem to know who we are."

Bates explained that he had called Colonel Pantolini, then introduced himself.

"Please also allow me to introduce Senators Jonathan Dillard and Reginald Christopher," Bates offered, "both representing our state of Utah. They have a vested interest in the activities taking place at this facility, as you'll understand soon enough."

The men exchanged handshakes with the Marines, Dillard's smile of the professionally plastered variety while Christopher's seemed even more forced than usual for a politician.

"Thank you for coming," the senator said, his voice quiet and reserved. Even as he spoke the word, it was obvious to Hassler that, whatever the current situation here, Christopher had some kind of personal stake in it.

Of course, the term "vested interest" alone was enough to ratchet Hassler's concern up at least two notches. Though he had never visited the Hill Air Force Base before today, he had heard enough about the installation to know that its location in the Utah desert afforded it a seclusion enjoyed only by a handful of military bases around the country. It was at bases like this, and others such as those at Groom Lake in Nevada, Twentynine Palms in California, and the Yuma Proving Grounds in Arizona, where some of the most highly guarded military secrets were held and where classified experiments and operations were conducted.

Many of those activities were, of course, feints designed to feed disinformation to would-be conspiracy theorists who spent their time trying to sneak onto such installations and expose government cover-ups. Still, the truth was that only a few locations around the country were ideal for the sort of work that demanded utmost secrecy. Hill was one of them.

Somebody's made a mess out here in the middle of nowhere, and we've been called in to clean it up. Hassler felt the twinge in his gut as he reacted to the troubling thought. *Wonderful.*

Eyeing Hassler, the professor turned and indicated Rolero with a nod of his head. "Gunnery Sergeant, I believe you and my head of security know one another."

Hassler forced his expression to remain neutral as his own attention focused on Rolero. "We worked together a few times."

Still offering her tired smile, Rolero tilted her head in an almost coy manner as she regarded him. "Oh, come on, Hassle. Is that all I get, even after all this time?"

Inwardly, Hassler bristled at the use of the nickname. It was a natural distortion of his name, one that had followed him throughout his life. Drill instructors at Parris Island in particular had used it with glee during his Marine recruit training. He had always tolerated it from those few close friends who joyfully ignored his requests to refrain from using it, but coming from her it sounded like the taunt he knew it to be.

Refusing to take the bait, he instead offered a noncommittal shrug. "It's all I'm allowed to say. You know that."

He had last seen her in Bosnia, where she had been a junior CIA operative and he had been a sergeant and an assistant recon team leader. Over the course of six months, their paths crossed on several occasions as mission directives repeatedly called on the agency to draw on Marine recon assets for their frequent intelligence-gathering missions.

Then, of course, there were the other "collaborations," the ones just between the two of them, which occurred at roughly the same intervals as their missions together. Hassler almost smiled as he recalled the volatility of those encounters, like the firefights in the Bosnian wilderness.

Hello? he chided himself. *Yeah, you. Back to work, jackass.*

As if sensing the tension brewing between Hassler and Rolero, Bates cleared his throat. "Well, Captain Sorensen, I want to thank you and your men for coming out here on such short notice." Motioning for everyone to take seats at the table, he made his way back to his own chair at the far end of the room.

"Part of the job, Professor," Sorensen said as he lowered himself into one of the dull gray conference chairs. "You're definitely right about the short notice, though."

It was an understatement, though one Sorensen would not be explaining to anyone in the room, of course. The order to get ready for another departure had come within an hour of Third Platoon's return from Colombia, while the Marines were still transferring their gear from the air station at Camp Pendleton back to their operations center.

Though lacking in detail, the information the team had received was unambiguous in its urgency, notifying the captain that he and one recon team, no more than nine men in all, were to be on a plane within one hour for transport to a location that would be revealed at a later, more appropriate time. With little hard data to go on, Hassler had ordered Maddox and his men to gear up as though preparing for a full mission.

There had been time enough only for the Marines to draw fresh ammo and other consumables to augment their individual gear before boarding the plane.

"As you've no doubt already deduced," Bates said as he reached for a carafe on the table and poured himself a glass of water, "we have a rather inconspicuous installation here."

The professor was only just able to finish his sentence before he was overcome by a momentary coughing fit. "My apologies," he said after a moment. "I'm afraid that while my mind is still reasonably sharp for a man my age, my body has a different opinion on the subject." He offered a weary smile, and Hassler watched as Bates pulled a medicine bottle from the pocket of his lab coat and extracted two ovular, bright blue pills. Swallowing the pills, he chased them with water from his glass.

After giving the professor time to take his medication, Sorensen asked, "You don't get sightseers or other curious types?"

"None that I've ever heard of," said Bates. "In addition to Ms. Rolero's teams, the air force is responsible for maintaining a perimeter of ten miles in all directions from our project site, using a combination of roving patrols and active listening devices, motion and heat sensors, and so on. They aren't briefed into the specifics of what they're guarding, of course."

Chiming in, Rolero said, "The blanket of protection around this place makes Groom Lake look like it's staffed by mall cops."

It was a safe bet that, given Rolero's predilection for working with Special Ops groups, most of her security contingent had seen time in line units of the army or Marines. The majority of those would have seen some kind of combat, as Rolero preferred to work with veterans who had logged real "trigger time" in the field.

Definitely no rent-a-cops walking around here.

"I'm well aware that your normal duties require you to travel all over the world and deal with all manner of trying chaotic situations," Bates said, and Hassler noted the quick glance to Senator Dillard, as if the professor were seeking approval for his next words. "Believe me when I tell you that this assignment is unlike anything you've taken on before, and it's very likely that you'll never be required to do something of the sort for the remainder of your careers."

"Sounds like my first marriage," Maddox quipped.

Dillard offered a polite, if tense, smile. "The reason you're here," he said, "is that a situation has developed which requires the talents of individuals such as yourselves. I'm afraid we've had a few mishaps that have proven to be more than our own security people are capable of handling."

Hassler caught Rolero's jaw tightening in response to the senator's words, and so did Bates, with the professor quickly reaching out to pat her on the arm. "Not to dismiss Ms. Rolero or her team, of course. Even they could not have been expected to anticipate the difficulties they ended up facing."

Despite Bates's attempt to mollify her, Hassler knew that Dillard's remarks had gotten under her skin. Whatever had happened here, it had taken her by surprise, something Hassler knew from past experience was not something she handled well.

I don't know if this is getting better by the minute, he mused, *or worse*.

"That," Maddox said, "is one mean-looking son of a bitch."

Hassler nodded as he studied the creature in the photograph that Professor Bates had displayed upon the conference room's wall. It wasn't so much the armorlike hide, or the thick, jagged nails on the massive forepaws, that bothered him. Even the rows of razor-sharp teeth didn't give the gunnery sergeant pause.

It was the eyes that bothered him.

Positioned high on the face, they were wide and round, staring directly into whatever camera had captured the image. They weren't crazed or even hostile. But they were intelligent. It stood to reason that these things had been bred to be of superior aptitude and ability to anything else roaming New Eden. The simple revelation that they had left the artfully constructed habitat that should have confined them was enough to tell Hassler that he and his Marines would not be confronting garden-variety junkyard dogs.

God help these pricks if they're holding out on us.

"*Another* pack of genetically engineered animals running around a man-made jungle?" Mad Dawg whispered to Hassler as a guard standing near the door raised the conference room's lighting. "Man, they gotta start giving us something else to do. If I had a dollar for every freaky supercreature I've had to take out with this here zap gun—"

"Shut up, Maddox," Hassler growled. Now, if *he* had a dollar for every time he had to tell Maddox to close his pie hole, he could have retired long ago.

"If what's happened here is somehow leaked to the public," Dillard was saying, "it'll undermine the legitimate good we're trying to do here."

"It's been my experience," Captain Sorensen said, "that most things done in the name of good or right are rarely kept beneath a veil of secrecy."

This time Hassler had to restrain himself rather than Mad Dawg. He so wanted to leap over the conference table and shake Sorensen's hand. The captain was an artist when it came to putting slimy politicians in their places.

While Bates waxed scientific about saving the environment, and Dillard tried and failed not to ooze glee at the thought of the money and power this project could generate, Hassler indulged in his own thoughts about the promise of this technology. He was no scientist, but there had to be some sort of medical application for all of this. There had to be. Hassler had read enough about cloning and DNA research over the years to gain a healthy respect for the potential such work held with regard to its ability to identify the causes of various debilitating and currently incurable diseases.

With this kind of knowledge, how much longer would Dad have had to hang on before someone could have helped him?

Hassler had watched his father, once a vibrant man with a striking physique and an even more imposing intellect, ravaged both mentally and bodily by the relentless onslaught of Alzheimer's disease. Very little of the man remembered so fondly from his childhood remained by the time he had finally, mercifully, succumbed to death early the previous year. Naturally, Hassler feared the disease's hereditary nature. With the effects of the affliction forever seared into his mind, he had vowed more than once not to stand by and wait for the end should he be similarly afflicted.

Only now, it was quite possible that, during the remainder of his lifetime, cures could be found for ailments such as cancer and Alzheimer's, to name just two. How much time remained before such fantasies became reality? It boggled the mind.

His mind, at any rate.

Not that any of that mattered right now, of course.

"So, these harbingers, or whatever you call them, that attacked the outpost," Hassler said. "Where are they now?"

Rolero replied, "According to her reports, Dr. Christopher said that there were a few instances where the things tried to force their way into the complex, but the outer doors seem to be holding. They haven't heard anything since . . . yesterday."

There was no missing the pause, and Hassler could not help but feel sympathy toward her for the loss of her people. Shannon Rolero had many qualities of which he did not approve, but she was no slacker. She took her work seriously, and the fact that even she was caught off guard by the ferocity of the creatures that had killed her security team was not lost on him.

"How many of these things are we talking about?" he asked once Bates completed his dissertation.

"Twenty-one, we think," Bates replied. "We originally deployed twenty-five to the environment. They're all male, so they're incapable of breeding. We know of at least three that have died, apparently from complications arising from their gestation in our laboratory, and we think one more may have been killed by the others. So far as we've been able to tell, the remaining animals travel in packs of five or six, like wolves or lions."

Wonderful, Hassler mused.

"How are Dr. Christopher and the others holding up?" Maddox asked.

Though Senator Christopher had remained virtually silent to this point, Hassler observed the man visibly perk up at the mention of his daughter. "Um, they seem to be doing fairly well, all things considered."

Turning in her seat to face Maddox, Rolero added, "They've got enough rations to hold out for a few more days, but they've only got the one portable radio to maintain contact. It's battery-operated and has a hand crank for emergencies, but at least we can talk to them whenever we want to."

"They'd been cooped up inside the facility for three weeks before all of this," Bates added, "so you can imagine they were starting to feel a bit cagey already. This certainly didn't help matters any."

Rolero nodded. "You can be sure they'll be damned happy to see us, though."

It took a moment for that to sink in, but as realization dawned Hassler had to force himself to remain seated. "What did you say?"

"I'm going with you," the security chief replied. Rising from her chair, she began to pace the room. "I'll concede that my people can't compete with your team's training or even your firepower, but there's more to it than that. You don't know the area, and even if you did, you're still not prepared to deal with the region's special considerations. Just rubbing up against the wrong plant can kill you, Captain."

Pausing as she came abreast of Hassler, she made a show of giving him the once-over. "Be sure to wear a cup. Wouldn't want you to damage anything important out there."

"According to you," Hassler countered, "we should be in and out of there in no time. Why the concern all of a sudden?"

Still giving him the eye, Rolero replied, "If things go bad, we might find ourselves on the ground for longer than we expected, and that's not good for you and your men, Hassle."

"What do you mean by that?" Sorensen asked.

It was Bates who provided the answer. "Every member of the project who's expected to spend extended periods inside New Eden has undergone a regimen of inoculations designed to counteract the effects of exposure to toxins and other poisonous substances found in the environment. The vaccination program takes weeks to complete, time we obviously don't have in your case, I'm afraid."

"Whoa," Maddox said, placing his hands on the table. "Nobody said anything about getting contaminated." Looking to Rolero, he added, "Listen up, lady. I'd just as soon not walk out of there and have my dick drop off an hour later, if it's all the same to you."

Shaking his head, Bates replied, "We have other medications which can provide temporary protection, of course. They've all been tested thoroughly and used successfully by several members of the project. They'll allow you to traverse most of the region for forty-eight to fifty-five hours before symptoms of exposure begin to manifest themselves."

"Upon your exit from New Eden," Rolero added, "you'll undergo a thorough decontamination procedure and be given medications to counteract any possibility of infection, as well as neutralize any remaining inoculants in your system."

Sorensen turned to face Hassler, the expression of doubt on his face unmistakable. "What do you think, Gunny?"

Frowning, Hassler was unsure of just what to think. "Hard to say, sir. This ain't exactly up our alley."

"I appreciate your concerns, Mr. Hassler," Senator Christopher said, leaning forward until his forearms rested on the table and with his hands clasped in front of him, "but I would consider it a personal favor if you went in to retrieve my daughter."

Recalling the overhead images Bates had showed them earlier, with their detailed depictions of the compound that was the location of the subterranean observation station, Hassler felt doubt facing off against sympathy. Even if things went totally to shit, the most time they should spend on the ground was a couple of hours. If necessary, they could hole up with Dr. Christopher and her companions until the cavalry arrived.

Hassler nodded to Sorensen. "I say we go for it, sir."

Pounding his hand on the table in mock frustration, Maddox said, "Oh sure, go for it, just like that." He made a show of wagging an accusatory finger at Hassler. "If anything happens to the Mad Dawg's schwatz out there, Lisa's gonna have your ass."

Hassler smiled. "Maybe you'll get lucky and rub up against something that'll make it grow."

CHAPTER TEN

Even through the muffling effect of the patrol boat's insulated passenger cabin, Maddox still heard the churning of the watercraft's engine as the boat moved away from its mooring pier and into the deeper water of a man-made inlet.

The compartment in which the team found themselves was almost the same size as the interior of a commuter bus. Despite those dimensions, the cabin still felt cramped, mostly owing to the presence of painted aluminum equipment cases, each the size of a household refrigerator laid down on its side, which were bolted to the center deck plating from one end of the compartment to the other. Jump seats constructed of canvas webbing were secured to the bulkheads on either side, interrupted at two-meter intervals by additional vertical storage lockers running from floor to ceiling. The arrangement reminded Hassler of the interior of a military transport plane.

"The boats are used mostly for conducting water-based experiments," Rolero had explained during the briefing, "but they come in handy for moving bulk supplies or a science team to a couple of the remote observation stations." With hulls designed to resist possibly corrosive elements found in the river, the patrol boats also were designed to protect occupants from airborne contaminants while working inside the region.

Not exactly Disney World, is it?

Hassler rubbed his upper left arm, which still throbbed with a dull ache from the inoculations he had received at the hands of the EDN project's medical staff. Each of the Marines had received injections followed by a quartet of tablets containing medicines to combat expected side effects such as nausea and elevated temperature.

"The skipper doesn't know what he's missing," Maddox said, noting Hassler's action. "Lucky bastard." Captain Sorensen had escaped the painful battery of shots, the vaccines apparently incompatible with prescription medication he was forced to take after registering positive on a tuberculosis-detection test earlier in the year. The revelation meant that Sorensen could not accompany the team into the EDN region, a decision the captain had protested but which was enforced by Professor Bates.

In addition to the vaccinations, the professor had also insisted on the small tags currently worn by each Marine on his fatigue jacket. Similar to those used by workers operating in and around nuclear reactors, the tags would change color when exposed to various contaminating agents. While the area immediately surrounding Observation Station Four was supposed to be free of hazardous toxins, Bates had insisted on the additional precaution. Hassler approved of the extra measure.

Which didn't mean that he actually trusted Bates, of course.

Turning in his seat, Maddox looked around the cabin's interior, which had been sealed during the trip in order to reduce the risk of exposure to airborne contaminants. The doors on either side of the compartment would remain sealed almost until the moment the rescue party disembarked from the craft. "Fucking sardine can," he muttered, his movements drawing the attention of the boat's crew chief, a burly Latino man Rolero had introduced as Eddie Munoz.

"Something you need?" Munoz asked.

Maddox nodded. "Yeah. You gonna open the casino once we hit international waters? I've been saving up for this vacation all year."

The crew chief said nothing, his expression revealing the same lack of amusement Hassler had observed from most of the EDN personnel they so far had encountered. Frowning in disapproval, Munoz shook his head and turned back toward the rear of the compartment.

"Probably no refreshments, either," Maddox said, shrugging. "Cheap pricks." His sardonic sense of humor had gotten him into trouble on more than one occasion with various superior officers, but Hassler rarely cared about such things. With combat tours in Somalia, Afghanistan, and Iraq, David "Mad Dawg" Maddox was a first-rate recon Marine and team leader, and if having him in the platoon meant allowing him the random smartass comment, so be it.

"Hey," he said to Hassler, "I read on the Internet that there are as many as fifty thousand people living in Utah who supposedly have polygamous relationships. I hope we get this op over with pretty quick, so I can go find three or four more wives of my own." Shrugging, he added, "Maybe it'll spice things up back home."

"That, or else Lisa'll just kill you," Hassler replied as he checked the flaps on various pouches attached to his assault vest, noting as he did so the rhythmic rocking of the boat as it accelerated into a wider part of the channel. Rising from his seat, be moved to stand near the passenger cabin's forward window, and was in time to see a massive steel mesh gate—stretched across the artificial waterway—parting in the middle so that the boat might pass through. Hassler's eyes scanned the six different signs mounted on the gates, each one warning of restricted access, authorized personnel only, and high-voltage danger.

"To keep people out, or something in?" Maddox asked as he glanced out the window at the jungle that lay beyond the fence line. Shaking his head, he said, "This is without doubt the weirdest fucking place I've ever seen. Looks like Cambodia, except that all the trees are colored like Boston in October."

Still looking through the window, Hassler could not help but agree with his friend's assessment. Was the odd coloring of the vegetation the result of its artificial nature at the hands of EDN scientists, its exposure to the various toxic pollutants saturating the region, or both?

"It's obviously some next-level shit going on in here," Maddox said. "You can always tell how secret something is by the number of gag orders they make you sign. My wrist hasn't hurt that much since I was thirteen and found my dad's porn collection."

Everyone on the team had been required to complete a series of nondisclosure agreements as part of their preparations. They had signed similar forms for uncounted missions over the years. It was simply a factor of the job, after all. Just one more odd and perhaps even dirty little secret to keep.

"So what do you think about all this?" Maddox asked, nodding his head in the direction of the surreal environment they were entering. "You figure some of the science guys got a hard-on watching too many movies, and now they've got dinosaurs or some other weird shit like that running around in there?"

Pausing to consider the question as he listened to the comforting thrum of the patrol boat's engine, Hassler replied, "If you mean do I think they've got stuff they're not telling us about, the answer is yes." He nodded to the back of the passenger compartment, where Rolero sat with the two security agents she had brought with her. "It wouldn't be the first time she'd held back on info before a mission." He offered a mischievous smile. "Besides, if it was just dinosaurs, she probably would have taken care of those all by herself."

Maddox glanced toward the rear of the passenger area. Even though it would be impossible for anyone to overhear their conversation unless they were sitting right next to him, he still leaned closer to Hassler before asking, "What's the deal with you two, anyway?"

"She was in Bosnia with the agency. She showed up one night during a poker game, flashed a roll of bills and held up a bottle of bourbon, and asked to sit in. None of that 'Gee, this is my first time' bullshit, either." Hassler chuckled at the memory of the evening's events. "She cleaned out the other three guys at the table inside of an hour, and I was hanging on by a thread. Oh, and she was drinking that bourbon like it was water. The next thing I know, it's morning, I've got a hangover, and I'm lying naked on the floor of her hooch."

"Ah, the good old days," Maddox offered with a wicked smile. "So, what happened?"

Hassler felt his body shift as the boat turned to starboard. "Couple of weeks and it was over, but man, what a ride." He could not help but smile as he recalled the handful of memorable nights. "Anyway, we broke it off with no hard feelings, both of us figuring it wouldn't work long-term, and it was business as usual for a while. We continued running recon patrols, snatch-and-grabs and all that. On the last job, we kidnapped a suspected Serb spy and brought him back for interrogation. The grab went down fine, and we delivered him to Rolero and her superiors."

The memories of the mission remained as vivid as if they had occurred yesterday. In particular, Hassler could still see the expression of abject terror on the man's face as he was taken from his bed in the middle of the night. The prisoner had steadfastly proclaimed his ignorance of anything relating to the insurgence and escalating violence plaguing cities and villages across the Bosnian countryside. Hassler had seen it all before, of course, and had not been fazed by the man's unending appeals.

"Rolero's people worked the guy over pretty good," he said after a moment. "I wasn't there during the interrogations, but I heard the screaming." He stopped again, clearing his throat as he recalled the unsettling shrieks of agony echoing through the thin aluminum walls of the Quonset hut that had served as one of the CIA's offices at the airbase outside of Tuzla, the Bosnia city where Task Force Eagle had been headquartered.

"Typical company horseshit," Maddox said, gazing through the window at the unnatural jungle environs passing to either side of the patrol boat. "Same kind of crap got them in trouble in Iraq. Like Abu Ghraib."

"Only this time they didn't get caught. They killed him." Hassler swallowed a lump that had formed in his throat. "It was only after it was too late that we found out we'd snatched the wrong guy."

"You mean you screwed up?" Maddox asked, his near whisper barely audible over the whine of the boat's engine.

"No way," Hassler countered. "He was the right target, according to our briefings. Intel was where it went bad." He sighed at the memory of it all. More than a decade had passed since the incident, one of many clandestine operations in which he had participated during his tenure with Force Recon, and yet it still burned with vicious clarity in his mind.

"Since the entire operation was illegal in the first place," he said, "Rolero and her people were more than content to cover it up. The man's death was never publicly reported. His family never learned the truth, so far as I know." Glancing once more over his shoulder at Rolero, he added, "It wasn't just that we'd made a horrible mistake, it was the callous way in which it was just swept away. Wrong guy? Well shit, sorry 'bout your luck, brother. Young, inexperienced dumbass that I was, I tried to make things right. I went to Rolero, tried to get her to at least have us acknowledge the man's death and compensate the family somehow. That wasn't gonna happen, of course. Operational security, blah blah blah."

"How'd she react to that?" Maddox asked.

Grunting in half-remembered irritation, Hassler replied, "First she told me to fuck off, then she got nasty. Took a swing at me, got a pretty good shot in, too." He could still feel the white-hot pain shooting through his face as she broke his nose with that first strike. "I hit back, and the next thing you know we're going at each other like a full-blown street fight. Only thing that stopped us from killing each other was our bosses prying us apart." Laughing in spite of himself, he offered a half-smile. "Come to think of it, the sex was like that, too."

"You always were a charmer," Maddox said.

"The whole thing still got buried," Hassler replied, "and Rolero was reassigned. I don't know where she ended up. A few weeks later, my team was rotated back to the States. That was the last time I saw her, until this morning." Rolling his eyes, he added, "Of all the gin joints in all the world, and all that shit."

On the far bulkhead, a red indicator light began flashing, a signal from the driver telling the passengers that the patrol boat was approaching the designated landing point. "Here we go," Hassler said, nodding toward the light.

"Two minutes!" Munoz called out over the boat's howling engine as he stepped toward the passenger compartment's starboard door.

"Rock on," Maddox said, pulling himself to his feet but remaining slightly hunched over in light of the low overhead inside the cabin. He gave his own gear one more quick visual inspection before turning his attention to Sergeant Lipton, his assistant team leader. "Saddle 'em up, Bobby."

"You got it," Lipton replied before beginning to issue a series of preinsertion instructions to the other five Marines.

Closing the Velcro flap of his Interceptor flak jacket and shrugging a couple of times to make sure it did not bind in the shoulders or under his arms, Hassler rose from his seat to tap the shoulder of another Marine, Corporal Michael Takemura. "You ready to go, Tak?"

"Lead on, Gunny," the younger man said, his wide smile threatening to envelope his entire face. Not a member of Maddox's Team Two, which Hassler and Captain Sorensen had selected to accompany them on the mission, Takemura was Third Platoon's special equipment NCO as well as Hassler's assistant. A quiet and unassuming young man, the corporal was one of the more gifted Marines in the platoon when it came to explosives, even more so than the unit's other professed "master blaster," Corporal Kerry Stewart.

Takemura was arguably the smartest Marine in the platoon, with college degrees in history and computer science. He was a voracious reader, and it was a virtual certainty that he would have at least one book tucked in his rucksack, which would be thicker and contain more words than the last four books Hassler himself had read. The corporal was well versed on a variety of subjects, particularly military history, and Captain Sorensen had recommended him for a commission on several occasions. The corporal had politely declined the offer for reasons he chose not to share, apparently content to continue serving as a recon Marine.

Hassler suspected that it might have something to do with the man's interesting lineage, which included a grandfather who had served as an officer aboard the *Akagi*, the Japanese aircraft carrier at the forefront of the surprise attack on Pearl Harbor. While Takemura's heritage was uncommon knowledge, it was entirely possible that someone somewhere in the higher echelons of command had learned of it and was holding it against the young Marine, stifling his opportunities for promotion or advancement. Nothing overt had ever been said, of course, but Hassler's cynical nature always had thought otherwise.

"One minute!" Munoz shouted, reaching out to grip the handle of the door.

After the events of the previous rescue attempt, Rolero had decided to treat the landing zone as though the Marines would be landing under fire. The boat would pull up alongside the landing dock located one hundred meters from the observation station and remain on station just long enough for the rescue team to disembark. Once the team was out, the patrol boat would exit the area and remain on station in the middle of the channel, its driver on standby until the call for extraction was issued.

Already feeling the vibrations of the boat's engine as it throttled back, Hassler reached up and held on to a support bar as he observed his people go through their final preparations, untroubled by the small yet legitimate hazards the next few minutes presented. Inserting into hot landing zones—by plane, helicopter, parachute, and even the occasional boat or submarine—was a frequent aspect of their training, to the point that each man in the recon platoon could go through the entire sequence of events blindfolded.

Hassler took one last check of his comm gear to ensure that his throat mike and earpiece were operating, as well as verifying once more that all of his vest's pouch flaps were sealed and that his Beretta pistol was secure in its holster on his right thigh. Tugging his soft camouflage boonie hat down on his head, he moved to take his place near the door. As the highest-ranking Marine, he would be the first one to disembark.

The patrol boat was slowing almost to a crawl now, and Hassler could see the sloping terrain of sand and rocks rising up and away from the waterline at the channel's edge. Open ground led to a path cut into the jungle, tracking a short distance to where he could see another, larger clearing beyond the trees. Twenty meters in front of the bow, Hassler noted a boathouse constructed of aluminum siding and painted a flat gray. Hazardous materials and fuel-storage signage decorated the exterior of the structure, along with warnings against smoking, open flames, and so on. The building appeared to be intact and secure.

Even with his mind focusing on the mission at hand, Hassler found himself drawn to the oddly shaped and colored vegetation in the terrain before him. However strange and unfamiliar it might have looked from the photographs shown to him by Professor Bates, or even as he had seen it during the boat ride in from the main operations center, seeing it up close was something altogether different. Whereas he recognized hints and traces of normal trees and other foliage in his surroundings, most of that was quashed by the eerie shapes, tints, shadows, and sounds of the alien jungle.

"It's like another world, isn't it?" he heard Rolero call out, and he turned to see her standing behind him.

Nodding, Hassler replied, "You're not kidding." Out of habit, he noted her weapons and equipment as though he were inspecting one of his Marines. Like the other two members of her team, Rolero was dressed in black battle dress and full assault vest. In addition to the Glock pistol in the holster under her left arm and the combat knife in its scabbard strapped to her right thigh, she also carried an M16 slung across her body in a manner that allowed the weapon to hang vertically along her right hip.

"Sure you got the right guys for this?" he asked. "I figured you'd want to call in the Space Patrol or Captain Kirk, or maybe even the Men in Black."

Rolero shrugged. "They're not in my Rolodex. You are."

"You kept my number," Hassler said, making no effort to hide a teasing smile. "I'm touched."

"Yeah, well trust me," she said as she nodded toward the door and whatever waited for them outside it, "you ain't seen nothing yet."

Hassler felt the forward motion of the boat slow still more as the driver reversed the engine, churning the water around the craft as it angled toward a landing dock. His muscles tensed in anticipation of the insertion, his right hand grasping his M4A1 assault rifle tightly across his chest while his left held on to a support handle near the open door. Glancing through the porthole, he saw the gap between the boat and dock closing with each passing second, the boat beginning to move sideways to come in parallel to the wooden platform.

The flashing red light was replaced by a static green indicator at the precise instant Munoz yanked on the handle to the door. As it slid open and out of his way, Hassler saw murky brown water just over the transom, less than a meter from the bottom edge of the door. The boat's driver had brought the watercraft into position with pinpoint precision.

Moving even before he heard Munoz shout "Go," Hassler made the short jump from the boat to the landing dock. The soles of his combat boots clattered along its wooden surface and his legs absorbed the slight impact as he hit the ground with practiced ease. With the sounds of the boat's revving engine already increasing behind him, he remained hunched over as he moved forward, off the dock and onto the uneven terrain of the shoreline. Keeping his attention on the jungle less than fifty meters in front of him, be brought the M4 up and sighted down its barrel in search of targets.

The first thing about his surroundings to grab his attention was the *smell*.

Sharp, acidic odors assailed Hassler's nostrils, at first reminding him of a chemical-processing plant he once had infiltrated as part of a sweeping mission during his first recon tour in Iraq. So thick—and potentially harmful—were the noxious fumes permeating the air on that occasion that he and his team had donned their field protective masks, hoods, and gloves.

This was different, he decided. The scents he now was picking up were not nearly so overpowering and yet still palpable. Drawing air into his lungs, he detected a bittersweet tang as he inhaled. He likened it to the sensation of trying to breathe during heavy pollen season in the forests surrounding his unit's training area during his time at Camp Lejeune in North Carolina.

Yeah, except there, the pollen didn't give you cancer.

Pushing the unwelcome thought from his mind, Hassler turned his head to see Maddox to his left, the staff sergeant's movements a mirror of his own after departing the boat. Takemura and Corporal Anthony Sortino were behind him, moving into their proper positions and scanning their flanks for threats as the team moved forward. Rolero followed after Sortino, with Sergeant Bobby Lipton bringing up the rear.

"Everybody's out, Gunny," Lipton's voice whispered in Hassler's earpiece at the same time he heard the sound of the boat pulling away from the dock, the rumble of its engines and the wake it caused in the channel breaking the otherwise serene silence of the landing. "Eleven up and moving."

"Boathouse is secure," Maddox said, and Hassler caught sight of the staff sergeant running back to the clearing after first ensuring that nothing was hiding behind the far side of the building. That completed, Maddox moved into position to lead his team—Sergeant Daniel Artiaga, Corporals Stewart and Marks, and the two security agents Rolero had brought with her, Dana Garbuz and Brody Carpenter—up the short trail toward the far side of the glade and the main entrance to the observation station. "I've got the stairwell in sight."

According to the information supplied by Rolero, the outpost, which was the equivalent of a small office building, was cocooned in concrete and steel and buried below the surface of the clearing. Even the garage that held two specially designed maintenance vehicles was underneath the dirt. Only a series of ventilation shafts, along with an array of cameras and observation ports—most of which were camouflaged by facades carved and painted to resemble rocks—was visible above ground.

"Going right," Hassler said, the barrel of his M4 leading the way as he moved toward the remnants of the transport vehicle dispatched during the earlier rescue operation. Despite the unsettling evidence presented by the video feeds from that failed attempt, Rolero had insisted on verifying the fates of each of the people she had sent in to retrieve Dr. Christopher and her companions.

With Lipton, Sortino, and Takemura spreading out to assume defensive positions between the truck and the open ground behind them, Hassler drew closer to the front of the decimated vehicle. He noted the shattered glass littering the ground on the starboard and the blood-splatter patterns all over the cockpit's interior.

"Judging from the video," Rolero said as she stepped beside him, "we figure one of the harbingers must have gotten to the driver, then broke through the canopy to go after somebody else."

Hassler pointed the muzzle of his rifle through the open window. "Driver's gone. You think the things took him?"

"From what we saw," Rolero replied, "there's no way he could have survived the attack." She shook her head. "The harbingers are carnivores, though they were supposedly designed to feed only on other EDN-created animal life. By the looks of things, they've found something else they like to eat."

They stepped to the starboard crew door, and Hassler looked inside to see that the truck's passenger compartment was in similar condition. The frames for the seats had been ripped from their mountings, and wiring and other equipment hung in tatters from the ceiling as well as bulkhead panels. Dried and darkened blood streaked and sprayed across everything, along with fragments of what Hassler recognized as skin and muscle tissue, no doubt from one of the luckless security personnel. The stench of copper permeated the compartment, the smell of death stinging Hassler's nostrils.

Something about the earlier attack had been gnawing at Hassler since he first heard about it from Professor Bates. As he studied the scene of carnage before him, he realized now what it was that bothered him. "The truck's engine was running during the attack," he said. "It had to be making a hell of a racket. Most animals would haul ass away from here when it showed up, but not these things. Pretty damned aggressive, even for what you and Bates already told us."

Maddox's voice sounded in his ear. "Gunny, we're at the main entrance, and the hatch's been forced. Something really tore the shit out of it. If it was those things, well, let's just say I'd like to avoid pissing them off."

Hassler turned away from the trashed vehicle, his eyes scanning the clearing in search of the other team. He saw five figures at the far end of the glade, dispersed in a semicircular fashion near the concrete parapet leading down to the observation station's recessed outer door. "Any activity inside?" he asked.

"Not that I can see," Maddox replied, "but we did find signs of . . . well, we found some remains on the ground outside. Not much, just blood along with some ripped clothing and bone fragments. We think it might have been one of Rolero's people."

Hassler saw Rolero's reaction to the unpleasant news, a response born as much from anger as from anguish. He could appreciate her feelings, having witnessed the deaths of people under his command on far too many occasions.

Still, she recovered quickly, concealing her momentary emotional lapse beneath her professional veneer once again. Reaching for the headset clipped over her right ear, she replied, "Thank you. Any luck contacting the science team?"

"Affirmative. Stewart's already got them on Tac Two," Maddox replied, referring to the secondary radio frequency Hassler had established for the operation prior to their departure.

"Good. Tell them to sit tight, and that we're coming to them," Hassler said.

In and out, he reminded himself as he studied the boundary of the jungle at the clearing's far end. *Ten minutes, tops. Piece of cake, right?*

For some reason he could not fathom, the perimeter of the glade seemed to have encroached perhaps a bit closer since he last scrutinized it. He saw nothing out of the ordinary, save for the abnormal terrain of New Eden itself, of course. In the distance, he heard what might be a bird squawking, but other than that it appeared that he and his team were alone out here.

The hairs on the back of his neck told him otherwise. Something, from somewhere within the dense cover offered by the jungle, was watching them. He was sure of it.

The sooner they got the hell out of here, the happier Hassler would be.

"Jesus, Mary, and Joseph," the middle-aged Hispanic man said as Hassler opened the door to the station's billeting section. "Are we glad to see you." He stepped closer, extending his hand in greeting. "Paul Sanchez."

Hassler moved through the doorway and took Sanchez's proffered hand, noting as he did so the room's other two occupants, Joshua Griffin and Elizabeth Christopher. Griffin was perhaps fifty-five or sixty years old, with a beer belly drooping over his faded jeans and long gray hair pulled into a ponytail. Christopher, however, was an attractive blonde in her early thirties, wearing sweats that almost succeeded in cloaking her trim, athletic physique.

"Donovan Hassler," he said, shaking Sanchez's meaty hand. "Everybody okay?"

"All things considered, I think we're okay," Christopher replied. "It's been a long couple of days, though."

Hassler replied, "I'll bet."

With Maddox's team providing rear security, Hassler had led Rolero and his own squad into the station, treating the interior of the complex as they would any other interior during a building-clearing operation. The Marines and Rolero had covered one another's movements past doors and intersections in the underground passageways, constantly on the alert for signs that any of the harbingers might still be inside the station. Despite the team's precautions, the sojourn down to the outpost's living quarters had proven uneventful, much to Hassler's relief.

"Everything's secure on this floor," he heard Rolero say from behind him as she entered the room. "Power's off to the elevator, all the doors on this level are sealed."

Hassler nodded in approval. "Good," he said as he keyed his headset. "Lipton, you three stay near the stairwell. Keep your eyes and ears open. We'll be heading your way in a couple of minutes."

"Roger that, Gunny," Lipton's voice replied in Hassler's ear.

Looking back to the three scientists, Hassler asked, "You ready to go?"

"Absolutely," Sanchez replied, a dark scowl clouding his features. "The sooner I can get my hands on Bates, the better. That son of a bitch's got some explaining to do."

"There'll be plenty of time for that later, Paul," Christopher said as she stepped around Hassler and walked toward Rolero. "Hey, Shannon," she said, reaching out with both arms to embrace the other woman. "I'm so sorry about Rory and Sean, and the others."

To Hassler's surprise, Rolero returned the hug, her toned arms wrapping around the scientist. "Thanks. I'm sorry about Dr. Watts . . . Alicia."

Reining in her emotions, Rolero released Christopher and turned to Hassler. "I don't know about the rest of you," she said, her familiar hard expression firmly in place once again, "but I don't see a reason to hang around here any longer."

"Amen to that," Griffin said, reaching for a large red duffel bag sitting near one of the bunk beds. "I've been packed for two days."

Hassler smiled at the man's remark. Though there was no denying the fatigue and anxiety in their worn expressions, he was impressed that even in the face of the ordeal they had confronted, the three scientists were maintaining good spirits overall. There would be mourning for those lost during the past days, of course, but for now Elizabeth Christopher and her companions seemed only a little the worse for wear.

"I can't say I blame you," he replied. Nodding to Rolero, he said, "Let's get a move on, then."

CHAPTER ELEVEN

Jane Hamilton heard the whine of the patrol boat's engine increase and felt the vibration translated to the steering wheel she held in her right hand as she maneuvered the craft around to head upstream toward ObStat Four's landing dock.

"Ground Team Two," she called into her helmet microphone, "we're en route to your position now." Glancing at her wristwatch, as well as verifying the patrol boat's current speed from the gauge on the console before her, she added, "ETA three minutes. What's your status?"

A male voice replied through her helmet speakers. "All quiet on our end, Transport One," it said, and Hamilton recognized it as belonging to the Marine who had tried to engage Eddie Munoz in flippant conversation during the ride in to the observation station. "Fourteen for extraction. Everybody'll be standing by when you get here." She had originally dismissed the man as just another smartassed jarhead with too many muscles and not enough brains. None of that came through now, with the Marine all business as he offered his situation report.

"Acknowledged, Ground Team Two. Hang tight." She glanced to her right to see her partner, Dylan Vandegrift, nodding in confirmation as she negotiated a bend in the river. "Time to get this show on the road."

Vandegrift replied, "Roger that." Shaking his head, he added, "Good thing, too. I was starting to get dizzy."

She offered a tired smile at the weak jest. "No kidding." Shannon Rolero's order to patrol a two-mile circuit up and down the river from the observation outpost had grown dull within minutes of getting under way after the successful insertion of the rescue team. Still, there was no denying Rolero's reasoning, given what had happened to the first rescue team sent in to retrieve Dr. Christopher and the rest of the observation contingent. Rolero had decided to take no chances this time around, ordering Hamilton and the river boat away from the landing dock just in case the creatures, whatever the hell they might be, decided to pay a return visit to the observation station.

"Didn't take them long, did it?" Vandegrift asked as he looked out the window at the jungle passing to either side of the boat.

Hamilton shook her head as she steered the boat to keep it in the middle of the river as it came out of the bend. "Nope. I figured that Marine in charge was just talking shit like most of them tend to do, but it looks like he walks the walk."

Her remarks were born more from playful interservice rivalry than from any true animosity. She had run into her fair share of cocky infantry types during her army tour, of course. Her own status as a female military pilot, stepping into what had long been male territory, certainly had added to the tension. Handling those situations had always been easy for Hamilton, though, her skills and confidence due in large part to her having grown up with three brothers, each of whom had played football from the moment they could fit into a set of pads. By comparison, army grunts had proven surprisingly easy to endure.

So too had the group of recon Marines, though for different reasons.

Each of them had boarded her boat with the swagger of the professional soldier, though in their defense Hamilton was able to tell that it was more than simple bravado. There had been no attempts at displaying their machismo for her benefit, only polite greetings as they came aboard and quickly and efficiently took their seats in the passenger compartment.

These were not men who spent their days training in the hope that they would one day be called upon to employ untested skills in a real operation. From their quiet, practiced dialogues with one another to their economical movements as they checked their weapons and equipment, and even to the way their well-worn camouflage uniforms molded to their hardened physiques, it was easy to see that the men had proven their mettle under fire.

The African-American sergeant commanding the team, Hassler, had proven to be as good as his word, with one of his people contacting Hamilton for extraction less than ten minutes after the rescue team had entered the station. The report from the rescue team indicated that they had encountered no resistance or other difficulties while moving in to locate the survivors of the observation group. All that remained was one more quick

157

landing followed by sixty to ninety seconds as the Marines and their charges ran to the dock and boarded the patrol boat—assuming Hassler and his team were as proficient at extracting from a landing zone as they appeared to have been during the insertion—and they would be on their way home.

Still, from her experience, it was when you thought that everything was going your way that your luck usually changed, and almost always for the worse.

For the first time, Hamilton cursed the necessity of keeping the boat buttoned up while in transit through the EDN region. Its current configuration did not allow for the M60 machine guns that might ordinarily be mounted in the access doors located on either side of the boat's passenger compartment just aft of the wheelhouse doors. What if they needed to project covering fire as they approached the landing dock?

Quit whining and work with what you have.

"Munoz," she called out over the boat's internal communications system, "get your rifle and get on the port-side door. When we hit the dock, shoot anything with more than two legs that even looks at us funny."

"You got it, boss," Munoz replied, and Hamilton looked over her shoulder to see the crew chief scrambling across the troop compartment to where his M16A2 rifle was strapped to the port-side bulkhead.

"We kill one of Bates's zoo animals," Vandegrift said, "especially if it's not trying to kill us, he's gonna have our asses."

"Fuck Bates," Hamilton snapped, though her eyes automatically moved to check the comm settings and confirm that their conversation was not taking place on a frequency that might be overheard by the professor or anyone else back at Central Operations. "After what happened to Jake and the others, we're not taking any chances. Rolero will back us all the way on this." In her opinion, the worst thing that could happen from any action taken during the operation was her dismissal from the security detail.

Better than getting killed.

Looking through the windshield, Hamilton saw the dock getting closer as the boat approached a final bend in the river. "Here we go," she said as she eased the throttle forward, increasing the boat's speed in anticipation of the turn she would need to make in order to line up with the dock.

"Dawg, where are we?" Hassler asked as he climbed the steps leading from the observation station's main entrance to the grassy clearing. Shannon Rolero was right behind him, with the remainder of his team and the three EDN scientists bringing up the rear.

Turning from where he crouched near the top of the stairs, his M4 lying across his knees, Maddox replied, "Boat's inbound, Gunny. Be here in a minute or so." As Hassler reached the last step, the staff sergeant hooked a thumb over his left shoulder. "Pilot's making her final turn toward the dock now."

Hassler nodded in approval. "Works for me. Your team boards first." After directing Sergeant Lipton and the rest of his team to assume defensive positions around the perimeter Maddox had already established with his own men, he turned to Christopher and her companions. "Doctor, this is Staff Sergeant Maddox. I'd appreciate it if you stayed right on his ass all the way to the boat, and do whatever he tells you until we're out of here. Understand?"

"Certainly," Christopher replied. Her response was echoed by Sanchez and Griffin, and once again Hassler gave silent thanks that everything about this mission seemed to be unfolding in textbook fashion. In hindsight, he expected that Professor Bates, Senator Christopher, and Shannon Rolero in particular would review their decision to bring in an outside team as an overreaction.

Job's not done yet, he reminded himself. *Congratulate yourself later.*

Hassler would not truly relax until they were back at Central Operations, of course, but he did not like that he had allowed himself to slip from "tactical mode" while still on the ground, even for an instant. You lose your focus and even the easiest assignments go sour.

Looking up, he noted that the sun was already nearly straight overhead, and that the temperature had increased several degrees even in the short time since the team had first entered the observation station. Jungle humidity, as odd as that sounded considering he was standing in what once was the middle of the Utah desert, was already working its way under the lightweight material of his camouflage uniform. It was going to be a hot day

He cast furtive glances toward the tangle of alien vegetation encircling the clearing, reminded once again of his team's exposed position. Given the distance to the edges of the glade, Hassler did not believe that anyone . . . any*thing*, rather . . . could sneak up on them out here on open ground. Still, he recalled the video images captured during the first rescue attempt and what they had revealed about the harbingers' startling speed. If the creatures were to attack them, there would be only seconds to mount any kind of a defense.

His attention was drawn to the south, from where he now could hear the sounds of the boat as it maneuvered upstream toward the landing dock. It was still faint, but gaining in volume with each passing second. Turning to Christopher, he exchanged smiles with the attractive scientist.

"Right on time," he offered.

"Now we're talking," Maddox added as he rose to his feet. Touching the fingers of his left hand to the slim microphone positioned near his mouth, he said, "Team Two, prepare for evac. We're boarding the boat first." Despite the staff sergeant's update to his charges, the other Marines of his team maintained their defensive postures. None of them would move from their established positions until Maddox actually gave the order to pull out.

Hassler noticed Joshua Griffin stepping toward him, the doctor's expression one of worry. "Is there enough room for all of us?" he asked.

"It'll be a tight fit," Hassler replied, "but it'll carry everybody." He reached for one of the canteens strapped to his equipment harness. He was in the midst of extracting the container when a warbling, shrieking cry erupted from somewhere in the jungle, almost loud enough to obscure the sounds of the approaching boat's engine. Hassler felt his gut tighten in response to the obviously inhuman sound.

"Well, that's new," Paul Sanchez said from where he stood next to Christopher and Griffin. The three scientists, along with all of the Marines, were turning to look toward the northern edge of the clearing, from which Hassler was certain the unsettling noise had come.

Bringing his rifle up, Maddox said, "It doesn't sound like anything I heard on the video they showed us."

A similar wail filtered through the trees, only this time it was from Hassler's left, the same direction from which the boat was approaching. The cry was also fainter, suggesting that it originated from farther away.

"They didn't make noises like that before," Christopher replied.

Movement to his left flickered in Hassler's peripheral vision, and Hassler turned to see the boat moving beyond

161

the trees. It was moving at a steady clip, no more than fifty feet from the dock by his estimate.

"Taxi's here," Maddox said.

"Thank God," Griffin replied, making no attempt to hide the relief in his voice even as, from somewhere in the distance at yet a third location, another of the chilling shrieks echoed through the jungle.

Keying his mike, Maddox called out, "Team Two, pull back to my position." To Hassler he said, "Time to make like a baby, and head out."

· Hassler did not smile at the lame joke, his attention drawn to the river and the sounds of the approaching patrol boat. Because of that, he was able to see the exact instant that the mission, which had unfolded flawlessly to this point, went utterly and irrevocably to hell.

Jane Hamilton also heard the bizarre cry, at the same moment something struck the boat.

"What was that?" Vandegrift shouted as the boat tilted to the right, his voice echoing in cramped confines of the wheelhouse but loud enough also to be heard even beyond the muffling effects of her the boat's engines.

She ignored him, reacting more from instinct than conscious thought to maintain control of the now-listing boat. There was resistance in the steering wheel, as though something was fighting her for command of the craft.

"Feels like it's stuck," she called out, her eyes sweeping the console for any indication of malfunction from the array of dials, gauges, and digital readouts before her. "Give me a hand here, Dylan."

"Holy fuck!"

Hamilton heard Munoz's high-pitched cry just as it was drowned out by the screeching din of tearing metal.

It was followed a second later by the sounds of the boat's engine, no longer buffered by the insulated hull.

And overwhelming all of that was another bloodcurdling cry, just like the one she had heard seconds earlier, only louder and much closer and sending a jolt of unrestrained dread coursing down her spine. Despite everything demanding her attention in the wheelhouse, Hamilton jerked her head in the direction of the horrific shriek.

Something was clawing its way inside.

The hole in the side of the bulkhead, no more than two feet behind Vandegrift's seat, was already the size of a basketball and growing with each second. Hamilton saw what looked like a massive hand gripping the edge of the compromised hull section and bending the steel plating aside as though it were cardboard.

"It's one of those things!" Munoz shouted as he scrambled away from the port-side door, fumbling his M16 in his hands as he fell over crew seats in a desperate attempt to distance himself from the creature.

"Get it off!" Vandegrift cried, fear lacing every word and driving the pitch of his voice up several notches.

Insane!

Hamilton's mind screamed the word over and over, her attention split between maintaining control of the boat and keeping her eyes on the rapidly growing gap in the side of the bulkhead. Where had the damned thing come from? Had it actually jumped from the shoreline to the boat?

Ahead of them, the distance between the boat and the dock and boathouse was dwindling with each passing second. If Hamilton was not careful, she would very quickly find herself with little to no maneuvering room.

Sharp, piercing reports of M16 rifle fire echoed in the confines of the boat's passenger compartment as Munoz unleashed two three-round bursts at the creature. Hamilton flinched as she heard copper-jacketed lead pinging off the inside of the cabin, and the stench of expended gunpowder filled the air.

"I'm hit!" Vandegrift screamed, jerking in his seat and reaching up to clamp his upper left arm. His eyes and mouth were squeezed tightly shut in response to the pain, and Hamilton could already see blood seeping through her copilot's gloved fingers from where the bullet had torn through the man's biceps.

"Munoz!" she shouted even as she yanked the steering wheel to port to avoid running headlong into the landing dock. "Stop it before you kill us all!"

"It's inside!" she heard the crew chief call out even as more movement over her right shoulder registered in her peripheral vision. Then something large and heavy slammed into the bulkhead just behind her seat.

Oh Christ . . .

Hamilton didn't have to look, hearing instead the frantic thrashing of the harbinger as it lunged about the interior of the passenger compartment. Then Munoz screamed again, a bone-chilling cry of agony that dissolved into a choking, gurgling sound she could only just hear over the thrumming of the boat's engine.

"Munoz!" she shouted, trying to twist around to see what was happening behind her but unable to do so while strapped into her seat.

To her right, Vandegrift was scrambling to pull himself from his own seat while at the same time trying to extract his pistol from the shoulder holster under his right arm. His left hand did not seem to be cooperating, his movements no doubt hampered by his wounded arm.

Then something dull and dark swept across her vision, and Vandegrift's head was torn from his body, slamming against the glass of the crew door to his right before bouncing off the control console directly in front of Hamilton. It ricocheted off the edge of the copilot's chair before rolling down toward the passenger compartment. Blood sprayed across the interior of the wheelhouse as Vandegrift's headless body, still gripped by spasmodic reactions, twitched in its seat. Blood poured from the gaping maw that once was the top of the man's neck, staining his flight suit in a blanket of dark crimson.

Hamilton's mouth fell open in shock. Gripped by terror and the unmitigated violence of the sight before her, she froze, the stench of death washing over her and clawing its way up her nostrils and holding her immobile in its unyielding grasp.

Then there was another blur of movement, big and fast and coming directly at her.

"What the hell?"

Hassler grabbed Christopher by the arm and halted her advance toward the loading dock. He and the rest of the group watched the boat churning up a sizable wake as it sailed past the loading dock and headed directly for the boathouse.

From where he stood, he could see at least two large figures, hulking creatures that at first glance resembled monsters from some old movie he might have watched as a kid, moving in and atop the patrol boat's passenger cabin. He only had time to glimpse dark, thick hides and long, sinewy limbs before the boat's speed and direction took it out of his line of sight.

"It's those things!" he heard Josh Griffin shout from somewhere over his left shoulder.

"Everybody back!" Maddox shouted as the boat crashed into the side of the structure at full speed, its arrow-shaped prow puncturing the wall facing toward the river and opening a gap in the siding. Steel screamed against comparatively flimsy aluminum as the boat plowed deeper into the building.

Hassler knew what was coming even before Maddox and Rolero turned and dove for the ground. A massive fireball erupted as the boat ruptured fuel-storage tanks stored inside the boathouse, shredding the building and flinging a cloud of burning debris in all directions as a roiling dark cloud billowed upward from the center of the explosion. The shock wave from the explosion washed over Hassler an instant before the thunderous cacophony reached his ears. He heard shrapnel peppering the jungle, some of it even reaching the low grass of the clearing.

"Anybody hurt?" Hassler called out as he pulled himself to his feet. A chorus of negative reports answered him and he sighed in relief. Most of the Marines had been caught in the open and were unable to find shelter as the boat crashed, resorting instead to dropping prone to the ground and covering their heads with their arms.

Dusting herself off from where she had been unceremoniously dumped, Rolero stared with an expression of barely contained fury at the sphere of fire growing rapidly up around what had been the boathouse. "Damn it! That's three more people."

Hassler knew full well the emotions she was dealing with at the moment, as he too had lost good people while on assignment. While he firmly believed that the majority of those deaths were a natural consequence of the dangerous jobs he and his Marines did, every so often there was a different kind of death. That was the hardest kind to accept—the deaths that were due to a failure by someone higher up in the chain of command. Every type of job had its opportunists, of course, but in his line of work the poor grunts on the bottom of the food chain stood to lose a lot more than a steady paycheck when some muckety-

muck on top got drunk on ambition. Hassler had periodically sought vengeance on power-crazed superiors in the
past, so he could sympathize with Rolero's anger.

*Too bad there's no way to show it that she wouldn't take
wrong.*

"Speedy little—well, big—motherfuckers, aren't they,"
Maddox said as he stepped out onto the ground. The
creatures were scary, but the worried look on the normally
unflappable staff sergeant's face was scarier still.

Despite any misgivings he might harbor, Maddox immediately turned to the task of reestablishing their defensive perimeter. The area around the buried observation station was still not secure, and given the events of
the past few moments it would be unwise for the
Marines to let their guard down even for a moment.

The smell of burning fuel reached Hassler's nostrils,
mixing with the already acrid scent of the surrounding
jungle, reinforcing the sensation that he was standing in
the midst of an oil refinery or perhaps a chemical plant.
For a brief moment he wondered what sort of damage
the noxious conglomeration of vapors—combined with
the toxic environment of New Eden itself—might be doing to his lungs.

This is what I get for giving up smoking.

"Hey," Corporal Takemura said as he pulled himself to
his feet and moved back to where Hassler was standing.
He pointed to the crash site. "Look at that. As hot as that
fire is, and none of the trees around it are burning."

Studying the flames that were continuing to devour
the remains of the boathouse, Hassler saw that, indeed,
none of the vegetation surrounding the fire had been
blackened from the intense heat. The flames did not appear to be spreading.

"Another characteristic of our artificial jungle,"
Christopher replied as she brushed dirt from her

clothes. "As part of the various experiments conducted during the early years of the project, the outer bark of the trees and much of the vegetation throughout the region was engineered to absorb the heat from any ignition source, gradually spreading it and dissipating it until the fire can no longer sustain itself. It *can* burn, but only after it's been treated with a special accelerant developed by our labs."

Turning to the doctor, Hassler asked, "What's the point of that?"

It was Paul Sanchez who said, "The idea was to engineer trees that could be planted as replacements for those cleared during logging operations. In the event of a forest fire, the tress would work to contain the blaze, rather than allowing it to spread too rapidly before firefighting crews could get to it."

"An additional benefit," Christopher added, "was a reduction in the need to start controlled burns as a means of thinning out overgrown areas—fires which sometimes spiral out of control after they're set." Shrugging as she shook her head, she added, "Seemed like a good idea at the time, anyway."

"Aw, no campfire means no luau on Fantasy Island tonight," Maddox snapped, his expression falling even before Hassler could level a withering gaze at him. "Right, boss, ain't the time for being a smartass."

"So what now?" said Josh Griffin.

Sanchez replied, "We'll have to secure another way out. Have them send in another boat."

"I'm not sure that's a good idea," Rolero said. "We'd be risking the same thing happening again. I've already lost two teams of people. I'm not going to lose another one going about this half-assed. We need a new plan."

Shrugging, Hassler offered, "I agree. Have them send in a chopper from Hill." He figured a helicopter could be dispatched from the main landing field of the air force base and be here within the hour.

"Absolutely not," Rolero countered. "No one there is qualified."

"Now, see, *there's* an idea I'm gonna drop in the suggestion box soon as we get home," Maddox said, anger lacing his voice. "Teach *flying* in the air force." He held up a hand before the security chief could retort. "I know, I know. They're not briefed into the fun and games you all are playing out here."

Further discussion was interrupted by another shrill cry from somewhere in the jungle. Though distant, it was still obvious to Hassler and everyone else that the sound had come from behind where the destroyed transport truck still sat. The echo from the first call was still dissipating when it was answered by another and then by a third shriek. All around the glade, the members of the recon team raised their weapons and aimed into the dense undergrowth, and even Hassler found himself searching the trees beyond the remains of the still-burning boathouse in search of anything remotely resembling a threat. The racket continued for several seconds before fading altogether.

Still sighting down the barrel of his M4 and studying the tree line, Maddox said, "Well, wasn't that a nice kaffeeklatsch."

"You're not seriously suggesting that they were communicating, are you?" Griffin asked, shaking his head in disbelief. "None of the animals we developed as part of the project have anything approaching that level of intelligence."

Eyeing Rolero as he replied, Hassler said, "Yeah, and nothing you developed is supposed to kill people, either."

He saw the look on her face, knew that she recognized his own questioning expression for what it was. "Don't go there, Hassle. Whatever this shit is about, I'm as much in the dark as you are."

"First time for everything, right?" Hassler asked, turning away from Rolero before she might even offer any sort of response. "For what it's worth, I'm with Maddox; it sounded to me like they were yammering back and forth."

There was more to it even than that, he decided. Something about the way the harbingers seemed to be alternating their cries, each building on the frenzy initiated by the one preceding it, suggested a pattern. His gut told him it was a simple give-and-take, somewhat similar to what he and the others had heard earlier and yet possessing a new quality that had been lacking before the attack on the boat.

And then it hit him.

They were celebrating.

CHAPTER TWELVE

"What you're suggesting is ridiculous," Professor Bates said after listening to the situation reports submitted by Rolero and Hassler, his voice sounding hollow as it was filtered through the portable radio's built-in speakers. "The behavior you describe is simply not a characteristic that was bred into the harbingers. We designed them to be aggressive, of course, but that was in keeping with the role they were expected to play when deployed during post-decontamination operations."

"But you said they were demonstrating remarkable adaptive capabilities," said Elizabeth, reaching for the microphone Hassler held in his hand. "Couldn't this be just another unexpected development?"

Through the speakers, Bates replied, "If it is, then it would certainly be unprecedented. The only way to be sure would be to conduct a whole new battery of tests along with further observational studies from the field, but we can't really concern ourselves with that now, Elizabeth. My primary concern is getting you and the others out of there safely."

Fucking liar, Hassler thought as he wiped sweat from his forehead. He, along with his team and their charges, had returned to the observation station's barracks room. With the outpost's main power still out and the already-overtaxed backup generator turned back on just a few minutes ago, the air inside the room was still thick and warm.

And Bates was just adding more hot air to the mix. The trouble with this guy, Hassler decided, was that he wasn't just an ordinary liar. Bates instead phrased his answers and statements in a manner that allowed him to remain truthful while artfully avoiding anything that might later be denounced as a straightforward untruth. It was a skill that required more self-discipline to master than mere lying, and Bates's performance was every bit as polished as Hassler might normally expect out of Christopher or Dillard. However, the senators had remained largely silent throughout the entire conversation with the rescue team.

Thank God for small favors.

"What about borrowing a chopper from Hill?" Hassler heard Captain Sorensen ask. "I understand that you've got security concerns surrounding this project, Professor, but hell, I'll fly the damned thing myself."

"I don't know if that's a good idea, Skipper," Hassler said, earning him a host of questioning looks from Elizabeth and everyone else in the room.

Sorensen asked, "What do you mean, Gunny?"

Waving off the questions he knew Maddox would be throwing his way, Hassler replied, "I know this sounds crazy, sir, but based on what we saw of the attack on the rescue team and the boat, it's like the harbingers were driven to attack them. Most animals run from loud noises, but these things didn't give a damn about the racket the boat's engine was making. If anything, they acted as if the sounds were inciting them, stirring up their shit, or whatever."

Elizabeth added, "I have to agree, Geoffrey. We noticed the same thing when the harbingers first appeared here at the station. Remember how they went after the external cameras and other equipment? We think they may have gone after the main power junction because of the rhythmic humming of the transformer."

There was a pause for several seconds before anyone said anything on the other end of the radio. In his mind's eye, Hassler envisioned a gaggle of science types standing around, listening to his report, and nodding their heads with eager interest as he described the activities of their pet project.

No one, of course, offered anything in the way of information.

Four million postgraduate degrees are probably walking around that building, and no one has anything to say about the fucking creatures they bred. Wonderful.

His gut told him that these geeks' apparent inability to offer any sort of quantifying information had little to do with their technical prowess. Instead, he guessed that Bates's people, despite their instructions, were long accustomed to keeping potentially sensitive information to themselves while in the presence of nonproject personnel. He was sure that all manner of conversations would be taking place later, when they were able to talk more freely.

Once we're out of here, I don't give a damn what they do.

"Assuming we go with that theory," Sorensen said, "for now, anyway, what are you suggesting, Gunny?"

Hassler replied, "I don't think a single chopper's enough, Skipper. Bring in one for extraction, and at least one more to provide cover from the air. Everybody armed full-out and ready to blow the shit out of anything that twitches."

"Out of the question," Senator Dillard said, his first words since the conversation had begun, which provoked an exaggerated show of Maddox pretending to hammer his head into the nearby wall. The act evolved into the staff sergeant miming the motions of hanging himself as Dillard proceeded to describe a host of security problems that greatly concerned him and about which Hassler gave less than one-tenth of a damn.

"If what you've been telling us all along is true, Senator," Hassler said, "then it's obvious that we've underestimated the dangerous potential of these harbingers. Based on what's already happened, we have to step up our methods if we're to have a decent chance at completing the mission successfully."

An icy blast might as well have come from the radio speakers. "I beg your pardon, Sergeant," Dillard said. "Did you just suggest that I've been lying to you?"

"Chuckles done challenged you to a duel. Think you can take him?" Maddox mumbled, as the gang surrounding Dillard presumably tried to soothe the senator's tender feelings.

"Did I hear what I think I heard on your end, Gunny?" Sorensen asked.

"I'm afraid so, sir," replied Hassler, glaring at Maddox, who gave a little wave to the comm box.

"Did he actually say something constructive?" Sorensen asked.

"As constructive as usual, sir."

Maddox looked questioningly at Hassler and whispered, "Shut up, Mad Dawg?"

"That's the general idea," Hassler grumbled back.

Meanwhile, Dillard had started ranting again.

Hassler cut him off. "First, Senator, my rank is gunnery sergeant. Second, I wasn't implying anything. I'm flat-out saying for the record that I don't think we've been given the whole scoop here."

Over the comm channel, and as if sensing that the confrontation between Hassler and Dillard was on the verge of spiraling out of control, Sorensen asked, "What about bringing in some of our own assets? Helos from Pendleton?"

Bates, unsurprisingly, countered that suggestion. "The security concerns are too great. However, we can order in helicopter support from our facility at Nellis. Our personnel and equipment, and already briefed into project security."

While Hassler accepted the idea on the face of it, his main problem with the suggestion was the time involved. It would be well after sundown before the choppers arrived from Nevada, and he was far from happy about staying here that long.

Christopher seemed to echo his concerns. "Elizabeth and the others have already been out there too long as it is. We can't just leave them out there exposed for another day."

"There's still the security issue to consider," Rolero said from behind them, entering the room after returning from checking on the generator, and Hassler figured the radio must have been loud enough for her to hear the last part of the conversation as she came through the door. "The loss of personnel or equipment not assigned to the project, no matter how thorough our own containment procedures might be, could still generate inquiries that might expose us to more scrutiny than we are prepared to deal with, particularly now."

Hassler knew from talking to her that Bates and Dillard were scheduled to appear before a congressional panel next month, where they would detail everything that had been accomplished over the project's lifetime. Though the senator had not said as much, Hassler figured that it also meant Bates would be lobbying for funding to continue his team's work.

And we can't have bodies scattered all over the place when we're asking for money, now, can we?

"Don't worry, Doc," Hassler said as he wiped more beads of perspiration from his face and wondering once more where the hell the air-conditioner might be hiding. "If we die out here, none of us'll breathe a word to St. Peter."

"Speak for yourself," said Maddox.

To Sorensen, Hassler continued, "Skipper, I've got my issues with the helo option. We'll be safe enough down in this can until they get here, but that's not what I'm worried about. This clearing, as large as it is, is still pretty cramped when we're talking about a helicopter extraction."

"What about ObStat One?" Rolero asked. "That'd be a safer location for a chopper to land."

Bates's voice seemed to take on the tone of a proud parent or mentor as it filtered through the radio speakers. "An excellent suggestion, Shannon, though I'm sure you understand the difficulties involved with that course of action."

"Somebody want to clue the rest of us in?" Hassler asked.

"Observation Station One is the largest such facility inside New Eden," Bates replied. "It was designed for long-duration assignments, sometimes as much as several months. It was the first station we built, and it's aboveground instead of buried."

"It would mean going overground to get there," Elizabeth added. "Ten or twelve miles, if we stay on the service roads."

"What about contamination?" Hassler heard Sorensen ask. "Aren't those zones saturated with toxins and other hazardous elements?"

Bates replied, "Not every zone is a biohazard, Senator. We can provide a route that minimizes their exposure to the more dangerous areas, and the observation station should have enough protective equipment to outfit the entire group."

"Don't forget the maintenance trucks," Rolero offered. "There's still one in the garage here. We can use that to travel, but it won't carry all of us."

Hassler didn't like the fact that the movement would leave the rescue team as well as their charges exposed as they made their way to the other observation station. Still, he preferred the idea of the more secure landing site.

"It'll take us four to five hours to get there," he said. "If we're gonna do this, I'd like to get moving so we can be there well before dark."

"Roger that, Gunny," Sorensen said. "Load 'em up and move 'em out. I'll see about getting you a ride out of there."

"Aye, aye, Skipper. Hassler out." As the communication ended, he dropped the microphone on the table next to the radio's base unit, shaking his head. "Christ," he said as he rubbed his temples with his fingers, aware of the headache that was beginning to take root behind his eyeballs.

"Looks like we're taking a stroll through the park," Maddox said. "I'll get on it." To Rolero, he asked, "Got a gear locker around here somewhere?"

Rolero nodded. "I'll show you," she replied as she led him and the other Marines back into the hallway, leaving

Hassler alone with Elizabeth and her friends Sanchez and Griffin.

"It was a good day when I woke up this morning," he said, offering a smile to the scientists. "Honest."

Elizabeth returned the smile. "Well, no matter what happens, I'm grateful you came to get us." It was a sentiment echoed by her two companions.

Nodding in appreciation, Hassler still felt his jaw tightening. "I've got to tell you, Doctors, if any of my men comes out of here with anything more serious than jock itch, your boss is going to wish he'd opted for pizza delivery as a career."

Sanchez nodded. "I'm right there with you, partner, but you heard those morons. You know those senators are already figuring out how to keep from stepping into what's looking to be one big pile of shit."

Hassler knew the man was right, just as he knew he was treading on thin ice himself with regard to his verbal sparring match with Dillard. Still, the senator had sounded nervous during the exchange. Perhaps he held less power in Washington than he believed, or maybe he simply did not want to get into a pissing contest with an angry Marine.

More likely, Dillard had decided to wait for a more opportune time, during which he would make whatever phone calls and rattle whatever cages were necessary to make Sorensen's life unpleasant.

Can't concern myself with that crap right now, either, Hassler reminded himself. He would worry about the possible consequences of his tiff with Dillard and Bates only after he, his men, and the three scientists had been successfully extracted from the EDN region.

With any luck, some of these animals were bred to eat politicians. Now, that would be a useful application of technology.

"Never can get a taxi when you need one."

Despite his less than stellar mood, Hassler still smiled at Maddox's latest attempt at humor as it rang in his earpiece. "Yeah, the way things are going they'll have run out of, whaddya call it, foie gras by the time we get to the observation center."

"Could get ugly," Maddox agreed.

Walking down the middle of the path of packed dirt and gravel that was one of the network of service roads running throughout New Eden, Hassler maintained an even, steady pace. Only Rolero was ahead of him, leading the way through the artificial jungle to Observation Station One by means of the map that Professor Bates had transmitted to her personal digital assistant. With her on point, Hassler left a five-meter gap between them, an interval duplicated by Sergeant Lipton as he walked behind him.

Wiping the side of his face, Hassler sniffed and discovered yet another unidentified odor permeating the air. The heat and humidity seemed to be stirring up the legion of odd scents cast off by the surrounding vegetation, ranging from mild and pleasant—including something Hassler had likened to cotton candy—to sour and potent like battery acid or chlorine, to say nothing of the various aromatic mixtures he had sniffed while walking down the road.

Following after the sergeant was the maintenance vehicle obtained from the recessed concrete bunker that served as a garage of sorts at ObStat Four. The SUV, with its high, square shape, wide, flat hood along with fat, thickly treaded tires, was a cross between a large cargo van and a Hummer, the military's standard general-purpose vehicle for more than two decades. The truck's exterior offered no embellishments, but Hassler saw enough scratches and dents in its dull, green paint to suggest that the vehicles were well used. Pressurized and sealed to protect occupants from the hazardous environments of the EDN region's various zones, the truck's passenger area could seat five comfortably, as well as a driver and passenger up front.

After stocking the truck with a variety of protective equipment and clothing at Dr. Christopher's direction, Hassler had decided that she and her companions, along with Rolero's two security people, would ride inside the vehicle. Takemura was manning the wheel with Corporal Artiaga riding shotgun, and Hassler had also taken the precaution of positioning Corporal Sortino on top of the truck. That left Rolero, himself, and Lipton on the ground in front of it and Maddox, along with Corporals Marks and Stewart, providing rear security.

"What I wouldn't give for a pizza," Hassler said to Maddox, his stomach having already reminded him that it had been several hours since he had last eaten. The energy bar he'd taken from the pocket of his assault vest had staved off the hunger pangs for a while, but it was no substitute for a decent meal.

Or a beer, he mused as he reached up to wipe sweat from his face before tugging the brim of his boonie hat down a bit tighter on his head. The sun was now almost directly overhead. He had already opened the closure on his flak jacket in a weak attempt to cool himself and he was grateful for the slight breeze moving through the trees.

"Good luck calling for takeout," Rolero said. "Except for those programmed to operate on specific frequencies, no cell phone will work anywhere in New Eden. That includes the operations buildings as well as out here." Looking over her shoulder, she added, "Operational security, and all that."

"Figures," Maddox said. "Of course, that means no telemarketers. Sweet."

Following Christopher's instructions, Hassler had decided to rotate the Marines in and out of the truck in an effort to minimize their exposure to environmental hazards. Once they approached one of the more perilous areas, those outside the vehicle would don protective gear, but both Rolero and Christopher had proclaimed their current location as safe for humans.

So far, the tag he wore on his uniform jacket had remained a neutral white, but that did not stop Hassler from glancing at it every five minutes. Additionally and despite his best efforts, he could not keep himself from periodically glancing at the dull-faced field watch on his left wrist. Even the second hand seemed to move with agonizing slowness, as if time itself were taunting him.

"Don't worry," Rolero said, and he looked up to see her smiling at him as she walked backward. "You've got plenty of time."

The rescue team had been on the ground for just over four hours and on the move from ObStat Four for about an hour, but Hassler was still concerned about whether their temporary inoculations would protect them for their whole sojourn. Bates said the vaccines given to them would be effective for close to two days, but Hassler had not been convinced. Any number of factors could affect that estimate, such as an individual's metabolism or reaction to some other medication in their system, or even just a natural resistance to the compounds Bates's people had administered.

"I'll be worry-free once we're out of here," he replied, returning his attention to the unreal jungle around him.

The broken, uneven surface of the road was making the journey slow going, giving Hassler plenty of time to scrutinize his surroundings. Here too the foliage here spanned a variety of colors and shapes, from normal lush greens to bright oranges and yellows and even blues and violets. Trees and bushes bore only passing resemblance to anything he had seen in other forests or jungles. His eyes caught sight of one thin and gangly tree in particular, with bright crimson bark and broad, blue-tinged leaves along with branches that looked as if they had twisted themselves into a dome shape and begun growing back in on themselves.

Something crunched beneath his boot and Hassler instinctively hopped to one side. He looked down to see what looked to be a beetle, its bright red and green shell crushed and glistening with a film of glistening wet fluid.

Then he caught the smell of burning rubber.

"What the fuck?" he said as he saw the thin wisp of smoke trailing upward from his boot. Rubbing the bottom of his foot into the dirt so that he carved a small, narrow trough into the service road, Hassler quickly realized that whatever had stuck to the bottom of his boot was still eating through its hardened sole.

"My god-damned boot is melting," he shouted as he bent down to untie the boot's laces.

A shadow fell across the dirt in front of him. "Lift up your foot," Rolero said, and Hassler did as he was told just as the security chief brandished what looked to be a small aerosol can. She pressed the can's nozzle, releasing a thick ribbon of pale yellow fluid that coated the bottom of his boot and covered the small bubbling hole Hassler could already see penetrating the rubberized Vibram tread. Within seconds the smoking stopped, and he noted that the hole seemed to be getting no bigger or deeper. He felt no pain or heat on the bottom of his foot, and allowed himself to breathe a sigh of relief.

"Jesus," he said. "What the hell was that?"

Returning the spray can to a pouch on her equipment vest, Rolero replied, "Many of the animals here have acidic blood. It's a by-product of the toxic waste all over this place." Smiling, she added, "I'd avoid stepping in any droppings you might stumble across, if I were you."

"Gives a new meaning to the term 'deep shit,' I suppose," Maddox's voice echoed in Hassler's earpiece, and the Marine chuckled in spite of himself.

They were coming to a bend in the narrow road, and Rolero had turned to face ahead when she abruptly stopped. She raised her right hand and made a closed fist, a silent signal indicating for the column to halt. Hassler repeated the signal for Lipton's benefit, and he heard the sounds of the maintenance vehicle's brakes squeaking as Takemura brought the oversized SUV to a standstill.

Holding his breath, Hassler watched as Rolero began to move slowly forward, her rifle up and pointed out ahead of her, but maintained his own position. He listened for any telltale signs of danger, but heard only the sounds of the vehicle's engine as well as the high-pitched hum of insects and the rustling of leaves and branches in the slight breeze.

After a moment, he saw Rolero relax, the muzzle of her weapon dropping as she turned back to face him and offer a thumbs-up. "It's okay," she said, though she kept her voice at a normal level instead of trying to compensate for the increased distance between her and Hassler. "Come check this out."

"Everybody hang tight," he said into his mike as he moved to join her. Advancing toward the bend in the service road, he smiled as he got his first look at what Rolero had seen. "I'll be damned."

Fifty yards ahead of them, a large herd of hulking creatures milled across the width of the road. Covered in short beige hair, they were tall but not overly so, Hassler noted. He guessed that several of the animals stood five feet or more at the shoulder, their broad bodies supported by four squat, heavily muscled legs.

They were coming from the trees from the right and moving across the road, walking two or three abreast and continuing on into the jungle seemingly without a care in the world. A few of them had broken from the herd and stood to either side of the path, their long snouts and wide mouths grazing in the tall grass. Several of the creatures had taken to lying on the road's packed dirt, most of them prone and unmoving though one was on its back, twisting and squirming as if scratching an itch. A host of groans and grunts emanated from the herd, which seemed totally oblivious of the humans' presence or the approach of the vehicle.

"*Garnerlopes*," Rolero said by way of explanation. "Named by the doctor who created them, Theodore Garner." She shook her head. "Stupid name."

"What are they supposed to be?" Hassler asked.

Nodding in the direction of the herd, the security chief replied, "Basically, they're genetically engineered livestock. They're like a second cousin of the malanters Professor Bates told you about before, but this breed is supposedly impervious to infections."

Hassler had heard of genetically improved vegetables, corn and such, which had been slowly yet steadily making their way into the marketplace over the past few years. He also knew about meat that had been treated with radiation to ward off possible sources of disease or other infection, but this took the concept of artificially improving food to a whole new level.

"Using procedures developed as part of the Genesis Protocol," Rolero continued, "it takes about two months to create one of these things, and another month for it to reach maturity. Imagine the impact that would have on getting cheap beef to market faster."

"A shitload of farmers would be on the welfare rolls," Hassler retorted, but before Rolero could respond he added, "Unless farms are converted to raise these in addition to or instead of regular livestock."

"Bingo," Rolero said.

Still wary of their surroundings, Hassler waved the barrel of his M4 toward the garnerlopes. "Are they dangerous?"

Shaking her head, Rolero replied, "Not in the slightest. They're like cattle or horses on a farm, with lots of exposure to humans, and they'll make a hole for us as we get closer."

Satisfied with that, Hassler turned to look back to where the rest of the group still waited and waved his arm for them to proceed forward. As the column started heading toward them, he turned back to Rolero with a mischievous smile. "They taste any good?"

Rolero shrugged. "Some of the science guys say they make great steaks and whatnot, though I can't say I've ever had a garnerburger. We'll see about getting you one when we get back."

Hassler was about to say something when he noticed a change in the way the herd was moving about. A few of the garnerlopes had raised their heads and were now looking about, sniffing and snorting as if they had caught wind of some new scent.

There was something else, too.

"Listen," he said to Rolero, keeping his voice low. He had almost not caught it, but watching the garnerlopes had pushed his senses to an even higher state of alert, and now he realized that the almost innocuous background sounds of insects teeming in the jungle was gone now. Even the breeze seemed to have stopped.

"Something's up, boss," he heard Maddox's voice whisper in his earpiece. Turning slowly so that he faced the oncoming group, he saw that the staff sergeant and the other Marines on the ground were scanning the vegetation on either side of the service road, weapons up and pointing toward the trees. On top of the maintenance truck, Corporal Sortino had risen to a knee and pulled his M4 to his shoulder.

They were being watched. Hassler could almost feel the hot ache between his shoulder blades. It was a sensation he had experienced uncounted times before, usually in the seconds leading up to an ambush.

He flinched as several of the garnerlopes cried out, and there was no mistaking the anxiety in the sounds the creatures made as the herd began to scatter. Their flight instinct had taken over. The animals bolted into the jungle.

"Aw, shit," Maddox said. "This can't be good."

"Everybody stay cool," Hassler snapped, his eyes searching the dense undergrowth. Sweeping the muzzle of his rifle from left to right as he scanned the trees, he felt his right forefinger wanting to rein in the slack on the M4's trigger.

In his earpiece, he heard Corporal Marks whisper, "Gunny, I think I've got something."

Resisting the urge to look in that direction, Hassler instead kept his focus on the jungle directly in front of him. He sensed rather than saw the dark blur streaking between the trees to his right, a flash of black registering in his peripheral vision.

There was no time even to shout a warning.

CHAPTER THIRTEEN

The dark mass exploded from the trees, soaring through the air and arcing across the open ground separating the jungle from the service road.

Hassler whirled in its direction in time to see the harbinger land with a booming thump on the hood of the maintenance vehicle. Sunlight reflected from its slick black hide as the front end of the SUV buckled under the creature's weight, collapsing in on itself. The force of the impact snapped the vehicle's forward axle and the whole truck shuddered as the engine died. Still atop the truck, Sortino was thrown off his feet and landed heavily on the vehicle's roof.

"Out of the way!" Hassler shouted as he sighted down on the harbinger. Sortino was scrambling to regain his footing and bring his own rifle up, unable to fire it but instead swinging it like a baseball bat at the creature. The thing was too fast, lashing out at the corporal, whose weapon and right arm went flying into the nearby grass. Blood poured from the stump of his arm and he screamed in shock as he stumbled backward, pain not even having the chance to set in. The harbinger swiped at him again and more blood sprayed out. The animal's razorlike claws furrowed deep into the man's face, neck, and chest, tearing through his flak vest as though it were toilet paper.

Sortino's body was still falling from the truck as Hassler fired. He was sure the first few rounds tore into the thing's hide, but it seemed not to care as it crouched down and swung again, this time punching through the vehicle's windshield directly in front of the driver's seat. Glass shattered as the harbinger's thick, muscled arm disappeared up to the shoulder through the window.

"Gunny!" he heard Lipton's voice in his ear. "On your left!"

Hassler heard the call at the same instant the sounds of rustling bushes and snapping branches reached him. Turning to the source of the commotion, he was in time to see another harbinger lunging from the jungle. Running upright, it was bearing down on him with incredible speed. He fired without truly aiming, spraying rounds in an arc from right to left as he brought his weapon around.

Every shot missed but still the creature reacted to the gunfire, altering its trajectory to pass to Hassler's left. Sensing the animal swinging at him, Hassler ducked to his right and felt the rush of air as the harbinger's clawed hand passed through the space occupied by his head a heartbeat earlier. As the animal dashed past him he caught a whiff of pungent odor that was foul like death.

Falling to the ground and stirring up dust and dirt as he rolled to come up on one knee, Hassler fired after the thing as it bounded across the road and disappeared into the jungle. His M4 bucked one last time before the rifle's bolt locked to the rear, signaling an empty magazine. To his left, he heard the distinctive sound of Rolero's M16 and turned to see her firing into the trees where the harbinger had vanished.

"Watch your back!"

Hassler had no idea who shouted the warning as three more of the creatures burst from the jungle close to where he was looking, on the side of the road opposite from where the original attack had come from. No sooner were they on open ground than they separated, spreading out in what Hassler took to be a flanking maneuver as they headed for the now halted column.

Behind the wrecked vehicle, Maddox, Stewart, and Marks were already firing, their shots missing by wide margins as the harbingers sprinted with fantastic speed. So fast were the animals' movements that only the Marines' training and instincts prevented them from catching each other in a frantic crossfire.

Not that it mattered.

A shrieking cry pierced the air as one of the harbingers darted between Marks and Stewart. Then Marks went down, his legs dropping one way as his upper torso tumbled the other, his body separated at the waist by another of the creatures' lightning strikes. Blood rained onto the ground, darkening the dry, pale dirt as the dead Marine collapsed.

"Damn it!" Hassler shouted, angry and stunned all in the same instant. "Everyone find cover!" Amid the escalating chaos, he found himself running toward the vehicle, firing on the run as Lipton, Stewart, and Maddox fell back from the truck. Even as he gave the order Hassler knew it was fruitless. Out here in the open, there was no protection or place to hide.

The harbingers were unbelievably fast, each assault taking only seconds as they bounded from the jungle and lashed out at targets before racing back into the relative protection of the trees. Everyone with a rifle was firing after them, and Hassler could hear the occasional cry of pain when someone got a hit, but no one was doing any kind of significant damage so far as he could tell.

"Fucking things have hides like Kevlar!" Maddox yelled above the noise. "I know I'm hitting them, but it's not doing shit!"

No sooner did the last attack end than the next one began. This time the creatures lurched from the trees behind the team, two of them coming up from the rear. Hassler saw Maddox and Stewart dive to either side of the road in desperate attempts to dodge the charging harbingers, but the animals seemed focused on something else. It took him an extra second to realize what they were after.

The truck.

"No! Stay inside!" he heard Maddox call out and looked over to see the SUV's driver's-side passenger door slide open. Dana Garbuz and Brody Carpenter hopped out, each turning to fire their M16s at the oncoming harbingers. Incredibly, their shots had some effect, causing the creatures to alter their attack course to avoid the spray of bullets.

One of them changed direction and dashed off into the woods to Garbuz's right while the other jumped up and out of the way, landing heavily on the roof of the SUV behind Carpenter and buckling its metal plating. Carpenter pushed Garbuz to the ground before whirling around to confront the creature, but the thing moved with uncanny speed. The agent had no time even to raise an arm in a futile act of self-defense before the thing grabbed his head in one of its massive front paws. Carpenter

190

screamed in terror and pain as the creature launched itself toward the trees, pulling the man along with it.

Hassler tried to track it with his own rifle, the M4 spitting rounds after the creature as it and Carpenter disappeared into the dense undergrowth. He fired his weapon dry, conscious of the fact that he might hit Carpenter but seeing no alternative to trying to catch the animal with a lucky shot. His bullets tore into bushes and trees in vain.

A snarling cry from somewhere to his right and behind him made Hassler spin in that direction, turning to see another harbinger running from the jungle, its feet churning up grass and dirt as it sped across the open ground between it and where Garbuz still lay sprawled in the dirt.

"Garbuz!" he shouted. "Look out!"

She never had a chance.

Both Lipton and Maddox opened fire on the creature, and this time both Marines scored hits. The harbinger actually stumbled from its headlong charge, coming almost to a standstill and giving Hassler his best look yet at one of the creatures. It stood nearly upright on its massive jointed legs, its long thick tail dragging in its wake. Its arms were coils of muscle, ending in huge hands with those thick, long nails that were capable of inflicting such horrendous damage. Rows of sharp teeth glistened from within its elongated snout, the most prominent feature of the animal's narrow face.

The creature's hesitation was fleeting. After curling itself into a ball, it sprang up on its powerful legs to leap over Garbuz and the disabled SUV and into the trees on the far side of the road, letting loose a chilling, warbling cry as it vanished into the foliage. Gunfire erupted from all directions as everyone still on their feet trained their weapons on the fleeing harbinger.

Rifles emptied within seconds and the sounds of violence faded, with Hassler fumbling for another magazine even as he kept his eyes trained on the trees where the last animal had disappeared. From that direction he could hear the sounds of cracking branches and heavy feet crunching on dried leaves as the creatures ran through the jungle, each of the sounds punctuated by a series of shrieks and grunts that seemed at once agitated, possibly pained, and most definitely pissed off. Within moments, even those noises dissipated into nothingness.

Looking around, Hassler saw Maddox and Stewart along with Garbuz, Lipton, and Rolero scanning the trees all around them, their weapons reloaded and lifted to their shoulders as they awaited the next attack wave. Rifle barrels tracked wherever the shooter was looking, ready to fire on anything that revealed itself from the cover of the jungle.

Hassler felt sweat running down his face, chest, and back, but he ignored it. Several seconds passed with only the sounds of his own rapid breathing and his pulse racing in his ears to keep him company. He blinked several times to keep perspiration out of his eyes, sighting down the barrel of his M4 as he swept the weapon from left to right and examined every tree, every bush for some sign that it might be concealing a threat.

He saw nothing. As abruptly as it had started, the attack was over.

It was several more seconds before he finally relaxed the slightest bit, lowering his rifle even as his heart was still doing its best to hammer through his chest wall. The silence itself was deafening in the aftermath of the firefight, the smell of spent ammunition hanging in the stifling, humid air.

"Everybody okay?" he called out after a moment, turning to make eye contact with those who had survived the attack, and consciously avoiding gazing upon those who had not.

Rising from where he had been kneeling in the grass in the closing moments of the skirmish, Maddox removed his boonie hat and wiped his face with it. Seeing Hassler looking at him, the staff sergeant shook his head tiredly but said nothing, the enormity of what they had just experienced still holding him in its grip. Similar looks marred the features of the other Marines as well as Garbuz. Only Rolero, her eyes wide and her jaw taut, seemed able to muster any words.

"I think we're in deep shit, Hassle."

The smell of death permeated the thick afternoon air, the fetid stench of voided bowels and bladders assaulting Hassler's nostrils as he looked down upon the four bodies lying on the road, arranged side by side and covered with olive drab ponchos, the best the Marines could do given their limited resources. Genetically engineered insects had already begun to gather over the remains.

In addition to Marks and Sortino, Corporal Takemura had been killed when the first harbinger punched though the truck's windshield and struck him in the face, breaking his neck with the single blow. Sitting next to Tak, Corporal Artiaga had suffered several cuts across his face and hands from flying glass but was otherwise uninjured. The damage to the truck caused by the other creature landing on its roof had resulted in more death and injuries, as well. Josh Griffin suffered massive head trauma when he was struck by the collapsing roof, killing him instantly.

"Three minutes," Maddox said as he moved to stand next to Hassler. "That's how long the whole thing took." Like Hassler, the staff sergeant wore his M4 slung over his shoulder with the weapon riding along his right hip, his forearm resting casually along the handle on the rifle's upper receiver. Shaking his head, he added, "I'm telling you, I haven't seen things go to hell that fast since Somalia."

Though he had not seen action in that war-torn region, Hassler had witnessed enough combat operations gone bad to relate to his friend's comment.

"What about the rest of your situation, Gunny?" Captain Sorensen said, his voice sounding small and hollow in Hassler's earpiece. There was an additional element of concern in Sorensen's tone, no doubt brought about by his discontent at not being able to join the rescue team. He had listened to the report with paternal compassion as Hassler detailed the losses they had suffered and his initial reflections on the attack. Though he did not say so, Carpenter's death in particular still haunted him, the unfettered terror of the security agent's final screams still echoing in his mind.

"The truck's useless so far as transport goes, sir," Hassler replied a moment later, describing the ease with which the harbinger had disabled the vehicle and the ferocity it had unleashed on the thick safety glass of the windshield. His mind's eye replayed those seconds once more, this time inserting the frightened face of Corporal Michael Takemura, sitting helpless in the truck's driver's seat in that shocking instant before his grisly death.

Which brought him to his next point of concern. Loath as he was to accept it, this was one instance where removing the bodies of their slain comrades would be impractical, at least for the moment. "The way I see it, sir, we'll have to bury the bodies here, at least until we can secure the area and get them out for proper burial." It was as much an attempt to preserve some modicum of dignity for the deceased as it was a desire to protect their remains from foraging animals, be they harbingers or something else.

"No need to explain, Gunny," Sorensen replied. "Do what you can for them now, and we'll get them out as soon as we can." Pausing a moment, the captain said. "The helos Bates called in from Nellis should be here before dawn. Can you make it to the observation station?"

Glancing at his watch and noting the time before looking to the sky to see how far the sun had descended toward the horizon, Hassler said, "I don't think we can get there before dark, sir, and if we're going to be stuck out here overnight, I'd just as soon spend the time between now and sundown setting up some kind of fortified position." He had no idea what form such a position might take, given their surroundings and the limited nature of materials and time available to them, but anything was better than nothing.

"I don't like the idea of you spending the night out there at all," Sorensen said. "Those inoculations they gave you are only supposed to be good for a day or two, and that's under ideal conditions."

"I don't like it either, sir. We're gonna haul ass to that station just as soon as we can. Dr. Christopher tells me that there's a fully stocked infirmary at the station. She's not sure if they have any of the same drugs we were given originally, but she figures there's probably something that will cover us until the cavalry gets here. It's not the best plan, but it's the best one we've got."

"Story of our lives," Maddox said, listening to the conversation on his own radio. Without further prompting from Hassler, the staff sergeant moved off to where Sergeant Lipton had taken up position on a makeshift defensive perimeter around the wrecked SUV, and Hassler could hear him issuing instructions on setting up something more secure.

After taking his leave of Sorensen with the assurance that he would report in at hourly intervals, Hassler switched off his radio to conserve the unit's batteries. As he pulled the headset from his right ear and left it to dangle on his shoulder, he heard footsteps behind him and turned to see Rolero, Christopher, and Paul Sanchez walking toward him. Sanchez was sporting a dark bruise on his left cheek thanks to being thrown about the inside of the truck during the attack, but had been fortunate enough to avoid more serious injury. Christopher also had been spared for the most part, except for a drab green field dressing Sergeant Lipton had applied to her right forearm where she had sustained a deep cut.

"How are you doing?" Rolero asked, doing a decent job of keeping her emotions in check.

Hassler offered a shrug. "Better than some, I suppose." Turning to study Christopher, he saw the anguish over the loss of her friend and coworker on her face. She appeared less a highly educated geneticist than she did a frightened child. Hassler felt an instinctive need to reach out and hold her, to protect her from the dangers surrounding them.

Easy on the stereotypes, he reminded himself. Despite her appearance, Elizabeth Christopher had not comported herself like a fragile waif. Indeed, she and her companions had already overcome more than their share of adversity.

"Mr. Hassler," Sanchez said, "I wanted to say that I'm sorry about . . . what happened to your men."

Nodding, Hassler replied, "I appreciate that. I'm sorry about your friend, too." As he spoke the words, he made a conscious effort not to look where the bodies had been placed on the ground. Instead, he offered a tired smile to the scientist, "And please, call me Donovan."

Sanchez smiled at that. "Then call me Paul." Then his smile faded. "We've unloaded the protective gear, and I'll run checks on everything before it gets dark. I'll clean out the inside of the truck as best I can, too." Waving toward the vehicle's interior, he added, "There's some equipment in there we can use when we're setting up camp. A few motion sensors we can put out, stuff like that. Nothing fancy, just some things we use when we're doing field scouting exercises, but maybe it'll give us some warning if anything comes calling."

Buoyed somewhat by that revelation, Hassler replied, "That's great, Paul. Be sure to let Maddox know about those." Turning back to the group, he eyed Rolero and Christopher. "It'll be slow going on foot. If you've got any suggestions on making the walk any shorter, I'm all ears."

Though Christopher said nothing, Rolero reached into the side pocket of her black fatigue trousers and extracted her PDA. Holding it up, she said, "If we stay on the road, we'll pass through at least one very hazardous zone. I'll have Central Ops feed me a more detailed map of the area so I can see about maybe finding an alternate route."

"Works for me," Hassler said before looking to Christopher. "Doctor? Any suggestions?"

Christopher did not react to his question, instead surprising him by moving around the Marine until she had an unblocked view of the deceased. She regarded them in silence for several moments, brushing a lock of her blond hair from her eyes before crossing her arms over her chest as if experiencing a chill. When she turned back to look at Hassler, there was a new set to her jaw and a glint of anger in her eyes.

"I don't care what Bates told you," she said, "but no one I've worked with on this project would have created anything like the . . . like those things that attacked us."

"I'll second that," Sanchez offered, apparently indifferent to the abrupt change of subject, "and I don't buy that bullshit line about being specially created for cleanup operations. You don't need monsters like that for rounding up toxic bunny rabbits or whatever we use to reclaim contaminated areas."

"For what it's worth," Hassler said, "I'm sure there's more to all of this than we've been told. Any doubts I had about that were flushed during the last attack."

"What do you mean?" Sanchez asked, his brow wrinkling in confusion.

Hassler knew that what he would say next would sound odd even to the most open-minded individuals, including these scientists who had been involved with the incredible creations he had witnessed since arriving here. Still, after what he had observed of the harbingers, both on the video of the previous rescue attempt as well as what had just happened to him and his team, what he needed now was someone else's perspective on his gut feeling.

"Look, I'm no scientist or even an expert on animal behavior," he said, indicating the jungle to the right of the disabled truck with a wave of his left hand, "but the first harbinger came from over there." Turning, he pointed to a spot farther along the road but on the opposite side of the packed dirt trail. "Then the next one came at me from this direction. I've been on the giving and receiving ends of enough ambushes to recognize one when I see it. The first two strikes were designed to distract us from the main assault on the heart of the group."

Nodding toward the wrecked SUV, Rolero said, "Once the truck was out of commission, we were sitting ducks."

"Exactly," Hassler replied. "If you think about it, they should have killed at least two or three more of us. Me, Garbuz, and Maddox were just plain lucky, that's all."

"They don't have to possess superior intelligence to launch a coordinated attack," Christopher said, shaking her head. "Dogs and wolves, even tigers, have been known to pursue prey in similar fashion."

Removing his boonie hat so that he could wipe sweat from his face, Hassler said, "Bates said they were bred to be adaptable, and smarter than anything else you've created. Maybe they're even smarter than he's been letting on."

"Even if that's true," Sanchez said, "what the hell reason could he or anyone else have to create them? What do you do with something like that?"

"Oh, I'm betting you could ask ten different people in Washington that question and come up with fifteen answers," Rolero said.

Christopher still appeared adamantly against the idea. "It's insane." Waving her hands about, she seemed almost to be trying to convince herself that what she was saying was true. "I mean, yes we've been conducting experiments to enhance the intelligence of certain animal species in New Eden, but what you're suggesting is something else entirely. It's malevolent. It's . . . it's . . . evil."

Hassler agreed that it was a sinister notion to harbor. On the one hand, he believed the Genesis Protocol and the majority of the people involved in its creation were decent souls, holding sacred the best interests of the planet and those living upon it. Even during the short time he had been exposed to the project, he had seen enough to convince him of its potential to correct many of the environmental blunders humanity had committed.

Despite that, he also was aware of those who walked the corridors of government and military power and how many of them spent their days plotting and planning, either for their own gain or else in pursuit of some twisted goal that they somehow convinced themselves was just and proper. Someone, somewhere, had to have seen other uses for the work being performed here, even if those directly involved with it had not.

Wouldn't be the first time something well-intentioned had been perverted for someone's agenda, now, would it?

"Regardless," Rolero continued, "if what you're saying is true, then there's no sense talking to Bates about it. He's liable to keep his cards close to his vest as long as he possibly can, even if it means a few Marines and even some asshole security types buy it out here."

Hassler agreed with that assessment. Of course, he was familiar enough with Rolero's modus operandi to know that she could very well be lying straight to his face about this whole thing.

Besides, if she's right about Bates, she's up to her ass in the same alligator pit as the rest of us.

"Hey, Gunny," he heard Maddox say from behind him, and turned to see the staff sergeant standing in a small patch of bare soil to the side of the road, adjacent to the maintenance truck. Pointing to the ground, he waved for the group to join him. "Come check this out."

As he drew closer, Hassler saw what had attracted Maddox's attention. Several dark spots stained the otherwise sallow dirt and loose gravel, bracketed by scrape marks and a distorted footprint that most definitely was not human. The blemishes appeared to have a pallid red hue despite having already dried in the afternoon sun.

"This was where the harbinger was when me and Lipton opened up on it."

Having apparently shaken off her earlier anxiety, Christopher crossed to where Maddox was crouching. She dropped to one knee in order to better study the stains. "Blood."

"It's too pale to be blood," Maddox responded, reaching down to touch it, but Christopher grabbed his wrist before that could happen.

"Don't touch it," she said. "Remember what Rolero said before? Given the nature of what the animals are forced to eat out here, even their blood can be dangerous if you come into contact with a sufficient quantity."

Yanking his hand back, Maddox nevertheless made an attempt to be nonchalant about the revelation. "Oh, yeah. Good tip. Thanks, Doc."

Christopher stood up and brushed dust from her pants leg. "In addition to the properties you'd find in good, old-fashioned Mother Nature–brand blood, the stuff we manufactured contains a variety of genetic-resequencing enzymes that facilitate rapid growth. It's part of the reason the different breeds reach maturity so quickly."

"Well, that answers my main question, I guess," Hassler said, encouraged by Maddox's discovery. "When I shot at that first one, I was sure I'd hit it, but the damned thing didn't seem to care. My first thought was that the rounds weren't strong enough to punch through their hides." He nodded to the bloodstains. "But it looks like we can do some damage after all. The question now is how much firepower will it take to drop one of those things?"

"It might just be a case of hitting it in the right spot, or with enough rounds," Maddox said. "The one we shot did seem to stumble a bit when we hit it, though I have no idea which shots hurt it the most. The head's probably as good a spot to try as any."

"One another thing," Hassler said. "Bates said they've been moving around in groups of five or six, but I counted at least eight of them during the attack." Shrugging, he added, "They were moving pretty fast, so maybe there really weren't that many, but if there were, then they're not traveling like he thinks they are. I'm hoping we don't have to test that theory, but something tells me we're not gonna be that lucky."

He cast a glance over his shoulder toward the western horizon, noting that the sun had almost dropped to the tops of the tallest trees. Darkness was coming fast, and he had no doubt that it would be an anxious night even if nothing else happened. Worse, an even more stressful day undoubtedly awaited them tomorrow.

Assuming they survived until morning, of course.

CHAPTER FOURTEEN

Hassler had to admit it: These science types could be helpful. Christopher and Sanchez had assisted the Marines in the wood-gathering operation, pointing out which trees could safely be cut down without risk of exposing the group to any toxins or other pollutants contained in the leaves or bark. A chainsaw and manual bow saw from the vehicle's tool locker had made easier the job of removing the flame-retardant bark so that the wood itself could be burned.

As he removed his boonie hat and used it to brush himself off, Maddox glanced around the encampment that had taken shape during the past several hours before looking to Hassler. "Be it ever so humble, eh?"

Nodding in agreement as he surveyed the camp's perimeter, Hassler replied, "It'll do, I suppose."

Unlike what he would have done had he and his team found themselves on the ground during a regular mission, Hassler had elected to erect the group's makeshift camp with its center in the middle of the service road. Ordinarily he would have preferred to stay inside the tree line, using the foliage for cover and concealment. Likewise, the idea of a fire would never even have crossed his mind, as it would have been little more than a beacon in the night advertising their position to an enemy force.

Standing in the middle of the makeshift camp, Hassler allowed his ears to tune in to the chorus of sounds emanating from the surrounding jungle. For comfort, or maybe just for the hell of it, he tried to convince himself he was standing in the forests of northeastern North Carolina while on a training exercise, or perhaps the colder and more hazardous terrain of Bosnia or even the humid rain forests of South America. But the bizarre clicks and bellows of the even more bizarre wildlife undercut the fantasy.

Opening his eyes, Hassler regarded the totaled maintenance vehicle, the interior of which Sanchez and Christopher had spent the afternoon cleaning as best they could, removing blood and other evidence that anyone had been killed inside earlier in the day. Christopher was lying underneath a makeshift tarpaulin strung from the near side of the truck, trying to get some rest of her own, but Sanchez had volunteered to man one of the defensive positions Hassler had ordered put into place.

Looking around the perimeter of their encampment, Hassler could make out the fighting holes that had been dug more or less on the four points of the compass, each approximately fifteen to twenty meters from the fire. Two of the holes had been dug directly into the packed dirt of the service road, with the others carved out of the soil and knee-high grass offered by small clearings separating the road from the tree line. A pair of heads peeked out of each of the holes on the road to the east and west. Lipton manned the hole in the clearing to the north by himself, waiting for Hassler to join him there once he was finished, while Corporal Artiaga would presently be joined by Maddox.

His gaze lingered on the freshly turned earth just off the side of the road, ten meters from the rear of the maintenance vehicle, which was the current resting place for the remains of Josh Griffin and the three Marines lost during the earlier skirmish. Given the harbingers' apparent taste for human flesh. Hassler had given the reluctant order to have the bodies burned before burying them.

It was only a temporary measure, he knew, necessitated by the team's need to move quickly, but despite all of Sorensen's assurances he still felt that he was breaking the cardinal rule of soldiers and Marines on battlefields throughout history: that no man was to be left behind.

Of course, the burial detail had served only to remind everyone that the body of Brody Carpenter had not been recovered, and Hassler forced himself not to think of the gruesome fate that had befallen the hapless security agent.

Pushing the depressing thoughts from his mind, if only for a short while, Hassler found a seat atop an equipment case that had been pulled from the truck. Picking up his M4, he laid the rifle across his thighs and dropped the magazine before ejecting the round sitting in the weapon's chamber.

"Murphy's Law bites us on the ass again, I see," Maddox said. "Right on schedule. Consistency. That's what I love most about this job."

Proceeding to clean his rifle, including the M203 grenade launcher he had taken from the weapon that had belonged to Corporal Marks, Hassler asked, "How's the gear Sanchez gave us working out?"

"Pretty good, all things considered," Maddox replied, all business again as he pulled his boonie hat back down on his head. "They're directional listening mikes, designed to pick up noises within a fifty-degree arc that rose above a preset decibel level. Nothing as sophisticated as anything we've seen during various shoot-and-loots, but they should do the job."

Hassler nodded in approval. The five passive sensors would not cover a complete circle around the perimeter, but along with the network of trip wires and improvised booby traps the team had laid out, they would be enough to assist the Marines manning the fighting holes. As for the fire, it had been built with the intention of keeping any animals away from the camp, but it would also not be an impediment to the Marines' ability to see at night, as each man's weapon was equipped with a thermal sight that would let him home in on a target's body heat.

Sniffing the air, Maddox said, "What the hell is that smell? I've been in outhouses in Georgia during the summer that didn't smell this bad."

Hassler laughed. While the odor—which reminded him of a cow pasture—did not seem nearly as foul as Maddox described, the air did seem to carry with it a tinge that lingered on his tongue, like an orange not yet ripened.

"I swear," Maddox said as he pulled one of his canteens from his belt and untwisted its cap, "I know we're standing in the middle of West Nowhere, Utah, but other than the trees and shit looking like something out of a *Scooby-Doo* cartoon, this could be the Philippines or Colombia."

"Funny you should say that," a voice said from behind Hassler. "Josh claims . . ." The voice paused. "Josh used to claim we got our color palette straight from *Josie and the Pussycats*."

Turning on his makeshift seat, Hassler saw Elizabeth Christopher walking toward them, running a hand through her hair in an attempt to smooth it. She had a sad little smile on her lips and puffy, dark circles under her eyes.

"Good evening," Hassler said as she settled herself on another of the equipment crates, crossing her arms in front of her as if trying to ward off a chill. "Couldn't sleep?"

Christopher offered another halfhearted attempt at a smile. "Not really." Glancing around the stack of equipment pulled from the truck, she asked, "Is there anything to drink?"

"That crate to your right," Maddox replied, pointing to a small box near the woman's feet. Rummaging around in the crate, Christopher extracted a bottle of water.

After taking a long pull from the bottle, she looked to Hassler. "I don't remember if I've actually thanked you for coming to get us."

"Don't thank us just yet," Hassler said. "We're not out of the woods, in more ways than one." Finished with the quick cleaning of his weapon, he began reattaching the grenade launcher.

"Still," Christopher replied, "I appreciate all the effort. I know Paul does, too, and so . . . so did Josh." Her expression fell as she uttered the last word, her anguish still open and raw at having lost yet another friend.

Hassler did not blame her, of course. While death, whether it be his own or that of someone he knew, was something he had come to accept as not only a possibility but a probability given his line of work, it was not something to which he had ever grown accustomed to witnessing. What he had learned was not to be unfeeling toward such tragedy, but instead to compartmentalize and wait to express those emotions until after the mission was over.

Elizabeth Christopher, fortunate soul that she was, had not faced the need to develop such inner defense mechanisms. With luck she never would, at least not after tonight.

"How long have you been with the project?" he asked, checking his weapon by reinserting its magazine and chambering a round before ensuring that the M4 was on safe.

Still sipping water from the bottle, Christopher shook her head. "Five years. I've been a project manager for three." Her eyes seemed to glaze over for a moment before she added, "I can't believe I've been here that long and I had no idea about those . . . those things."

"Is Professor Bates normally the type of guy who keeps secrets from his own people?" Maddox asked.

Christopher frowned. "I didn't think so." Shrugging, she added, "Then again, the people who make the best liars and secret keepers are the ones who don't let on that they're doing it, right?" She shook her head again, this time releasing a tired sigh. "Makes me wonder what else I don't know."

Any reply Hassler might have offered was cut off by the sound of a single rifle shot from his left. He jumped to his feet, rifle at the ready as he looked in the direction of the weapons fire. "This is Hassler," he said into his lip mike. "Everybody stand fast. Stewart, what's the story over there?"

"Got movement, Gunny," the corporal replied. "We didn't get a good look at it, but whatever it is, it's big."

Hassler glanced to where a portable worktable and a rugged control console had been unpacked from one of the equipment crates near the rear of the maintenance vehicle. The table featured five small computer monitors, one for each of the listening devices deployed around the camp's perimeter. None of the screens were showing signs of having detected anything. Whatever it was that Stewart and Sanchez had seen, it had not set off any of the sensors.

Then a bright flash illuminated the jungle straight ahead of him, and Hassler raised his M4, the weapon's muzzle already pointing in that direction. The flare continued to burn, lighting up the surrounding foliage and silhouetting the form of Corporal Artiaga as the young Marine brandished his own rifle.

Peering through his weapon's thermal sight, Hassler caught the corporal's body heat, but nothing else. Whatever had tripped the flare, it had already moved beyond the range of the sight, the ability of which was already hampered by the thick jungle undergrowth.

Sneaky fuckers.

"Everybody hang tight," he said, making sure to keep his voice steady. "Don't fire blind. Wait until you've got your shot." The fight that afternoon had resulted in the expenditure of enough ammunition to give Hassler cause for concern. Even though the unused ammo from their dead comrades had been redistributed, they still could not afford to fire blindly.

His weapon pulled to his shoulder, Maddox crouched as he moved across the open ground toward Artiaga's fighting hole, leaving Hassler and Christopher standing near the maintenance vehicle and the equipment cache.

"Listen," Christopher said, looking to her right. "Did you hear that?"

At the same time, another voice, Rolero's, whispered in Hassler's ear. "Hassle, we've got movement at our one o'clock. Had it in my sights for a second, but then it was gone."

Hassler was turning to face up the road to where the security chief was sharing a hole with the other member of her team, Dana Carbuz, when one of the portable status monitors beeped for attention.

"The mikes are starting to pick them up," he called into his radio. "Everybody stay frosty. Lip, you okay?"

"Not seeing anything yet, Gunny," the sergeant replied, "but I can hear something off in the distance."

He could hear it, too. The same kind of grunting noises they had heard before, at the observation station and in the waning moments of the earlier attack.

They're screwing with us.

As silly as the notion sounded to him, everything happening right now suggested to Hassler that the harbingers were testing the camp's perimeter. Rather than the random, unruly ferocity that a herd of wild animals might unleash, this felt like a calculated, staggered series of probes, looking for weaknesses and openings they might exploit.

Behind him, the displays on the status screens were screaming their alerts, flaring off and on in a fury of their own and working in concert with the unsettling animal noises to create bedlam. One second one monitor would sound an alarm, indicating that its respective listening mike had detected sounds within its monitoring arc, only to fall silent the next moment in lieu of another sensor. The entire setup seemed to be going haywire.

Something heavy crashed through the jungle to his left and Hassler did not need the sensors any longer. Instinct brought his rifle up, experience told him where to point it, and when he looked through the thermal sight, a large orange-red blob flared in the viewfinder. It was moving, but now he had it.

His finger pulled the trigger nanoseconds ahead of his brain's command to shoot, the M4 bucking in his shoulder as he fired four rounds. He was rewarded by a scream of pain, a bloodcurdling cry unlike anything he had heard since entering this otherworldly place.

The reaction was immediate. All around him Hassler heard branches snapping and leaves rustling as something big and fast tore through the thick underbrush at breakneck speed. A chorus of shrieks and wails echoed through the trees, and at various points of the compass darkness vanished as trip flares were triggered, which in turn evoked even more cries of surprise and fright.

"Jesus Christ," Maddox's voice sounded in his ear. "Way to stir up the shit, boss."

More weapons fire erupted from the fighting holes, controlled bursts as the team went after whatever targets presented themselves. Hassler heard no more cries like what had greeted his own shots, but other shrieks and calls drifted from the trees. He swept his rifle from left to right in a circle, but saw no thermal images other than the members of his team.

"I think they're pulling back," Rolero said, her voice low and tight. "I can hear them running away."

"Hold on," Hassler replied, not saying anything else until he had completed two more sweeps of the perimeter with his rifle. Looking toward the worktable, he saw that all five of the status monitors had gone quiet, no longer registering readings from the listening devices. After at least a minute spent rechecking the computer readouts, he reached for his lip mike.

"Anybody got anything?" he asked, and received a chorus of negative replies. He strained his ears but heard nothing untoward coming from the jungle. Indeed, even the insects were resuming their disparate harmony of clicks, chirps, and high-pitched whining. Pulling his left hand from his rifle, Hassler glanced at his watch to check the time.

2134.

"Shit," he breathed. The entire action had taken less than three minutes.

It was going to be a long night.

Much to Bates's relief, Jonathan Dillard retained the presence of mind to wait until the door to the professor's office was closed before unleashing his hourly tirade.

The scientist allowed the senator's invective to flow smoothly in one ear and out the other for a few minutes, until propriety demanded he respond.

"I'm well aware our people are out there all night. They'll have to defend themselves as best they can," Bates said as he began to pace his familiar circuit around the perimeter of his office. Feeling a bit light-headed, he wiped his brow before checking the clock on the wall, remembering that it was past time for his medication. Reaching into his pocket, he extracted the small vial of turquoise blue pills as he moved to the carafe of water situated on the small conference table in the corner of his office.

I hate these things, he mused with no small amount of bitterness as he downed the pills along with half a glass of water. They were his penance, he knew, the price he paid for having lived so long in the first place. The attempt at consolation, one Bates had uttered to himself countless times over the years, failed to reassure him just as it had on every single one of those previous occasions.

As Dillard stepped around Bates's desk, his expression was one of unqualified amazement. "They've already lost five people, Geoffrey. Somebody has to step up and answer for this."

"You're as responsible for what's happened here as I am," Bates said.

"I didn't create the damned things," Dillard said, his voice seething.

"No, you simply ensured that the funding was in place for their creation," Bates replied, the indictment bouncing off the soundproofed walls of his office. Feeling his own ire rising in response to the senator, he caught himself before his temper could escalate any further.

Instead he sighed, feeling the joint burden of fatigue and resignation beginning to weigh on him. Turning away from Dillard, Bates made his way back to the conference table, falling more than sitting down into one of the chairs. He removed his glasses and rubbed his eyes with the heels of his hands.

"We created the harbingers to be aggressive and adaptable to their environment," he said. "On those points, they've far exceeded even our most hopeful expectations. They're rate of development is unprecedented."

It was a true statement, and one he offered with no small amount of pride despite the unfortunate events of the past few days. Indeed, he and other senior members of the project had even gone back and amended certain components of the Genesis Protocol based on their observations of the harbingers since their introduction to New Eden, which would only have contributed to the animals' continued advancement.

I gave you what you wanted, and now that things have gotten a little messy, everyone involved wants to make sure their hands stay clean.

Bates had seen his share of that same attitude during all of his dealings with the government and the military. Though the harbingers were not exactly what had been requested, they still had proven to be more than worth the time and expense that had gone into creating them. He wondered what the reaction at the Pentagon would be when those individuals who knew of the project found out just how successful their twisted little idea had become.

Wiping his brow, Dillard replied, "Yes, but until now they've only had the other animals and your science contingent to deal with. It's obvious they've adapted to become the alpha males out there just like you intended, but this is different." Pointing toward the main floor of the operations center, he added, "Those Marines are trained in jungle warfare and special tactics, and they're not stupid. You heard Hassler and Rolero on the radio before. They're starting to figure shit out."

Bates nodded in agreement. It was obvious the combat-tested Marine sergeant had recognized that the creatures were not acting like mindless animals, or even employing a simple pack mentality like those of dogs or wolves. He had seen a quality in the harbingers that had unsettled him, and if he had been underestimating them before then it was doubtful he would do so again. That was, of course, what a successful warrior did when confronted with a formidable enemy.

"In that case," Bates said after a moment, "then the harbingers will most likely adapt, as well."

CHAPTER FIFTEEN

As Hassler walked, he once more attempted to adjust the shoulder straps of the respirator pack that was part of the awkward ensemble he was wearing. It was just one of several things contributing to the garment's overall discomfort.

Covering him from head to toe and constructed from a type of synthetic polymer if he had correctly understood Dr. Christopher, the suit shared only moderate similarities to the Mission Oriented Protective Posture garments currently used by the military. While those suits were semipermeable, allowing air to filter through after being strained of chemical or biological agents by charcoal lining the material—theoretically, at least—what he now wore succeeded in separating him hermetically from the bizarre environment surrounding him.

It was a single piece, starting with leggings that went on over his own feet and shaped themselves to the contours of his boots, and ending with a formed helmet featuring a three-sided faceplate that afforded Hassler an almost unobstructed view and permitted the use of his peripheral vision. Thin yet durable rubber gloves sheathed his hands, their material still thick enough that he had to release the trigger guard on his rifle in order to allow his finger access. Unable to wear their assault vests on the outside of the suits, the Marines had been forced to make use of pouches on the garments' accompanying equipment belt to hold extra magazines for their rifles and other miscellaneous items.

Naturally the garment was airtight, requiring the pack unit on his back to act not only as a supplier of oxygen but also a regulator of the suit's internal environment, cooling him as best it could in the jungle heat. So far the pack appeared to be doing its job, but Hassler knew that the worst of the day's oppressive heat was still hours away. Because of that, he was thankful for the rig's "camelback" bladder system, which allowed him to drink water and refill his reservoir without compromising the suit's integrity, while a similar system allowed for the storage and removal of bodily waste.

The suit's main downside was in how the sealed helmet amplified the sound of his own breathing, making it difficult to listen for any signs of something trying to sneak up on them from the jungle. Likewise, it was impossible to move through the brush with anything approaching stealth while wearing the damn thing.

Looking over his shoulder and seeing Christopher walking behind him, he said, "If wearing this all the time is a job requirement, then my hat's off to you. It's only been an hour or so and I'm ready to rip it off and run screaming into the jungle."

Christopher smiled through her own helmet's faceplate. "It's something you get used to after a while. I mean, I've heard that. Personally I hate wearing the damned things. I was hoping we might avoid having to use them at all, but . . ." She shrugged, letting the sentence trail off into silence.

The requirement to don the cumbersome gear had come sooner than Hassler would have liked, with the team's journey taking them off the packed surface of the dirt road and guiding them over broken terrain through a forested area that did not appear to be as overgrown with vegetation as the more alien zone in which they had spent the previous day. Unlike that region, the forest in which Hassler currently found himself resembled a place he might conceivably have found on this planet. Trees grew more or less vertically, their branches jutting outward in all directions from their trunks and often sagging under their own weight.

For a moment the familiar environment was comforting, and he found himself relaxing just a little. But the similarities between this forest and any other he had ever visited quickly ended. According to Christopher and Sanchez, the leaves dangling from the trees here were poisonous to the touch, their contaminated nature producing the equivalent of a nerve toxin that, if introduced to exposed skin, would almost certainly prove fatal. Further, the scientists had warned that inhalation of pollen released from trees or vegetation here was also hazardous.

This place is just plum full of laughs, ain't it?

As if comprehending the awkward silence she had caused, Christopher said, "Come to think of it, the longest I've ever had to wear one of these things was sixteen hours. Doesn't sound all that bad, until you realize you can't eat while wearing it, and there's only so much the suit does so far as bathroom breaks are concerned. Not exactly pampered treatment, especially for the ladies, if you catch my drift."

"Point taken," Hassler said, turning and offering a smile, "and complaint withdrawn, Doctor."

"Please, call me Elizabeth," Christopher replied. "Some people call me Liz, but I usually smack the shit out of them. Except for Shannon, that is. I figure it's not good policy to hit people who can probably kill you with a paper clip."

"Sound thinking," Hassler offered. "In that case, the name's Donovan."

"You don't like 'Hassle'?" Christopher asked, her tone containing an element of mild teasing.

"I can kill you with a paper clip, too."

"Fair enough. Donovan it is."

Satisfied that he had won the day, at least so far as his name was concerned, Hassler asked, "How are you holding up?"

Elizabeth nodded. "Okay, all things considered. Obviously the things that . . . that have happened over the last couple of days aren't something I'm used to dealing with." Her expression softened somewhat, her eyes dropping to look at the ground. "Mostly I feel sad, for the people we've lost and their families. I don't know what to think or say about that." Looking up at Hassler again, she asked, "What about you? How does . . . I mean, about your men. Are you okay?"

Drawing in a long breath, he replied, "I'm upset, if that's what you mean, but I can't dwell on it right now. There'll be time for that later."

Hassler looked up to face Rolero, who was still walking at the same steady pace she had established an hour earlier. Just as she had yesterday, the security agent had taken the point position, using the digital map downloaded to her PDA as a guide.

"Where are we, Shannon?" he asked.

"About six hundred meters from where we're supposed to pick up the road again," Rolero replied. "If we stick to this pace, we should be there in half an hour."

She, along with Hassler and Elizabeth, had studied the map the previous evening, working with personnel from Central Operations who were intimately familiar with the network of service roads and footpaths crisscrossing the EDN region. The joint brainstorming session had yielded a route through the artificial environs that would take the rescue team and their charges to Observation Station One.

The course was not entirely free of risk, but it minimized the amount of time the group would have to spend wearing containment suits. That part of the equation eased Hassler's concerns, if only marginally. He was worried about the way the suits hampered mobility, to say nothing of the physical drain the team members would experience the longer they were forced to wear the protective garments in the oppressive jungle humidity.

"How far to the station once we're back on the road?" he asked as he stepped around a knee-high, bright yellow and brown bush with leaves oozing a thick lime green mucus. He had no way of knowing if the viscous slime was capable of eating through his suit, but after his run-in with the beetle the previous day and the damage inflicted on his boot, Hassler was taking no chances.

"I figure we can make it before lunch," Rolero replied.

Hassler nodded in approval, though she could not see him. "Works for me," he said as he wrinkled his nose. In addition to protecting him from the toxic vegetation surrounding him, his suit also was doing an admirable job of containing his own body odor, which of course was suffering from the past twenty-odd hours spent sweating in response to jungle heat and humidity. He was more than ready to shuck the garment and, hopefully, get behind some kind of fortification while they waited for the helos to arrive. "Did you get that, Skipper?"

"Roger that, Gunny," Sorensen replied. With the requirement to wear the suits as they traversed this part of the region, Hassler had elected to keep the team's radios locked on the frequency he would normally have used to contact the captain with his regular status reports. The result was an open line that could be heard by personnel monitoring the channel back at Central Operations.

After suffering through two more probing actions by the harbingers during the night, the team had gotten under way at first light. The results of those two encounters were the same as the first instance, with the creatures running around the outer perimeter of the camp while setting off the motion sensors and the odd trip wire. Only Maddox and Corporal Stewart had seen anything that presented itself as a target, with both Marines firing at the fleeting figures and coming up dry.

As for the harbinger Hassler was sure he had hit during the first infiltration attempt, a search had been conducted of the area where he thought he had engaged the creature. Sergeant Lipton reported finding more traces of what passed for blood in EDN animals, but no body. Either Hassler had not seriously wounded it, or else the harbinger had managed to escape.

Or, maybe his buddies came and got him.

"So, tell me something, Donovan," Elizabeth asked as she pushed aside a long, sinewy branch—the bark of which reminded Hassler of half-cooked pizza crust—in order to step up alongside him, "how long have you been doing this? Serving in the military, I mean."

"Going on fifteen years now," Hassler replied, pausing to scan the trees and their equally strange-looking foliage before adding, "Went in right out of high school, which I almost didn't finish, by the way. I was a screwup as a teenager, but my older cousin gave me the kick in the ass I needed. Started out in the infantry before I volunteered for recon, and I've been doing that ever since." Turning so that she could see his face through the helmet's visor, he asked, "What about you? What makes a person decide to become a genetic engineer, or whatever you call it?"

Smiling at that, Elizabeth replied, "My doctorate is in molecular biology, and I started working for the government about seven years ago. Plenty of money in government-funded research, you know."

"Oh yeah, I can imagine," Hassler said as he stepped over a thick tree root covered in burnt-orange moss that had grown up out of the ground. "So that led you here?" Was it his imagination, or had the branch moved of its own accord in response to his passage?

You're paranoid.

Oblivious of his unspoken worry, the doctor nodded. "More or less. It's not as though you answer an ad in the paper to come and grow your own animals. Professor Bates recruited me while I was working at MIT, and the rest, as they say, is history." Indicating the surreal forest with a wave of her gloved hand, she added, "When I first came here, most of this work had already been done. The environment, I mean. I was brought in to observe various experimental animal and plant life, how they reacted to whatever we subjected them to, make recommendations and so on. I haven't actually created anything, at least not yet."

"Is that something you want to do?" Hassler asked.

"Of course," she replied. "The uses for the knowledge we've gained here are staggering. We could repopulate endangered species, or re-create something that's already become extinct. Imagine what we could learn if we could duplicate a species of animal that died out thousands of years ago."

Unable to resist the easy opening, Hassler said, "Didn't they make a movie or two about something like that? I seem to recall things not going very well for those scientists." Waving a hand to indicate the jungle around them, he added, "Of course, they only concentrated on animals that might be dangerous, as opposed to killer bushes and weeds and other shit like that."

Elizabeth took the mild tease in the spirit with which it was intended. "This is real life, friend, and we're not looking to open a theme park here. Imagine being able to reproduce a specimen of early man, using remains found at archaeological digs around the world as a guide." She once more pointed to the trees and brush around them for emphasis. "The Genesis Protocol isn't just about fixing some of the problems we've created for ourselves. It can also answer questions about where we came from."

Holding up his hands in mock surrender, Hassler said, "You don't have to convince me, Doctor. I've seen enough to think there's a lot of good that can come out of all this." His expression then lost some of its warmth. "At the same time, I see a lot of ways that things going on here can be misused." Then, remembering that he was talking on an open line, he added, "Right now, though, I'm only worried about the things that can get us killed."

The pair walked in silence for more several minutes, their only interaction coming when Elizabeth pointed Hassler toward certain vegetation or bugs that he should avoid stepping on or brushing up against. Each bush that he sidestepped seemed even more alien to him than the last, with garish colors and thin, sinewy branches twisting and extending in directions that only heightened the sensation that he was walking on another world or through the center of someone's dark and demented nightmares.

"You can say it if you want to," Elizabeth said after another minute or so. Looking over to her, Hassler saw that she was keeping her attention directed toward the ground. "I figure you've been holding back out of consideration for my feelings."

The odd statement caught Hassler off guard. "What do you mean? Say what?"

She raised her head to meet his gaze. "Tell me that what's happening here is our punishment for playing God."

Hassler shook his head. "Thought never crossed my mind."

"Really?"

He shrugged. "I'm not all that religious, to be honest with you." It was an honest response. In the time since he and his team had arrived here, the idea that God or anyone else might be visiting retribution upon those assigned to the EDN project had not occurred to him. In fact, having heard Elizabeth give voice to the notion, he found it silly.

Okay, maybe not completely silly.

"Interesting," Elizabeth said. "Given our penchant for biblical references around here, I'd have thought that an obvious statement for you to make. You certainly wouldn't be the first."

"I like to be different," Hassler replied, turning to walk backward for a few steps as he scanned the rest of the group walking behind him. They had emerged from the more dense area of the forest and he was able to see every member of the team, their orange or yellow containment suits doing an admiral job of harmonizing with the curious palette of colors dominating the vegetation in this area.

Stewart was closest to him in the column, followed by Lipton, Sanchez, Corporal Artiaga, and Dana Garbuz. As usual, Maddox was bringing up the rear, making sure to turn and look in all directions every few paces as they walked and ensuring that nothing could sneak up on them from behind.

Hassler's slower pace while looking back to observe the rest of the team allowed Stewart to close some of the gap between the two Marines. As the corporal approached, Hassler noted something about the man that seemed wrong. He looked pale and his cheeks appeared sunken, as though he might be fighting off illness.

"You okay?" Hassler asked.

"Stomach's bothering me a bit," Stewart replied, his voice somewhat muffled in spite of the otherwise clear communications circuit. He sucked on the small tube positioned near his mouth before adding, "It helps when I sip water."

As he stepped closer, Hassler noted an irregular blemish on the man's right cheek. "What did you do to yourself?" he asked, making a motion to indicate Stewart's face. The blemish was bright red, appearing at first to be a blood blister, but its haphazard pattern of small swellings was not consistent with what he knew of such afflictions. "Looks like a rash or something."

By now other members of the team were walking up, and out of habit Hassler worried about them being bunched up too closely together.

Guess the harbingers *won't lob grenades at us*, he mused. Nevertheless, he motioned for the rest of the column to keep walking after Rolero, even though Dr. Elizabeth stayed behind to examine Stewart's face. Maddox, bringing up the rear, stopped when he got to the trio.

"What's the scoop?" he asked.

"Oh God," she said, leaning in as far as her bulky helmet would allow. "He's showing signs of exposure."

"Exposure to what?" Hassler said, his eyes widening. To Stewart he asked, "Did you rip your suit?"

Anxiety began to show on the corporal's face. "No, Gunny. Everything's still sealed." He held up his left arm so that Hassler could see the status gauge affixed to his suit's sleeve at the wrist. "No leaks."

"Gunny," Sorensen's voice sounded in his ear. "What's wrong?"

"Dr. Christopher thinks that Stewart may have been contaminated somehow, sir," Hassler replied. "Wait one, please."

Still hovering over Stewart, Elizabeth asked, "You said your stomach was queasy? Nausea and skin sores are normal first signs that you've been exposed to something out here, usually something airborne."

"How can that be?" Hassler asked. "None of our tags showed anything before we suited up, and we've been wearing these damn things for two hours. What could he have come into contact with?"

Shaking her head, Elizabeth said, "I don't know. Unless . . . " Turning, she locked eyes with Hassler. "Unless the vaccinations you were given before coming in here are starting to weaken."

"What the fuck?" Maddox asked. "I thought that stuff they pumped into us was good for at least two days."

"That's an estimate," Elizabeth said, "based on a whole slew of factors that really don't mean much right now." To Hassler, she said, "If this is what's causing his symptoms, then it's going to get worse over the next few hours if left untreated."

Over the radio, Sorensen asked, "Can you do anything for him there, Doctor?"

"Not while we're stuck in these suits," the doctor replied. "ObStat One has medical facilities, but the main hospital would be better. We need to get him and the rest of your team out of here as soon as possible."

Stopping himself from offering a smartassed response to the obvious nature of her observation, Hassler said, "We're working on that, Doctor. Shannon, you getting this?"

In his earpiece, he heard the security chief reply, "Yeah. We're still about two hours away. We can chop some of that down if we pick up the pace."

Any reduction in the time to get to the observation station would be negligible so long as they were encumbered by their suits, Hassler knew. How much time did they have before Stewart's condition deteriorated or, worse yet, before any of the other Marines started to present symptoms?

Hassler forced the thought away. There was only a single option available to them at the moment. Turning to Stewart, he asked "Stew, you okay to keep humping it?"

The corporal nodded. "Semper Fi, Gunny. Let's get the civilians out of here."

Seeing the hint of mounting fear in the young man's eyes. Hassler patted him on the shoulder, proud of Stewart's commendable attempt to maintain his bearing. He was an experienced Marine, and understood the virtue of keeping positive morale during an op, especially when things turned dicey. Despite what he was facing personally, Stewart was striving to stay focused and continue with the mission.

Satisfied with that, Hassler waved for Maddox to resume his position at the rear of the column. "Okay then. Let's haul ass."

Unlike the outpost from which Hassler and his Marines had extracted Dr. Christopher and her team, Observation

Station One had not been designed to blend into the jungle background in any way. Straight lines, right angles, pale concrete, and dulled metal stood out against the haphazard contours of the surrounding jungle. That the blatantly artificial structure might present such a contrast amused Hassler, considering that everything down to the smallest weed protruding from the soil here had been created as a result of the machinations of humans.

The team stopped at the edge of the open field playing home to the compound, dominated by reddish yellow clay only sporadically populated with patches of pale blue weeds, which to Hassler resembled the fake grass one might use to decorate a child's Easter basket. Ignoring this latest and admittedly tame example of New Eden's alien vegetation, he took his first good look at the wall surrounding the building. Twenty feet high, it reminded him initially of a prison, but he decided that the moat, at least thirty feet wide and forming a circle around the station, gave the structure a distinctly medieval air.

"Were you expecting an assault by an angry barbarian horde or something?" he asked Elizabeth as the rest of the team spread out in a line to either side of them, all the while fighting the urge to try and wipe sweat from his face through the faceplate of his helmet.

"Maybe not at first," Elizabeth replied. "Given how things have been going the last few days, though, I'm not gonna complain."

"Amen to that, sister," Maddox said as he came up behind them "I'm ready to peel out of this overgrown condom, and far be it from me to whine to the host about the accommodations."

Smiling at that, Elizabeth said, "We'll be able to take off the suits once we're inside." She pointed toward the moat. "A word of warning, though. No swimming."

"Let me guess," Hassler said as he regarded the murky brown water. "Acid."

Elizabeth nodded. "Close. The water is mildly acidic, but it's diluted by a filtration system running from inside the compound. That's not the big problem, though." She indicated the moat again, and Hassler looked in time to catch sight of something disappearing beneath the surface of the water.

"Uh," Maddox said, "what was that?"

"Like some of the birds we've created, those animals are engineered to eat fish that we might introduce into lakes or streams contaminated by industrial waste. They're more of an experiment than anything we might actually deploy, but they're capable of living in the most polluted water. We could drop them off the coast of Huntington Beach and they'd be right at home."

Maddox shrugged. "Yeah, but that might cause a bit of a public relations problem with the grand populace of southern California. Not that it's a deal breaker or anything."

Noting Stewart's slumped posture, Hassler walked over to the younger Marine, seeing that the rash on his face had grown larger and more pronounced. "You okay?"

The corporal looked up. "Yeah, I think so. Dizzy, is all."

Hassler indicated the rash. "Does it hurt?"

"Not really," Stewart replied. "It's kind of warm, but it doesn't itch or anything. Good thing, I guess. Otherwise I might be scratching my face off."

"Now that just might be an improvement," Hassler said, offering the lame joke as he clapped the man on the back. "Hang in there. We're almost to the house." Rising to his feet, he turned to walk back to where Maddox and Elizabeth were standing when something made him stop.

A sound?

No, he decided. He had not heard anything unusual. Nothing had caught his eye, but he stood in place and studied the surrounding jungle anyway, seeing only the outlandish tapestry of trees and underbrush, which was much thicker here than in the area through which the group had passed earlier, thereby affording better cover and concealment. Additionally, the abnormal shapes and colors made it that much more difficult for him to pick out shapes or silhouettes that might be out of place. For all he knew, something could be standing two feet inside the tree line and it would be all but invisible.

Something's out there.

His eyes and ears might be compromised by his protective suit's damnable helmet, but his gut and the hairs on the back of his neck were telling him everything he needed to know.

They were being watched.

"Let's move it out, Shannon," he said, bringing his weapon up to emphasize his point. The other Marines saw the action and mimicked it, their attention turning back to the jungle they had left behind. Once again following Rolero's lead, the team fell back into their column formation for the final leg of their journey.

"Skipper," Hassler said into his lip mike, "we're at the compound. We should be inside in a couple of minutes."

"Excellent," Sorensen replied over the radio channel. "Professor Bates recommends that all of you go through decontamination procedures once you're inside. Dr. Christopher knows what to do."

"Roger that."

Covering the last hundred meters or so should have been a simple exercise, but Hassler knew it was complicated by everyone's senses ratcheted up to a heightened alert. He could sense the renewed focus as the team continued to check their flanks and rear, searching for threats.

Thankfully, none appeared.

"Everybody spread out," he said as the team approached the compound's single entrance. "Defensive line facing the trees." The team immediately reacted to the order, with Lipton guiding Sanchez and Garbuz to proper positions along the hastily defined perimeter.

Turning to examine the entryway, Hassler nodded in approval. Built atop a natural land bridge that dissected the moat, the entrance was essentially a tunnel of steel mesh large enough for one of the maintenance vehicles to pass through.

"Nice," he offered.

"The cage has two layers, and the exterior layer is electrified," Rolero explained as they drew closer. "Keeps animals from jumping onto it and getting close enough to scale the wall." She pointed to where a squat column of metal rose from the ground adjacent to the near end of the tunnel. "That houses a keypad for opening the gate."

Noting the access panel on the front of the panel, complete with lock, Hassler asked, "Got the key?"

Rolero shook her head as she extracted a combat knife from a sheath on her belt. "Nope. Guess I'll have to be creative."

"Whatever works," Hassler said. "Just get us the hell inside." His instincts told him that they were not yet in the clear. Something was about to go down. He could feel it.

His instincts were right.

CHAPTER SIXTEEN

Two harbingers broke from the tree line less than forty meters to the team's right and sprinted toward them. Hassler could see spittle flying from their mouths and sunlight reflecting off rows of gleaming, sharp teeth.

"Two o'clock!" Maddox yelled. Dropping to one knee, the staff sergeant fired the first shots as he unleashed a barrage of M4 fire. At least some of those initial rounds scored hits on one of the creatures, for Hassler saw the blood spray from the impacts even as the animal shrieked in shock and pain before dodging to its left to avoid being hit again.

It was enough to allow other members of the team to draw beads on the animals, and an instant later the air erupted with gunfire, with both harbingers stumbling under the force of the multiple bullets tearing into their leathery skin. Despite the wounds being inflicted upon them, the creatures continued to press forward. One of the harbingers finally fell in the face of the onslaught, crashing heavily to the earth at the same time its companion changed direction and fled back into the trees.

Even as he fired after the retreating animal, something about the attack felt wrong to Hassler. It seemed too quick, too simple, and not nearly as ferocious as anything the Marines had seen since their arrival. The harbingers obviously had been keeping to the cover offered by the dense undergrowth to conceal their movements. Why had they not attacked sooner?

They're suckering us.

The thought screamed in his mind at the same instant he detected movement to his left. Hassler swung the barrel of his M4 in that direction in time to see three more of the harbingers lunging from the underbrush. They were farther away than the first pair, but the distinction was negligible when factoring in the creatures' speed.

"Son of a bitch!"

Grabbing Elizabeth by the arm, Hassler pulled the doctor behind him before taking aim at the onrushing harbingers. He lost a precious second or two getting his gloved finger situated inside the weapon's trigger guard but finally managed to fire, catching the first creature in the head. Rounds punched through the animal's tough skull and it lurched to its left, actually stumbling and losing its balance.

That action was enough for Dana Garbuz to bring her own weapon to bear, the security agent unloading a full magazine at the creature. As close as she was, less than ten meters away, most of the fifteen to twenty rounds caught the thing in the upper chest and head. It flailed backward before tripping over its own feet and falling clumsily to the ground, where it continued to twitch and shudder for several more seconds.

"Dana!" Sanchez screamed, his voice tight with near-panic. "Watch out!"

Reacting to the warning, Hassler caught the harbinger moving to his left from the corner of his eye but was unable to do anything in the heartbeat it seemed to take the animal to lunge across the open ground and pounce on Garbuz. The woman screamed in abject terror as the harbinger pushed her down, pinning her beneath its weight as its teeth and claws slashed across her body. Blood-soaked fragments of her containment suit were thrown everywhere, which only seemed to fuel the animal's efforts to tear her to pieces.

"No!" Sanchez cried out, turning to run to her aid, but Hassler grabbed him by the arm and held him back even as Garbuz's horrendous screams faded mercifully away. The harbinger, as if realizing that its prey was no longer alive and capable of mounting any kind of defense, halted its slaughter, its head perking up as if searching for a new target.

It was enough for Corporal Artiaga to step forward and bring his own weapon up, firing the M203 grenade launcher attached to his rifle. The projectile caught the creature full in the chest before it detonated, the sound of the explosion muffled through the layers of Hassler's suit helmet. Pieces of the creature's torso and head spattered in all directions. The other two harbingers, obviously frightened by this new development, scampered off at different angles, the sounds of snapping branches and crunching leaves following after them as they plunged back into the jungle.

"Nice job," Hassler called to the younger Marine, his voice actually cracking from the strain of witnessing Garbuz's ghastly death even as he searched the trees for any indication that the harbingers might be rallying for another try. "Key up another one like that if you can," he offered as he pulled a 40mm grenade from the bandolier slung over his left shoulder and inserted it into the breach of his own rifle's M203. "Rolero, get that fucking door open. Lipton, you lead the rest of the group inside."

"Got it," the security chief replied as she backed away from the line, moving toward the stanchion concealing the protected keypad.

"What do you want me to do?" Elizabeth asked.

Hassler said, "Go with her. I want you inside right behind Lipton."

As the doctor turned to run after Rolero, Sorensen's voice rang in Hassler's ear. "Gunny, what's your status?"

"They're strafing us," Hassler replied, his attention remaining fixed on the tree line as he dropped the magazine from his M4 and quickly fumbled a replacement from one of the pouches on his belt. Once again, the thick jungle growth was doing a fine job of concealing any sign of the creatures' presence. Where the hell were they? "It's different from yesterday." The previous day's attack had been much more ferocious, with the harbingers seeming to feed off the carnage they were inflicting on the team.

Then he heard the unmistakable clamor of something large and bulky moving somewhere beyond the initial cover of vegetation, sounding like a herd of cattle trudging through the brush. He caught flickers of movement between the squat, twisted trunks of the trees as the things drew closer, seeming more like shadows than actual beings.

"Here they come again," he called out as the first harbinger emerged from the jungle at a sprint, followed by four others lunging out onto the open ground at different points along the perimeter. Despite the distance separating them, Hassler could see the bullet wounds inflicted on three of the creatures, though they seemed not to be hampered by their injuries.

Tough little bastards.

He fired first, with the rest of the team quickly following his lead. The harbingers seemed to anticipate the counterattack, spreading out and changing the path of their advance almost before Hassler could pull the trigger. Even as he felt the M4 buck against his shoulder, his instincts told him that the animals were trying to hem them in, drawing their prey closer together and making it easier for them to attack.

"Don't bunch up!" he shouted over the weapons fire. Taking aim at one harbinger, he pulled the trigger and saw the rounds tear into the animal's dark flesh. It howled in pain and anger, bounding away from the gunfire and heading back toward the safety of the trees.

Around him, other members of the team were having similar success, driving other creatures away from them and back toward the jungle. Turning to his right, Hassler saw one of the things angling for a run at Stewart, closing the gap between them with mind-numbing speed.

"Stewart! Watch out!"

The corporal saw the attack coming and ducked instinctively to his left, his movements carrying him down the bank of the moat and up to his knees in the dark, muddy water. It was enough to spoil the harbinger's aim, though, the creature swinging its massive arms at the Marine but missing before changing direction and heading off as if in search of different prey.

What the hell?

Hassler's mind screamed the question. Was the harbinger avoiding the water?

Movement to his right caught his attention and he saw one of the harbingers leap forward, its muscles coiling and releasing like an Olympic long jumper. Momentum carried it forward as though it had been launched from a catapult, and it landed heavily near Maddox, dirt and dust flying upward from the impact points of its feet.

Facing in another direction as he fired at another of the creatures, Maddox was still able to sense the more immediate threat. He lunged away in time to avoid the savage swipe of the harbinger's left hand and its gleaming claws. Rolling on the ground, he brought his rifle up and fired at the advancing creature. Bullets ripped into the harbinger's leg and chest, the thing halting its advance as it screamed out in reaction to its injuries.

Without thinking, Hassler turned toward the harbinger, his firing hand moving to the trigger of his weapon's grenade launcher and pulling it before he really had a chance to aim the rifle. The M4 kicked as the grenade was fired, closing the distance between him and the animal in scarcely a heartbeat before striking the harbinger in the back.

The resulting explosion was muffled but still effective, the projectile shredding the creature apart just above the crotch. Blood, bone, and tissue sprayed everywhere, some of it landing on Maddox's legs and lower torso.

"Fuck me!" Maddox suddenly exclaimed. As he jumped to his feet, Hassler could see smoke coming from those parts of his suit that had been hit by blood spatter from the harbinger. "This shit's eating through my suit!"

Hassler yelled "Get in the water!" but Maddox was ahead of him, turning and running for the moat only a few meters behind the team's defensive line. He plunged in up to his chest, his rifle held in both hands above his head. Ignoring the continuing firefight going on all around him, Hassler sprinted for the bank to see if he could help his friend.

"You okay?"

As quickly as he entered the water, Maddox had turned and was scrambling back toward shore. He nodded to Hassler. "Yeah. I don't think it got through the suit in time. Now get me the hell out of here."

"Stay there!" Hassler shouted as he saw movement among the trees once more. Turning toward to the rest of the team, he called out, "Everybody into the water! Move!" As fast as he could while wearing the containment suit's insulated gloves, he ejected the spent cartridge from the M203 while fumbling another grenade from his bandolier.

The team reacted to the order as the first of the harbingers emerged from the jungle once more, firing at the moving targets and falling back from their positions toward the slick mud near the water as carefully they could. Lipton, following his instructions to oversee the movement of the group into the compound and with the help of Sanchez, was directing traffic, indicating for everyone else to move past him as backed into the waist-deep water. Sanchez mirrored the sergeant's movements, each man covering the other's retreat with his rifle.

"What the hell are you doing?" Rolero called out from where she worked to pry open the access panel protecting the gate's entry keypad.

"They don't like the water," Hassler replied as he pulled the M203's slide closed. Looking over his shoulder to where Rolero was still working on the access panel, Hassler asked, "What's up with that door?"

"Almost got it," she replied, not turning from where she had jammed nearly half of her knife's eight-inch blade into the panel's seam.

"Sanchez," Hassler snapped, not taking his eyes off the tree line, "You're in first. Everybody else on you. Lipton, cover their asses."

Maddox was the first to spot new trouble. "Here they come," he called out, pointing to an area of the otherworldly jungle nearly fifty meters away where first one harbinger and then nine more appeared from the cover of the trees. Instead of charging forward, they stopped as soon as they were visible, standing just to the side of the service road.

"Looks like you stumped them, boss," Maddox offered.

By now all of the creatures were halted on the road and looking in the team's direction. A few of them sniffed the air with their elongated snouts, while others swayed slightly on their massive legs or flailed their tails about. To Hassler, it seemed as though all of the creatures were uncertain as to what to do next.

All of them, except one.

Standing at the front of the pack, its wide, dark chest a crisscross of fading, puckered scars, the harbinger was as rigid as a statue. No flaring of its nostrils, no twitching of its claws. Its tail drooped to the ground as if offering balance for the creature's formidable mass.

And its eyes were locked on Hassler.

"Oh my God," Elizabeth said, her words little more than a croaked whisper.

Ignoring the comment, Hassler stared down the harbinger, studying its eyes. There was more going on behind them than simple instinctive fury, of that he was certain. Elements of fear and anger, perhaps due to the firepower that had killed four of its companions? Maybe, Hassler decided, but he also sensed there was something more.

Comprehension? Possibly.

Determination?

That was it.

His first instinct was to give the command to open fire, though something told him that would be useless. At this range and given their uncanny speed, it was unlikely that a new counteroffensive would succeed in bringing down any more of the things. Further, given the team's current position, Hassler was not yet convinced that the harbingers were as much afraid of the water as they were examining their options before deciding they could handle getting wet for a few moments if it meant having access to an easy kill.

Something tells me they might learn to live with it.

A metallic snap sounded from somewhere over his left shoulder, and he glanced over to see that Rolero had succeeded in opening the panel and was now frantically entering an access code to open the gate. A second later, an electronic buzz echoed from the tunnel leading to the observation station, and the double gate began to swing open.

"Got it!" Rolero called out, sheathing her knife and pulling her M16 back up as she directed Elizabeth and Sanchez along with Lipton through the widening entry.

His eyes still fixed on the harbingers, Hassler illogically waited for the pack's apparent leader to do something, offer some sign that it did indeed understand what was happening. While it did not move even the slightest bit, several of its companions were watching the goings-on at the gate. Their eyes narrowed in apparent suspicion as Elizabeth and the others ran across the bridge toward the compound's inner door, shifting their weight and waving their tails with a bit more fervor.

And yet, none of them moved.

Attention shifted back to him when he raised his rifle and aimed the grenade launcher in their direction. A few of them crouched down, as if preparing to jump out of the way of anything fired at them. In sharp contrast, the pack leader remained absolutely immobile.

They understand. Son of a bitch, they understand!

"Nice and easy," he said, keeping his voice low and quiet, "one at a time, move to the gate. Rolero, if they start this way, close it and get the hell inside." As he expected, the security agent offered no protest. She knew how the game was played, after all.

In his peripheral vision he saw Stewart stepping out of the water and moving toward the gate, with Artiaga following after him as soon as the corporal was in the tunnel. Risking a look over his shoulder, Hassler saw that Elizabeth had run across the bridge and was opening a service door leading through the concrete wall and into the compound.

While all of this activity took place, the harbingers held their ground, their leader never once moving his eyes from Hassler.

"I think he likes you," Maddox said as he crossed behind him on his way to the gate.

"I don't believe this," Elizabeth said. "Their behavior is like . . . " Her voice trailed away, and Hassler looked to her. Sensing his gaze on her, the doctor shook her head. "It's like nothing I've seen before. I just don't understand it."

As Maddox stepped into the tunnel, Hassler turned his attention back to the harbinger as he stepped up the bank, feeling mud and water running down the outside of his containment suit as he sloshed out of the moat.

No sooner had he cleared the water than the harbinger moved.

It turned and loped back into the jungle, never once looking back as it vanished into the trees. The others followed after it, a few of them looking over their shoulders as animals in retreat normally did, ensuring that nothing was following them.

"Get the hell inside, Gunny," Maddox said, standing at the entrance and keeping his own rifle trained on where the harbingers disappeared into the jungle. In response to his friend's summons, Hassler stepped into the metal cocoon forming the entry tunnel to the compound and Rolero keyed the sequence to close the gate.

"Nine o'clock!"

The metal barriers had started drawing together when a lone harbinger lunged from the jungle to Hassler's left. Bent low, it ran on all four appendages as it scrambled across the open ground toward the gate. Hassler pulled his M4 to his shoulder but held his fire as he watched the creature's approach, the gates having closed far enough that it could not pass through without coming into contact with their electrically charged exterior. If the thing wanted inside, it would have to force its way in.

It tried.

Hassler winced as the harbinger touched the gates, sparks flying from the electrified steel mesh when the creature's hands made contact. The creature howled in protest and pain at the sudden shock as it jumped back from the barrier. It paused, glaring through the metal latticework at Hassler, who was tempted to shoot the thing through the gate. Before he could decide one way or the other, the harbinger turned tail and ran back into the jungle.

"Somebody needs to find these assholes a new hobby," Maddox offered.

"Yeah, well maybe later," Hassler said as he caught sight of something moving near the tree line. Looking back to Maddox and Rolero, he nodded his head in the direction he'd been watching.

Another harbinger had reemerged and was standing in plain view on the road. This time it stood alone, with no sign of the others. Hassler saw the scars on its chest and recognized it as the pack's apparent leader.

Once again, their gazes locked, and he saw the determination in the creature's eyes at the same time a single thought whispered in his mind.

This ain't over yet.

Observation Station One was a more impressive visual sight than the other outpost, Hassler decided, if nothing else than because the majority of it was above ground.

The station's main feature was a large three-story building sitting in the center of an expansive courtyard. It reminded him of a prison, with even rows of narrow windows set into pale gray concrete. Only the topmost level of the structure broke from the design, with large, tinted plate-glass ports overlooking the compound.

As for the courtyard itself, it consisted mostly of gravel and dirt. Hassler saw no grass or weeds of any sort peeking up among the loose rock and soil, making him wonder if the ground here either had been treated to prevent such growth or was one of the few areas within the EDN region that had never been altered from its original desert topography. In fact, aside from the odd metallic scent permeating the air and lingering on his tongue, Hassler could almost believe they finally had left behind New Eden's bizarre environs.

"Between the wall and the moat," Maddox said as he completed his report of the security sweep he and the other Marines had conducted, "we should be safe. The thing that hit the gate seemed pretty pissed about it, so hopefully they'll stay away, but Dr. Christopher has already showed us the main observation deck and I've got Artiaga cleaned up and manning the console that controls the camera and alarm systems. Once the rest of us go through decon, we'll rotate in shifts."

"Outstanding," Hassler said, nodding in approval before a worried frown creased his features. "How's Stewart?"

"The doc's giving him the once-over now." Grimacing, he added. "The rash on his face has gotten worse, and it's spreading all over his body."

Hassler's stomach quivered at the memory of the festering pustules that had erupted across the unfortunate Marine's body. He currently occupied a bed in the station's medical clinic that had been sealed off with a protective plastic shroud. The doctor's prognosis for Stewart's recovery at last check was not good, a thought upon which Hassler tried very hard not to dwell.

"What about the others? Anyone else show anything?"

Maddox shook his head. "Nothing I know about. Christopher said she'd have a full report for you in thirty minutes."

Upon entering the compound and determining that it was secure, Hassler had made it his next priority to assess Stewart's current condition and ensure that no one else in the group had been exposed to anything during the sojourn through the jungle. Fortunately, the observation station was equipped for just such measures.

Elizabeth and Sanchez had already begun the process, directing the Marines through the decontamination area that acted as a foyer to one entrance. Stripping out of their gear and uniforms so that they could be cleaned separately, each of the men had next passed through special decon showers. Afterward, the doctors conducted tests to see if anyone else had begun to exhibit any symptoms of exposure like those Stewart had demonstrated. Hassler had shown no signs of infection, and Maddox seemed healthy enough.

"At least we're out of those damn suits," Maddox said as he rolled up the sleeves on the blue jumpsuit Elizabeth had provided, along with athletic shoes, for each member of the group. "My whole body was starting to smell like one of Lipton's boots."

The Marines' uniforms and equipment had been cleaned and were in the process of drying, and Hassler had already ordered weapons maintenance once their gear had been declared free of contaminants. Even though Captain Sorensen had informed him during his last report that the helicopters had departed Nellis Air Force Base and would be here by midafternoon, Hassler had learned from experience that you did not let your guard down on a mission until your feet touched ground at home base. Until that happened, he and the rest of the team would proceed as though they were on their own for the foreseeable future.

"Seen Rolero?" Hassler asked.

Maddox replied. "Not since decon. She seemed pretty upset over losing Garbuz."

The security chief had not said anything since before taking her turn through the decontamination process. She had held out as long as possible, and at first she had wanted to go back outside the compound to retrieve the body of Dana Garbuz; that plan had been thwarted when she checked the security cameras and saw that the woman's remains were gone, no doubt snatched up by the harbingers. Understandably angered over the loss of yet another of her people, Rolero had elected to distance herself from the rest of the group, at least for now.

For a brief moment, Hassler considered seeking her out in an attempt to offer some comfort, if only a shoulder to lean on, but he dismissed the idea. She wouldn't want that. At least not from him.

Quit bullshitting. Just admit you don't want anything to do with her, and get on with life.

"Get anything to eat?" Hassler asked in an attempt to change the subject. According to Elizabeth, the station's kitchen was fully stocked, including a walk-in freezer, with just about anything on the menu that the team might want.

Shrugging, Maddox replied, "Nah, not yet. Figured I'd wait until the doc was through poking and prodding everybody. Besides, after sweating my ass off in that suit all morning, I can't say I'm all that hungry. What about you?"

Hassler shook his head. "First I want to check the perimeter again. Make sure there's nothing those things can exploit." The final minutes of their last run in with the harbingers had been playing in his mind since they entered the compound, and he had not been able to shake the feeling that the creatures were playing some sort of game. They had employed deliberate tactics of ambush and misdirection, acting nothing like wild animals stalking prey.

He knew how ludicrous the idea sounded, but he was also sure he had not mistaken the sheer resolve in the eyes of the pack's leader.

Another check of the compound eased his concerns, at least for the moment. Satisfied with that, he made his way with Maddox to the observation station's main control room, which reminded Hassler of the bridge of an aircraft carrier. Large bay windows dominated the far wall, offering a view, beyond the station's protective wall and moat, of New Eden's eerie jungle.

In addition to a pair of standard desks, each with its requisite suite of binders, phones, and unruly piles of paper, the room sported three large curved consoles facing the windows, each with a chair and a quartet of computers. Hassler could see that the various monitors provided video feeds from the compound's external cameras as well as an array of status displays that he had no hope of understanding.

Artiaga was sitting at one of the consoles, and turned in his seat upon hearing Hassler and Maddox enter. "Hey, Gunny," he offered.

"Anything going on out there?" Hassler asked.

The younger Marine shook his head. "All's quiet."

Nodding at the report, Hassler was sending the corporal in search of the kitchen when he heard the sounds of running feet, echoing in the hallway and increasing in volume with each step. Seconds later, Elizabeth appeared in the doorway, and Hassler noted the fatigue in her eyes, along with a hint of both anxiety and sadness, and perhaps even something else he could not quite identify.

Guilt?

"Jesus," he said. "Elizabeth, are you all right?"

"We've got another problem," she replied. "Stewart's condition is worsening. The rash is spreading across his body, his fever's climbing, and he's started to suffer from chronic nausea and vomiting. I'm treating him with medicines we have here, but we have to get him to the hospital at Central Ops. Also, Sergeant Lipton has started to show signs. I found a rash on the back of his thigh. It's small, and I'm treating it, but once it starts the only thing I can do here is slow it down."

"What about the stuff they gave us?" Maddox asked. "The vaccinations or whatever. Can't you just give us a booster or something?"

"No," she said. "It's too soon since your initial inoculation. Another dose might trigger cardiac arrest or maybe even a stroke."

Looking at Hassler, Maddox offered a frustrated sigh. "And the hits just keep on coming."

"How much time do we have?" Hassler asked.

Rubbing her face, Elizabeth said, "Lipton's only just begun to present symptoms, but for Stewart, based on the speed of his deterioration, I'd say hours at most. Nightfall, maybe midnight if we're lucky, but the longer we have to wait to start the treatments, the worse his chances are of recovering fully."

Forcing himself to maintain his bearing, Hassler tried to think logically through the situation. "The choppers will be here in an hour," he said, "we should be back at the base an hour after that. That's enough time, right?" Even as he asked the question, he knew it would be close.

Of course, we don't have a choice, do we?

As if reading his mind, Elizabeth nodded, "Yeah, but the margin for error is pretty damned slim."

Turning from the doctor, Hassler crossed the control room to the large windows overlooking the compound. Leaning against the glass, he closed his eyes and let the warmth of the late-morning sun wash over him. The tendrils of fatigue were reaching up for him, taunting and teasing as they attempted to draw him into their depths, but he ignored them. Despite their current position of safety, alleged or otherwise, there were still too many details to juggle before the helicopters arrived.

You can sleep on the plane ride home, he reminded himself. *Get back to work.*

When he opened his eyes again he found himself looking over the wall of the compound and toward the tall trees, perhaps seventy to eighty meters away at first guess. The trees, as odd-looking and off-colored as any he had seen since arriving in New Eden, were not what caught his gaze.

Instead, he saw only the harbinger.

"I'll be god-damned," he breathed.

He heard footsteps behind him before Maddox asked, "What?" Then, seeing what Hassler saw, added, "Oh hell no. You can't be serious."

Looking around the office, Hassler spotted a pair of binoculars, a fancy model incorporating a digital camera, staged on a shelf below the windows. It took him several seconds to figure out how the gadget worked before he could focus it on the tree line.

The harbinger, its chest scars showing up in sharp relief thanks to the binoculars, sat among the high branches of one of the taller trees. It stared across the expanse separating it and Hassler, apparently looking directly at him.

"What the hell is it doing? Maddox asked.

"It can't see us," Elizabeth said. "The windows are tinted on the outside."

Still peering through the binoculars, Hassler said, "Tell him that."

Even as he continued to study the creature and it remained motionless, its gaze unwavering as if hell-bent on peering directly into his soul, Hassler could not shake the feeling that harbinger knew exactly what it was doing.

Turning away from the window, Hassler saw that Elizabeth's attention was riveted on the creature sitting in the nearby trees, and once again he was sure he sensed an air of shame or burden weighing on her.

"What is it," he asked.

Not taking her eyes from the harbinger, Elizabeth shook her head and offered a resigned sigh, as if coming to some decision before turning to stare at Hassler.

"Get Bates."

CHAPTER SEVENTEEN

One of the nicer features of the observation station's control room, Hassler decided, was its video-conferencing abilities. For one thing, it allowed him to study Geoffrey Bates and figure out just how to make the lying bastard break.

"Okay, enough with this horseshit," Hassler said as he, Maddox, Rolero, and Elizabeth stood before the large plasma screen mounted to the control center's rear wall. The screen itself displayed an image of Bates flanked by Captain Sorensen as well as Senators Dillard and Christopher. "Professor, I think it's way past time you told us everything you know about these harbingers."

On the screen, Bates said, "I don't understand, Mr. Hassler. I've provided you with all the relevant information regarding the animals."

"Yeah, well relevant's a subjective term, ain't it?" Maddox asked as he reached up to wipe perspiration from the side of his face. "Any pezhead can see there's more to these pets of yours than what you've been telling us."

"I don't know who you think you're talking to, Marine," Dillard snapped, obviously annoyed at Maddox's blunt statements, "but I would advise you to remember the chain of command, and just how far down the ladder you are."

"Feel free to hump your way out here and explain it to me, Senator," Maddox replied, unimpressed with the politician's bravado.

Next to Bates, Sorensen ordered, "Secure it, Maddox," but to the professor and Dillard he said, "That said, I think you're full of shit, too. What are my people dealing with out here?"

When Bates hesitated for a moment, Elizabeth stepped closer to the screen.

"Don't make them ask you again, Geoffrey. It's time you told them the truth. The *complete* truth, this time."

Drawing a deep breath as if to calm himself, the professor said, "Even during the earliest phases of the Genesis Protocol's development, particularly when we were designing animal life to thrive in various areas of New Eden, some of my colleagues and I began to see additional uses for what we were creating. Not the specific species, mind you, but the concept as a whole.

"For example, what if we could breed an animal to be smart enough that it could accept training and perhaps even the ability to learn rudimentary skills far beyond the grasp of even the most intelligent animals living on Earth today? I don't mean search dogs, or teaching chimpanzees to work simple sequences of buttons and switches or training dolphins to retrieve unexploded torpedoes. What we were envisioning far exceeded those limited parameters."

"Let me guess," Hassler said, shaking his head in mounting disgust, "somebody had the bright idea for you to grow something that could be used by the military." Sighing, he reached up to wipe his face and felt moisture.

Damn jungle heat.

Nodding excitedly, Bates actually smiled. "Yes, exactly. Very astute, Mr. Hassler. The military options alone were enough to justify one of the Pentagon's special warfare offices funding a limited and highly secret series of experiments entailing a new variation on the Genesis Protocol."

"Harbin," Rolero suddenly said, earning her confused stares from everyone else in the room, to say nothing of Sorensen and Senator Christopher.

"Victor Harbin?" Hassler asked. "I know that name. He was a director of special warfare studies at the Pentagon in the early nineties." As he recalled, a lot of the training and equipment advances over the last decade had come about because of Victor Harbin's recommendations and commitment to improving the way SpecOps units did their jobs.

Rolero replied, "Yeah, but some of his ideas could be a little out there. You-all probably never heard half the stuff he came up with."

"I remember the name, too," Sorensen said. "He died a couple of years ago, right?"

"Along with his chauffer," Dillard said, "when his car slid off the road during a snowstorm and fell into the Potomac River on his way home from work one evening. There was talk for a while that he might have been killed because he was about to go public with some pretty damaging information regarding various classified Special Ops missions. Such revelations would have been embarrassing for the president and several others, to put it mildly. One rumor even suggested that the CIA had been ordered to silence him." Looking to Rolero, he asked, "You wouldn't know anything about that, would you?"

"Absolutely nothing," Rolero replied, and Hassler noted that her tone, facial expression, and body language offered no clue as to whether she was being truthful, lying, or simply choosing to elicit a feeling of uncertainty in the senator.

It was an effective tactic, Hassler decided, suppressing the urge to smile. Instead, he turned his attention back to Bates. "So, the harbingers were his idea."

"Precisely," Bates said. "It was Victor who first envisioned some of their proposed capabilities, such as being able to enter areas contaminated as a result of nuclear, biological, or chemical warfare. They would be able to operate without risk in areas toxic to humans and other ordinary animal life. Further, the harbingers' intelligence might be cultivated to a point where they could undertake a variety of tasks while still being under human control. Traveling into enemy territory and carrying out reconnaissance, for example, along with search-and-rescue and even certain types of surveillance and counterinsurgency operations."

"We used to call those search-and-destroy missions," Maddox quipped.

"Yes," Bates replied, unfazed by the comment, "and other such assignments requiring a high degree of intelligence and reasoning, abilities far beyond anything we had developed to this point. While unable to communicate with us, at least not through language of course, we theorized that they could be trained to operate various types of equipment. Digital cameras, long-range listening and recording devices, remote-operated observation drones, things of that nature."

"And how did you achieve this?" Senator Christopher asked, his expression a mask of shock and disbelief.

Shaking his head, Bates replied, "In reality, we didn't. In addition to combining traits from a number of predatory species, we also latched on to the idea of incorporating certain components of human DNA into the formulae we were deriving using the Genesis Protocol. Additionally, we encoded specific genetic blocks to prevent them from progressing beyond a predetermined level of intelligence. In simpler terms, we attempted to invoke a deliberate impediment to their learning abilities."

"Can't have the children getting smarter than their parents, now, could we?" Rolero asked.

"That is essentially correct," Bates replied, taking the statement in stride. Hassler could see that the professor was now most definitely in his element. "We also decided that additional limitations would be necessary in order to maintain control over them, not only during their development and testing within New Eden but also when they became operational. For example, we encoded an aversion to crossing bodies of water, which you witnessed firsthand during your last encounter."

"Which you could have told us about a day or two ago," Hassler said bitterly. "So we could have camped near a river or pond."

"Wouldn't have worked, Hassler," Rolero interjected. "The closest bodies of water along our route were in really toxic zones."

Bates continued his monologue, seemingly oblivious of the interruption. "Oh, that first generation looked great, strong, fast, all of the predatory instincts, but none of the intelligence or learning abilities on which we were counting. Ultimately, the experiment was labeled a failure, and we confined the test subjects to a remote sector of New Eden."

"That obviously wasn't the end of it," Elizabeth said, and Hassler noted that the line of her jaw had tightened.

"What we didn't realize," Bates replied, "is that it was only our initial tests that were unsuccessful. The increased intelligence simply took longer to evolve than anticipated. Progress was slow at first, but thanks to periodic exposure to humans the manifestations of these characteristics soon began to accelerate. The interaction was enough to spark various learning processes such as mimicry, repetition, and so on. With these eventual triumphs, we were able to go back to development and revise our approach accordingly in order to produce a second generation of harbingers which were far more advanced than their predecessors."

"I knew it," Elizabeth said, her voice hard and cold. "I didn't want to believe it, but after watching those things, every time they attack, learning from their previous mistakes, applying different tactics and adapting to what they see. I can't believe you went ahead with that project."

Realization dawned for Hassler. "You knew about this?"

Her shoulders slumping, the doctor nodded. "I read a file about it, back when I first became a project manager. Some of what they'd proposed was interesting, and a few of us thought it that at least parts of the research could be incorporated into other facets of the project."

She looked to Hassler, and he saw that her eyes had begun to water. "We decided against it, though, because just like some of the people involved in the original studies, we thought it might be too dangerous." A single tear streamed down her left cheek as turned back to Bates. "But you did it despite the risks and you've been keeping it a secret from us for years."

The tears were coming freely now as she turned to Hassler. "I recognized some of the traits they were exhibiting early on, but I wasn't sure." She stopped, shaking her head. "No, that's not right. I didn't want to believe what I was seeing, but . . . " Further words were lost as Elizabeth broke down, covering her hand with her mouth and weeping openly as she turned and fled from the room.

"You son of a bitch," Senator Christopher said to Bates, his voice trembling with barely contained fury.

Bates paused to wipe his brow before continuing, "As for the harbingers, their demonstrated ability to learn through observation and mimicry, coupled with their already impressive predatory characteristics and their heretofore latent aptitude, was truly beginning to blossom. I made the decision to once again isolate them to a specific area of the region. The special markers we'd encoded were supposed to have been enough to keep them confined to their designated zone, along with my orders against any further direct human contact. All observations were to be done remotely, from concealed stations like the one Dr. Christopher and her team were using when all of this began."

Hassler decided from his own study of Bates's facial expressions and eye movements over the past few minutes that the professor was being truthful, at least with the information he had provided to this point. Still, there were still questions demanding answers.

"So," Rolero said, "either they were responsive to your methods of controlling them, or they weren't. Which is it, Bates?"

There it is, Hassler thought as he saw the change, albeit subtle, in the professor's expression. *Now we're getting to it.*

Bates said, "As we began to realize the true scope of their capabilities, to say nothing of their ferocity, the idea of what they might do if unleashed beyond the confines of New Eden was alarming, to say the least."

"So what's stopping them?" Sorensen asked. "Obviously keeping them penned up in their own corral didn't work, so what stops them from hopping the fence or whatever surrounds this jungle and heading out into the desert?"

"No animal developed within New Eden can survive in the outside world," Bates snapped. "It's a genetic certainty and failsafe that's encoded into the DNA of every living thing out there."

"If these damn things have shown me anything so far," Hassler said, "it's that they can adapt. Who's to say they can't learn to live without whatever chemical you pump into the animals they hunt and kill for food?"

Sighing audibly, Bates replied, "That is a possibility, certainly. Only time will tell, I suppose."

Maddox, obviously getting fed up with the entire conversation, shot a disgusted expression at Hassler before saying, "Why wait around for that? You said yourself they were too dangerous to risk letting them escape, so why take the risk? Either confine them to someplace more secure, or, better yet, hunt them down and kill them."

"There are obvious and, I hope, understandable reasons why we chose not to destroy the harbingers, at least at first," Bates replied. "Our wish to study what we had created was certainly the driving priority."

Rolero could only shake her head in disbelief. "All this time, with our people moving all over the region conducting experiments, and you never warned us about these things? How could you not say anything?"

Bates's gaze dropped again, and he paused to wipe his face before continuing. "Up until the first attack, we believed them to be confined to their own area of New

Eden. They had never shown signs of being able to leave their quarantined sector, or even of being interested."

"But even after that first attack," Senator Christopher countered, anger lacing every syllable, "there was still time to warn the rest of your people, and yet you never said a word. What about the people lost over the past three days, Professor?"

To Hassler's surprise, Bates and even Dillard had the common decency, or perhaps just common sense, to avoid any attempts at refuting what the senator was saying. While he held no sympathy whatsoever for Dillard, Hassler almost felt a tinge of pity for Bates as he hung his head in the face of the verbal onslaught, but it was quickly squashed under the memories of the Marines he had lost in the last twenty-four hours.

"I'm truly sorry about that. I simply don't know what to say," the professor said.

"I do," Rolero countered, speaking for the first time in several minutes. "Maybe you did want to destroy them, and maybe you didn't. You may have argued the point, and you might even have been pretty aggressive about it, but I'll bet a month's salary that you were overruled." Pointing an accusatory finger at Dillard, she asked, "Isn't that right, Senator?"

Unfazed by the allegation, Dillard nodded. "We're talking about decades of research and development, Ms. Rolero, to say nothing of billions of dollars of taxpayer money funding the effort."

"I'd have preferred you cured cancer, or maybe just fix the potholes in my neighborhood," Maddox replied, his expression deadpan.

As if sensing the discussion going off-tangent again, Bates held up a hand to quell the senator. "There is one thing that has bothered me about the harbingers since the reports of the first attack," he said. "Despite the predatory instincts with which we imbued them, we also encoded an underlying territoriality, in part as a further means of keeping them controlled within the region. While it's possible to believe that they may have chosen the area near Observation Station Four to mark as theirs to defend, it's most curious how they seem to have abandoned this practice in favor of . . . well, the only way I can put it is to say that they're stalking you and your team, Mr. Hassler."

"Doesn't seem all that complicated to me," Hassler replied. "From my experience, animals tend to react in one of two basic ways when something more assertive or threatening sets foot on their turf. Either they become fearful and retreat, or else their own protective instincts kick in and they get more aggressive. Even after all of the genetic scrambling you've done, it doesn't look as though you've figured out a way to deal with that basic trait."

The professor nodded. "We've considered that, of course, but I think you'll admit that there's more at work here than that, certainly far more than we ever anticipated."

"Well, you keep telling us how smart they are," Rolero challenged, "but how smart are they really? Smart enough to figure out a way to get in here?"

"I'd rather not hang out long enough to find out," Hassler said. "What's the status on the helicopters?"

Pausing to look at something off-screen, perhaps a clock or computer display, Sorensen replied, "They should be here within the hour, Gunny. Once they refuel, they'll be on their way to you. I take it that the current plan is still in effect?"

"Roger that, Skipper," Hassler said. "One chopper provides air support while another drops in. We all climb in and haul ass. Keep it simple." Looking around at the haggard faces of Maddox and the others, he added, "With your permission, sir, I'd like to give my team a chance to get some rest. It's been a long couple of days so far."

Sorensen nodded. "Understood, Gunny. I'll be in touch when the choppers set down."

The image on the screen faded, to be replaced by a computer-generated schematic of the observation station's interior rendered with white vector lines on a black background. The internal structure of the building's different levels, which Hassler had already taken the time to memorize, was represented in softer blue lines, with exits illuminated in yellow.

"The guys on my softball team are never gonna believe this," Maddox said, eliciting a smile from Hassler and rolled eyes from Rolero.

"That son of a bitch."

The three of them turned to see Elizabeth, standing in the doorway, her eyes red-rimmed. While part of him wondered if he should be angry with her, Hassler could not bring himself to levy upon her any blame for what he and his people had experienced.

She's endured plenty herself. Even if she was guilty of anything, she's paid her dues, and then some.

"All this time and I never had a clue. Not one." Shaking her head, she asked, "What in God's name would possess him to create those things?"

"I'm sure the intentions were good, at least in the beginning," Hassler said, wiping the back of his sleeve across his forehead and noting that it came away dark with perspiration. "Then imaginations and egos got in the way, to say nothing of the government stepping in with a Christmas wish list once he and his partners proved the concept could work. I imagine the money involved in such a funding effort was more than enough to soothe any misgivings he might have had."

To Rolero, Elizabeth said, "Shannon, I don't know what to say. I should have said something earlier, but I didn't want to believe what I was seeing. I should have known, should have realized that something like this was possible, but I never considered that someone like Geoffrey would be capable of . . . " Once more, tears welled up in her eyes. "I'm so sorry."

In a startling display of warmth and compassion, Rolero crossed the room and pulled Elizabeth into a hug. "It's not your fault, Liz. You didn't make the decision to create those things, and you haven't been lying to us all these years. This is on Bates. Do you understand me?"

Holding the embrace for a few more seconds, Elizabeth finally pulled away. She moved across the control room, dropping into a chair and smacking her fist atop a nearby desk. "We were supposed to be working toward a righteous goal," she said, waving toward the windows and the jungle beyond the compound. "We were trying to help us, the entire planet, and he took everything that was supposed to be good and perverted it, and why? So the military could have another weapon? Don't you people have enough?"

As soon as she spoke the words, she caught herself, holding out a hand in entreaty. "I'm sorry, that wasn't fair. You and your men are good people, Donovan. I know it's not right to lump you in with what they're doing. I'm just angry, at him, at myself, at everything about this place."

"If I had to guess," Rolero said, "Bates probably had to offer something in exchange for the funding and time needed to do what the project was meant to address in the first place. He gives them what they want—in this case, the harbingers—and they let him do what he wants."

Elizabeth seemed to consider that for a moment before replying, "I wish I could believe that. I want to believe I haven't wasted years of my life here."

"Somehow," Hassler said, offering a small smile, "when this is all said and done, I don't think you'll be able to say that about you or anyone else who worked on this project." Casting a glance toward the windows, he added, "All we have to do now is make sure we get out of here so we can put that to the test."

Everyone flinched as an alarm blared, echoing off the windows and walls of the control center. Hassler, Maddox, and Rolero all reached for the weapons slung over their shoulders while Elizabeth immediately turned and moved toward one of the three control consoles. Grabbing a wireless computer mouse situated next to a keyboard, she used the device to move a cursor to a flaring indicator on one display monitor.

"What is it?" Hassler asked, checking the safety on his weapon even as he saw Elizabeth bolting for the door.

"It's Sanchez!" she shouted over her shoulder. "He needs help in the clinic!"

The alarm was louder in the corridor as Elizabeth ran ahead of Hassler. Despite his own running ability he was no match for the doctor, who sprinted the length of the passageway outside the control room and plunged through the doorway leading to a stairwell. Taking the stairs three at a time, she was down to the second level and out into the corridor before Hassler had even reached the third-floor landing.

He heard the chaos of several different alarm indicators sounding as he and the others approached the medical section. Entering the clinic's anteroom, they found Elizabeth standing near the doorway leading to the patient treatment area. It had been sealed off with a makeshift airlock constructed from a framework of lumber around which had been wrapped sheets of plastic. On the other side of the transparent barrier was Paul Sanchez, dressed in a bright yellow containment suit and standing over the convulsing form of Corporal Kerry Stewart, who was only barely recognizable as a human being.

"What's happening?" Hassler asked, his eyes riveted to Stewart's lesion-riddled body, which lay atop a gurney and sported a web of wires connecting him to a suite of medical monitors as well as tubes channeling fluids and medicines into his body.

"Heart failure," Elizabeth asked, already moving toward an equipment locker where another containment suit was stored. "Paul's trying to give him some adrenaline, but he needs help."

Stewart was jerking and twitching violently in his bed, his movements threatening to tear out the various needles inserted into his arms and legs. Sanchez, by the looks of things, was trying to hold him still long enough to stick him in the chest with a large needle.

"What can we do?" Maddox asked, his eyes wide with worry at the same moment the shrill chorus of beeping was replaced with first one and then another steady, droning tone.

Other alarm indicators quickly fell into the same pattern, and Hassler turned back to the doorway to see that Stewart had stopped moving. Sanchez had abandoned the cardiac needle and was now applying cardiopulmonary resuscitation, alternating compressions of the patient's chest with squeezes of an airbag placed over Stewart's mouth.

Hassler reached for the plastic sheet, intending to plunge through the improvised double curtains and run in to assist Sanchez, but was stopped by Elizabeth's harsh warning.

"No!" she said as she stepped toward him. She had finished shrugging her way into her containment suit and pulling the helmet over her head as she reached for the switch to activate her environment pack's air-circulation system. As she stepped toward the doorway, Sanchez looked up, holding out a hand and indicating for her to wait.

"It's too late," he said, his voice muffled through the helmet of his suit. "He's gone." Without saying anything else, he began switching off the array of monitors surrounding the patient bed before slowly drawing a sheet up and over Stewart's now stilled form.

"Damn it," Maddox whispered, shaking his head as he turned away from the scene. Hassler exchanged saddened, defeated looks with Elizabeth before turning to Rolero, whose eyes he saw were red-rimmed and moist around the edges.

"I'm sorry, Donovan," she said, her voice low and lifeless.

Looking through the plastic at Sanchez, Hassler asked, "Paul, what happened?"

Still confined to his suit until he could pass through a decontamination procedure, Sanchez replied, "His kidneys had already started to shut down and I had to put him on life support, which is when I sounded the alarm. Then his heart just gave up, and there was only so much I could do. I'm really sorry."

"You did what you could. I appreciate that," Hassler replied, feeling a wave of fatigue and despair reaching out for him. He wiped his face and ran the back of his hand across his forehead, drying the perspiration that had formed there before turning to Maddox. "Dave, we need to make arrangements for transporting the body. We're taking him with us when we leave."

He was just able to get the words out before the room spun away and he felt himself falling, a sensation that was confirmed when he hit his head on the tiled floor.

"Whoa! Gunny, you okay?" he heard Maddox calling before he felt hands on him, running over his body and checking for injuries before helping him to a sitting position.

"I'm fine, I think," Hassler said, wincing as he reached for the back of his head where he had hit the floor. "A little dizzy, though." He jerked involuntarily when Elizabeth, who had removed her containment-suit helmet and unzipped the heavy garment's upper torso section, reached out and grabbed him by the wrist before pushing back the sleeve of his jumpsuit. "Hey, what's going on?"

Still holding his harm, Elizabeth looked down at him, an expression of worry in her eyes. "It's started."

Freeing his arm from her grasp, Hassler twisted it until he could see the underside of his forearm.

Just above his wrist, a rash had formed.

CHAPTER EIGHTEEN

Bates was already waiting for Dillard when the senator entered his office.

"I take it you've heard the news?" the senator asked.

Sitting behind his desk, Bates said nothing as he poured himself a glass of bourbon from the bottle he had retrieved from his liquor cabinet. He took a sip and released a troubled sigh.

"Yes," he finally said. "Corporal Stewart died. Elizabeth transmitted the results of blood tests she was able to run using the station infirmary's equipment, and it was as I had feared. One of the compounds administered to Stewart during the vaccination procedure appears to have been defective." He had already ordered a more comprehensive series of tests performed on the vials containing the medicines administered to the unfortunate Marine, and he planned to direct an autopsy of the man's body upon its return.

After first crossing to the corner armoire containing Bates's liquor stash and retrieving a glass, Dillard took the bourbon bottle and poured himself a generous portion. He said nothing for a few moments, and Bates noted the look of contemplation on the senator's face as he sipped his drink.

"It's only going to get worse, Geoffrey," he said finally. "Hassler and another of his Marines are showing signs of infection. Chances are that we'll get them back here in time for them to be treated, but what about afterward?"

"I'm not sure I understand what you mean," Bates said, as he drained the last of the bourbon from his glass. In truth, he knew precisely to what Dillard was referring, but he was waiting to see if the senator actually would come out and say it.

Dillard regarded him with raised eyebrows, as if suspecting that Bates was testing him. "Once this is over, how can we know the Marines will keep their mouths shut about what they've seen here? About what they've endured?"

"They've signed nondisclosure agreements," Bates said. "They're sworn to maintain the secrecy of what they've seen here, at the risk of prison sentences. Captain Sorensen and his men are accustomed to maintaining operational security during missions. This is no different."

He took another sip from his drink but almost spit up the bourbon as a he was gripped by a brief coughing spasm. Wiping his mouth, he checked the clock on the wall and shook his head as he reached for the vial of pills in his pocket.

"Do you really think so?" Dillard countered. "I mean, I think we can agree that this isn't like anything these Marines have faced before. Captain Sorensen has lost half of his men, with a very real possibility that the others could also die. If they'd been killed in combat or on some secret mission into a foreign country or behind enemy lines, that would be one thing. But we're not exactly talking about that, are we?"

Reaching across the desk for the bourbon bottle, Dillard refilled his glass. "It's not just that those men died, Geoffrey," he said after taking a sip of his drink. "The manner in which they were killed, coupled with the argument that at least some of those deaths might have been prevented if we'd been more forthcoming about the harbingers, is what makes this dangerous."

"The harbingers are one of the prime reasons we have such tight security around here in the first place, Jonathan," Bates countered. "They're also why your peers in Washington continue to fund us, as you well know. After all, simply saving the planet isn't profitable. It's that sort of thinking that led to the development of the harbingers in the first place, correct?"

To his credit, Dillard had the good grace not to appear offended or bewildered. "We've had enough late-night conversations for me to know that you don't truly believe that. The work you do here will one day be lauded as a defining moment in human history, Geoffrey. But, no matter how much good comes from the knowledge and technology collected here, we both know just how easily it can also be perverted for evil purposes. That's the reason for the security."

Once more he upended his glass, swallowing its contents before releasing a contented grunt. He said nothing for a moment, instead pausing to stare at the bottom of the empty glass still in his hand, and Bates fancied he could see the wheels turning behind his friend's eyes.

"And you think the Marines are a threat to that security," Bates said, pushing Dillard in the direction he already knew the senator was heading.

Slowly, Dillard nodded. "Yes, I think so. What's happened here is simply too big for them to keep to themselves. We have to take steps to ensure containment."

"I'd argue that the harbingers have done much for us in that regard already," Bates countered, finding no joy in the statement. "But I can tell by the way you're fidgeting about that we have to take this even further. You're thinking we have to act so that this whole thing can just . . . fade away." Setting his glass down atop his desk, he locked eyes with Dillard. "You're suggesting we eliminate the rest of the rescue team."

"I said no such thing," Dillard countered. He even displayed the proper amount of indignation at the notion, a tribute to his finely honed acting skills, Bates decided.

"No, you didn't," Bates said, waving away the senator's spurious ire. Rising from his desk, he clasped his hands behind his back as he crossed his office until he could once again peer through the window overlooking the central operations center. He noted the number of unoccupied workstations on the main floor. In accordance with his instructions, the men and women who normally manned the center were getting some much-deserved rest, with only a skeleton crew watching over things for the time being. Bates had ordered the stand-down once the Marines and their charges had made it safely inside ObStat One.

Of course, his generosity and compassion for the long hours his staff had been working also reduced the likelihood that anyone overheard what he had told the rescue team about the harbingers. Keeping that concealed from all but the handful of staff members directly involved with that aspect of the EDN project was proving to be an increasingly worrisome burden, as well.

When he spoke this time, he did so without turning from the window.

"People like you don't give such orders in plain, unfiltered language, do you? It's all about parsing every syllable so as to avoid even the appearance of liability. You want this situation resolved, and you've already voiced your concerns that the people most likely to be involved in a potential security breach can't be trusted to maintain their silence. Ergo, the only course of action open to us would seem to be forcing that silence upon them by other means." Now he did turn from the window, his eyes boring into Dillard. "That is what we're talking about, isn't it?"

Not that he needed the senator to respond, of course.

"Fortunately for you," Bates continued as he stepped away from the window and began his habitual pacing around the perimeter of his office, "achieving this end requires no extra effort on your part. We have only to wait for the problem to resolve itself."

Frowning, Dillard regarded him with evident confusion. "What are you talking about?"

"Sergeant Hassler is already displaying signs of exposure," Bates replied, "and it seems likely that the remaining Marines will begin to present similar symptoms within the next few hours. Given the speed with which Corporal Stewart succumbed to contamination and assuming we offer no means of treatment, I estimate that all of the Marines will be dead by tomorrow evening."

When Dillard's mouth dropped open this time, Bates was forced to confess that he was not certain whether the senator was acting or instead reacting from genuine shock. "Are you suggesting we abandon them in there?"

"No," Bates said, his tone impassive. "We simply delay the helicopter extraction for a few more hours, perhaps due to weather or mechanical problems or whatever explanation works best. We do so until such time as we know every member of the rescue team has been contaminated. Once that's happened, we bring them out and transfer them to our medical section, where after extensive observation and after trying everything we can to save them, they will yield to the effects of infection and die. A tragedy, to be sure, but still an unavoidable consequence of protecting our work here."

The words were coming all too easily, Bates realized even as he spoke them. There was no hesitation due to remorse. Was he so blinded by the years of effort he had expended in this place, so protective of what he and others had accomplished, that he could so dispassionately justify what amounted to simple murder?

"Call it what you want," Dillard said, "but it's still abandoning them." Wiping his face with his right hand, the senator shook his head. "Jesus, if that ever got out, they'd string us up."

"You know precisely what has to happen here, the benefits to you if it does happen and the consequences if it doesn't," Bates said with a withering gaze at the senator. "If you can't summon the intestinal fortitude to admit that much, at least show me the courtesy of not pretending as though you don't know what the hell we're talking about."

To his surprise, Dillard had no response to the sharp rebuke. The silence, fleeting though it would be, was still refreshing. It gave him precious moments to think.

Of course, the ultimate decision would come from somewhere in the echelons of power above him. Dillard, despite the timidity he was now exhibiting, had been keeping in close contact with his comrades in Washington and apprising them of the situation here. His next report would doubtless include the highlights of this clandestine conversation and the recommendations it spawned. Bates had no doubt that the senator was using whatever influence he had to ensure the security of the EDN project, no matter the cost.

Therefore, someone else would make the call, someone else would take the responsibility. The effort to ensure that no one could ever be blamed for the decision or, in fact, ascertain that such a decision ever was made, would eclipse tenfold the energy expended to actually issue the order.

Still, it was Bates who was carrying out the will of those unseen faces lost somewhere in the corridors of power, their only connection to him being the funding they authorized so that he might continue his work here.

You despicable son of a bitch.

Near the window once again, he searched operations center until he spotted Reginald Christopher seated at a desk in a small office situated just off the main floor, speaking into a phone while gripping the receiver in both hands. It was easy to guess that the senator was once again talking to his daughter, perhaps trying to offer some measure of parental comfort as the final hours of her ordeal played out.

He'll be a problem, Bates thought with mounting resignation. *That much is certain.*

Finding his way back to the bourbon still sitting on Bates's desk, Dillard refilled his glass. "What about Rolero, or Christopher and Sanchez?" he asked. "How do you suggest we handle them?" Even before Bates could reply, the senator held out a hand. "Wait, you're not thinking of . . . ?"

"Certainly not," Bates countered, perhaps too quickly. "Rolero is a soldier who follows orders, an experienced intelligence operative who's known her fair share of unpleasant assignments. I'm not the least bit worried about her. As for Elizabeth, she's like one of my own children." Even as he said it, he knew that the situation could easily evolve to the point where maintaining project security required taking steps even more unpleasant than those he already had proposed.

"She and Sanchez didn't know about the harbingers," Bates said, "but that can be handled through normal channels. There are a number of project initiatives under way that even senior staff members don't know about. They'll continue to be understandably upset as they've been to this point, but they'll adapt." Shrugging, he added, "They won't know the details of how we handle the Marines, of course."

"And if they don't adapt?" Dillard pressed.

Sighing in resignation, Bates nodded. "Then they'll present another problem that will have to be resolved," he said as he stared through the window down to where Senator Christopher still sat in the small office. He shook his head, disgusted with himself for employing the euphemistic language, but he was unable to give further voice to the despicable thoughts currently haunting his mind.

The phone on Bates's desk rang, emitting a sequence of five electronic beeps before the unit's speaker automatically engaged. "Professor Bates," a voice said, "we've just been informed that the helicopters from Nellis are on final approach and should be landing in less than five minutes."

Glancing at his watch, Bates noted that the helicopters were even arriving ahead of schedule. "Thank you," he said, and was rewarded by a single beep signifying that the connection had been severed. To Dillard, he said, "And so it begins."

From where he stood near the desk, his hand still holding his empty bourbon glass in a death grip, Dillard said, "Wait, what about Sorensen? You know he's going to want to ride out for the extraction. How do we handle him?"

Still standing before the picture window, Bates looked down to see the Marine captain crossing the operations floor. The man was moving with purpose, no doubt having just been informed of the helicopters' imminent arrival. Dillard was right, of course.

Sorensen could very well pose a problem.

The force of the Black Hawks' rotor blades whipped the air around William Sorensen as he stepped outside the hangar that sat adjacent to the helipad. Renegade grains of sand and dirt were being flung in all directions, and Sorensen felt some of it beating against his uniform as well as stinging the exposed skin on his arms, neck, and face. He had to shield his eyes as the pair of helicopters, flying in a tight, precise formation, descended to a landing on the concrete pad fifty feet in front of him.

He waited as the pilots powered down their machines and climbed out of their cockpits before both crews crossed the pad toward the hangar. Six people, four men and two women, each dressed in a black flight suit lacking patches or other ornamentation save for a name stitched in white block lettering above the right breast pocket. One of the pilots, a man perhaps ten years older than Sorensen himself and with the name "Branton" embroidered on his flight suit, smiled from behind a pair of aviator's sunglasses as he approached and extended a hand in greeting. The man's teeth were so bright that Sorensen had to resist the impulse to raise a hand in order to block the glare.

"How you doing, Captain," the man said. "Sam Branton. I'll be your pilot this afternoon."

As he took the man's hand, Sorensen saw the faded yet still puckered scar running down the left side of Branton's face from the temple almost to the jawline.

Whatever had hit him, it had to have been a miracle responsible for keeping him alive.

"Chicks seem to dig it," Branton said, noting where Sorensen's eyes had gone.

After introducing the rest of his crew and the crew from the other helicopter, he said, "What say we see what we can do for you today?"

"How soon can you be ready to pull chocks?" Sorensen asked.

Standing next to Branton, the other Black Hawk's pilot, an attractive black woman named Amarie Thompson, said, "An hour, tops. We need to refuel and run a systems check. We hit some heavy wind coming across from Nellis, and I want to make sure the sand didn't worm its way into anything delicate."

"Fair enough," Sorensen replied, resisting the urge to look at his watch and revise the schedule he kept in his head. He did not want his people to stay in New Eden one second longer than was absolutely necessary, but one did not rush or short cut preparations. Such reckless action only invited disaster. "Time's a bit of a factor here, so I'd appreciate it if we could head out as quickly as possible. Whatever I can do to help, you've got it."

"No worries, Captain," Thompson said, offering her own winning smile. "We've been briefed into the situation and understand the need for speed. Tell your people to sit tight, and that we'll be on our way in no time."

Buoyed by the woman's air of confidence, Sorensen smiled. "Outstanding." Looking to Branton, he added, "Sam, I'd like to ride out with you, if that's okay."

"The more the merrier," the pilot replied, "but we were told that some sort of vaccinations would be required before we could enter the restricted area."

"My guys had to go through the same thing before they left, too." Sorensen briefly recounted the problems encountered during the inoculations, engendering a look of concern from Branton.

"You sure that's such a hot idea, going in without the shots?" the pilot asked.

Sorensen shrugged. "I've got people on the ground in trouble, and I'm tired of sitting on my ass." He had weighed the risks to his own health by venturing unprotected into the EDN region, deciding that the exposure time would be minimal if the same protocols observed by the first team were heeded. "I figure the docs can check me out when we get back and take care of anything I pick up along the way."

"That sounds like what I used to say in Thailand every payday weekend," Branton quipped. "I figure you're safer here." Turning to his people, he said, "Okay, folks, let's get cracking."

As the Black Hawk crews turned to their various duties, Sorensen noted that other teams from inside the hangar were already gathering around the helicopters. A fuel truck was maneuvering into position while maintenance techs opened various panels along the choppers' fuselages. Sorensen watched the practiced choreography with satisfaction, impressed at the skill and efficiency with which each member of the crew carried out their individual tasks.

Things were shaping up well, he decided.

"You folks seem to have everything covered here, so I'm going to check in with Bates while you finish up out here. An hour, you said?"

"Call your bookie," the Black Hawk pilot replied, offering a mock salute as he walked through the doorway and left Sorensen alone outside the hangar.

As Sorensen turned to head back to Central Operations, his thoughts turned to the remaining members of his team. How were they holding up? Had anyone else begun to exhibit signs of contamination thanks to the team's prolonged exposure to the EDN region and its debilitating effects?

His boots tapped against the tarmac as he approached the door leading back to the main operations center. Reaching for the door handle, he stopped short of entering the building.

Two men, one black and the other Latino and both dressed in black fatigues, waited just inside the door. The black man, obviously in charge, nodded at Sorensen in greeting. He was big, bodybuilder big, with hair cut almost to the scalp. He wore small gold hoop earrings in each ear, and the sleeves of his fatigue jacket had been rolled to a point above the elbow so that Sorensen could see the man's muscled forearms. The bottom edge of a tattoo, which appeared to be a stiletto highlighted in white, peeked out from beneath the left sleeve.

"Captain Sorensen," the man said, offering his hand as well as a professional smile, "I'm Jason King, Shannon Rolero's second-in-command, and this is my assistant, Ed Gutierrez. Professor Bates asked us to come and find you. He's waiting for you in CentOps."

Two men to come and find me?

Sorensen felt the hairs on the back of his neck stand up. Without moving his eyes from King, he was still able to discern that each man was armed with a pistol, Berettas if they were consistent with what he had seen other guards carrying. Both weapons remained in the holsters at the men's right hips, their handgrips facing to the rear and telling Sorensen that both men were right-handed. King's belt also sported a knife near his left hand, a short, straight blade with a black handle secured in a ballistic nylon sheath.

"Well, here I am," Sorensen said, holding his hands away from his body. "I was just talking to the chopper crews."

King nodded. "No problem, sir. The professor wants to go over the details of the rescue mission with you and the pilots before things get under way." He indicated the corridor behind him with a wave of his right arm. "If you'll accompany me?"

"Sure," Sorensen replied as he followed the security agent into the building. As they marched down the passageway, their bootsteps echoing off the polished black-and-white linoleum floor, Sorensen noted out of habit that Gutierrez was more to his right side than directly to his rear and walking just far enough behind him that the captain could not see him in his peripheral vision. That served only to further heighten Sorensen's awareness of his surroundings.

Something's up.

Alarm bells went off in his brain when they came to an intersection and, instead of turning right and heading for Central Operations, they continued to walk straight ahead, toward an area of the building Sorensen had not yet visited.

"Where are we going?" he asked, noting as he did so that King's shoulders seemed to tense in response to the question.

"Professor Bates asked me to bring you directly to his office," the man replied, still composed and professional. The answer was smooth and delivered without hesitation, a passable lie for anyone not listening for it, Sorensen decided, especially considering that Bates's office also lay in the direction they should have turned back at the intersection.

Maybe it's a shortcut, he told himself. *Yeah, and it takes two guys to find it.*

Turning at another hallway junction, the trio proceeded down another stretch of corridor. Doors lined either side of the passageway, each bearing a label with a combination of numbers and letters which Sorensen was sure meant something to someone somewhere. There was nothing else to distinguish the doors, though Sorensen noticed that the hinges of the doors were mounted on the outside so that they swung outward to open.

A few of the doors featured magnetic card readers mounted on the wall next to them, and it was one of these that King approached, slowing his pace as he reached into his breast pocket to extract a cardkey. He inserted the card into the reader's slot and the unit beeped, after which the door responded with a click and King reached for the handle to pull it open, allowing Sorensen to see the room beyond.

"I don't understand," he said. The room was a no-frills affair, consisting of a square conference table and suite of six chairs surrounding it.

"Please step inside, Captain," King replied, all the warmth now gone from his voice. "The professor will be with you shortly."

Holding his ground, Sorensen said, "I thought we were going to his office."

That's when it happened.

Gutierrez moved with some stealth, almost enough to avoid Sorensen's sensing his approach. Only the whisper of cloth rubbing against cloth gave him away. The skin on Sorensen's neck prickled at the precise instant the man's right hand clamped on his shoulder, but by then it was too late.

Sorensen's first move was quick and sloppy, flexing his right arm and sinking his elbow into Gutierrez's abdomen. The guard grunted more from surprise than pain, but it was enough for Sorensen to reach up with his left hand and grasp the other man's wrist. Pivoting on his heel, the captain struck out with his elbow again, this time with more force and purpose as he connected with Gutierrez's nose. He heard cartilage crunch and a few drops of blood sprayed forth as the man's head snapped back.

The guard stumbled away from him but Sorensen ignored him, already hearing King approaching from the front. A blur of black in the corner of his eye made him duck to his right just as King's fist sailed past, missing him entirely and pulling the security agent off-balance. It was enough to expose his left flank to attack and Sorensen took the opening, punching the other man in the kidney even as he reached for the still-outstretched arm.

King tensed from the blow but did not stagger or falter, jerking his arm away from Sorensen before the Marine could secure a decent grip. Sorensen saw the knee coming up and lowered both hands to deflect the strike. He managed to raise his arms to protect his face as King punched at him again, and this time he was able to grab the other man's arm. Twisting down and around until he could push the arm up and against his opponent's back, Sorensen held it by the wrist up near King's shoulder blades.

The action forced King to cry out in pain as he bent at the waist rather than risk breaking the arm. Using his grip on the man's wrist to direct his movements, Sorensen turned him toward the still-open door, at the same time reaching around to retrieve King's pistol from the holster at his waist.

He froze when his vision filled with another pistol barrel, huge and black as it leveled itself less than six inches from his face.

"Let him go," Gutierrez said, blood running from both nostrils and his eyes watering from the pain of his injury.

Sorensen noted that the hammer on the Beretta was cocked and the man's finger was resting on the trigger.

"What the fuck is going on?" he asked, hissing the word between gritted teeth. He still held King's arm immobilized, but knew that any attempt to take the other man's weapon from him would fail, and would only leave him open to a renewed attack from King.

Instead of answering the question, Gutierrez stepped closer until the pistol's muzzle rested just below Sorensen's left eye. "I said let him go. I won't ask again." Sorensen heard the pain lacing the man's words, knew that he would pull the trigger if pressed.

He let King go and stepped back, holding his hands up and tensing in anticipation of the security agent's retaliation.

Twisting the ache from his arm, King turned to face Sorensen. "Lucky for you Bates just wants you put on ice for a while."

"Where is he?" Sorensen asked, standing firm. "What's this all about?" Why would Bates want him detained? Something had obviously happened during the past hour that gave the professor cause to view him as a threat, but what? He was aware of no security protocols he had breached, no restricted areas into which he might have trespassed.

King shook his head. "Don't know. Said he'd be along later, and told us to make sure you didn't get yourself into any trouble while you wait." Holding up his left hand, he indicated the small room with one meaty finger. "Now, you can put your own ass in that room, or else I do it for you."

Glancing to where Gutierrez appeared to be hoping King gave him the okay to shoot, Sorensen slowly moved toward the door, his mind still racing to fathom just what the hell was happening here. Either Bates believed he had done something improper, or else he was moving proactively to prevent him from doing something which might cause the professor headaches later.

Is this about the extraction? It had to be, he decided as he followed King's order to remove his equipment vest, which included his team radio and sidearm. Nothing else made sense. Some kind of problem had presented itself, something which was hampering the forthcoming rescue attempt. Even if that were the case, to Sorensen that still did not seem like cause enough for detention.

"What about my people?" he asked as he stepped inside the room. "When are they being retrieved?"

Throwing Sorensen's vest over his shoulder as he reached for the door, King shrugged. "I don't know, and I don't care. I just do what the boss tells me."

The mission's not going forward for some reason, his mind screamed at him, and *Bates figures I'll be pissed about it. He needs me out of the way so I won't cause a shit storm.*

"You tell Bates that if anything else happens to my people, I'm gonna make an ashtray out of his skull."

Gutierrez said nothing in response to that, but King chuckled. "Big smack. I like that," he said as he began to close the door. "You might want to think about getting past me first, though. Got anything special in mind for that?"

"Not really," Sorensen said, shaking his head. "You're light work. If you're lucky, I'll just feed your balls to my dog."

Smiling, King laughed again. "Honey, hush. You're getting me all excited. You just stay here and make yourself comfortable. There'll be plenty of time for us to work out all this confusion later." With that, he pushed the door closed.

Just before the lock engaged, Sorensen was able to get out one last pledge.

"Count on it, prick."

CHAPTER NINETEEN

Hassler was feeling it now.

The fever had crept on up on him, so gradually that he had at first chalked up to the effects of the jungle heat and humidity. That notion faded when he saw how the rash on his left forearm had grown while others had appeared on his legs and chest, eclipsing his dark skin in favor of angry red sores. His joints had started to ache, knees and elbows followed by the irritating sensation that somebody was stepping on the back of his neck.

Final confirmation came from David Maddox.

"Jesus, Gunny," the staff sergeant said as Hassler entered the control room. "You look like shit."

"Too bad I don't feel that good," Hassler replied as he made his way across the room to where Maddox was manning one of the workstations. Handing his friend one of the two bottles of water he had brought with him from the station's kitchen, he asked, "How are Lip and Artiaga?"

Maddox shook his head. "Both of them popped rashes an hour or so ago."

"And you?"

"Just lucky, I guess," the staff sergeant replied. "Though I've got to tell you this is one time I feel bad about bringing up the rear."

"I just hope that voodoo concoction the doc is giving us will hold us over." The treatments administered by Dr. Christopher were designed to slow the progression of the debilitating effects the Marines were experiencing, but they were temporary measures at best, not much more effective than the vaccinations given to the team prior to the start of the rescue operation.

"Once we're back at mainside," Hassler continued, "the medical staff has everything they need to take care of us. By this time tomorrow, you'll have all you need for a whole new batch of bullshit stories."

Even as he said the words, he battled with his own doubts. The horrific images of Corporal Stewart's final hours still burned in his mind, more gruesome than almost anything he had witnessed in any of the combat missions in which he had taken part. He wanted answers about that, even if he was never able to share that information with anyone beyond the team.

Checking his watch, Hassler noted that he was overdue for their hourly check-in with Central Operations. Captain Sorensen had been manning a station in the main control center, receiving regular updates on the team's condition as well as monitoring the progress of the helicopters flying in from Nellis. "The last time I talked to the skipper," he said, "the Black Hawks were supposed to arrive within the hour." That meant that they were most likely on the ground now, probably refueling and preparing to head into the EDN region.

At least, Hassler hoped that was what was happening. Staring through the large windows overlooking the compound and searching the not-so distant jungle for signs that the harbingers might still be observing them. He pointed to the workstation Maddox occupied. "Get mainside on the horn. Let's find out when the taxi's coming."

"Amen to that," Maddox replied as he swiveled his chair around. "Artiaga showed me how to work this thing, but I don't think he accounted for my particular level of dumb-assedness."

"Can't blame him for that," Hassler replied as he watched the staff sergeant fumble with the computer's keyboard for a few moments. "It's easy to underestimate that sort of thing."

Maddox offered Hassler both a headset and a flipped middle finger. "You're on," he said as he donned a headset of his own.

Slipping the set over his head, Hassler said into the microphone, "This is Hassler."

A voice other than the one he had been expecting replied, "Hello, Mr. Hassler. This is Professor Bates. Captain Sorensen had to step away for a few moments to address another matter, but asked that we stand by for your scheduled report. You're a bit late, though. Is everything all right?"

"We're holding, I suppose," Hassler replied, providing a brief recap of his own condition as well that of Lipton and Artiaga. "Any time you want to send in the choppers, we're ready to go."

Bates said, "They arrived just a little while ago and their crews are going through preflight checks. I expect they'll be ready to get under way in a half hour or so. Our medical staff is already standing by to treat you and your team."

"Sounds like a plan, Professor," Hassler said. "If you don't mind, may I ask what's keeping Captain Sorensen busy?"

There was a slight pause before Bates answered, "He didn't say much, just that he had to take a call from your commanding officer. Something about a new mission your team is being assigned down in South America. He did not go into specifics."

Now it was Hassler's time to pause. Even if such a conversation truly were taking place between Sorensen and Colonel Pantolini, there was no way the captain would divulge details from that call—locations of impending operations in particular—with anyone not cleared into the team's activities.

Bates is lying. What a surprise. What did the professor have to gain by engaging in such a deception? Hassler did not know, but he trusted his instincts. Further, the look on Maddox's face told him that his friend was having similar thoughts.

"No rest for the weary, I guess," he said, rolling with it and adopting what he hoped was a casual yet tired tone.

"Considering everything you've had to deal with to this point," Bates replied, "to say nothing of the losses you've suffered, I'd say you've more than earned a respite. Hopefully the captain is lobbying for that on your behalf. In the meantime, just sit tight, Mr. Hassler. Help is on the way."

The connection severed, leaving Hassler listening to dead air. "What do you think of that?" he asked as he removed the headset. The lump of uncertainty he'd felt in his gut when Bates brought up Sorensen's call was growing larger by the moment.

"I think the good professor is full of shit," Maddox replied. "Something screwy's going on back there."

"Something screwy is going on here, too."

Both Marines turned to see Elizabeth walking into the control room with a PDA in her hand and a frown on her face. Hassler noted the dark circles under her eyes, knowing that like the rest of the group she was starting to feel the pronounced effects of fatigue. He figured that she, along with Sanchez, had to be even more tired than the Marines, considering how long they had been dealing with the situation that had begun at Observation Station Four.

To say nothing of that fifty-pound pack full of guilt she's humping.

"What's wrong?" Maddox asked.

"The local computer network's been disconnected from the main system back at CentOps," Elizabeth replied. "I was trying to send the latest reports on your people's condition to update Dr. Redina, but my messages are being bounced back."

"Some kind of server problem?" Hassler asked. Though he was by no means a computer expert, he knew enough to ask the right questions. "Maybe a line's down somewhere between here and mainside?"

Elizabeth shook her head. "The network is all wireless. We've got repeater towers scattered all throughout the region." Holding up her PDA for emphasis, she added, "Another thing. Normally, we can use these to tie into the system and give us direct access to the network even if we're nowhere near a workstation. It's not working, either."

"Something with your login info, then?" Maddox asked.

Frowning again, Elizabeth replied, "Thought about that, too, so I had Paul try his access. No dice." Stepping closer to the work station, she pointed to the computer terminal near Maddox. "Try logging in with the administrator account."

With her watching over his shoulder, the staff sergeant used two fingers from each hand to peck out the administrator login name and password. Hassler saw that his efforts were rewarded by a screen blank except for two words in bright crimson: access denied.

"That code should grant rudimentary access at a minimum," Elizabeth said. "My code should grant top security access to all but a few upper-echelon directories accessible only to Bates and a few others. We've been shut out, deliberately."

Not liking what his gut was telling him now, Hassler reached for the earpiece and lip mike to his own radio that still dangled from his equipment vest. Activating the unit and setting it to the team's command frequency, he keyed the mike. "Oscar-Four-Sierra, this is Echo-Seven-Hotel," he said, using his and Sorensen's call signs.

There was no response.

"Either his radio's off, or else he's not wearing it," Hassler said after he repeated the call two times, knowing that Sorensen would never ignore such attempts to contact him. Turning to Maddox, he said, "Get Bates back."

"Hundred bucks says no answer," another voice said, and Hassler turned to see Rolero leaning against the doorway leading from the control room. Her arms were folded across her chest, and she was regarding the others with an expression mixed of equal parts amusement, fatigue, and resignation.

"You know what this is about?" Hassler said, hoping she did not say what he figured she had to say.

Rolero pushed off from the doorjamb and stepped into the control room, nodding to Maddox. "Go ahead, give it a go."

Hassler and the others watched the staff sergeant try to reestablish contact with Central Operations. Rolero even stepped up to the station in an attempt to help.

"We're not getting a connection," Maddox finally said.

"I have an idea of what's going on," Rolero replied. "I'm betting that Bates or that weasel of a senator," she paused when she saw Elizabeth's questioning look. "That being Dillard, of course, are getting cold feet about this whole thing. My guess is that Stewart's death was the straw that broke the camel's back, and now they're taking steps to . . . sanitize the situation."

"What does that mean?" Elizabeth asked.

Shaking her head, the security chief replied, "It means that Dillard and, to a lesser extent Bates, considers the death of a few Marines to be acceptable losses if it maintains the security of the project."

"That's insane," Elizabeth said. "Geoffrey would never sanction that."

"Uh, may I point out that this is the same guy who oversaw the creation of a squad of genetically engineered lizards that could be trained for special warfare operations, and kept it a secret from you?" Maddox said, making no attempt to mask his sarcasm.

Annoyed at the Marine's remark, Elizabeth countered, "That's one thing, but you're talking . . . you're talking about murder. Geoffrey couldn't do that. I refuse to believe it."

"But it can be made to look like an accident," Rolero said, looking to Hassler. "After all, you and your team are already showing signs of infection. What if we don't get out of here for a few extra hours? What does that mean for your chances of recovery?" She pointed to the radio on Hassler's vest. "Interesting how Captain Sorensen is suddenly incommunicado, too, isn't it?"

"So you think they corralled the skipper?" Maddox asked.

Rolero replied. "I would. If this is the way Dillard and Bates choose to go, then Sorensen's a problem unless he's contained."

While Hassler suspected Dillard was capable of anything, he would still need the support not only of Bates but also other members of the EDN staff. Based on what he had learned since arriving here the previous day, only a handful of people would even seem to know about the harbingers and whatever other clandestine activities Bates was overseeing. All such effort surely was couched within the legitimate research and development work being carried out by the majority of personnel assigned to the project, which meant that most of the science and support staff also would be oblivious to any decisions made in regards to various illicit endeavors.

"What about Elizabeth and Paul?" Hassler asked. "They're not infected, so Bates would have to tell them something, right?" Pointing to Rolero, he added, "What about you, for that matter?"

"You know how it works, Hassle," Rolero replied. "You feed the nonplayers a bullshit cover story and if that doesn't work, well, things go bad." She shrugged. "Bear in mind that I'm not saying Bates would be a big fan of the idea, but he knows who pays the bills. He'd roll over, not without a fight, but he'd go."

"Now you're saying he'd have us killed, too?" Elizabeth said, her disbelief evident with every word. "You can't be serious, Shannon."

Hassler knew she was. "That still leaves you, Rolero."

Running a hand through her short black hair, the security agent actually smiled in response to the question. "I'm a soldier, Hassle, and I follow orders, just like you do. I've followed orders in the past that I disagreed with, or that I was sure were illegal even though they served a higher purpose or greater good or some other such horseshit. If Bates had included me on all of this and it came down that you had to be dealt with in order to contain the security situation, I'm being honest when I say I'd consider it long and hard before acting."

"That's a whole lot of jabbering that doesn't really answer the question," Maddox said. He reached for the M4 lying near his left hand on the workstation table. "So, let me ask it another way. Are you with us, or do I have to consider long and hard whether to empty this clip into your ass?"

Hassler, tensing as Maddox went for his weapon, allowed himself to relax somewhat when it became clear that Rolero was making no moves for the pistol under her left arm.

She always could play it cool.

"Let's not forget one thing," she said, her voice taut and angry. "He sent me out here with you and didn't tell me what we were up against. Add to that the fact that I've also lost a bunch of my people to those things Bates created, and guess what? He and Dillard owe me big time." Looking to Hassler, she added, "I figure they owe you, too, and it'll be easier to make them pay up if you're helping me. Deal?"

"Deal," Hassler replied. "Of course, we're not going to make anyone pay up anything until we get out of here." Sighing, he shook his head and turned away from Rolero to find himself looking through the room's front windows again. He was about to say something else but the words died in his throat as his eye caught sight of something outside the compound.

"Son of a bitch."

"What?" Maddox said, coming out of his own chair.

Looking around, Hassler found the binoculars he had used earlier. He brought them to his face and waited the few seconds necessary for the auto-focus feature to wash away the fuzzy picture in the unit's viewfinder.

The harbinger was back, sitting once again among the branches of the same tree it had earlier occupied. Once again, it was staring directly toward the control room windows.

Staring directly at *him*.

No sooner did Senator Christopher appear in the doorway to his office than Bates knew his plan was going straight to hell.

"What's going on?" the senator asked without preamble. "The helicopters have been here almost an hour. Why haven't they left yet?" For the most part, Christopher seemed to have regained his bearing, the anger he had earlier displayed now shrouded by a veil of cold determination.

Seated behind his desk, Bates attempted to affect an air of quiet composure. "Refueling and routine preflight checks, Senator," he said. "Given the weather they had to contend with on the way here from Nellis, it's prudent to run through such inspections to ensure the craft are in working order."

"I watched them do all that already," Christopher countered. "They've been ready to go for at least thirty minutes. What's the holdup?"

Christopher was simply too suspicious now, was asking too many questions. If left unchecked, he would either stumble across information Bates did not want him to have, or else he would have to be told what was happening in an attempt to maintain secrecy.

The only problem Bates had with either option was that he did not trust the senator to keep his mouth shut. While he had only known Christopher a short time and believed that the man might be persuaded to see the larger picture with regard to the Marines, there was no way he would ever be talked into sacrificing his own daughter for the sake of the project.

And you would be an irredeemable bastard to even suggest such a thing, he mused, knowing that he had perhaps already committed far too many unpardonable sins over the life of the EDN project to ever be considered for salvation.

One more would make very little difference.

Making his decision, Bates said, "Don't worry, Reginald. I'm as worried about Elizabeth as you are, to say nothing of the others, and I want them back here as quickly as possible. I think it's time we got started doing just that." Reaching for his phone, he casually pressed a button that did not access a line but instead sent a signal directly to whichever phone he programmed to be the recipient.

"We're launching the rescue mission?" Dillard asked, and Bates could hear the unspoken question in the senator's voice.

Bates nodded. "That's right. We've wasted too much time as it is." To Christopher he said, "Captain Sorensen will be monitoring the entire operation from a private conference room. Perhaps you'd like to join him there?"

The question seemed to put Christopher at ease, but Dillard's eyes nearly bugged out of their sockets. A stern warning look from Bates kept him silent.

"Yes," Christopher replied. "That would be great. Thank you." Pinching the bridge of his nose, he added. "I apologize for my outburst, Professor. I'm simply worried about Elizabeth."

"Quiet understandable, Senator," Bates replied.

Drawing a deep breath, Christopher leveled a hard gaze. "Be that as it may, don't get the idea that I'm forgetting everything that's happened here so far. When this is over, there are going to be hard questions to answer." Turning to glare at Dillard, he added, "For a lot of people."

"All in due time," Bates said as he rose from his seat and crossed the floor of his office to open his door, allowing the ambient sounds of activity from the main operations floor to filter into the room.

Stepping into the hallway, he heard footsteps from his right and turned to see Jason King walking down the corridor. He had pressed his uniform to remove the wrinkles and polished his boots to their customary high shine and eliminating the scuffs they had received during his brief skirmish with Captain Sorensen. He had fared better than Gutierrez, whose nose had been broken during the fight.

Bates had at first been reluctant to trust King with taking care of Sorensen, but his worry had been short-lived. The man was essentially a mercenary, one of several recruited by Rolero from the small pool of people she had come to trust during her career of covert activities. The senior positions within Rolero's security organization were held by professionals just like King. So long as they were paid, they would do what they were told without raising too many nagging questions.

For once, Bates was thankful for such a plain, unencumbered outlook.

"You sent for me, Professor?" King asked as he approached, his expression and demeanor once more the consummate professional.

Bates indicated Christopher with his hand. "Yes. We're about to send the helicopters in to get our people, and the senator would like to observe the operation with Captain Sorensen. Would you show him the way, please?" He glanced toward Dillard, who at the moment was doing everything possible to maintain his composure.

Nodding, King replied. "No problem, Professor." To Christopher he said, "Senator, if you'll follow me?"

"Yes, of course," Christopher said. He turned and offered a final hard stare at Bates, but said nothing further before King led him down the passageway.

Dillard waited until they were out earshot before saying anything. "What the hell are you doing?"

"I am containing the situation, Jonathan," Bates replied as he turned to go back into his office.

Dillard extended his arm, blocking Bates's path. "You can't be thinking of . . . well, I mean . . . "

"You can't even say it, can you?" the professor snapped, his anger now all but clouding his emotions. "If it makes you feel better, I don't wish to do anything of the sort. That much will be up to Christopher, but for the time being I need him out of my way."

The hand Dillard brought up to wipe his face was shaking. "I don't know if I can go through with this, Geoffrey. I mean, I didn't count on . . . all of this."

"Perhaps you need guidance from our friends in Washington," Bates replied, an element of mocking in his tone. "I'd definitely be interested in hearing what they have to say about this." He knew that the actions he had taken to this point had already been tacitly approved by those officials overseeing the EDN project, but eliminating one of their own?

In truth, Bates knew that he could not kill Christopher, or Sorensen for that matter. While he admitted that the notion seemed like the most effective way to handle the situation, once he actually faced the prospect of ordering the cold-blooded murder of another human being, he could not bring himself to do it. Further, he suspected that Dillard would never be able to summon the fortitude necessary to make such a decision. Therefore, if such an order were to be given, Bates resolved that it

would have to come from one of Dillard's faceless companions, wherever they might be hiding.

Not that it absolves you of anything, you craven hypocrite.

As if reading his thoughts, Dillard asked, "You think
they'd sanction this? Go that far just to save their own
necks?"

"I think we both know that if what we're doing here,
be it the project itself or the steps we're taking to preserve
it, is made public in anything resembling a negative
light, they'll cut both of us loose." Leaning closer so that
he was all but whispering in the senator's ear, Bates
added, "Face it, Jonathan, your future depends on this
entire mess being cleaned up as quickly and quietly as
possible."

Likewise, Bates knew that the same was true for himself, as well.

CHAPTER TWENTY

Guilt was eating at Clifford Meyer.

Seated at his workstation along the central operations center's uppermost tier of consoles, Meyer chewed at his fingernails while doing his best to pretend that he was immersed in the quartet of computer monitors before him. The urge to look up and over his shoulder toward the windows of Bates's office was overpowering. He felt a hot ache in the middle of his back, right between his shoulder blades, and was sure it was being generated by the heat of the professor's fierce, suspicious gaze.

It's not supposed to be like this, damn it!

Serving as the senior operations technician for more than five years and responsible for overseeing the computer and communications networks not only for Central Operations but also the observation stations scattered throughout New Eden, Meyer had only been a spectator for the bulk of the project's successes since his

arrival. While he knew he had no hope of ever understanding the tremendous scientific advances that had
created New Eden and its complex system of artificially
engineered plant and animal life, the excitement he felt at
being a part of something with such historic and endur-
ing potential had never diminished.

If it worked as planned, every single living thing on
the planet would benefit from the work being performed
here. Of that, Meyer had believed since first taking this
assignment, there was much to be proud.

That's the way it should be, anyway.

As a senior staff member, Meyer quickly found his ide-
alism tainted as he was briefed into the various secret activities Professor Bates oversaw, some of them going back
years. The harbingers in particular had been an alarming
concept to him, as they flew in the face of everything
upon which the rest of the project was founded.

Still, he had come to accept with no small amount of
disappointment that those in power were not funding
the development of the Genesis Protocol for anything as
noble as curing the ills they and others like them had inflicted on the planet. There was always a catch, and for a
while he was able to comfort himself with the knowledge
that such endeavors, hypocritical though they were to
the project's basic concept, were necessary evils if the rest
of the EDN effort was to be allowed to continue.

Still, Clifford Meyer believed a line had to be drawn
somewhere. Further, he knew that Professor Bates and
the cadre of staff members involved in the project's more
covert aspects had now stepped over that line.

He had scarcely been able to keep his seat during the
briefing held by Bates for his inner circle. The professor's
plan for "handling" the Marines was nothing less than
evil. It had taken nearly all of Meyer's self control to
avoid speaking up against the idea, and his disbelief had

only mounted as he listened to Bates describe the steps he had already taken. Confining Captain Sorensen? Preparing quarantine facilities where the remaining members of the Marine rescue team would be interred under the pretense of treatment but which would instead act as a prison until toxic contamination conquered their bodies? Hearing it very nearly had made Meyer sick to his stomach.

So why the hell didn't you speak up when you had the chance?

Movement to his right attracted his attention, and Meyer turned his head to see Jason King leading Senator Christopher out of the operations center. A few minutes earlier, he had noted the senator entering the elevator at the rear of the control room which would take him to the level housing Bates's office. No doubt the man, worried about his daughter, had gone to ask the professor yet again about the status of getting her and the others out of New Eden.

What sort of lie had Bates and Dillard used to placate Christopher? Meyer was certain the professor would not have revealed the truth, not now when so many variables were still in play. Still, he must have said something to calm the senator, as Christopher seemed to be not the least bit agitated as he followed King away from CentOps.

You idiot.

The only thing that made sense right now was for Bates to "contain" Christopher in the same manner that he had taken care of Captain Sorensen. Though neither Bates nor Dillard had come out and said as much, the only logical manner to effectively deal with Sorensen would be to kill him. Did that now apply to Christopher as well? If that were true, it meant that King was escorting the oblivious senator to a holding room.

You have to do something.

His heart pounding as the notion of what he might do to affect the current situation took shape in his mind, Meyer once more became acutely aware of his surroundings. What if he was being watched? What if Bates had somehow picked up on his reticence during the briefing and was waiting to see if he acted upon it? If Meyer was not careful, he could well stumble into whatever trap the professor might have laid.

You're paranoid, he chastised himself. Perhaps that was true, he decided, but it did not mean he was wrong.

With as casual an air as he could muster, Meyer tapped a string of cursory commands to his computer terminal, inquiring about the status of all active users and processes currently operating within the network. To his relief, he found nothing which might indicate that his own station was being monitored by someone else. According to the access logs, Bates was not even logged into the system at the moment.

Stalling one last time, Meyer rose from his desk, using the pretense of refilling his coffee cup as a means of checking out the rest of the room. Those few people working at various stations around the operations center were intent on their own tasks and therefore ignored him. To his relief, there was no one in the small kitchenette with whom to exchange small talk, which allowed him to fill his cup and exit the room without incident.

As was his habit, he made a circuit of the room on his way back to his desk, first crossing in front of the array of monitors dominating the operations center's forward wall before walking past the room containing the network's main suite of hardware components. A quick check of the status monitors mounted on the wall outside the room told him that all systems were functioning at nominal levels, leaving him with nothing to do except climb the stairs past the first and second tiers of workstations and return to his own desk. That action allowed him to casually glance up toward Bates's office, and he was relieved to note that the professor was nowhere to be seen.

Thank God.

Meyer knew that Bates could not make use of the security detail's main holding area without raising suspicion, and had ordered Sorensen to be isolated inside one of the smaller conference rooms. Meyer had been responsible for overriding the security protocols for the door lock, ensuring that Sorensen could not get out or that anyone else could not open the door without express authorization from Professor Bates. He had also deactivated the room's intercom and phone systems as well as the fire alarm control, effectively cocooning the Marine captain from the rest of the building.

What was turned off could just as easily be turned back on.

Fueled by determination and the knowledge that he might somehow be able to mitigate or change the heinous events unfolding around him, Meyer turned his attention to his workstation. His fingers danced over his keyboard as if possessed of their own consciousness, the commands he entered rushing through the computer network to undo some of the work he had earlier performed. Within seconds, the system returned the response messages he wanted. After entering a final string of commands, he donned his phone's headset in time to hear the ringing tone on the other end of the connection he had established.

William Sorensen waited, holding the door handle down to keep the lock from engaging and with his ear next to the door as he listened for the approach of King and his new charge, Senator Christopher. Within moments he was rewarded by the sounds of footfalls echoing in the corridor beyond the door.

"Captain Sorensen's in here, Senator," came King's somewhat muffled voice as the footsteps stopped, and Sorensen heard minor scuffing against the floor tiles as the security agent halted before the door. "You'll have everything you need to observe the extraction."

"Will I be able to talk to my daughter?" Christopher said, his voice quieter and harder for Sorensen to hear through the door.

"Of course," King replied, and Sorensen imagined he could almost hear the lie.

He listened as the man inserted his cardkey into the reader, waited as the reader beeped acknowledgment of the card's embedded access codes, his muscles tensing in anticipation of what was next to come. Even with the door separating them Sorensen still heard the click of the lock disengaging as King pulled on the handle and opened the door.

"What the fuck?"

Only able to guess where King might be standing and wondering just for an instant if the man's mouth was open in shock as he beheld an empty conference room, Sorensen pushed his own door open and lunged across the corridor. Coming up behind King, he threw all of his weight into his first kick to the larger man's back, sending him face first into the edge of the partially open door.

Senator Christopher had the presence of mind to stumble back and out of the way as King cried out in pain, instinctively reaching for his face as it struck the door. He spun around to face his attacker, blood streaming from his nose. Sorensen gave him no quarter as he closed in for another strike, this time lashing out at the injured man's face with the edge of his right hand even as his left punched King in the groin.

The security agent grunted in renewed agony but maintained his footing, lashing out with his right arm in a feeble attempt to defend himself. Sorensen parried the blow easily, twisting the arm up and away before slamming the heel of his right hand into King's face. Blood spattered in all directions and King made a wheezing, hissing sound like air escaping from a balloon before dropping in an unconscious heap to the floor.

"What the hell is going on?" Christopher asked as Sorensen bent over King's prone form and removed the man's pistol belt before rummaging through his pockets. Other than a small two-way radio clipped to his shirt and the keycard lying near the door, which Sorensen quickly retrieved, the security agent carried nothing else of value.

"There's been a change of plans, Senator," Sorensen replied as he took hold of King's legs and dragged the unconscious man into the conference room. Indicating for Christopher to follow him, he closed the door behind them, offering a modicum of temporary privacy.

The plan, hastily put into motion with the unexpected assistance of Clifford Meyer, had been enough. With only moments to act, Sorensen had asked the control technician to unlock the door to his conference room as well as the one across the hall, banking that King would be caught off guard by the misdirection long enough for the captain to get the drop on him.

On the conference table, the phone was still active, one indicator flashing a steady red. He punched the button next to the light, activating the phone's speaker mode. "Meyer, you still there?"

There was a pause before the tech responded in a quiet voice, "I'm here, Captain. Are you all right?"

"Better now, thanks to you," Sorensen said as he bent over King once more and undid the man's belt before turning his attention to his boot laces. "Nice job, by the way."

After being locked inside the conference room, Sorensen had quickly exhausted every potential means of escape or attracting attention. The room's single door had proven strong enough to resist breaking through, and there was no means of accessing the locking mechanism in an attempt to pick or otherwise circumvent it. The phones on the conference table had been disconnected, as had the intercom system and even the fire alarm trigger mounted on the room's rear wall. Sorensen was not carrying a lighter or matches to test the fire sprinklers hanging from the ceiling, but he suspected that those had been deactivated as well.

Enter Clifford Meyer.

"Any idea where the helicopter crews are?" Sorensen asked as he set about binding King's hands and feet with the laces from the man's boots.

Meyer replied, "Flight crew prep quarters. Bates instructed them to remain there until he gave the order to start the mission."

Excellent, Sorensen thought. It meant that Branton and his people were close to their birds, and could probably get to them without attracting too much attention. "Can you contact them, give them instructions that the mission's on and they should leave as quickly as possible?"

"Yeah, I think so," Meyer replied. "They're basically just waiting for the word to go, anyway. I have to be careful, though. I'm in the open here."

"Captain," Christopher cut in, "I demand to know what's happening here."

Satisfied that King was immobilized, Sorensen used the agent's belt as a makeshift gag before dragging him to the rear of the conference room. In terse, brief statements he relayed what he knew of the current situation as provided to him by Meyer.

"They were going to kill you?" Christopher asked, his expression a mask of disbelief. "What about me?"

Shrugging, Sorensen was unable to resist a wry smile. "Welcome to the party, sir." Turning back to the phone, he said to Meyer, "Cliff, tell Branton that I'm on my way to the pad. I should be there in a minute or two."

"You got it," Meyer replied. "Should I tell him what's going on?"

"Hell no. It's better if they don't know about it, at least not until my people are back here." Sorensen was making a calculated guess, based on what Meyer had told him, that the majority of people working in the building were oblivious of what Bates had put into motion. While the security people were obvious risks, Sorensen was chancing that Branton and the rest of the Black Hawk crews had been told only that they were on standby until their mission was put into play.

If you're wrong, this'll be over before it starts.

"Okay, Cliff," he said once more into the phone, "we're heading out. What's the quickest way to the pad from here?" It took two tries before he decided that he had committed Meyer's directions from the conference room to the helipad to memory.

He was about to sever the connection but held up at the last instant. Sighing, he added, "Listen, if this doesn't work out, I want you to know that I appreciate what you've done. You're taking a huge risk helping me this way."

Meyer hesitated again before answering, and when he did Sorensen was sure he thought he heard a note of vindication in the man's voice. "It's the least I could do, Captain. I'm . . . I'm sorry for everything that's happened. When this is over, I know I'll probably be in as much trouble as Bates, but . . . "

"Don't worry about it," Sorensen said. In truth, he was unsure as to the depth of the man's involvement in Bates's various questionable activities, and for the moment did not care. "We'll work all that out after this is over. Right now I need you to focus on helping me get those choppers airborne, and not getting caught while you do it. Got it?"

"Got it," Meyer replied. "I'm notifying Branton now."

Nodding in approval, Sorensen said, "One last thing. Get a hold of Gunny Hassler out at the observation station. I want him to know the cavalry's on the way."

"I'm on it," the tech said, "but it could take me some time to do that without tipping anyone else off."

"Whatever you have to do," Sorensen answered. "Thanks again," he added before hanging up and offering a quick, silent prayer that Meyer could make contact with his team without compromising his own safety.

As he moved toward the front of the room, he looked to Christopher. "Let's go, Senator," he said, waiting for the older man to join him near the door.

"Where are you taking me?" Christopher asked.

"To the helipad," Sorensen replied. "I'm gonna make sure those choppers take off."

Opening the door, he paused and listened for signs of activity in the corridor. Satisfied that none of King's people were lurking nearby, he pushed the door open. "Follow me," he said as he stepped out of the conference room and headed down the corridor in the direction indicated by Meyer. Rather than attempting to be covert, Sorensen simply walked down the passageway, looking as though he had every right to be there, the senator at his side.

They turned left at the first intersection, and Sorensen saw the hallway Meyer had described, perhaps fifty feet long and featuring a dozen doors along with a junction to another corridor. Also as the tech had described, the passageway ended at a metal door with a rectangular window set into it at eye level. Sunlight was evident through the window, and Sorensen smiled at that. The helipad lay in that direction.

"Just act natural, Senator," he whispered as they walked. So far they had seen no one else in the corridor, but he was taking no chances. As simple as his hastily concocted plan was, Sorensen knew that it would all go in the toilet if they happened to be spotted by a member of the security detail.

Such as the one who turned in to the hallway from the intersection he and Christopher were approaching.

Forcing his expression to remain neutral, Sorensen did not even break stride as the security agent walked in their direction. The senator, to his credit, also kept walking, though the captain sensed Christopher's anxiety ratchet up a notch. Sorensen felt his entire body coiling in preparation as the guard's face first registered confusion and then recognition.

"Son of a bitch," he said as realization dawned, and he reached for the pistol at his hip. As his hand fumbled with the holster, his fingers catching on the flap's plastic catch, his eyes lowered, just for an instant.

That was all the opening Sorensen needed.

He closed the gap between them, his left foot lashing out for the man's gun hand before the pistol could clear the holster. Sorensen heard the Beretta clatter to the floor even as he stepped closer and punched the man in the face. The guard's head snapped back in reaction to the strike. Grabbing the guard by the front of his uniform, Sorensen all but picked the man off his feet and slammed him into the wall. The guard's head struck the painted concrete and he went limp within seconds, his body slumping in Sorensen's hands before the captain let him fall to the floor.

"Damn it," he breathed as he bent to check the guard's condition. To his relief he found a pulse. Too many people had already died in this place.

"Nice to see they're still training you guys the right way," Christopher said.

"Your tax dollars at work," Sorensen replied as he used the keycard he had taken from King to open a nearby door. To his relief, the room was a walk-in storage closet housing a variety of office and janitorial supplies. It was not the perfect place to stash the unconscious guard, but it would do.

After securing the guard and retrieving his fallen pistol, which Sorensen tucked into the back of his waistband, he and Christopher encountered no further resistance as they exited the building. On the helipad, the two Black Hawks were powered up, their rotors already turning at full idle. The power of their engines drowned out the other sounds and churned up air-whipped sand at them as he and Christopher ran across the tarmac. Sorensen saw the figures of the flight crews through cockpit windows. One of the pilots noticed his approach, tapping his partner on the shoulder and pointing in Sorensen's direction.

Running to the nearest helicopter, he was happy to see Sam Branton opening the door to the cockpit and jumping out of the craft, his face all but obscured by his helmet and dark sunglasses. There was no mistaking the annoyed expression clouding the portions of his face that Sorensen could see.

"What the hell is going on, Skipper?" he asked, shouting to be heard over the Black Hawk's engines. "First they give us the go, then somebody else tells us to stand down, then the first guy tells us to ignore the second guy. What's this all about?"

"There's no time to explain it all, Sam," Sorensen yelled in reply. "The guy in charge is trying to fuck my people over, and I need your help to get them out of there."

Frowning, Branton shook his head. "Bates?"

"Yeah," Sorensen answered, looking over his shoulder back the way they had come, expecting to see the entire tarmac flooded with security people any moment. "I don't know the whole story yet, and frankly I don't give a damn. I just want my team out of that fucking jungle."

"I thought that guy was an asshole the first second I laid eyes on him," Branton replied, much to Sorensen's relief. Flashing another of his sixty-watt smiles, he added, "Rest easy, jarhead. The Night Stalkers are on it. You coming?"

Sorensen shook his head. "No." Indicating Christopher, he said, "But I'd appreciate it if you took the senator here for the ride. His daughter's in there, too." Turning to Christopher, he said, "Sir, I figure the safest place for you is on this bird."

The relief was evident on Christopher's face; he was no doubt comforted by the idea of traveling out to personally retrieve his daughter. The moment of comfort passed, though, as he locked eyes with Sorensen.

"What about you?" he asked.

Sorensen shook his head, and he felt emotion draining away as he considered the actions he was planning. "I'm going to go have a little talk with Bates."

Watching from a safe distance as the Black Hawks lifted off and turned toward New Eden, the captain allowed himself a momentary sigh of relief. If all went according to plan, his people would be out of the bizarre artificial jungle in less than an hour.

All that remained was to ensure that they were safe when they arrived.

CHAPTER TWENTY-ONE

Pulling the headset from his ear, Maddox dropped it on the desk in disgust. "Everything's working on our end, so far as I can tell."

"Cutting us off," Hassler said. He wiped sweat from his face and winced at the ache in his elbow and shoulder resulting from the motion. "Wouldn't that attract attention somewhere else in the system?"

Rolero replied, "Not if our feeds were rerouted so as to appear normal. There's only a handful of people on the staff who could do that, though."

"Bates?" Elizabeth asked.

The security chief shook her head. "Nope. It'd have to be one of the senior techs. Meyer, or maybe Lyman." She paused a moment before adding, "No, Meyer's part of Bates's inner circle, which means he's probably the only one of the tech support staff who's clued in to what's going on."

Hassler could not care less who was responsible for dropping the net on the station's communications. That was the least of their problems right now.

The rash covering much of his arms, legs, and chest was becoming sensitive to the touch, and Elizabeth had wrapped him in gauze bandage to prevent the rash being aggravated by rubbing against the material of his uniform. She and Paul Sanchez had also given him medication to dull the pain, a measure that was proving to be less than successful.

Noticing Hassler's discomfort, Maddox said, "You okay, Gunny?"

"Remember those four days in Cancún last year?" Hassler asked, mustering a tired smile.

Maddox cringed as he recalled the impromptu vacation the team had enjoyed following a particularly hair-raising mission into South America. "So you've got the hangover from hell without the fun that caused it?"

"Please. I wish I felt that good," Hassler quipped as he rose from his chair. Looking to Paul Sanchez, who had entered the room a few minutes earlier, he asked, "Any updates on Lipton and Artiaga?"

Sanchez shook his head. "No change, thank God." Waving toward the window, he added, "They're walking around the compound, said they wanted to get some fresh air."

"Good," Hassler replied. At first he was concerned about the Marines being outside the building, but he knew that both men were armed and also would have their radios if something worth reporting came along. "Anything else you can tell me about them, or me, for that matter?" He held up his right arm for emphasis, the bandages just visible underneath the cuff of his sleeve.

Elizabeth said, "Based on what Paul and I have seen, all of you should be fine if we can get you to the main infirmary in the next couple of hours." Her expression fell as she spoke the words. "That is . . . well . . . "

Hassler took comfort in the concern Elizabeth was showing. Though she, Sanchez, and Rolero did not face the same risks as the Marines, each of them had spared no opportunity to share their sympathy and anger over the current situation. Even Rolero, who always put the mission first regardless of consequences, surprised him. Ten years ago, she may well have been the first one to support any action to protect the secrecy of a classified operation, up to and including her own death were that to become a necessity. Hassler shared that mindset, at least for the most part, and so at first he had wondered what had made the former CIA operative change her mind.

Simple, he reminded himself. In the past, when she had been called upon to put her life at risk for reasons of national security, Rolero had done so with the full knowledge of the dangers and rewards involved. Were she to die on a mission, she could make that sacrifice knowing she and those she commanded had made the decision of their own free will.

Such was not the case here.

Far too many of her people had died because of unknown hazards. Rolero had not been given the chance to knowingly accept the risks of this particular job, and neither had her people. A fundamental line of trust, one that had existed in military units since time immemorial and that was meant to ensure the highest probability of success during even the most hazardous missions, had been crossed. While the uniforms and the mission might be different here, so far as Rolero was concerned it was an infraction from which there could be no redemption.

And Hassler agreed with her.

Rising from her seat behind the computer workstation, Rolero walked across the control room to where

Hassler stood near the window, gazing once more over the compound's protective wall and toward the jungle beyond.

"See anything?" she asked.

Hassler shook his head. "No." He indicated the nearby trees with a wave of his hand. The harbinger had until just a short while ago been sitting atop one of the high branches. It had remained there for hours, motionless and staring with unrelenting intensity directly at the station's observation windows, as if able to peer through the dark tinting that should have obscured the interior of the room from view. "I stood here for maybe half an hour, watching that damned thing," he said. "I turned away for a second and when I looked back, it was gone. The fucking branch wasn't even swaying or anything. It was like it just disappeared." It was but the latest demonstration of the creatures' apparent stealth abilities, one that admittedly had unsettled Hassler.

"Part of you has to admit that the idea behind those things is fascinating," Rolero said after a moment. "Think about it. Trained animals that could be sent into hazardous areas to conduct covert operations, and smart enough to relay their findings back to a home base? It's pretty amazing stuff when you think about it."

Hassler briefly entertained and then quickly discarded the mental image of a harbinger sitting in front of a computer while it transmitted digital imagery or audio recordings to its handlers. "Hey, if they want to send them after drug lords or other scumbags, that's fine with me. I was getting tired of that crap, anyway. My concern is when the cute little buggers kill their masters and head out into the countryside."

Shrugging, Rolero said, "Maybe the plan's always been that humans are what will have to contain them if a situation gets out of hand."

"Well, count me out," Hassler said. Reaching for the half-empty bottle of water he had brought with him from the desk, he drained its contents in his latest attempt to slake his growing thirst. He was running a temperature and continuing to sweat like a pig, a consequence of his infection, and it was vital he maintain good hydration.

He was about to go looking for more when a beeping tone sounded from the workstation Maddox was using for a footrest. The unexpected alert all but sent the startled Marine tumbling out of his chair.

"What the hell is that?" Hassler asked.

Pointing to one of the computer screens embedded into the console, Maddox replied, "It's the comm system. Somebody's plugged us back in. I'll be damned." He reached across the desk to push the control button to activate the connection. "Hello?"

"Um, hello?" a tentative voice said in a low voice, little more than a whisper. "This . . . this is Clifford Meyer. I'm technical coordinator for the EDN project. Who is this?"

The response to the man's voice was electric, as Hassler and the others crowded around Maddox. Perhaps now they could get some answers.

"This is Dave Maddox, and boy, are we glad to hear from you," the staff sergeant said, exchanging smiles with the rest of the group. "Think you could maybe tell us just what the hell is going on out your way?"

Everyone in the room listened in as Meyer offered an explanation for the events of the past few hours, their emotions coursing through shock and anger in reaction to Bates's plans before returning almost to their initial elation as they learned the helicopters were finally on the way.

"Oh my God," Elizabeth said, shaking her head in disbelief.

Standing next to her, Sanchez wrapped an arm around her shoulder as he exchanged looks with Hassler. "If he's willing to write you guys off, then it's a sure bet he'd do the same to us if he thought we were going to be a problem."

"He's dead," Rolero said, her voice low and tight. "I swear to God, the first thing I'm gonna do when we get back is put a bullet in his head."

Hassler was tempted to tell her that she might have to take a number, but opted against it. She was entitled to her fury, he decided, given the number of people she had lost to the harbingers. If nothing else, the raw, unguarded moment seemed to tell him that Rolero had been truthful all along about her knowledge of the creatures and her feelings of animosity toward Bates for leaving her and her security detail exposed.

If she wanted to cap the professor, Hassler was not about to get in her way. If Bates was lucky, she *would* shoot him in the head and offer him a merciful escape from her wrath.

Otherwise, I'm getting some popcorn, an air horn, and a good seat.

"When are the choppers due?" he asked.

"Eighteen minutes," Meyer replied, his voice still subdued. No doubt the man was doing everything he could to mask his activities from Bates or other prying eyes.

Nodding in approval, Hassler was almost able to forget how crappy he felt for a moment. "Give the pilots our radio frequencies," he said before providing the tech with the necessary information. "I want to be able to talk to them directly if I have to."

"You got it," Meyer answered. "I have to get off this line now, but I'll be in touch. Hang in there, okay?"

"We'll be here," Hassler said as the connection went dead. He turned to the group. "Looks like we finally caught a break. I want to be out of here in nineteen minutes. Maddox, you and I'll go and get Stewart." He knew that Elizabeth and Sanchez had already sealed the man's remains inside the EDN equivalent of a body bag, but he had reserved the duty of transporting the dead Marine from here to himself and the staff sergeant, the gesture as close as he could come to honoring the tradition of carrying the body of a fallen comrade from the field of battle.

"Lipton, Artiaga," he said as he keyed the radio clipped to his equipment harness. "Choppers are inbound, ETA eighteen minutes. Hotfoot it back inside and grab any gear you've got lying around in here. We're rallying at the building's main entrance."

"Outstanding," Lipton called out a moment later. "You got it, Gunny. We'll be there in . . . "

A dull thump echoed through the radio connection at the same instant the lights in the control room flickered and the displays on all of the computer monitors wavered. At the same instant another pulsing alarm erupted from one of the workstations. Instead of a warm, inviting beep, this tone was loud and sharp, its meaning evident with each piercing note.

Alarm.

"What?" he asked, looking to anyone who might provide an answer as Rolero and Maddox both bent over their respective workstations.

"There's been an overload somewhere," Rolero called out without turning from her consoles.

"Gunny!" Lipton shouted over the radio. "Something's going on near the main gate! Sparks and shit are flying everywhere."

The flickering lights returned to constant illumination and the computers resumed their normal displays, though Hassler noted that one of the screens near Rolero was highlighted with several more crimson indicators.

"Breakers have flipped for the lines running to the gate. The security cage is out, but main power's still online."

"What caused the overload?" Elizabeth asked, and Hassler felt his pulse quickening as he imagined possible scenarios and answers to the doctor's question.

Leaning over the desk and tapping queries into her keyboard, Rolero shook her head. "I don't know yet."

"Holy shit," Maddox said from his own station. "Gunny, you need to see this." As Hassler and the others moved to stand behind him, the staff sergeant pointed to one monitor that was split into four images alternating black-and-white feeds from the twenty video cameras positioned around the compound. Entering commands to his computer terminal's keyboard, he froze the feed rotation so that a single view, the one covering the compound's main entrance, enlarged to fill the screen.

"No fucking way," Hassler breathed as he watched at least six harbingers moving erratically around the entrance to the security cage protecting the entrance to the compound.

Not just around the cage, but also over and on it.

"What is that?" Elizabeth asked, pointing to something in the screen's upper-left-hand corner. It was a dark object, partially obscured by the cage's steel mesh network, which conspired with the camera's angle to all but hide it from view. As Hassler and the others watched, one of the harbingers scrambled up the mysterious object and onto the top of the cage.

"It's one of them," Hassler said. "It must have tried to jump on top of the cage and gotten electrocuted. That's what caused the overload."

"Jesus Christ," Maddox said as he ran toward the window, his M4 in his hands. "They've figured out that the fence is off, and now they're walking over the cage like it's a fucking bridge. They'll cross and jump over the damned wall."

"I've got another angle," Rolero called out from where she had moved to Maddox's workstation. Hassler turned to the monitor, and felt his jaw go slack as he watched two harbingers running across the top of the protective enclosure.

Hassler grabbed his radio mike. "Lipton, the things are coming over the wall near the main gate. Get back inside, now."

The only reply to his summons was weapons fire, muted through the sound of the heavy glass of the window. Running over to the large port, Hassler strained to look in the direction of the main gate, but could only curse that the layout of the station prevented him from being able to see that area of the compound.

"Gunny!" Artiaga's voice shouted in his earpiece. "They're coming over the wall!"

Geoffrey Bates was furious.

"Who gave the order for those helicopters to leave?" he shouted into his phone. "I specifically ordered that they were not to leave until I gave my personal authorization."

"I don't have the answer to that, Professor," the harried voice of the flight operations director replied over the phone's speaker. "They acknowledged my order to stand down, but then left a minute or so later. One of my men saw two people running out to the choppers right before they took off."

"Who the hell was that?" Dillard said from where he sat in front of Bates's desk.

Her voice carrying a distinct element of nervousness now, the FOD replied, "One of the men was wearing a camouflage uniform, sir, so I suspect it was one of the

Marines. The other man was wearing a dark business suit, and I'm told he boarded one of the choppers."

"Sorensen and Christopher," Bates hissed through gritted teeth as he punched the button to sever the line. "Damn it." It was obvious that the Marine officer had somehow overpowered King when the security agent had brought Christopher to the conference room where he was being held, and then taken the senator out to the helipad so that he could ride along on the trip to retrieve his daughter.

"We should have killed Sorensen when we had the chance," Dillard said.

"We've got other things to worry about right now. Sorensen obviously had help in his escape," Bates replied distractedly.

"What are you talking about?" Dillard asked.

Bates shook his head in disgust. "Even if he was able to get away from King and get Christopher to the pad on his own, someone else sent instructions to the pilots."

"Sorensen could have done that once he was out of custody," Dillard countered.

Was the man simply incapable of reasoned thought? "The flight director said that the pilots had received in-structions to take off." He moved from behind his desk toward the windows overlooking Central Operations. "She didn't provide that clearance, which means that they were contacted directly. Sorensen would not have had access to a communications system or even the frequencies the pilots were using. Someone else took care of that."

The only logical answer was that a member of the project staff had provided Sorensen with that necessary assistance.

Looking out over the main floor of CentOps, he saw the cadre of technical support staff working at various consoles along the three tiers of workstations. A trio of lab technicians, two women and a man, were gathered near the front wall of display monitors, with one of the women pointing to something on one screen and talking to her colleagues. Despite everything that had happened during the past few days, the scene before him was as close to routine as he might normally expect. Clifford Meyer, the project's senior technical coordinator, was as usual hard at work at his station, his omnipresent headset worn over his right ear as he pored over the quartet of computer monitors arrayed before him.

Meyer.

It was the only answer that made sense. The man's command of the project's computer and communications network was unmatched, and he also possessed full knowledge of the current situation. He would be the ideal person to assist Sorensen, particularly from a remote location.

"It was Meyer," Bates said as returned to his desk and punched the button on his phone that would connect him with the security office.

Dillard's face was a mask of horror. "If that's true, then he knows everything. He would have told Sorensen, and he might even have told the others. He's a security threat."

"Thank you for stating the obvious, Jonathan," Bates replied with undisguised sarcasm as he waited for someone in the security office to answer the damned phone.

"Security," a male voice said as the line connected. "Chavez speaking. What can I do for you, Professor?"

Dispensing with any sort of preamble, Bates said, "I want a security detail sent to CentOps immediately. Take Clifford Meyer into custody."

"May I ask why, sir?" the man asked, confusion evident in his voice.

"He's become a security liability, I'm afraid," Bates replied, biting off each word. "Arrest him. Now."

"Understood. A team's on the way, sir."

Severing the connection, Bates turned the laptop computer occupying one corner to face him. He entered his login information and waited for confirmation.

"What are you doing?" Dillard asked.

"Seeing who else might be helping him," the professor replied as he entered a query to access the system's communications logs. Available only to senior project members, the logs recorded information about every voice or electronic interaction transmitted over the network.

Dillard said, "Aren't you jumping the gun a bit? What if he's not the one?"

"Then this will rule him out," Bates answered, though instinct told him his suspicions were correct. Given the limited amount of time that had passed since he had issued his instructions and Sorensen had gotten free, the list of potential suspects with all the necessary knowledge and skills was very short.

Entering a search on the Meyer's name, Bates called up a record of every communication the tech had performed in the last six hours. Once he had that, he would be able to access transcripts of all conversations Meyer had conducted.

Assuming he hasn't already covered his tracks.

The laptop's screen went blank.

"Damn it!" Bates shouted, slamming his fist on the desk hard enough to jostle the phone and laptop as well as various other articles cluttering the workspace. "He's locked me out!" Running back to the window, he looked down to the uppermost tier of consoles on the main floor, searching for Meyer.

The tech was staring up at him, his expression a blend of fear, uncertainty, and triumph.

"That smug little bastard," Dillard said from where he had moved to stand next to Bates, the uncharacteristic level of anger he was displaying also harboring more than a hint of panic. "He'll ruin everything."

"He already has," Bates replied, his own ire rising with each passing moment as the full weight of what Meyer had done began to register. If the tech had succeeded in warning anyone outside the project's sphere of control about what was happening here, then his troubles were only just beginning.

"Come on," Dillard called out as he headed for the door. "I want to know everything he's done."

Bates was not surprised when the senator reached for the door handle and found it locked.

CHAPTER TWENTY-TWO

The harbingers were in the compound.

"Is the building secure?" Hassler asked as he crossed the control room to stand behind Maddox, who was once more hunched over the array of computer monitors dominating his workstation.

"Everything looks tight, boss," the staff sergeant replied. He pointed to one computer monitor displaying a schematic of the station's interior. All exits were displayed in blue, indicating that they were closed and locked.

"What about the roof?" Hassler asked. His concern was not that the creatures might gain access to the structure's interior through one of the doors but that they might climb the stairs or the latticework enclosing them in order to get up on the roof.

Maddox called up video feeds from the roof, all of which showed nothing but an empty expanse of concrete only occasionally broken up by electrical boxes or ventilation-shaft covers. "All clear so far."

Keying his lip mike, Hassler said, "Lipton, what's the story out there?"

There was pause before the sergeant replied, and when he did Hassler heard the sounds of his and Artiaga's M4s as they engaged targets. "We've counted at least six coming over the wall, Gunny, but there might be more. They're running all over the fucking place!"

"Where are you?"

Again a pause. "We found some cover near a storage building about thirty yards from the west-side fire door. We can see it, but it's open ground between us and there."

"Hang tight," he said as he turned at the last intersection in the corridor. "I'll be there in a minute."

"Hurry if you can, Gunny," Artiaga piped up. "We're running low on ammo."

Hassler had feared that the ammunition situation might bite them in the ass. The remaining ammo and supplies from their deceased comrades had been redistributed among the surviving members. That had been augmented with a small cache of ammunition from the station's weapons locker. Still, it still was not enough for them to mount any kind of prolonged defense against an enemy as fierce and unrelenting as the harbingers.

"Stay here and watch my ass on the cameras," Hassler ordered. "I'll get Lipton and Artiaga and bring them up. Once I'm inside the building, you get everybody on the roof." Pausing, he added, "Including Stewart."

Maddox nodded, his jaw taut. "You got it."

"I'll go with you," Rolero said. "They'll need cover, and so will you, to keep any of those things from getting inside if nothing else."

Tempted as he was to decline the offer, Hassler instead nodded in agreement. From the layout of the compound he had memorized while sitting in the control room, he was sure of the approximate location where Lipton and Artiaga were pinned down. The protection there would be minimal, with only a handful of large metal crates and assorted heavy equipment parked nearby to offer meager cover. If the harbingers got it in their heads to attack in force, the Marines would not stand a chance.

"Okay," he said. "Dawg, call the choppers and tell them we're going to Plan B."

The contingency plan that he, Maddox, and Rolero had devised once the harbingers got into the compound involved using the roof of the building as the extraction point. According to Rolero, the building's structure was capable of supporting a helicopter. Additionally, the Black Hawks were armed with everything they would need to engage the harbingers from the safety of the air. All the team had to do was get to the roof and hold their positions long enough for the choppers to arrive.

Oh, Hassler's mind chided him. *Is that all?*

After ensuring that everyone had their instructions and with Rolero following close behind him, he navigated the three flights of stairs and several lengths of corridor separating him from his destination. As he ran, Hassler was aware of the burn in his legs and chest and that his breathing was becoming more labored. He was already running a fever owing to the effects of his exposure to the EDN's hazardous environment, and the additional exertion was beginning to wear on him, even though he knew he really had not done anything yet. While this might well be the final push before the team was rescued, his gut told him that it would not be as simple as waiting for the helicopters to spirit them from this place.

"I'll never bitch about close-quarters drills ever again," he said, more to himself than Rolero. The intense live-fire exercises, which tested a team's ability to engage and defeat an enemy within a confined, enclosed space, had never been one of Hassler's favorite training evolutions. Still, the practice maneuvers, performed over and over uncounted times until every man knew not only his own moves but could also anticipate each step of his teammates, had saved his life in places like Afghanistan, Iraq, and Colombia.

He shook off the sensations of fatigue as he caught sight of the fire door. "There it is," he called over his shoulder. Already he could hear the sounds of skirmish growing louder as he approached the door, Lipton and Artiaga firing single rounds now, their diminishing supplies of ammunition no doubt forcing them to be more selective with their targets. The occasional high-pitched shriek of the harbingers was also audible.

Stopping at the door, Hassler thumbed off his M4's safety and verified that a round was loaded into his rifle's M203 grenade launcher. "I'll go outside, you stay at the door and keep it from locking."

"Got it," the security chief replied. "Ready when you are."

Satisfied that this was as good as it was going to get, Hassler took a deep breath and kicked at the door, his boot striking the handle running across it at waist level and sending it opening to his right. He lunged through the opening and dodged to his left, crouching down and keeping his back to the wall. Rolero held the door open with her body, scanning the area to Hassler's left that he could not see.

"On your right!" Artiaga shouted, and movement from that direction made Hassler turn in time to see a dark figure scrambling across the open ground directly toward him. The bright afternoon sunlight reflected off the harbinger's lean, muscled body, giving its hide the look of freshly oiled leather. Its eyes, high on its head, were locked on him as it closed the gap between them.

He heard weapons fire from Lipton and Artiaga's position as he spun to face the onrushing creature, pulling the M4 to his shoulder and depressing the trigger. The rifle's buffer absorbed most of the recoil as the rounds found their mark, striking the harbinger in the head and chest. An angered, wounded cry echoed off the wall of the building as the animal changed direction and leaped out of the line of fire, its massive legs sending it thirty feet across the compound to land on the roof of the small storage building the other Marines were using for cover. Lipton and Artiaga were already scrambling away from their place of questionable concealment as the harbinger stumbled and fell atop the roof, clearly slowed by the injuries the three Marines had inflicted.

"Get out of there!" Hassler shouted as he targeted the creature through the blocky sights of the M203 and pulled the trigger. The other two Marines dashed across the open ground as the grenade arced away from him and slammed into the roof of the building. It detonated less than three feet from the harbinger, tearing away a sizable portion of the structure's upper wall and roof. Hassler felt the concussion from the blast as fragments of concrete and aluminum ballooned into a dusty cloud.

The harbinger had caught most of the blast as well as the storm of shrapnel it created, falling from the roof to land in a heap in the gravel bed below. Pink blood oozed from numerous shrapnel wounds covering the creature's body, and while it bucked and twitched where it lay on the ground, it was making no attempt to regain its feet. Hassler took aim on the animal's head and fired five rounds into it, catching the harbinger in and around its right eye and ceasing its movements for good.

"Got another one!" Rolero shouted, and Hassler turned to see another of the creatures approaching from his left. Rows of sharp, gleaming teeth lined its long, narrow mouth, which appeared to smile at him as it closed the distance.

His ears rang with the cacophony of M16 fire directly over his head as Rolero opened up on the harbinger, emptying her rifle's magazine. Bullets ripped into its head and upper torso. Pale red blood sprayed in all directions as the animal, howling and screeching in pain, tried to retreat, but the security chief had wounded it enough that it was unable to escape, instead falling limp to the gravel-laden ground.

Lipton and Artiaga used the opportunity to finish their mad dash across the compound, slamming themselves against the wall next to Hassler. Both Marines looked bedraggled and ready to shit their pants, but otherwise none the worse for wear.

"How many more?" Hassler asked as he ejected the magazine from his rifle and inserted a new one, trying not to dwell too much on the fact that he had only two left in his vest pouches. His concern was not eased when he reached for the bandolier slung over his left shoulder and found only three grenades hanging there.

"At least six," Lipton answered, "but once they started coming over the wall we got the hell out of there." Hassler heard the fatigue in the younger Marine's voice, the first sign of weakness the sergeant had shown. Was exposure to New Eden's hazardous ecosystem finally beginning to affect him? What about Artiaga? How was he feeling?

Hang in there just a little longer. The plaintive wish was as much for his Marines as it was for himself.

"Maddox!" he yelled into his lip mike. "Where are the rest of them?"

Instead of the staff sergeant, Paul Sanchez replied. "We count at least five near the main door, three on the south wall, and three heading toward . . . "

"Time to go!" Rolero shouted just as Hassler heard the sounds of something heavy and fast skittering across gravel to his right and turned to see the harbinger coming around the corner of the building.

"Get inside," he told Lipton and Artiaga, firing rounds at the approaching creature as two more came into view. Rolero held the door open as the Marines dove inside.

Pushing Rolero in ahead of him, Hassler turned and aimed at the ground in front of the creatures as he fired the grenade launcher. The projectile detonated at the foot of the lead harbinger, vaporizing it in a cloud of bone, gravel, pink blood, and dark muscle tissue. Its frightened companions scampered back the way they had come, giving Hassler the precious seconds needed to get inside and close the door behind him.

"We're back inside," he called into his radio as he led the group back through the corridor. "How long until the choppers get here?"

"About seven minutes," the staff sergeant replied. "I've already notified the pilots of the new plan. It's all over but the waiting, boss man."

Yeah, right.

"Okay, we're on our way to the roof using the west fire stairs," he reported. "Seal everything else except for your route up, and then seal that once you're there."

Hassler heard the fatigue in his voice. The contamination he had suffered was beginning to take its toll. How much longer could he hold out before his body failed him and he was helpless to defend himself?

There has to be a better way to make a living.

"Mr. Meyer, you need to come with us, please."

Clifford Meyer turned in his seat to see a pair of security agents, dressed in their normal black fatigues with the cuffs of their trouser legs tucked into the tops of their black tactical boots. The agent who had spoken to him was a tall Caucasian man, his bald head sitting atop a neck thick with muscle. His EDN access badge listed his name as Hiltz. The man's partner, a Latino woman who looked like a smaller version of Shannon Rolero, stood to Hiltz's right and slightly behind the man, her hands clasped behind her back. The name on her badge read ARAGUZ.

"What's the problem?" Meyer asked, doing his best to maintain a calm outward composure.

Hiltz replied, "Professor Bates has ordered that we take you into custody, sir." The tone of the man's voice left no doubt that he meant business.

"I don't understand," Meyer said, certain that his efforts to feign ignorance were as transparent to the security agents as they were to him. "This has to be some sort of mistake."

Having monitored the call but unable to stop it in time, Meyer could only wait for this moment to arrive. He had briefly considered making a run for it, but knew that would likely prove to be a hopeless venture. Instead, he had elected to remain at his station, putting into motion a variety of initiatives that would, he hoped, help Dr. Christopher and the Marines trying to rescue her and the other members of the EDN staff.

He had succeeded in cutting Bates off from the rest of the facility, severing his phone and computer connections and locking him in his office. Further, he had disabled the alarms and other preprogrammed phone connections to the security office, hoping the action would slow down any calls for reinforcements. The lockouts were all encoded through an encrypted phantom user account he had forged and provided administrator access with clearance to the entire EDN computer and communications network. Only he would be able to cancel the measures he had put into place. If the circumstances were different, he might even have been proud of the work he had done.

Taking a step forward, an action that actually blocked out some of the light coming from behind him, Hiltz said, "Mr. Meyer, let's not make this more difficult than it has be. Please, stand up."

Did they know that he had helped Captain Sorensen escape? He doubted it, though he was less certain about their knowledge of his role in deploying the Black Hawks. He had contacted the pilots directly, bypassing the flight-operations director, which he knew was a risky maneuver. Even though he was able to mask certain movements through the computer and phone networks, there still would be smart questions asked by smart people who would waste little time fitting together the pieces of the puzzle.

Hence Bates's call to security.

His mind racing through a host of potential excuses he might offer, Meyer nodded and rose from his chair, removing his headset and laying it down on his desk. Hiltz stepped forward and placed a firm hand on his arm, as if worried that Meyer might make a run for it.

"Let him go," said a voice from behind the agents.

Sorensen saw the relief on Clifford Meyer's face, which was canceled out by the surprise and anger on the faces of the security agents as they all turned to face him. Stepping forward, he aimed the barrel of his pistol at the man's head. "I said let him go. Do it now." Other members of the Central Operations staff overheard him that time, turning from their workstations to see what was happening at the rear of the room.

To the large agent's left, Araguz's right arm moved and Sorensen saw the fingers of her hand flexing as she tried to reach for the pistol on her hip. Turning his own weapon on her, he stepped forward.

"Don't," he warned. "You'll never get there." Anticipating a similar action from her partner, he added, "Look, I don't want to hurt anybody, but I'll put you down if you force me. Now, let Meyer go."

To his relief, Hiltz released his grip on the computer tech, who promptly turned and began to head toward him. Sorensen stopped him by holding up his left hand. "No," he said. "I need you to maintain contact with the choppers. How much time until they're at the landing site?"

Meyer paused, seemingly performing the calculations in his head before replying, "A little over four minutes now, I think." His voice was trembling, if only a bit, which Sorensen could understand. "But," he added, "things are getting kind of rough in there."

Not liking the sound of that, Sorensen asked, "What do you mean?" In response, Meyer offered a brief recap of the communications between the members of the rescue team he had overheard over the past several minutes and their status as the situation with the harbingers seemed to worsen with each passing moment.

Damn it, Sorensen thought. *And we're so close.*

"Keep me posted. I want to know the second those choppers are in position." As Meyer sat back down at his desk, Sorensen indicated for Hiltz and Araguz to move away from him and directed them to stand closer to the nearby wall, instructing them to keep their hands in plain sight at all times.

"What the hell is this about?" Araguz asked.

By way of reply, Sorensen posed his own question. "How much about what's going on are you clued in to?" he asked the agents.

Hiltz shrugged in irritation, the anger on his face unmistakable. "Clued in to how?" he asked.

"You know that your boss, Rolero, is in the bush with my people, trying to rescue members of the science team, right?"

Hiltz nodded. "We were told they ran into some kind of wild animals, and that there've been a few casualties."

Jesus, how much bullshit has Bates fed these people? "Yeah? And what about your people who went in for them first?"

Casting his gaze downward, the security agent replied, "They were attacked, too. Everybody was killed."

The man's expression turned from somberness to shock as Sorensen told him the truth. He offered them everything, including the cover story Bates had been giving to his own people.

Shaking his head in disbelief, Hiltz said, "You're saying Bates made these things and put them out in the jungle, and kept it a secret?"

Sorensen nodded. "It was a classified government project, one Senator Dillard was overseeing along with some buddies of his in Washington. It wasn't supposed to go down like it did, but it happened and now they want to cover it up." Shrugging, he added, "What's one more artificially grown animal around here, anyway? It's not as though it's the weirdest thing going on in this place, right?"

"Except for the part about the things killing people and Bates lying about it," Hiltz countered.

Indicating Meyer with a nod, Sorensen said, "This guy helped me, and he can prove everything I've been saying. Right, Meyer?"

Turning from his desk, the tech nodded. "Yeah, I can prove all of it." He pointed up toward the rear wall of the room, and Sorensen risked a glance to see Bates and Dillard standing before the office's bay window. Both men appeared to be livid and, at least in Sorensen's opinion, more than a little frightened.

"I activated the intercom to Bates's office," Meyer said. "They heard everything you just said."

Hiltz regarded the tech with no small amount of skepticism, but Sorensen thought he also saw the first signs of uncertainty in the man's face. No doubt he and Araguz had been close friends with at least some of the security people lost during the past three days. Further, they both worked for Shannon Rolero, who Sorensen believed would not hire people she did not trust and who were not in turn loyal to her.

"You think he's telling the truth?" Araguz said. The lilt in her voice as she asked the question told Sorensen that he had won her over, at least in part, but that she still had doubts and was waiting to follow her partner's lead.

To Hiltz, he said, "Look, I know it's a lot to take in, but right now I need your help. My people are going to need medical attention when they get here. So are yours, and I don't want to have to fight every person in this building to see that they get it." He lowered the Beretta's barrel so that it no longer pointed at the agents. "I need you to trust me, and I only know one way to demonstrate that." Engaging the pistol's safety, he offered it butt-first to Hiltz.

Stepping forward, the agent took the proffered weapon and regarded it for a moment before nodding. "Okay, we'll see where this goes," he said, his voice and expression remaining firm. "What do you want us to do?"

Sorensen replied, "First, I want the tarmac secured. I don't want any more surprises waiting for my people when those choppers get back." He glanced up to the windows of Bates's office. "In the meantime, I'm going to go have a little chat with the professor."

"You should probably take backup," Araguz said, still regarding Sorensen with no small amount of suspicion. "I'll go."

Sorensen nodded. "Works for me." Attempting to lighten the mood, he turned to Hiltz. "I don't think she likes me."

The other man replied, "It's not personal. She just hates jarheads." Drawing a breath, he offered the Marine the pistol he had taken. Sorensen accepted the weapon with a nod of thanks.

"Where are we, Meyer?" he asked as he holstered the pistol.

The tech replied. "Choppers should be over the compound any time now, Captain."

Almost over.

Nodding in satisfaction, Sorensen said, "Thanks. Outstanding work you did today, by the way." Meyer smiled at that, and when he turned back to his work Sorensen noted that the man seemed to sit a bit straighter in his chair.

As if noting the relief on Sorensen's face, Hiltz said, "If you're wrong, King's gonna play golf with my balls."

Sorensen sighed in relief, unable to suppress a smile. "Yeah, well funny thing about that. You should probably know that I put him out of commission for a little while."

To his surprise, Hiltz appeared to shrug off the notion even though his expression remained neutral. "Always thought he was an asshole, anyway."

CHAPTER TWENTY-THREE

Stalking back and forth before the windows of Bates's office, Dillard appeared to the professor to be little more than a caged animal. He held his arms close to his sides, his hands clenched into fists so tight they appeared as white as his dress shirt, the collar of which Bates saw was damp with the senator's perspiration. The man had loosened his tie and opened his shirt's top button, as far from an impeccable appearance as he had ever presented in all the years Bates had known him.

"Who the hell does that son of a bitch think he is?" Dillard growled, his attention focused beyond the windows and the main floor of CentOps below them. "The only thing he's going to accomplish is to destroy his career. One phone call from me and he'll be a janitor at some fucking weather station in Alaska."

Collapsing into the chair behind his desk, Bates felt sweat on his own forehead as well as under his arms and along the small of his back. He reached with a trembling hand into the right pocket of his lab coat and withdrew his medication. Fumbling two tablets from the vial, he dry-swallowed them, wincing at their rough-chalky texture as they worked their way down his throat.

"Odds are he's already contacted his superiors, Jonathan," Bates said as he wiped his brow. "No doubt those people will be escalating matters." There undoubtedly would be congressional hearings once the security surrounding the project was broken, he knew, to say nothing of the probability of criminal trials.

Dillard stopped his pacing long enough to glare at the professor. "There's too much value to what we've accomplished here for it to be consumed by all the ridiculous nonsense an investigation would bring, Geoffrey. There's too much at stake for it to be swept under the carpet."

What we've *accomplished?* His hand moving to loosen his shirt collar, Bates almost sneered at the senator. "I hope you'll be as enthusiastic to share the credit when they put us in jail, Jonathan." Drawing a deep breath in an attempt to calm himself, he continued, "Don't you understand? Nothing we've done here is worth killing people, good people who devoted their lives to something that might one day benefit all of us. Creating those monsters for your friends at the Pentagon wasn't so important as to forfeit those people's lives."

"Accidents happen," Dillard countered, his tone cold and devoid of emotion as he turned to look out the window. "As for the Marines, well, sometimes they get paid to die."

In frustration, he slapped the heavy Plexiglas with the palm of his hand, the impact's dull echo resonating through the office.

Bates felt his ire rising even as he studied the senator's back. "Damn it, Jonathan, these weren't accidents, and those Marines certainly didn't swear an oath to die at your whim. As for my own people, their deaths are on our heads, mine more so than yours."

There was only one thing that now could be done, the professor knew, a single act that might offer some slim chance at redemption for all that had happened here. The truth had to be told, all of it, so that deaths of the men and women caused by his failure to properly act would have some meaning.

"I'm not going to keep that to myself," Bates continued. "I'll testify to any committee they want to hold. I'll lay out everything—my involvement, yours, our Washington benefactors'. I'll do so without compulsion or the hope of securing a more lenient punishment for myself." He was tired of the lies, not only his own but also those belonging to the people with whom had had allied himself in order to realize the potential of New Eden and the Genesis Protocol.

Dillard turned from the window. "None of this will ever get out, Geoffrey," he said, but Bates heard an undercurrent of worry belying the words. "Too many people in Washington want this project to succeed. The harbingers may have been faulty, but that can be corrected. That's the whole point of this place, after all. We'll just grow a new batch and start over. I'll see to it personally, if I have to."

Bates knew it was not simple hyperbole. He could see desperation—fueled perhaps by desperation—in Dillard's eyes. Whatever action was required not only to keep the project active but also to ensure that the tragic events which had transpired here were forever buried from scrutiny, the senator would take it. Further, the idea that the machinations of senate oversight hearings and other congressional nonsense might well vindicate himself as well as Dillard disgusted Bates, as did the idea that the EDN project could be buried under yet another veil of secrecy while work continued toward creating the next generation of harbingers or perhaps something worse.

"No, Jonathan," Bates said as he opened his center drawer. "You won't." His right hand was still shaking as it closed around the grip of the small .38-caliber pistol.

I cannot allow that, the professor decided. *Not any longer.* While he was certain his own intentions might have been honorable in the beginning, regardless of whatever deals he might have made with whichever devils masqueraded as Washington bureaucrats, any sense of nobility he might have possessed had been abrogated the moment he allowed innocent lives to be endangered or sacrificed in order to protect the project's secrets.

The senator must have sensed the discussion taking this turn, because he was moving across the room even before Bates could clear the weapon from the drawer.

"You bastard!" Dillard shouted, his eyes wide with shock, fear, and betrayal. Despite his age and apparent lack of fitness, the senator was able to close the distance even as Bates struggled to rise from his chair. Dillard wrapped his hand around the barrel of the snub-nosed revolver as Bates was bringing the gun up in an attempt to aim.

Bates could only cry in pain as Dillard pulled the gun from his grasp, the other man stumbling backward a step at the sudden shift in his balance. The professor reached out in a feeble effort to retrieve the pistol but Dillard stepped away, turning the .38 around in his hand. As he looked down the gun's barrel, Bates could only hold up his hands in surrender.

"How dare you." The words hissed past Dillard's lips, his eyes glowering with rage as he stared down his outstretched arm, which now held the revolver. "You of all people should know that this is bigger then either of us. Even if you had killed me, it doesn't matter what happens to either of us. There'll be someone to take our places tomorrow. The project is too big now, and too important."

Feeling his pulse quicken and his legs begin to shake so badly that he feared they might no longer support him, Bates attempted to clear his throat. "You can kill me, Jonathan, but you can't kill everyone here. Someone else will simply do what needs to be done to make sure things are set right." He was certain Elizabeth would spearhead such an effort. She would know what to do.

Assuming she makes it out of there, he reminded himself.

Regardless, Bates was certain that Senator Jonathan Dillard, as cold and calculating a man as his chosen profession demanded, possessed little if any of the fortitude and dispassion required to take another life in cold blood.

He was wrong.

"One step at a time, Geoffrey," Dillard said as he pulled the trigger.

There was no mistaking the pistol shot even through the muffled walls surrounding Bates's office. Sorensen instinctively crouched down near the wall to his left, aiming his pistol toward the office door. Casting a quick look over his right shoulder, he saw that Araguz had followed his lead, dropping to one knee and her own weapon pointed in the direction of the professor's office.

"Shit," Araguz said. "They're armed?"

Sorensen cursed to himself. He had anticipated either Dillard or Bates possibly having a weapon in his possession, but he had not counted on one of the men apparently shooting the other.

What had happened? To Sorensen, the most likely explanation was that one of the men, obviously knowing they were facing possible criminal charges for what had taken place here, had grown desperate once they were locked in Bates's office. Both Bates and Dillard had much for which they would have to answer, but which of them considered the present situation and their prospects for the future so dire that they felt it necessary to kill in a frantic, last-ditch attempt to save their own ass?

No bet, he decided. *Dillard.* Sorensen had not trusted the scumbag from the moment he had first heard the man's name. The simple fact that the senator had called in whatever favors were owed him to secure the use of the Force Recon team was enough to tell the captain that Dillard was a man accustomed to getting what he wanted. He had grown used to the influence and prestige that far too many officials in Washington took for granted, and would likely balk at the notion of having that power removed forcibly from him.

In short, when cornered, with his freedom in jeopardy and perhaps even with his own mortality staring him in the face, Dillard would be dangerous.

Damn, Sorensen thought. *I should have taken that private-sector job when I had the chance.* So far as he knew, security consultants for Fortune 500 companies were rarely called upon to face down aggrieved and panicked politicians who might at least be marginal marksmen.

He flinched in response to another shot from inside Bates's office at the same time that sparks burst from the card reader situated at waist level on the wall to the right of the door. The reader emitted a tortured series of beeps as the door was flung open, revealing Jonathan Dillard, his face flushed and his eyes wide. In the midst of rushing from the office, he stopped short as soon as he saw Sorensen and Araguz standing in the hallway.

Sorensen, noting the small-caliber pistol in the man's right hand, pointed his own weapon at Dillard's face. "Drop it, Senator." To his right he noted Araguz as she entered his peripheral vision, her own pistol aimed at Dillard.

"Wait!" the senator all but shouted in response, making no move to raise his pistol from where it aimed toward the floor. His other hand was empty, and Sorensen noted the perspiration running down the sides of the man's face. Glancing past Dillard, the captain saw the prone form of Professor Bates on the floor near his desk. A dark red stain was visible across the older man's chest, soaking through his simple white dress shirt and spreading with each passing second.

"Senator Dillard," Sorensen said, "drop that weapon. Now." Even as he issued the command, he felt the tendons in his finger tightening, drawing in the slack of his pistol's trigger.

Holding his left hand out before him in a halting gesture, Dillard's upper lip quivered as he said, "Captain, let's . . . let's all just calm down, please. This situation has spun entirely out of control, and . . . and now it's time for us to regain our bearing. You have just cause to be angry, but I assure you that . . . "

Light reflected off the polished barrel of the pistol as his right arm moved.

Sorensen pulled the trigger.

The single bullet struck the senator just above his left eye. His next words faded into nothingness, his lips still moving even as the single thin line of blood trickled from the entrance wound and down his face. Dillard's expression melted into one of shock and the pistol fell from his hand as he collapsed to the dull gray carpet.

Moving closer to provide cover as Sorensen stepped forward, his pistol still aimed at the man's head, Araguz said, "Jesus. You just killed a U.S. senator. You know what that means?"

"You get to vote for somebody who's not such an asshole?" Sorensen replied as he reached for Dillard's fallen gun, tucking the .38 into the cargo pocket along his left thigh. A quick check of the man's pulse verified that the senator was indeed dead. Pulling himself to his feet, he entered the office and crossed to Professor Bates's still unmoving form.

The bloodstain all but covered the professor's chest, but Sorensen saw from the pained, irregular rising and falling of his chest that the man was still breathing. "Get a doctor or paramedic or whatever the hell you've got around here," he called out to Araguz as he holstered his pistol. Kneeling beside Bates, he reached for the fallen man's lab coat, pushing the flaps to either side before tearing at his bloody shirt.

"Oh my god," Sorensen breathed, nearly recoiling as he saw the obscene patchwork of scars, blemishes, and pockmarked discolored tissue—some old and faded and some newer and still raw and festering—covering Bates's exposed torso, cumulative evidence of a prolonged bout with some kind of hideous, debilitating disease. The hideous topography of his distressed and otherwise pale skin was highlighted in a sheen of deep, wet crimson radiating outward from the single dark hole just above his left pectoral muscle.

What the hell happened to him?

"The price I've paid for the good we've done here."

So low, so weak were the words that escaped Bates's lips that Sorensen almost did not hear them. He looked up to see the professor staring back at him, the other man's eyes dull and hooded, as if barely recognizing his surroundings. A thin line of blood trailed from his mouth, clear evidence that one of his lungs had been penetrated by the bullet from Dillard's gun.

Damn it. Sorensen reached down and pressed the palm of his right hand atop the bullet wound on Bates's chest, hoping he might stem at least some of the blood loss.

"Early tests during our . . . research were some . . . somewhat hazardous," Bates said, the words raspy and distorted. "I was one of . . . lucky ones. Able to create medicines to . . . cope with the effects." He managed a weak smile. "We got better at it aft . . . after a time."

Placing his hand on Bates's shoulder, Sorensen said, "Save your strength, Professor. Help's on the way." Looking around the office, he saw nothing that might be a first-aid kit or anything else he could use to treat the man's critical chest wound.

The medics won't get here in time.

How long had Bates suffered these debilitating effects? Years? Sorensen could not imagine. What other harm had his body suffered over the decades he had worked on the EDN project? Who else was infected in this manner? Were his Marines at risk of incurring similar permanent damage?

As if reading his thoughts, Bates said, "Your people . . . treated . . . if they get out in time." His right hand moved, feebly, to rest across Sorensen's forearm. "I'm sorr . . . sorry for everything. Tell her . . . tell Elizabeth . . . I'm sorry."

His hand fell to the floor at the same time Bates's eyes dilated and his head lolled to one side.

"Is he dead?" Araguz asked as she stepped into the office.

Rising to his feet, Sorensen nodded. "Yeah." As he looked through the windows and toward the bank of video monitors depicting various images from cameras scattered throughout New Eden, his thoughts turned to his people still fighting to escape the man-made jungle that Bates and his people—for reasons pure or errant—had created.

"And I just hope he's the last one."

CHAPTER TWENTY-FOUR

"Heads up, Lip!"

Hassler turned in response to Maddox's cry in time to see the fifty-five-gallon drum sailing over Lipton's head and crashing behind him. It bounced off the concrete before clattering and rolling across the roof until it came to rest against the parapet thirty feet away from the younger Marine.

The harbingers were coming up with new tricks.

It started with two creatures' initial assault on the roof after discovering that their prey had relocated there. Sanchez, able to access the station's computer network via the PDA he had brought with him, had used the handheld device to activate the building's fire-control system. He had closed and locked every fire door and hatch leading to the interior stairwells. Even though Hassler expected at least a few of the harbingers to get into the building from the ground floor, they would be flummoxed by the maze of corridors and all the barriers in their path.

It's not like they're mice looking for cheese in a maze, he reminded himself. *They know where we are.*

Per the plan Hassler had devised, the Marines had taken up defensive positions at the building's corners as Rolero and Sanchez provided whatever support they could while at the same time guarding the door leading back into the building. Elizabeth, armed with the M16 that at one time had belonged to Dana Garbuz and after receiving a crash course from Hassler in the weapon's operation, had taken up position a few meters from him.

The Marines had repelled the animals' first attempts to climb the exterior fire stairs, and though injuries had been inflicted they had not been able to dispense with any more of the animals. While Hassler knew that he and his people were at least somewhat protected by occupying the high ground, the harbingers' speed and agility were excellent equalizers. The creatures also had supplemented their direct assaults by throwing whatever they could find onto the roof—rocks, mostly, but there was the occasional larger object such as the fuel drum that had nearly decapitated Lipton. There seemed to be no rhyme or reason to the actions; to Hassler it seemed more like the creatures were venting frustration at not being able to reach their quarry.

"They should get these guys to test luggage for Samsonite," Maddox said over the radio just before a chunk of concrete perhaps twice the size of a basketball came hurtling over the parapet less than two meters from Hassler's position. The projectile thudded onto the roof behind him, and chips of concrete shrapnel peppered the back of his flak vest.

"Something tells me they're not too keen on that idea," he offered.

So far the attacks had been sporadic, one or two at a time, with the harbingers darting from various places of concealment and leaping onto the fire stairs' scaffolding. Even there the tactic appeared to be deliberate, as the creatures were able to use the latticework for cover as they climbed, requiring whichever Marine was closer to step out onto the stairs and aim straight down in an attempt to scare away the harbinger. The attempts were getting bolder with each iteration, and Hassler figured it was only a matter of time before the things figured out that their best course of action would be to attack en masse.

With any luck, we'll be long gone before that.

Further, each action to repel the things was costing the team precious ammo from their ever-dwindling supply. He was down to the few rounds that remained in his rifle and one spare magazine in a vest pouch, and he knew that the rest of the team was in similar straits. He had his Beretta in its thigh holster along with five extra mags that he had not yet used, but he doubted the pistol's effectiveness against the harbingers' thick hides. Only two high-explosive grenades remained for his M203, but knew he could not squander what had proven to be the most successful weapon against the creatures.

As a consequence of the ammo situation, Hassler had ordered strict fire discipline, waiting for a sure, clear shot or until one or more of the animals made a direct attempt to scale the building. Though a few had tried that tactic, the entire pack seemed to have learned from those attempts, with the harbingers restricting their movements away from the compound's open areas. They were using the walls of nearby structures for cover, or else stayed close enough to the main building that it required one of the Marines to lean over the roof's parapet in order to get a shot. Hassler had put a stop to that when he realized that it was putting team members at risk from the assorted flotsam the harbingers were flinging up at their quarry.

He was shifting his body in an attempt to find a more comfortable position when the compound in front of him abruptly dissolved into an unfocused haze, and he reached out to steady himself as the new wave of dizziness washed over him. Sitting down, he wiped his face with his shaky left hand as his stomach lurched in response to the latest bout of nausea.

"Donovan," Elizabeth said from where she crouched a few meters from him, "are you okay?"

"Queasy," Hassler replied, leaning back against the parapet and taking several deep breaths in an attempt to calm himself. The debilitating effects of his exposure to the EDN environment were becoming more pronounced, and he was once again aware of the sensitivity of the rashes that covered his body. It required a superhuman force of will to refrain from scratching the lesions until he reached bone. If not for the medications Elizabeth had given him and the other affected Marines, he probably would have done just that.

Suck it up, he scolded himself. *You're almost out of here.*

"Gunny," Lipton called over the radio, jerking Hassler's mind back to the situation at hand. "Choppers inbound from the west."

Even as the sergeant delivered the report Hassler's ears caught the first faint sounds of approaching helicopters. He looked to the west and saw two dark shapes flying over the treetops, heading straight for the compound and growing larger with each passing second. A moment later, a new voice sounded in his ear.

"Recon Marines, this is Black Hawk Romeo One. Do you copy?"

Sam Branton smiled as the Marine's voice replied in his helmet speakers.

"Roger that, Romeo One. This is Hassler. We're spread out on the roof, but the center's wide open for an LZ. Do you have a visual?"

"I see them," said Senator Christopher, pointing over Branton's shoulder from where he crouched just behind the cockpit. The bulky olive drab helmet he wore, which allowed him to communicate with the rest of the helicopter's crew, was at odds with his starched white dress shirt and dark trousers, but the senator did not seem to mind. He had shucked his suit jacket and tie and rolled up his sleeves, looking every bit like a buttoned-down politician trying much too hard to act like just one of the boys when visiting troops.

Branton knew better, having seen his share of such things during his own army days, and so was willing to cut Christopher slack given the current circumstances. The senator had discarded all worry about being exposed to the EDN region's dangerous environs, and had volunteered to do anything Branton needed during the extraction operation, up to and including manning a weapon if necessary. He wanted his daughter back and rather than issue orders from a position of safety had pledged instead to assist. That earned him more than a few points in Branton's book.

"Roger that, Recon," he said as he scanned the dull concrete building in the distance, able to pick out seven figures situated at or near the corners of the structure and leaving the entire middle area of the roof clear. "Looks good, partner. We'll be there in thirty."

"Be sure to keep your support well above the tree line, Romeo One," Hassler said. "These things are already climbing trees and walls. They might be ballsy enough to jump at you as you fly by if you're low enough."

Get the fuck out of here!

Despite the briefing he had been given by Professor Bates about the mysterious creatures attacking the Marines, Branton still found the whole thing hard to believe. Even the video footage he had seen left him with uncertainty, but he was not about to doubt the word of the Marine gunnery sergeant sitting in the middle of the shit.

The compound was in plain sight now, the simple concrete wall and ordinary-looking buildings contrasting sharply with their otherworldly surroundings. Viewing the pictures and video of New Eden during Geoffrey Bates's briefing had been unsettling enough, but flying over the artificial jungle and seeing its abnormal mixture of vegetation that looked like something his youngest son might draw for first-grade art class was something else altogether.

Those nondisclosure agreements were a waste of Bates's time and paper, he decided. *Who the hell's gonna believe any of this, anyway?*

"Romeo Two," he called into his mike, "you heard the man. Keep your distance when I head in. If anything pokes its head up, feel free to aerate it." Looking over his shoulder, he saw that his crew chief, Russell Whitaker, had already opened the starboard crew door and was prepping the door-mounted M60 machine gun for use in covering their landing.

Let's rock and roll, and all that shit.

After receiving an acknowledgment from Amarie Thompson, Branton turned to his own copilot, Juan Valenti. "You ready to play ball?"

Valenti, a stocky, barrel-chested Mexican man who all but filled the right side of the cockpit, nodded. "Oh yeah. Let's do it."

"Keep your eyes open for bad guys," Branton said, "or whatever the hell they are." He knew that getting the remains of the Marine recon team and their charges loaded would take several seconds. Despite the fact that he would be landing the helicopter on the roof, he had to figure one or more of Bates's pet monsters would make a play during the extraction process, especially if they were as crafty as the professor had described.

With Thompson's chopper veering off to provide air support, Branton eased the nose of his Black Hawk down as the distance to the compound continued to shrink. He could plainly see the people on the roof now and in his peripheral vision he saw other movement on the ground inside the compound, but when he tried to get a better look he caught only glimpses and hints of what might have been there.

Sneaky little pricks, aren't they?

"Jesus," he heard Christopher say as he pointed toward the cockpit windshield again. "Look at that. On the wall."

Looking to his left, Branton saw what he meant. "I got it," he replied as he caught sight of the dark shape running along the top of the wall. Despite its uncanny speed, he was able to make out a long, angular head and muscled body before the thing disappeared down into the compound.

He called into his mike, "Hassler, this is Romeo One. Stay clear of the LZ. I'm bringing her in hot."

"Roger that, Romeo One," the Marine replied, and Branton saw one of the figures near the far corner of the roof, a black man in camouflage utilities, wave in his direction.

The wall surrounding the compound slid beneath the helicopter's belly as Branton brought the craft in high and fast, maintaining altitude as long as possible and aiming for a fast approach. He was aware of dark figures scurrying across the open ground around the building but ignored them as he concentrated on his landing site. Below and ahead of him on the roof, he saw Hassler and another Marine scrambling from their positions and running to the near side of the building, brandishing their weapons to take aim at a target that Branton could not see.

"Be aware you've got hostiles on the ground, Romeo One!" a voice sounded in his helmet at the same time he felt something strike the left side of the Black Hawk. The only effect on the craft's flight was an all but indiscernible trembling in the controls transmitted to his hands. His first instinct was to yank up on the collective but he restrained himself.

"What the hell was that?" Valenti asked.

"The natives are going apeshit down here," replied another voice, one Branton did not recognize. "They're throwing anything they can find at you. You might want to abort and come around for another pass."

"They'll just be more riled up when I come back," Branton replied. "Let's do this. I'm starting my descent now."

He brought the Black Hawk into a hover directly over the center of the building, rotating the craft as it descended until its nose was facing back toward the west. His body objected to the abrupt maneuvers, straining against the harness holding him in his seat. It had been a long time since he had flown a helicopter in anything resembling combat conditions, and he could feel the adrenaline rush heightening as he guided the craft in for a landing.

The muffled reports of weapons fire reached him, and he spared a glance through the cockpit window toward the roof below him to see two Marines firing at something below his line of sight. Judging from the angle of their rifle barrels, one of the creatures had to be very close to the building.

"Pull up, Romeo One!" Hassler's voice shouted. "Abort!"

Branton did not think, did not question. His body simply reacted to the warning as he pulled up on the collective, halting the Black Hawk's descent. The chopper's engines howled in protest as he applied more power. He banked to his left, intending to swing around and circle the compound's perimeter before coming in for another pass.

"Look out!" Valenti shouted, only a second before the helicopter shuddered, the violence of the action so severe that the collective jerked from Branton's hand.

The chopper was less than ten meters above the surface of the roof when the massive chunk of concrete struck the rear of the Black Hawk, shearing away part of its tail rotor. Sparks flew as pieces of the titanium and fiberglass blades struck the helicopter's armored fuselage and the craft jerked in response to the attack before starting to spin clockwise.

"Rotor!" Hassler heard Branton shout over the radio. "They got the tail rotor!"

Without the tail to compensate for the main rotor, the chopper began to twirl as though ensnared in the violent, cyclic winds of a tornado. Hassler could only yell what seemed like a futile warning for everyone to get down, screaming in his lip mike to be heard over the helicopter's rotor wash. The scream of the Black Hawk's engines echoed off the walls of the compound as he caught glimpses of the two pilots in the craft's cockpit, struggling to maintain some control over the wounded helicopter.

"I'm cutting power," Branton said, and Hassler heard the engines die even as it continued its descent. Branton had guided the craft away from the center of the roof, dropping it near the eastern edge. Behind it, Lipton and Sanchez scrambled away as the chopper dropped with all the aerodynamic qualities of a stone to the roof below.

The force of the Black Hawk's impact was great enough that Hassler felt the roof shudder beneath his feet, and for a horrified instant he imagined the entire structure collapsing beneath him. The left forward landing wheel snapped, dropping the helicopter's nose to the ground, and Hassler heard the high-pitched metallic ping of metal skipping off concrete as the main rotor blades broke apart, sending pieces of jagged shrapnel spinning away from the point of impact.

"Romeo One is down," he called out over the comm net as the helicopter came to rest. "Everybody all right in there?"

Several seconds passed before Branton's voice came on the line. "Relax, Marine. We're here to rescue you." He was about to say more but the words were lost behind a string of ragged coughs, then, "I think we're okay."

Despite what he had just witnessed, Hassler was forced to appreciate the pilot's undiminished bravado. "Lipton, Sanchez, get them out of there."

"We're on it, Gunny," Lipton replied.

There was some other chatter on the link, but Hassler ignored it as he heard the now-familiar sounds of other harbingers wailing and grunting back and forth. Standing on the wall across the compound from his position, two of the creatures were jumping up and down like dogs excited that their master had come home. Their actions and cries were consistent with what he had seen of their earlier behavior. While there was no disputing that the animals were adapting to their environment, the claim could now also be made that they were relishing the role they were establishing for themselves in New Eden.

Another argument for nuking the place.

"Gunny," he heard Lipton say, "we've got everybody out of the chopper. One guy's got a broken arm and other one's cut on the forehead, but they'll be okay."

Acknowledging the report, Hassler called into his radio mike, "Romeo Two, requesting evac."

The female pilot, Thompson, replied, "We're swinging around now. Coming in from the south. Have your people ready."

"Roger that," Hassler said as he saw the helicopter making the turn for its approach to the building, coming in high for a fast descent to the landing site. Using hand signals, he indicated for the rest of his team to hold their defensive positions. With no air support, it would be up to them to protect the remaining Black Hawk as it attempted to land.

Here we go again.

"Got one on the stairs!" Rolero shouted, and Hassler turned to see her scrambling toward the edge of the roof and aiming her M16 at where he knew the fire-escape scaffolding was attached to her corner of the building. She fired two three-round bursts before running forward again.

"I winged it but it's still hanging on," she said, punctuating her report by firing again, letting loose another burst before Hassler saw that she was forced to reload. He heard her curse and she backpedaled, dropping the rifle's spent magazine as she fumbled for another one from the pouch near her hip. She cursed as she dropped the new clip, which bounced away from her as it fell to the ground.

Hassler knew what was coming, every sense screaming a warning to him as he raised his rifle at the precise instant the harbinger appeared over the parapet. It made the leap from the top of stairs at the third-floor fire door and landed twenty meters from him. Late-morning sunlight glinted off its leathery black skin as well as its rows of angled teeth, and its thick tail curled and twisted behind it as it stood before him on broad muscled legs. Saliva, or what passed for saliva in a genetically engineered animal whose blood had already proven to be a biohazard in and of itself, dripped from its long, angular mouth.

He was only dimly aware of the sound of the helicopter increasing from behind him before weapons fire erupted over his head and he saw massive bloody holes punching into the creature's body. Looking up, he saw that the Black Hawk had slowed to a hover and that a man was sitting in the open port-side crew door. Firing a door-mounted M60 as the chopper descended, the shooter was unleashing a steady stream of 7.62mm rounds that were more than sufficient not only to stop the harbinger in its tracks but also to knock it off its feet. What little remained of the creature's head and torso collapsed in a pulpy heap to the ground, small pyres of acidic smoke already rising from where the animal's blood stained the concrete.

"Time to go, people!" Thompson's voice echoed in Hassler's earpiece as the shadow of the helicopter crossed over him and he felt the updraft caused by its rotor blades. Scrambling toward the edge of the roof in order to give the chopper an unobstructed approach, he watched as the door gunner fired again, this time at a target somewhere on the ground.

Turning away from the Black Hawk, Hassler located Rolero on the opposite side of the roof, gathering Elizabeth and Sanchez and shepherding the scientists toward the helicopter. He watched in surprise as Elizabeth broke away from the others and ran to where Lipton and Artiaga were escorting the crew of the downed chopper. One of the men was not wearing a black flight suit like the others, and it took Hassler an extra second to realize that he recognized him.

Elizabeth's father. What the hell was he doing here?

It was simple, of course. The senator obviously had tired of standing around while others were sent to retrieve his little girl. That spoke volumes about the man's character in Hassler's opinion. Senator Reginald Christopher had apparently stepped up at the right time. As he watched father and daughter embrace in reunion, Hassler considered it a good omen.

God knows we could use one right about now.

"Come on!" he yelled, waving them and the others to hurry the hell up. Then weapons fire from his right reached him through the clamor of the Black Hawk's engines, and he turned to see Artiaga firing at another harbinger that had scrambled onto the roof.

"Jesus!" yelled someone behind Hassler whose voice he did not recognize. One of the chopper crew? "Look at it!"

The harbinger was advancing on them, and Hassler saw that it was carrying a nearly six-foot piece of what looked to be angled metal, steel or iron, in its massive left hand. It was swinging it back and forth across its body as it stalked forward, extending its deadly reach by the length of a grown man.

"You've got to be shitting me."

Artiaga was doing his best to fend off the harbinger, but depite his hitting the creature several times the thing continued moving toward him. It was closing in for the kill, but the corporal dropped to the ground as the creature leaped forward to pounce, rolling beneath it as the harbinger's momentum carried it past. It pulled up, turning itself around and searching for its quarry, this time too close to miss.

Running toward the fray, Hassler waved Artiaga to get clear as he aimed his grenade launcher and fired. The projectile punched through the harbinger's thick hide just beneath its left shoulder before detonating, blowing the creature off the roof in a cloud of skin, muscle, and bone.

"Get on the chopper!" he shouted as Rolero, Sanchez, and Maddox drew closer. They were carrying the sealed body bag containing the deceased Corporal Stewart, determined not to leave the dead Marine behind, while Rolero covered their retreat. Behind Hassler, the Black Hawk had set down on the roof. Its port side was facing him and the door gunner was still manning the M60.

"There's one!" Maddox called out, point to where another harbinger was just visible at the far end of the building, its head poking up above the parapet as if checking to see that the coast was clear. Like its companion, it was carrying a makeshift club, this one appearing to be a hunk of splintered wood.

Hassler almost fired at it but held back, conscious of his near-critical ammo situation. It was simply too far away to risk wasting rounds that would do little to harm it from this distance. The door gunner had no such compunction, opening up on the harbinger as it climbed onto the roof. The machine gun cut down its latest target with relative ease, chewing into its chest and head, pushing it off the roof and out of sight.

How many more are there?

The thought echoed in Hassler's ears as he felt himself losing his balance.

He dropped to his knees, his M4 falling from his grip and clattering away. He felt his pulse racing as his vision began to blur and the near-overwhelming urge to vomit swept over him. He collapsed forward, barely able to put his arms out and keep himself from slamming face-first into the concrete.

Not now, damn it!

He swallowed the bile rising in his throat, wincing at the sharp burning sensation that evoked as he shook his head in an attempt to shake off double vision. To his left, he thought he could make out Rolero pushing Sanchez toward the waiting helicopter, pausing only to take the man's M16 and sling it over her shoulder. Lipton and his charges were right behind him, but he slowed when Senator Christopher stumbled and fell, landing clumsily on his right knee.

Hassler saw the man's face contort in pain, heard his scream of pain even over the howl of the Black Hawk's engines. Two of the men from the crashed Black Hawk rushed to the aid of the falling man while Artiaga grabbed Elizabeth by the arm and pulled her toward the chopper. Maddox, having deposited Stewart's body aboard the craft, wasted no time in running forward to help Artiaga and the others with Elizabeth and her father. Lipton turned to fire, but the staff sergeant waved him off.

"Get on the bird, damn it!" he ordered as he took the senator by the arm and aided the hobbling man to keep running. Running toward Hassler and the helicopter, he yelled, "Time to haul ass, boss!"

A new threat materialized as a harbinger sprang over the parapet near the far corner of the building, another one following on its heels. A third one appeared from the opposite corner, this one wielding a length of pipe and bounding over the parapet to hit the roof at a full run. It galloped on all four extremities as it dashed across the open expanse of concrete.

"They're converging," Rolero yelled over the Black Hawk's rotor wash as she stepped closer to Hassler, taking up a kneeling stance and firing at one of the oncoming creatures.

He knew she was right even as he fumbled with shaking hands for his last 40mm grenade and loaded it into his M203. They were sitting ducks so long as the helicopter was on the ground. Double vision and all, he aimed the launcher in the direction of the first two harbingers and pulled the trigger.

The explosive's flight was short and low; the grenade arced only the slightest bit before slamming into the roof and detonating. Hassler felt wind on his face as the blast's concussion washed over him. The building shuddered beneath his feet as dust and chunks of concrete spewed into the air.

"That's it!" he yelled, looking over his shoulder to verify that everyone save for himself, Rolero, and Maddox was aboard the chopper. "Let's go!"

With his vision clearing, yet still somewhat off-balance, Hassler allowed Maddox to help him to his feet before pushing his friend toward the Black Hawk. He started to backpedal in that direction, being sure to give the M60 gunner a field of fire to cover their retreat as the harbingers emerged from the dissipating smoke cloud. The gunner fired again, taking one of the creatures in the head as its two companions scampered away, splitting off in opposite directions.

The gunner swung the machine gun to track after one of the animals, leaving the other one unmolested. Hassler saw it lunging for their position, saw that Rolero was holding her ground and covering their retreat.

"Shannon!" he shouted into his radio, bringing up his own rifle even as Maddox pulled him toward the chopper. The sounds of Rolero's M16 were only barely audible over the sound of the engines now, its short bursts at odds with the M60's deeper and more rapid cycle of fire.

Hassler was still struggling for a shot when the harbinger pounced on her.

Blood trailing from a dozen wounds she had inflicted on it, the creature rammed her with its full weight. Her rifle flew from her hands as she fell to the concrete, and the harbinger landed atop her, claws and teeth flashing in the sunlight. Rolero had time for a single scream that was all but lost in the fury of the Black Hawk's rotors before the creature's mouth closed around her throat, ripping skin and muscle away in a cloud of crimson rain.

No! Hassler's mind screamed the agonizing plea. *Not when we're this close!*

Maddox dragged him into the Black Hawk and he felt other hands reach out to pull him into the craft, his feet dangling from the open door. The echoes of the door-mounted M60 bounced off the walls as the helicopter rose into the sky.

"Hang on, everybody," Thompson's voice sounded in his ear. "We're putting the hammer down."

Hassler watched the roof of the observation station fall away as they gained altitude. He felt the chopper change direction, moving over the compound even as it continued to rise beyond the reach of any remaining harbingers. A few of the creatures were still scurrying about the compound, while the bodies of several others littered the roof of the building as well as the surrounding ground, evidence of the final fight that had been waged here.

"Gunny," Maddox said, tapping him on the shoulder before pointing through the open crew door. "Look."

A lone harbinger was watching them as the Black Hawk passed over the compound wall and left the station behind. It made no attempts to jump for the helicopter or to hurl anything at it. Instead, the creature appeared simply to be watching the craft's departure.

Hassler recognized the web of scars on its chest.

The leader. Light glinted off something in the harbinger's left hand, and Hassler saw that the creature held what looked to be a combat knife, perhaps something it had taken from the body of one of the Marines it or its companions had killed.

"Son of a bitch," he whispered.

The harbinger did not move as it watched the helicopter lift away, its eyes seemingly fixed on Hassler until the Black Hawk banked to starboard and he lost sight of it. This time, he decided, there was no denying the qualities present in its odd expression.

Understanding and resolve.

To Hassler, it was as though the animal not only had accepted the losses it had suffered today, but also that there would be opportunities for future victories. In addition to all of that, he was sure he sensed one other powerful vibe coming from the harbinger.

When and if those opportunities arose, it would be ready.

Shaking off the unsettling sensation, Hassler turned to regard the rest of the group seated in the helicopter's passenger area. Lipton and Artiaga looked beaten and tired, much as Hassler did himself, and no doubt they were gripped by similar effects of infection. Sam Branton and his own chopper crew sat quietly, their expressions offering mute testimony to their experiences of the past several minutes.

In the rear of the compartment, Senator and Dr. Christopher held each other in a firm embrace, with Elizabeth allowing the full weight of the past several days to finally slide from her shoulders as she sobbed into her father's chest. The elder Christopher merely sat in silence, holding his daughter close and stroking her hair, his eyes watering as he looked to Hassler and mouthed a silent *Thank you.*

Behind them, Maddox and Sanchez were shaking hands, though there appeared to be no joy in the gesture.

Hassler suspected that, like his own, their feelings of salvation were subdued by the fact that their rescue had come at such a tragic cost.

How high was that price? In addition to the lives lost here, Hassler had to wonder about the damage to be suffered by the EDN project itself. Decades of effort, striving to harness the vast potential offered by New Eden and the Genesis Protocol, might all be lost because of the selfish machinations of those consumed by their own agendas and drive for self-preservation.

And who would be responsible for repaying that debt?

That was a question he hoped to answer the minute they arrived at the base. There were scores to settle, not only for the Marines he had lost but for Shannon Rolero and her people, as well.

CHAPTER TWENTY-FIVE

Hassler was awakened by the jolt of the Black Hawk's wheels striking the concrete landing pad and the sounds of its engines powering down. How long had he been asleep?

As those around him began exiting the helicopter, he heard the voices of nearby people, lots of them, and turned his head to see dozens of onlookers standing behind yellow lines painted on the tarmac that indicated the safety zone surrounding the landing pad. To his shock, some were clapping, but many of them simply stood in silence, their expressions running the gamut from happiness and satisfaction to worry and even shame.

What the hell is this about?

"Donovan," a voice called out from behind him, and he turned to see Elizabeth Christopher moving across the compartment to him. "Are you okay?"

"What's going on outside?" he asked, surprised by how weak his own voice sounded.

Smiling down at him, her eyes still puffy and red from her earlier crying, Elizabeth replied, "Your welcoming committee."

The helicopter's engines were shut down and its rotors slowing to a stop as she helped him step down to the tarmac. Looking up, he saw that the crowd of people had grown much more animated at the sight of their friends as well as the Marines and helicopter crews who had rescued them. The next few minutes were a whirlwind as everyone disembarked from the helicopter, with people offering praise to the Marines and pilots. Hassler and his men thanked the Black Hawk pilots while the crew of the downed chopper voiced their own appreciation for being saved. Hassler was trying to maintain his bearing despite his depleted condition, and much of the interaction moved too fast for him; the only thing from the entire exchange that he seemed able to focus on was the smile of one of the pilots, Sam Branton, which seemed at least bright enough to use as a reading lamp if not a distress flare.

Some of the people, men and women alike, wept openly as they reached out to embrace Paul Sanchez. Others came to the assistance of Maddox as he, with the aid of Lipton and Artiaga, carried the remains of Corporal Stewart from the helicopter to a stretcher provided by a team of waiting medics. Only after they finished that task did the Marines allow anyone to turn their attentions to them. The medics wasted no time helping the two ill Marines onto other stretchers, already beginning the process of assessing their condition and administering various treatments.

"I had the pilot call for ambulances to take you and your Marines to our medical facility," Elizabeth said.

"Our doctors are already prepped and waiting for your arrival. You and your team should be fine."

"You can treat the symptoms?" he asked, grateful for the support she offered as she slung his arm around her shoulders.

She nodded. "Yes. They'll want to keep you here for observation until they're sure the contamination has receded, but based on everything I was told in flight, you should make a full recovery."

One of the medics, a blond man dressed in dark blue trousers and a white shirt, broke away from the group tending to the other Marines and walked toward the helicopter. Both his shirt and pants were outfitted with pockets from which protruded various tools, pens, and other assorted items. "Mr. Hassler?" he asked by way of greeting. "My name's Dale Burnett." He reached into the bag slung over his shoulder and extracted a small pouch from which he produced a hypodermic needle containing a dark green fluid. "We're getting set to transport you and your team to the hospital, but we're starting a counter regimen to the infection you're experiencing. This is the first in the series, and I need to administer it now."

Hassler nodded in understanding. "Whatever you say, Doc. You've already treated my people?"

"You're the last one," Burnett replied as he rolled up Hassler's right sleeve and began unraveling the bandage protecting the rashes on his arm.

Approaching them from behind the medic, Maddox said, "Can you believe they want to hold me, too? They're hoping to figure out why I never showed any symptoms. I told them it was because I'm mean, and it scared the bugs away, but these folks don't seem to be buying it."

Mustering a tired smile even as Burnett inserted the needle into his arm, Hassler replied, "Could be that you're just so full of shit there wasn't room for anything else." He winced at the slight burning sensation from the medication as it entered his bloodstream.

Damn, that hurts worse that the rash.

The staff sergeant shrugged. "Nah, I'm sticking with my story. Anyway, something tells me there's a lot of poking and prodding in my near future. I just hope the doctors are pretty."

"I know I am," Burnett said dryly. And for once, Dave Maddox couldn't seem to think of a reply.

Stepping back, Maddox indicated the Marines and other medics with a thumb over his shoulder. "They're taking Lip and Artiaga to the hospital and moving Stewart to their morgue. I'm going to stay with him until we can get him transported back to Pendleton."

Hassler nodded. "Go on. I'll be there once Doc Burnett here throws me into an ambulance." As his friend departed, he leaned back to rest against the Black Hawk's doorframe, aware once more of his mounting fatigue in the face of his condition and not minding one bit that Elizabeth was continuing to watch over him even as she was greeted by friends and coworkers.

"Here, drink this," she said as she offered him a bottle of water. "You're dehydrated. It'll get things started until the medics can fit you with an IV."

Accepting the bottle without protest, Hassler opened it and drained its contents, basking in the cool refreshing liquid. It did little to ease his overall discomfort, but it still tasted damned good.

"Got another one?" he asked.

"Coming right up," Elizabeth replied. Her smile was wide and bright; for the first time she appeared to be all but free of the fatigue, anguish, and guilt that had weighed on her during the past two days.

Pretty lady, he decided, finally allowing some of the tension from the mission to melt away. There was still much to do—medical treatment, debriefing, all of the unpleasant duties that came with the deaths of Marines under his command—but at least the danger had passed. He could let his guard down now, if only a bit.

"Mr. Hassler," said Senator Reginald Christopher as he approached, extending a hand in greeting. As with his daughter, Hassler saw the relief and sorrow in the man's eyes. "I don't know how to thank you for everything you and your men went through to rescue my daughter."

Taking the proffered hand, Hassler nodded in respect. "You're welcome, sir. Just doing our job."

Waving away the attempt at modesty, the senator placed a paternal hand on Hassler's shoulder. "You and I both know that what you endured was far above any call of duty you ever answered. It's a debt I can never repay, but I'll be damned if I don't try."

Hassler accepted the compliment, sensitive to the senator's relief over his daughter's safe return. This was not the appropriate time or place to debate what could and could not be done for those who had sacrificed their lives, either his Marines or the even larger number of EDN project staff killed during the past several days. There would be many such opportunities later, after the more immediate concerns were addressed.

He caught sight of Captain Sorensen making his way through the small crowd of people. Hassler began to rise to his feet but the captain indicated for him to stay seated.

"Good to see you, Gunny," he said.

"Same here, sir," Hassler replied. "Thanks for sending the birds to get us."

Sorensen shook his head. "Thank Clifford Meyer. That kid had some onions, doing what he did."

Hassler made a note to seek out the computer technician and thank him. Indeed, the man's efforts had been fraught with all manner of risks, especially considering what little Hassler had heard about the actions undertaken by Bates and Dillard—to say nothing of the acts they had contemplated taking.

"What about Bates and Dillard?" he asked. "Where are they?"

Sorensen shook his head. "They're dead."

Blinking several times as he digested the succinct reply, Hassler frowned. "Really? What happened?"

The captain shrugged. "Shit. That's what happened. Long story." To Elizabeth he said, "Except to say that Professor Bates asked me to tell you he was sorry, Doctor. For everything."

Hassler glanced over at her, and saw that she could offer only a silent nod in response to the sentiment. There were new tears in her eyes, no doubt generated as much from the tragedy of her friends' deaths as from the keen sense of betrayal she had to be feeling from a man she considered her mentor. Hassler knew it would be a long time before she came to terms with everything that had happened here as well as her role in all of it.

She'll be okay, he reminded himself. *She didn't do anything wrong. As long as she can convince herself of that, she'll make it all right.*

After taking another long drink from his water bottle and relishing every drop, Hassler looked to Sorensen. "So, what's next?"

The captain shrugged. "Damn if I know. I've already contacted Colonel Pantolini and apprised him of the situation, and after he picked his jaw up off the floor he told me to stand fast until he could run this up the chain of command." Shaking his head, he added, "I imagine there's going to be a shitload of congressional hearings, for starters."

Turning to Sorensen, Senator Christopher said, "I intend to see that the truth comes out about what happened here, Captain. I'll personally ensure that your men and those members of the project staff who died here are properly honored for the sacrifices they made."

"There's something else you can do, Dad," Elizabeth said, and Hassler saw how she had drawn several breaths in an effort to regain her composure. She pointed in the general direction of New Eden. "Shut it down. All of it. I don't care if I have to drive a bulldozer myself, but I want the whole thing wiped away. It's obscene."

The elder Christopher regarded his daughter, his expression heavy. "I think that might be a mistake, Elizabeth."

"Why the hell is that?" Hassler asked, making no attempt to temper his skepticism.

Indicating the crowd of project staffers still milling about nearby with a wave of his hands, the senator replied, "Too much time and energy has been expended, too many advances made, and too many sacrifices suffered for anyone to simply allow it all to be rejected out of hand. It only has to be defended from those who become blinded by the power it offers and who lose sight of why these people were assembled here in the first place." He sighed in resignation. "It has to be kept from people like Jonathan Dillard and even Geoffrey Bates."

Elizabeth shook her head. "I don't know, Dad. I mean, I agree with you to a point, but even if whoever's in charge of sorting out this mess decides that the project's to be kept open, the damage is still done. Besides, what's to prevent something similar from happening here again?"

Stepping forward, Christopher reached out until he could drape an arm across his daughter's shoulders. "Having the right person in charge, for one thing."

"I hate to say it," Sorensen said, "but I think he raises a fair point."

Nodding, Senator Christopher replied, "Assuming there's someone who'll try to see past the chaos this thing's sure to ignite in the near term. I think it'll be tough to find advocates once word gets out about what happened here."

"Maybe we can find a way to make it work," Elizabeth said as she pulled her father close. "We've come too far and accomplished too much to throw it all away now. We at least owe our friends that much." To Hassler, she said, "And your men, as well."

Hassler could agree with that. If such a feat was to be accomplished, then it would make for a more fitting memorial to those who had sacrificed their lives here than dissolving New Eden, shelving the Genesis Protocol, and allowing all of its accomplishments to simply fade into nonexistence.

Now, if only they can get the idiots in charge to see it their way.

Given his own experience with such people, Hassler held little hope for that actually happening.

Looking toward the sun, which was well on its way toward setting in the western sky, he saw that a line of ominous dark clouds was gathering on the distant horizon. A storm was brewing, it seemed.

An omen? Hassler pondered the question.

Damned if that ain't a sucker bet.

A SHADOW OF
THINGS TO COME

EPILOGUE

Full and bright as it hung low in the sky and flanked on either side as it was by the jagged peaks of distant mountains, the moon still offered ample illumination even as it caused shadows to stretch and distort along the lonely, narrow service road.

The group of five harbingers gathered near the edge of that road, where sand and dry, brittle grass gave way to dark, cracked stone that seemed strange and yet familiar to the creatures. Behind them, the shiny, smooth barrier that had stood at the outer boundary of their land for as long as any of them could remember now separated them from the lush, vibrant, teeming jungle that had been the only home any of them had ever known. None of the harbingers looked back the way they had come, their gaze and attention instead focused on the vast expanse of bland, foreboding desolation that lay before them.

For countless cycles of the sun and moon, the pack leader had watched from the concealment of the jungle as the smaller, fleshy creatures traveled down this path in their strange machines. They came and went as they pleased, intruding on its home and offering no measure of respect to those who already dwelled in this place. Intuition always had told it that the creatures were to be feared, and that as long as it remembered it had carried a sense that they were the masters of the world in which it lived.

Having defeated several of them in battle, the leader had decided such was no longer the case. Similarly, it had cast off the inherent trait—seemingly radiating from the core of its being—that made it fear whatever lay beyond the boundaries of its home.

This would not be the first time it and the others had stood here, contemplating a journey into the sprawling wasteland. Indeed, the pack leader had made several such attempts, all of which had ended in failure within one cycle of the sun and moon. Neither the meager amounts of water nor the rare small animals they had been able to scavenge seemed to offer any sustenance. Each tasted bitter and foul, inducing vomiting as the creatures expelled the unwelcome matter from their bodies. Eventually, ultimately, they had been forced to stagger and crawl out of the desert, drawn by instinct to the one place that seemed to offer safe haven: the jungle from which they had come. The unexplained debilitating effects diminished as they drank water and ate of the prey that always had sustained them.

Still, despite these defeats, the pack leader soon realized that the progress made traversing the desert seemed to grow with each excursion. The animals they ate and the water they drank still sickened them, though not with the same intensity as had been experienced during their first journey. Likewise, upon their return to the jungle after each failed attempt, it took less time to recuperate.

Perhaps, in time, they might not face the need to return home at all. It was this feeling that drove the leader to set out once more into the sea of barren sand and rock before them.

Alongside it, the other harbingers stood in silence, waiting for it to take the lead. Their loyalty was hard-won; the leader earned it first by defeating the other harbinger that had made a claim for the dominant position within the pack, and then as it was forced to defend its own place from those seeking to unseat it. The scars crisscrossing its body bore mute testimony to the ferocity of those challenges, as well as demonstrating to the others the strength it possessed by having survived those confrontations and its mettle to lead the pack.

The leader's massive right hand brushed across the container attached to the large strap suspended from its shoulder, both taken from the large, smooth-walled caves where the masters sometimes dwelled. It had watched the masters using such objects, and had discovered that the vessel could carry water, a notion the leader considered helpful in light of the journey they were about to begin. With that in mind, it had seen to it that the other harbingers each found a similar container.

Two of its followers carried the long, shiny objects they had obtained near the caves as well. The pack leader was not sure if they were the bones of some bizarre animal or branches from some tree it had never before seen in the jungle, but their usefulness as weapons could not be disputed, as already had been demonstrated. Likewise, the leader had found the strange, elongated tooth it had taken from one of the creatures the harbingers had fought and defeated. Reflecting the overhead light cast off by the moon, it seemed small and fragile in the leader's hand, though it was as sharp as the harbinger's own claws.

It might prove useful.

Offering a series of grunts and clicks to the pack, the leader listened as the sounds were echoed by the other harbingers before it stepped across the hard surface of the path used by the masters, once more leaving the safety of the jungle for the uncertainty of the seemingly endless desert and whatever might lie beyond it.

This time, the leader vowed, they would not return.

ACKNOWLEGMENTS

Thanks are due once again to John Ordover at Phobos Books, who came to me yet again with a question that started with, "Hey, wanna try something?" While the initial concept for *The Genesis Protocol* was John's, he gave me free rein to go crazy with the idea. What can I say? It was fun.

Another round of thanks for Kevin Dilmore, my writing partner on various projects, who helped me juggle my priorities as I finished this book while at the same time working with him on other efforts. Who knows, maybe you'll even get to see some of those one day.

And, of course, many thanks to my wife and soul mate, Michi, who continues to tolerate my peculiar mix of insanity.

ABOUT THE AUTHOR

Dayton Ward served for eleven years in the U.S. Marine Corps before entering the private sector as a software engineer. His professional writing career began with his short stories being selected for each of Pocket Books' first three *Star Trek: Strange New Worlds* anthologies. He is the author of the *Star Trek* novel *In the Name of Honor* and the science fiction novel *The Last World War*, and his short stories have appeared in *Star Trek: New Frontier—No Limits*, *Kansas City Voices Magazine*, and *The World's Best Shortest Stories*. With cowriter Kevin Dilmore, he has written short stories, several tales in Pocket's *Star Trek: S.C.E.* series, the *Star Trek: The Next Generation* novels *A Time to Sow* and *A Time to Harvest*, and the forthcoming (as of this writing) *Star Trek: Vanguard* novel *Summon the Thunder*. Though Dayton currently lives in Kansas City with his wife, Michi, he is a Florida native and still maintains a torrid long-distance romance with his beloved Tampa Bay Buccaneers. Visit him on the web at http://www.daytonward.com.

ALSO FROM PHOBOS BOOKS . . .

PHOBOS IMPACT . . . IMPACTING THE IMAGINATION

PHOBOS IMPACT
An Imprint of Phobos Books LLC, 200 Park Ave South, New York, NY 10003
Voice: 347-683-8151 Fax: 718-228-3597
Distributed to the trade by National Book Network 1-800-462-6240

PHOBOS IMPACT

An Imprint of Phobos Books LLC, 200 Park Ave South, New York, NY 10003
Voice: 347-683-8151 Fax: 718-228-3597
Distributed to the trade by National Book Network 1-800-462-6420

Sandra Schulberg
Publisher

John J. Ordover
Editor-in-Chief

Carol A. Greenburg
Executive Editor

Matt Galemmo
Art Director

Terry McGarry
Production Editor

Andy Heidel
Marketing Director

Hildy Silverman
Webmaster

Chris Erkmann
Advertising Associate

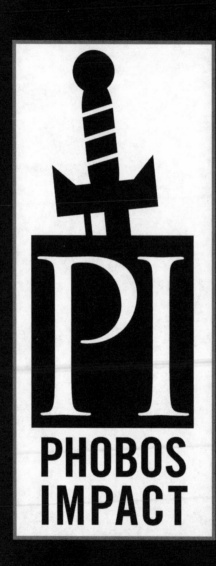